PURITY
IN
DEATH

Titles by Nora Roberts

HOT ICE
SACRED SINS
BRAZEN VIRTUE
SWEET REVENGE
PUBLIC SECRETS
GENUINE LIES
CARNAL INNOCENCE
DIVINE EVIL
HONEST ILLUSIONS
PRIVATE SCANDALS

HIDDEN RICHES
TRUE BETRAYALS
MONTANA SKY
SANCTUARY
HOMEPORT
THE REEF
RIVER'S END
CAROLINA MOON
THE VILLA
MIDNIGHT BAYOU
THREE FATES

Anthologies
FROM THE HEART
A LITTLE MAGIC

The Once Upon Series
(with Jill Gregory, Ruth Ryan Langan, and Marianne Willman)
ONCE UPON A CASTLE
ONCE UPON A STAR
ONCE UPON A DREAM
ONCE UPON A ROSE

Trilogies
Three Sisters Island Trilogy
DANCE UPON THE AIR
HEAVEN AND EARTH
FACE THE FIRE

The Irish Trilogy
JEWELS OF THE SUN
TEARS OF THE MOON
HEART OF THE SEA

The Born In Trilogy
BORN IN FIRE
BORN IN ICE
BORN IN SHAME

The Chesapeake Bay Trilogy
SEA SWEPT
RISING TIDES
INNER HARBOR

The Dream Trilogy
DARING TO DREAM
HOLDING THE DREAM
FINDING THE DREAM

PURITY
IN
DEATH

J. D. Robb

Doubleday Large Print Home Library Edition

BERKLEY BOOKS, NEW YORK

PURITY IN DEATH

A Berkley Book / published by arrangement with the author

ISBN: 0-7394-2939-6

**This Large Print Book carries the
Seal of Approval of N.A.V.H.**

We bow our heads before Thee, and we laud
And magnify thy name Almighty God!
But man is thy most awful instrument
In working out a pure intent.

—William Woodsworth

In friendship false, implacable in hate,
Resolv'd to ruin or to rule the state.

—John Dryden

Prologue

The heat was murder. July flexed her sweaty muscles, eyed the goal, and drop-kicked New York into the sweltering steam-bath of summer. Some managed to escape, fleeing to their shore homes where they could sip cold drinks and bask in ocean breezes while they did their business via telelink. Some loaded up on supplies and hunkered down inside their air-cooled homes like tribes under siege.

But most just had to live through it.

With humatures into the triple digits, and no end in sight, moods turned surly, deodorants failed, and petty annoyances elbowed even the mildest of souls toward violence.

Emergency medical centers were jammed with the wounded soldiers of summer, 2059. Many who, under normal conditions, wouldn't so much as jaywalk saw the inside of police stations and holding tanks, forced to call lawyers to explain why they had attempted to throttle a coworker, or shove a complete stranger under the wheels of a Rapid Cab.

Usually, once cooled off, they didn't know why but sat or stood, blank-faced and baffled, like someone coming out of a trance.

But Louie K. Cogburn knew just what he was doing, why he did it, and how he intended to keep right on doing it. He was a small-time illegals dealer who primarily hawked Zoner and Jazz. To increase his profit margin, Louie cut the Zoner with dried grass scored from city parks, and the Jazz with baking powder he bought in warehouse-sized bins. His target clientele were middle-class kids between the ages of ten and twelve in the three school districts closest to his Lower East Side apartment.

This cut down on travel time and expense.

He preferred straight middle-class as the

poor generally had their own suppliers within the family ranks, and the rich copped to the grass and baking powder too quickly. The target age group fit Louie's brand of logic. He liked to say if you hooked 'em young, you had a client for life.

So far this credo hadn't proved out for him as Louie had yet to maintain a business relationship with a client through high school graduation.

Still, Louie took his business seriously. Every evening when his potential clients were doing their homework, he did his. He was proud of his bookkeeping, and would certainly have earned more per annum as a number cruncher for any midlevel firm than he did dealing. But he was a man who felt real men worked for themselves.

Just lately if there'd been a wash of dissatisfaction, a touch of irritability, a jagged edge of despair after he spent an hour running his business programs on his third-hand desktop, he put it off to the heat.

And the headache. The vicious bastard of a headache no dose of his own products could ease.

He lost three days of work because the pain had become the focus of his world. He holed up in his studio flop, stewing in the heat, blasting his music to cover up the raging storm in his head.

Somebody was going to pay for it, that's all he knew. Somebody.

Goddamn lazy-assed super hadn't fixed the climate control. He thought this, with growing anger while his beady, reddened eyes scanned numbers. He sat in his underwear, by the single open window of his one-room apartment. No breeze came through it, but the street noise was horrendous. Shouts, horns, squealing tires on pavement.

He turned up the trash rock he played out of his ancient entertainment unit to drown out the noise. To beat at the pain.

Blood trickled out of his nose, but he didn't notice.

Louie K. rubbed a lukewarm bottle of home-brew over his forehead. He wished he had a blaster. If he had a goddamn blaster he'd lean out the goddamn window and take out a goddamn city block.

His most violent act to date had been to kick a delinquent client off his airboard, but the image of death and destruction fueled him now as he sweated over his books and madness bloomed in his brain like black roses.

His face was pale as wax, rivulets of sweat pouring down from his matted brown hair, streaming down his narrow cheeks. His ears rang and what felt like an ocean of grease swayed in his belly. Heat was making him sick, he thought. He got sick, he lost money. Ought to take it out of the super's hide. Ought to.

His hands trembled as he stared at the screen. Stared at the screen. Couldn't take his eyes from the screen.

He had an image of himself going to the window, climbing out on the ledge, beating his fists at that hot wall of air, at the noise, at the people below. A blaster in his hands, doling out death and destruction as he screamed at them. Screamed and screamed as he leaped.

He'd land on his feet, and then . . .

The pounding on his door had him spinning around. With his teeth bared he climbed back in the window.

"Louie K., you asshole! Turn that fucking music down in there!"

"Go to hell," he muttered as he hefted the ball bat he often took to recreation areas to insinuate himself with potential clients. "Go to hell, go to hell. Let's all go to hell."

"You hear me? Goddamn it!"

"Yeah, I hear you." There were spikes, big iron spikes drilling into his brain. He had to get them out. On a thin scream, he dropped the bat to tear at his own hair. But the pounding wouldn't stop.

"Suze is calling the cops. You hear me, Louie? You don't turn that shit down Suze is calling the cops." Each word was punctuated with a fist against the door.

With the music, the pounding, the shouts, the spikes all hammering in his head, the sweat drowning him, Louie picked up the bat again.

He opened the door, and started swinging.

Chapter 1

Lieutenant Eve Dallas loitered at her desk. She was stalling, and she wasn't proud of it. The idea of changing into a fancy dress, driving uptown to meet her husband and a group of strangers for a business dinner thinly disguised as a social gathering had all the appeal of climbing in the nearest recycler and turning on Shred.

Right now Cop Central was very appealing.

She'd caught and closed a case that afternoon, so there was paperwork. It wasn't *all* stalling. But as the bevy of witnesses had all agreed that the guy who'd taken a header

off a six-story people glide had been the one
who'd started the pushy-shovey match with
the two tourists from Toledo, it wasn't much
of a time sucker.

For the past several days, every case
she'd caught had been a variation on the
same theme. Domestics where spouses had
battled to the death, street brawls turned lethal, even a deadly combat at a corner glide-
cart over ice cones.

Heat made people stupid and mean, she
thought, and the combination spilled blood.

She was feeling a little mean herself at the
idea of dressing up and spending several
hours in some snooty restaurant making
small talk with people she didn't know.

That's what you got, she thought in disgust, when you marry a guy who had
enough money to buy a couple of conti-
nents.

Roarke actually liked evenings like this.
The fact that he did never failed to baffle
her. He was every bit at home in a five-star
restaurant—one he likely owned anyway—
nibbling on caviar as he was sitting at home
chowing down on a burger.

And she supposed as their marriage was
approaching its second year, she'd better

stop crabbing about it. Resigned, she pushed back from the desk.

"You're still here." Her aide, Peabody, stopped in the doorway of her office. "I thought you had some fancy dinner deal uptown."

"I got time." A glance at her wrist unit brought on a little tug of guilt. Okay, she was going to be late. But not very. "I just finished up on the glide diver."

Peabody, whose summer blues defied all natural order and managed to stay crisp in the wilting heat, kept her dark eyes sober. "You wouldn't be stalling, would you, Lieutenant?"

"One of the residents of our city, who I am sworn to serve and protect, ended up squished like a bug on Fifth Avenue. I think he deserves an extra thirty minutes of my time."

"It must be really rough, forced to put on a beautiful dress, stick some diamonds or whatever all over you and choke down champagne and lobster croquettes beside the most beautiful man ever born, on or off planet. I don't know how you get through the day with that weight on your shoulders, Dallas."

"Shut up."

"And here I am, free to squeeze into the local pizza place with McNab where we will split the pie and the check." Peabody shook her head slowly. The dark bowl of hair under her cap swayed in concert. "I can't tell you how guilty I feel knowing that."

"You looking for trouble, Peabody?"

"No, sir." Peabody did her best to look pious. "Just offering my support and sympathy at this difficult time."

"Kiss ass." Torn between annoyance and amusement, Eve started to shove by. Her desk 'link beeped.

"Shall I get that for you, sir, and tell them you've gone for the day?"

"Didn't I tell you to shut up?" Eve turned back to the desk, took the transmission. "Homicide. Dallas."

"Sir. Lieutenant."

She recognized Officer Troy Trueheart's face as it popped on-screen, though she'd never seen its young, All-American features so strained. "Trueheart."

"Lieutenant," he repeated after an audible swallow. "I have an incident. In response to . . . oh gosh, I killed him."

"Officer." She pulled his location on-screen as she spoke. "Are you on duty?"

"No, sir. Yes, sir. I don't know, exactly."

"Pull yourself together, Trueheart." She slapped out the order, watched his head jerk as if he'd felt it physically. "Report."

"Sir. I had just clocked off shift and was on my way home on foot when a female civilian shouted for assistance from a window. I responded. On the fourth floor of the building in question an individual armed with a bat was assaulting the female. Another individual, male, was unconscious or dead in the hallway, bleeding from the head. I entered the apartment where the assault was taking place, and . . . Lieutenant, I tried to stop him. He was killing her. He turned on me, ignored all warnings and orders to desist. I managed to draw my weapon, to stun. I swear I intended to stun, but he's dead."

"Trueheart, look at me. Listen to me. Secure the building, call in the incident through Dispatch and inform them that you've reported to me and I'm on my way. I'll call for medical assistance. You hold the scene, Trueheart. Hold it by the book. Do you understand?"

"Yes, sir. I should've called Dispatch first. I should've—"

"You stand, Trueheart. I'm on the way. Peabody," Eve commanded as she strode out the door.

"Yes, sir. I'm with you."

There were two black-and-whites, nose-to-nose, and a medi-van humped between them at the curb when Eve pulled up. The neighborhood was the type where people scattered rather than gathered when cops showed up, and as a result there was no more than a smattering of gawkers on the sidewalk who had to be told to stay back.

The two uniforms who flanked the entrance eyed her, then exchanged a look. She was brass, and the one who could well put one of their own rank's balls in the blender.

She could feel the chill as she approached.

"Cop shouldn't get hassled by cops for doing the job," one of them muttered.

Eve paused in midstride and stared him down.

He saw rank in the form of a long, leanly built woman with eyes of gilded brown that were as flat and expressionless as a snake's as they met his. Her hair, short and choppy, was nearly the same color and framed a narrow face offset by a wide mouth that was now firmed into one thin line. There was a shallow dent in a chin that looked like it could hold its own against a fist.

Under her stare he felt himself shrink.

"Cop shouldn't slap at a cop for doing hers," she said coldly. "You got a problem with me, Officer, wait until I do that job. Then mouth off."

She moved into the shoe box lobby, punched a finger on the Up button of the single elevator. She was already steaming, but it had little to do with the oppressive heat. "What is it with some uniforms that they want to bite your throat when you're rank?"

"It's just nerves, Dallas," Peabody replied as they stepped onto the elevator. "Most of the uniforms out of Central know Trueheart, and you gotta like him. A uniform terminates on his own like this, Testing's going to be brutal."

"Testing's brutal anyway. The best we can do for him is to keep this clean and ordered.

He's already screwed up by tagging me before he called it in."

"Is he going to take heat for that? You're the one who pulled him out of the sidewalk scooper detail and into Central last winter. Internal ought to understand—"

"IAB isn't big on understanding. So let's hope it doesn't go there." She stepped off the elevator. Studied the scene.

He'd been smart enough, cop enough, she noted with some relief, not to disturb the bodies. Two men lay sprawled in the corridor, one of them facedown in a pool of congealing blood.

The other was faceup, staring with some surprise at the ceiling. Through an open doorway beside the bodies she could hear the sounds of weeping and groaning.

The door across was also open. She noted several fresh holes and dents in the hallway walls, splinters of wallboard, splatters of blood. And what had once been a baseball bat was now a broken club, covered with blood and brain matter.

Straight as a soldier, pale as a ghost, Trueheart stood at the doorway. His eyes still held the glassy edge of shock.

"Lieutenant."

"Hold it together, Trueheart. Record on, Peabody." Eve crouched down to examine the two bodies. The bloodied one was big and beefy, the kind of mixed fat and muscle build that could usually plow through walls if annoyed enough. The back of his skull looked like an egg that had been cracked with a brick.

The second body wore only a pair of grayed Jockey shorts. His thin, boney frame showed no wounds, no bruising, no damage. Thin trickles of blood had seeped out of his ears, his nostrils.

"Officer Trueheart, do we have identification on these individuals?"

"Sir. The, um, initial victim has been identified as Ralph Wooster, who resided in apartment 42E. The man I—" He broke off as Eve's head whipped up, as her eyes drilled into his.

"And the second individual?"

Trueheart wet his lips. "The second individual is identified as Louis K. Cogburn of apartment 43F."

"And who is currently wailing inside apartment 42E?"

"Suzanne Cohen, cohabitation partner of Ralph Wooster. She called for aid out the window of said apartment. Louis Cogburn was assaulting her with what appeared to be a club or bat when I arrived on-scene. At that time—"

He broke off again when Eve held up a finger. "Preliminary examination of victims indicates a mixed-race male—mid-thirties, approximately two hundred and thirty pounds, approximately six foot one—has suffered severe trauma to head, face, and body. A bat, apparently wooden, and marked with blood and brain matter would appear to be the assault weapon. The second male, also mid-thirties, Caucasian, approximately one hundred and thirty pounds, approximately five foot eight, is identified as the assailant. Cause of death as yet undetermined. Second vic bled from ears and nose. There is no visual trauma or wound."

She straightened. "Peabody, I don't want these bodies touched. I'll do the field exam after I talk to Cohen. Officer Trueheart, did you discharge your weapon during the course of this incident?"

"Yes, sir. I—"

"I want you to surrender that weapon to my aide, who will bag it at this time."

There were grumblings from the two uniforms at the end of the hall, but she ignored them as she held Trueheart's gaze. "You are not obliged to surrender your weapon without representation present. You may request a representative. I'm asking you to give your weapon to Peabody so there's no question as to the sequence of this investigation."

Through the shock, she saw his absolute trust in her. "Yes, sir." When he reached down for his weapon, she put a hand on his arm.

"Since when are you a southpaw, Trueheart?"

"My right arm's a little sore."

"Were you injured during the course of this incident?"

"He got a couple of swings in before—"

"The individual you were obliged to draw on assaulted you in the due course of your duties?" She wanted to shake him. "Why the hell didn't you say so?"

"It happened awfully fast, Lieutenant. He rushed me, came in swinging, and—"

"Take off your shirt."

"Sir?"

"Lose the shirt, Trueheart. Peabody, record here."

He blushed. *God, what an innocent*, Eve thought, as Trueheart unbuttoned his uniform shirt. She heard Peabody suck in a breath, but whether it was for Trueheart's undeniably pretty chest, or the bruising that exploded over his right shoulder and mottled the arm to the elbow, she couldn't be sure.

"He got in a couple of good swings by the look of it. I want the MTs to take a look at you. Next time you're hurt on the job, Officer, make it known. Standby."

Apartment 42E was in shambles. Though from what was left of the decor, Eve imagined housekeeping wasn't a high priority of its residents. Still, it was doubtful the place was normally a minefield of broken glass, or the walls decorated with surreal paintings of blood splatters.

The woman on the gurney looked like she'd known better days as well. A bandage streaked across her left eye, and above it, below it, the skin was raw.

"She coherent?" Eve asked one of the medical technicians.

"Just. Kept her from going all the way under since we figured you'd want a word with her. Make it snappy though," he told her. "We need to get her in. She's got a detached cornea, shattered cheekbone, broken arm. Guy whaled on her good and proper."

"Five minutes. Miss Cohen." Eve stepped up, leaned down. "I'm Lieutenant Dallas. Can you tell me what happened?"

"He went crazy. I think he killed Ralph. Just went crazy."

"Louis Cogburn?"

"Louie K., yeah." She moaned. "Ralph was pissed. Music up so loud you couldn't think straight. Fucking hot. Just wanted a couple of brews and a little quiet. What the hell? Louie K., he mostly plays the music loud, but this was busting our eardrums. He's had it wailing for days."

"What did Ralph do?" Eve prompted. "Ms. Cohen?"

"Ralph went and banged on the door, told him to cut it back. Next I knew, Louie came busting out, swinging a bat or something. Looked crazy. Blood was flying, he was screaming. I was scared, really scared, so I slammed the door and ran to the window. Called for help. I could hear him screaming out there, and these awful thumping sounds. I couldn't hear Ralph. I kept calling for help, then he came in."

"Who came in?"

"Louie K. Didn't even look like Louie. Had blood all over him, and something was wrong with his eyes. He come at me, with the bat. I ran, tried to run. He was smashing everything and screaming about spikes in his head. He hit me, and I don't remember after that. Hit me in the face and I don't remember until the MTs started working on me."

"Did you see or speak with the officer who responded to your call for help?"

"I didn't see nothing but stars. Ralph's dead, isn't he?" A single tear slid down her cheek. "They won't tell me, but Louie'd never have gotten past him 'less he was dead."

"Yeah, I'm sorry. Did Ralph and Louie have a history of altercations?"

"You mean did they go at it before? Yelled at each other sometimes about the music, but they'd more likely have a couple brews or smoke a little Zoner. Louie's just a little squirt of a guy. He never caused no problems around here."

"Lieutenant." One of the MTs moved in. "We've got to transport her."

"All right. Send somebody in to take a look

at my officer. He caught a couple solids in the arm and shoulder." Eve stepped back, then moved to the door behind them. "Trueheart, you're going to give me a report, on record. I want it clear, I want it detailed."

"Yes, sir. I clocked off at eighteen-thirty and proceeded southeast from Central on foot."

"What was your intended destination?"

He flushed a little. Color came and went in his face. "I was, ah, proceeding to the home of a friend where I had arrangements for dinner."

"You had a date."

"Yes, sir. As I approached this building, I heard calls for assistance and looking up saw a woman leaning out of the window. She appeared to be in considerable distress. I entered the building, proceeded to the fourth floor where I could hear the sounds of an altercation. Several individuals came to their doors, but no one attempted to come out. I called requests for someone to call nine-eleven."

"Did you take the stairs or the elevator?" Details, she thought. She needed to take him through every detail.

"The stairs, sir. I thought it would be fas-

ter. When I reached this floor, I saw the
male identified as Ralph Wooster lying on
the floor of the corridor between apartments
42E and 43F. I did not, at that time, check
him for injuries as I could hear screaming
and breaking glass emitting from 42E. I responded to this immediately and witnessed
the individual identified as Louis K. Cogburn
assaulting a woman with what appeared to
be a baseball bat. The weapon was . . ."

He paused a moment, swallowed hard.
"The weapon was covered with what appeared to be blood and gray matter. The
woman was unconscious on the floor, with
Cogburn above her. He held the bat over his
head as if preparing to strike another blow.
I drew my weapon at this time, called for the
assailant to cease and desist, identifying
myself as Police."

Trueheart had to stop now, and rubbed
the back of his hand over his mouth. The
look he sent her was both helpless and
pleading. "Lieutenant, it all happened fast
from there."

"Just tell it."

"He turned away from the woman. He was
screaming something about spikes in his
head, about blasting out the window. Crazy

stuff. Then he lifted the bat again, shifting so it looked like he was going to strike the woman. I moved in to prevent this, and he charged me. I tried to evade, to get the bat. He landed a couple of blows—I believe it broke at that time—and I fell back, knocked something over, hit the wall. I saw him coming at me again. I yelled at him to stop."

Trueheart took a steadying breath, but it didn't stop the quaver in his voice. "He cocked the bat back like he was swinging for home, and I discharged my weapon. It's set on low stun, Lieutenant, the lowest setting. You can see—"

"What happened next?"

"He screamed. He screamed like—I've never heard anything like it. He screamed and he ran out into the hall. I pursued. But he went down. I thought he was stunned, just stunned. But when I got down to put restraints on him, I saw he was dead. I checked his pulse. He was dead. I got jumbled up. Sir, I got jumbled up. I know it was incorrect procedure to tag you before calling—"

"Never mind that. Officer, were you at the time you deployed your weapon, in fear for your life and/or the lives of civilians?"

"Yes, sir. Yes, sir, I was."

"Did Louis K. Cogburn ignore any and all of your warnings to cease and desist and surrender his weapon?"

"Yes, sir, he did."

"You." Eve pointed to one of the uniforms down the hall. "Escort Officer Trueheart downstairs. Medical attention for his injuries has been called for. Put him in one of the black-and-whites until the MTs can see him. Stay with him until I'm done in here. Trueheart, call your representative."

"But, sir—"

"I'm advising you to call your representative," she said. "I'm stating here, for the record, that in my opinion, after a cursory examination of the evidence, after an interview with Suzanne Cohen, your account of this incident is satisfactory. The deployment of your weapon appears to have been necessary to protect your life and the life of civilians. That's all I can tell you until my on-scene investigation into this matter is complete. Now I want you to go, get off your feet, call your rep and let the MTs take care of you."

"Yes, sir. Thank you, sir."

"Come on, Trueheart." The other uniform patted Trueheart on the back.

"Officer? Any of the beat cops know these dead guys?"

The uniform glanced back at Eve. "Proctor has this sector. He might."

"Get him," she said as she sealed up and walked into 43F.

"He's awful shook," Peabody said.

"He'll have to get over it." She scanned the room.

It was a filthy mess, smelling ripely of spoiled food and dirty laundry. The cramped kitchen area consisted of a two-foot counter, a mini-AutoChef and minifridgie. A huge tin sat on the counter. Eve lifted her brows as she read the label.

"You know, I just don't see our Louie K. baking a lot of cakes." She opened one of the two cupboards and perused the neat line of sealed jars. "Looks like Louie was in the illegals line. Funny, everything in here's neat as Aunt Martha's, and the rest of the place is a pigsty."

She turned around. "No dust on the furniture though. That's funny, too. You wouldn't figure a guy who sleeps on sheets that smell like a swamp would bother chasing dust."

She opened the closet. "Tidy in here, too. Clothes show a lack of fashion taste, but they're all clean. Look at that window, Peabody."

"Yes, sir?"

"Glass is clean, inside and out. Somebody washed them within the last couple weeks. Why do you wash your windows and leave— what the hell is this?—unidentified spilled food substance all over the floor?"

"Maid's week off?"

"Yeah, somebody's week off. That's about how long this underwear's been piled here." She glanced at the door when a uniform stepped in.

"You Proctor?"

"Yes, sir."

"You know those two dead guys?"

"I know Louie K." Proctor shook his head. "Shit—sorry, Lieutenant, but shit, this is some mess. That kid Trueheart's down there puking his guts out."

"Tell me about Louie K., and let me worry about Trueheart and his guts."

Proctor pokered up. "Small-time Illegals rat, went after schoolkids. Gave them samples of Zoner and Jazz to lure them in. Waste of air, you ask me. Did some time, but mostly he was pretty slick about it, and the Illegals guys never got much out of the kids."

"He a violent tendency?"

"Anything but. Kept a low profile, never gave you lip. You told him to move his ass along, he moved it. He'd give you a look now and then like he'd like to do more, but he never had the guts for it."

"Had guts enough to open Ralph Wooster's head, bash a woman and assault a uniform."

"Must've been sampling his own product's all I can think. And that's not profile either. He maybe smoked a little Zoner now and then, but he was too cheap to do more. What's out there looks like Zeus," Proctor added with a jerk of the thumb toward the corridor. "Little guy like that going nutso. But he never handled anything that hot I heard about."

"Okay, Proctor. Thanks."

"Guy sells illegals to schoolkids, world's better off without him."

"That's not our call." Eve dismissed him

by turning her back. She moved to the desk, frowned at the computer screen.

ABSOLUTE PURITY ACHIEVED

"What the hell does this mean?" she asked aloud. "Peabody, any new shit on the streets going by the name Purity?"

"I haven't heard of it."

"Computer, identify Purity."

INVALID COMMAND.

Frowning, she entered her name, badge number, and authorization. "Identify Purity."

INVALID COMMAND.

"Huh. Peabody do a run on new and known illegals. Computer, save current display. Display last task performed."

The screen wavered, then opened a tidy, organized spreadsheet detailing inventory, profit, loss, and coded customer base.

"So, according to the last task, and time logged, Louie was sitting here, very efficiently doing his books when he got a bug up his ass to bust his neighbor's head open."

"It's hot, Dallas." Peabody looked over Eve's shoulder. "People can just get crazy."

"Yeah." Maybe it was just that simple. "Yeah, they can. Nothing on his inventory named Purity."

"Nothing on the current illegals list by that name either."

"So what the hell is it, and how was it achieved?" She stepped back. "Let's take a look at Louie K., see what he tells us."

Chapter 2

He didn't tell her as much as she'd have liked.

The best she could determine on-scene with her field kit was that Louie K. had died due to neurological meltdown. That wasn't exactly the sort of term that elicited sage nods from the brass.

She passed the body off to the ME, flagged for priority.

Which meant, due to summer hours and summer glut, she'd be lucky if she got a confirmed pathology by the first frost.

She meant to push, calling in chips with the chief medical examiner.

Meanwhile she spoke with Trueheart's departmental rep via 'link, and danced the bureaucratic dance. She sent the still shaken rookie home, and ordered him to stand by for Testing.

Then she went back to Central to write, and rewrite, a detailed report on the incident that had resulted in two deaths and one critical injury.

And though her stomach curdled, she followed procedure and copied Internal Affairs.

By the time she got home, it was well past the dinner hour.

The lights were on, so that the urban fortress Roarke had built glowed like a beacon in the night. Green shadows from grand and leafy trees threw patterns on velvet grass and slid softly over rivers of flowers that were bright and bold by day.

The Lower East Side neighborhood that had eaten up most of her evening was a world away from this private paradise of wealth, of privilege, of indulgence.

She was almost accustomed to straddling worlds now without losing her balance. Almost.

She left her vehicle at the base of the stone steps and jogged up them more out of a desperate desire to shrug off the weight of heat than out of hurry.

She'd barely stepped in, taken that first breath of cool, clean air, when Summerset, Roarke's majordomo, appeared in the foyer like an unwelcome vision.

"Yes, I missed the dinner," she said before he could open his mouth. "Yes, I'm a miserable failure as a wife and a poor example of a human being. I have no class, no courtesy, and no sense of decorum. I should be dragged naked into the streets and stoned for my sins."

Summerset raised one steel gray eyebrow. "Well, that seems to cover it."

"Good, saves time." She started up the stairs. "Is he back?"

"Just."

A little annoyed she'd given him no opportunity to criticize, he frowned after her. He'd have to be quicker next time.

When she was sure he'd evaporated to wherever he'd appeared from, Eve paused at one of the house screens. "Where's Roarke?"

GOOD EVENING, DARLING EVE. ROARKE IS IN HIS OFFICE.

"Figures." Business dinner followup. She gave one blissful thought to detouring to the bedroom, jumping headlong into the shower. But guilt had her heading to his office.

The door was open. She could hear his voice.

She supposed he was refining the details of some deal he had going, most likely the one that had involved tonight's dinner. But she didn't care about the words.

His voice was poetry, seductive in itself even to a woman who'd never understood the heart of a poet. Wisps of Ireland trailed through it, adding music to what she assumed were dry facts and figures.

It suited his face, one that bore all that wild Celtic beauty in its strong, sharp bones, deep blue eyes, in the full, firm mouth that might have been sculpted by some canny god on a particularly good day.

She stepped to the doorway, saw that he stood at one of the windows, looking out while he dictated his memo. He'd pulled his hair back, she noted, all that thick black silk he usually wore loose so that it streamed nearly to his shoulders.

He still wore his dinner suit, black and

sleek, over his long, rangy form. You could look and see the elegant businessman, madly successful, perfectly civilized. He'd polished himself, Eve thought, but that dangerous Celt was still, always, just beneath the surface.

It still, always, allured her.

She caught a glimpse of it now as he turned, though she hadn't made a sound, and his eyes met hers.

"Sign Roarke," he said, "and transmit. File copy Hagerman-Ross. Hello, Lieutenant."

"Hi. Sorry about dinner."

"No, you're not."

She tucked her hands in her pockets. It was ridiculous, really, the way they continually itched to take hold of him. "I'm sort of sorry about dinner."

He grinned, that lightning bolt of charm and humor. "You wouldn't have been as bored as you think."

"You're probably right. If I'd been as bored as I thought, I'd have slipped into a coma. But I am sorry I let you down."

"You don't let me down." He crossed to her, tapped her chin up with his finger and kissed her lightly. "It adds considerably to my cache when I apologize for my wife, who's been called to duty on a case. Murder always makes lively dinner conversation. Who's dead?"

"Couple of guys downtown. Small-time chem dealer whaled on his neighbor with a ball bat, then went after a woman and a cop. Cop took him out."

Roarke lifted a brow. More, he thought. There was a deal more trouble in her eyes than her quick rundown warranted. "That doesn't seem like the sort of wrangle that would keep you on duty so late."

"The cop was Trueheart."

"Ah." He laid his hands on her shoulders, rubbed. "How's he doing?"

She opened her mouth, then shook her head and paced away. "Shit. Shit, shit, shit."

"That bad, huh?"

"Kid breaks his cherry it's tough enough."

Roarke stroked a hand over the fat cat that sprawled over the console, then gave Galahad a little nudge to move him along. "That's an interesting way to put it."

"There are cops who go through the whole life of the job without deploying. Kid's in uniform under a year, and he's racked up a termination. It changes everything."

"Did it for you? Your first termination on

the job," he added. They both knew she'd killed long before she had a badge.

"It was different for me." She often wondered if the way she'd started life made death somehow different for her.

A cold and personal insult.

"Trueheart, he's barely twenty-two and he's . . . shiny yet." Pity—a dark, slippery blossom—bloomed inside her. She crouched down, gave Galahad an absent scratch under the chin. "He won't sleep tonight. He'll go over it and over it and over it in his head. If I'd done this, if I'd done that. And tomorrow . . ." She rubbed her hands over her face as she straightened. "I can't block Testing for him. I can't stop the process."

She knew what it was. Stripped bare, monitored, questioned, forced to let machines and techs into your head. Into your gut like a tumor.

"Are you worried he won't pass through it?"

She glanced over, took the glass of wine he'd poured her. "He's tougher than he looks, but he's scared down to the bone. And he's swimming in guilt. Take all that guilt, all those doubts into Testing, they can drown you. And there's got to be an investigation. Internal."

"Why is that?"

She sat, gave him the details while the cat leaped up and kneaded a nest in her lap. It helped clear her mind to say it aloud, particularly to someone who caught on quickly and saw the full picture before you painted in all the lines.

"A uniform's stunner can't terminate under those conditions."

"Yeah." Eve nodded. "Exactly. It would have to be on full stun and jammed on the throat pulse. Even then it would take more than one jolt."

"Which means Trueheart's version of the events doesn't quite hold."

IAB wouldn't think so, she knew, and ran it through for herself as she would for them. "He was under serious duress. A civilian dead, another in extreme jeopardy, himself injured."

"Is that how you're going to play it with IAB?"

Yeah, he always saw the whole picture. "Pretty close to that." She drummed her fingers restlessly on her thigh, on the cat, sipped her wine. "I need the ME's report. But

there's no way it's going to come out Trueheart terminated with deliberation. Panic,
okay. He'll take a slap for panic, thirty days'
suspension, some mandatory therapy. I
can't get in the way of it. It's already dicey
for him because he tagged me instead of
calling it in through Dispatch. IAB smells
cover-up, and the kid's finished."

Roarke sat, sipped his own wine. "Have
you considered speaking to your old friend
Webster?"

She tapped her fingers on the arm of her
chair now and kept her gaze steady on
Roarke's. There might have been amusement on his face—or something else. It was
often tough to call.

Don Webster wasn't precisely an old
friend. He had been very briefly and years
before a lover. The fact that he, for reasons
that would never be clear to Eve, had never
gotten over that single night they'd shared
had caused a violent and fascinating altercation between him and Roarke.

It wasn't something she wanted to repeat.

"Maybe, unless you're thinking that'd be a
nice opportunity to pound his face in again."

Roarke sipped, smiled. "I believe Webster
and I have a reasonable understanding. I

can't fault him for being attracted to my wife, as I'm very attracted to her myself. And he knows that if he puts his hands on what's mine again, I'll break every bone in his body into small, jagged pieces. It works well for us."

"Great. Dandy." She said it between her teeth. "He's over it. He said so," she added and Roarke merely smiled again. Lazily now. Catlike.

"You know what, I've got enough to think about, so we're just not going to go there tonight. I want to call the commander," she said. "And I can't. I have to play this by every page in the book. Kid was dog sick after. Nothing I could do for him."

"He'll be all right, Mum."

Her eyes narrowed. "Careful. I'm the one who brought him in out of Homicide Lite. I put him in the hospital a few months ago."

"Eve."

"All right, all right. I put him in a situation where he ended up in the hospital. Now he's dealing with a suspicious termination. I've got a responsibility."

"You'd see it that way." He grazed his hand over the backs of her restless fingers. "That's what makes you what you are. And why he called it into you first. He was scared, he was shaken. The taking of a life isn't a simple matter for most, and it shouldn't be. Doesn't it make him a better cop that he felt something?"

"Yeah, and I'll use that, too. It just doesn't hang, Roarke. Just doesn't hang," she said as she got to her feet to pace again. Annoyed, the cat shot his tail into the air and stalked out of the room.

"No burn marks on his throat. If Trueheart had zapped him that way, there should have been marks. Why weren't there?"

"Could he have used another weapon, one with lethal power?"

She shook her head. "I don't know anyone less likely to carry a drop piece. If I'm wrong about him, where is it? It wasn't on him. It wasn't in either apartment. I had the recyclers checked. His call to me came in minutes after the termination. No time to think clearly enough to ditch one safely. Besides, when you go back through it, the whole thing doesn't make sense."

She sat again, leaned in. "Take this Louie K. The beat cop, the neighbors, even the woman he attacked all describe him as your basic lowlife wimp. Preyed on schoolkids.

He's got a sheet, but nothing on it with violence. No assaults, no batteries. No weapons of any kind in his flop."

"The bat?"

"He played ball. So he's sitting there in his underwear doing his books. Tidy books, filthy apartment. But not logically filthy. Cupboards are organized, windows are washed, but there's food and dirty dishes, ripe laundry tossed around. It's like he got sick or went on a bender for a week."

She scooped her hand through her hair as she brought the picture of his cramped little apartment into her head. Pictured him in it. Sitting in the heat at his desk unit, by the open window. Sweating through his Jockey shorts.

"He's got the music up to ear-blasting, nothing new according to neighbors. Ralph from across the hall goes over and bangs on the door. Again, nothing new. But this time, instead of turning the music down, Louie K. picks up his bat and beats his sometime drinking buddy to death with it.

"Cracks his skull," she continued. "Turns his face to jelly, beats down hard enough to crack a good, solid baseball bat. Neighbor outweighs Louie K. by better than a hundred pounds, but he doesn't get a chance to put a mark on him."

He knew she was seeing it now, pulling images into her brain of what had happened. Though she hadn't been there, she would see it. "It's tough to fight back if your brains are leaking out of your ears."

"Yeah, that's a disadvantage. But then, screaming all the while, Louie K. kicks in the neighbor's door and goes after the woman. Cop responds, and Louie goes for him."

"The heat can turn people."

"Yeah, it can. It brings out the mean. But the sucker was sitting there, doing his books. Making entries. Just like he did every evening about that time. It doesn't feel right."

Frowning, she leaned back on Roarke's desk. "You know of any illegal that goes by Purity?"

"No."

"Neither does anyone else. When I went into his apartment, his screen was on. It said Absolute Purity Achieved. What the hell is absolute purity, and how was it achieved?"

"If it's something new, why would a small-time playground dealer be in on the ground floor?"

"I've been asking myself that. The computer wouldn't identify, even with my authorization code. So I've sent it into EDD. Can't bring Feeney in," she mused. "Looks wrong to tag the head of Electronics Detective Division for a standard data search."

"You could've tagged me."

"Talk about looking wrong. Besides, you were working."

"So I was, and eating, which I imagine you weren't. Hungry?"

"Now that you mention it. What did you have?"

"Hmm. Chilled plum soup, crab salad, and an excellent grilled turbot."

"Huh." Eve pushed to her feet. "I could go for a burger."

"Somehow I knew that."

Later, Eve lay awake, staring at the ceiling as she reconstructed data, evidence, theory. None of it *felt* right, she thought, but couldn't be sure how much of that was influenced by concern over a young, promising cop.

He had a good brain, and an idealism that was as bright and shiny as polished silver. Purity, she thought again. If she had to use one word to define it, it would be Trueheart.

He'd lost some of that purity today. Some,

she knew, he'd never be able to get back. He would suffer for it, more than he should.

And she wasn't being a mommy, she thought, turning her head just enough to scowl at Roarke in the dark.

"Well then." He shifted toward her, sliding his hands unerringly over her breasts. "Since you've all this energy . . ."

"What're you talking about? I'm sleeping here."

"You're not, not with your mind racing around loud enough to wake the dead. Why don't I just give you a hand with all that energy?"

As he pulled her against him, she chuckled. "I've got news for you, ace. That's not your hand."

Thirty-six blocks away, Troy Trueheart lay in the dark, staring at the ceiling. No one shared his bed to offer comfort or distraction. All he could see, printed on the dark, was the face of the man he'd killed.

He knew he should take a departmentally approved tranq. But he was afraid to sleep. He'd see it all again in his dreams.

Just as he could see it all as he lay awake.

The splatter of blood and bone and worse all over the walls of that dank hallway. Even here in his tidy apartment, he could smell it. The way the heat ripened the stench of blood, of gore. He could hear the screams, the woman's no more than a howl of terror and awful pain. And the man's. Louis K. Cogburn. The man's screams like a wild animal's mad from the hunt. The voices of other tenants shouting out from behind locked doors. Calls booming up into the windows from the street.

And his own heart raging in his chest.

Why hadn't he called for backup? The minute he'd heard the woman calling for help, he should have called for backup.

But he'd rushed inside, thinking only to protect and serve.

He'd shouted back—he had, at least he had shouted as he'd rushed up those stairs for someone to call 911. No one had. He realized that now. No one had or cops would have come long before Lieutenant Dallas.

How could people stand behind locked doors and do nothing while their neighbor was crying for help? He would never understand it.

He'd seen the man in the hallway far beyond anyone's help. He'd seen that, felt his stomach lurch, and the blood roar into his head in a buzzing white noise that was the sound of fear. Yes, he'd been afraid, very afraid. But it was his job to go through the door. The open door, he thought now, go through it and into the screams and the blood and the madness.

What then? What then?

Police! Drop your weapon! Drop the weapon now.

His stunner was in his hand. He'd drawn it on the way up. He was sure of that. The man. Louis K. Cogburn. He had turned, the bloody bat hitched in both hands like a batter at the plate. Tiny eyes, Trueheart thought now. Tiny eyes almost disappearing in a thin face that was red from rage and secondhand blood.

Darker blood, fresher blood leaked from his nose. Just remembered that, he thought. Did it matter?

He'd charged. A madman in Jockey shorts who'd moved like lightning. The bat had come down on his shoulder so fast, so hard. Stumbled back, nearly lost the stunner. Terror, bright as blood.

The man. Louis K. Cogburn. He'd whirled

back toward the woman. She was down, dazed, weeping. Helpless. The bat swung up, high. A death blow.

But then he jittered. His eyes—oh God, his eyes—demon red, went wide, jumped inside his skull. His body jolted, jolted like a puppet dancing on string as he ran by. Out in the hall.

He danced, still dancing. Then he fell, sort of folded up and dropped, faceup to stare at the ceiling with those awful red eyes.

Dead. Dead. And I'm standing over him.

I killed a man today.

Trueheart buried his face in his pillow, trying to erase the images that wanted to play in his brain. And he wept for the dead.

In the morning, Eve put in a call to Chief Medical Examiner Morris and tried not to sound too snarly when she was forced to leave a message on his voice mail. If necessary, she'd make time to go down to the morgue and speak with him personally.

In fact, that was just what she was going to do—and get another look at Cogburn's body.

As much at it irked, she put a call into Don Webster in Internal Affairs. This time she didn't bother to play down the annoyance when she was transferred to voice mail.

"The Rat Squad's got some cushy hours. Us real cops are already on duty. Give me a call, Webster, when you toddle in for your day of riding the desk and sniffing up dirt on fellow officers."

Probably not smart to annoy him, she thought as she broke transmission. Then again, if she tried to sweet-talk Webster, he'd know she was up to something.

"Lieutenant." Cap in hand, Trueheart stood in her doorway. "You sent for me."

"That's right, Trueheart. Come in. Close the door."

She wasn't crossing any lines by calling him to her office prior to Testing. She was primary on the case.

That was her story, she thought, and she was sticking to it.

"Sit down, Trueheart."

He looked every bit as pale and hollow-eyed as she'd expected. Somehow he managed to stay at attention even seated. She programmed her AutoChef for two coffees, black, whether he wanted one or not.

"Rough night?"

"Yes, sir."

"You're going to have a rougher day. Testing's no walk on the beach."

"No, sir. I've heard."

"You better be up for it. Look at me when I speak to you, Officer." She snapped it out, watched his head come up and his weary eyes focus. "You put on the uniform, you pick up the badge, you holster the weapon and you take on everything that means. Was your termination of Louis K. Cogburn justifiable?"

"I don't—"

"Yes or no. There's no middle here, no qualifications. Your gut, Trueheart. Was the deployment of your weapon necessary?"

"Yes, sir."

"If you walked into the same situation to-day, would you again deploy your weapon?"

He shuddered, but he nodded. "Yes, sir."

"That's the core of it." She passed him the coffee. "You hold on to the core of it, you'll get through the rest. Don't try to out-think Testing. You haven't got the brass for it yet. Answer correctly, answer truthfully. And however they twist the question of justification, you deployed your weapon justifiably, to preserve the life of a civilian and your own."

"Yes, sir."

"Jesus, Trueheart, you're an agreeable bastard. At what distance were you from the subject when you deployed?"

"I think—"

"Don't think. How far?"

"Six feet, maybe five and a half."

"How many jolts did you give him?"

"Two."

"Did your weapon, at any time during the altercation, come in direct contact with the subject?"

"Contact?" He looked baffled for a moment. "Oh, no, sir. I was down and he was moving away when I deployed. Then he turned, moving toward me when I deployed the second time."

"What did you do with the drop piece?"

"The . . ." Pure shock jolted over his face. She watched it turn pink with what could only be indignation. "Sir, I had no secondary weapon, nor do I own one. I had only the street stunner, which I'm authorized to carry and which you took into evidence at the scene. Sir, I resent—"

"Save it." She leaned back. "If they don't ask you that question in Testing, I'll be surprised. You can bet your ass IAB will ask it.

And they'll push. So save the moral outrage for them. Don't you drink coffee, Trueheart?"

"Yes, sir." He looked miserably into the cup, then lifted it, sipped. His breath sucked in. "This isn't coffee."

"Yeah, it is. It's *real* coffee. Got a lot more going for it than that veggie crap, doesn't it? You could use the extra kick today. Listen to me, Troy. You're a good cop and with some seasoning you'll be a better one. Terminations aren't supposed to be easy. We shouldn't be able to shrug off the taking of any life like it was nothing or we skirt too close to being what we're here to put away."

"I wish . . . I wish there'd been another way."

"There wasn't, and don't forget that. It's okay to be sorry, even a little guilty. But it's not okay to feel anything less than absolutely confident that you did what had to be done given the circumstances. You let them see you're not sure, and they'll rip you up like a leopard does a gazelle."

"I had to do it." He held the coffee tight in both hands as if he were afraid it would jump out of his grip. "Lieutenant, I played it in my head a hundred different ways last night. I couldn't have done anything else. He'd have killed that woman. He'd probably have killed me and anyone else who got in the way. But I made mistakes. I should've called for backup before entering the building. I should have called it in to Dispatch instead of tagging you."

"Yeah, those are mistakes." She nodded, pleased he'd thought it through, picked it apart. "Neither of which would have changed the termination. But they were mistakes that may cost you a little shine. Why didn't you call for backup?"

"I reacted. The woman appeared to be in immediate jeopardy. I did shout orders for someone to call nine-eleven once I was inside, but I should have done so personally. If I'd been unsuccessful in stopping the perpetrator, had no backup en route, more lives could have been lost."

"Good. Lesson learned. Why did you call me instead of Dispatch?"

"I was . . . Lieutenant, I wasn't thinking straight. I realized both men were dead, that I had terminated the assailant, and I—"

"You were disoriented from the blows you received," she said briskly. "You had some concerns that you might lose consciousness. Your immediate thought was to report the homicide and the termination, and you did so by contacting the Homicide lieutenant you have worked with in the past. Are you getting this, Trueheart?"

"Yes, sir."

"You were in physical and mental distress. The lieutenant, to whom you relayed your situation, ordered you to secure the scene and stand until her arrival. You did so."

"It wasn't procedure."

"No, but it'll hold. Be sure you do. I didn't bring you in off sidewalk detail to watch you wash out."

"I'll get mandatory thirty-day suspension."

"Possibly. Probably."

"I can take it. I don't want to lose my badge."

"You're not going to lose your badge. Report to Testing, Officer Trueheart." She got to her feet. "And show them what you're made of."

She put in another nagging call to Morris, then decided to swing into EDD before she nabbed Peabody and headed to the morgue.

EDD always baffled her. How anybody got anything done when they were all pacing around talking on headsets or burrowed in cubes arguing with computers was beyond her.

And they rarely dressed like cops. McNab, the skinny fashion plate who was currently engaged in activities on and off shift with Peabody that Eve didn't like to think about, might have been the most outrageous of the bunch. But he didn't win by much.

She retreated as quickly as possible into Feeney's dull, workingman's office.

His door was open. He rarely shut it, even when he was, as now, scouring a subordinate over some screw-up.

"You think the units in here are for your amusement and entertainment, Halloway? You figure you can kick back and play a little Space Crusader on the taxpayers' nickel?"

"No, sir, Captain, I wasn't—"

"This department isn't your frigging toy box."

"Captain, it was my lunch break and—"

"You got time for lunch?" Feeney's basset hound face registered shock, amazement, and a secret joy. "Well, that's fascinating, Halloway. I can promise you for the next little while lunch breaks are going to be a fond, fond memory. You may not have noticed, since you've been so busy saving the virtual universe while you tuck into a sandwich, but we're jammed in here. Crime's soaring like the temps out there, and we, being duly sworn servants of the law, have to buckle our asses in and save the city before we move on to space and goddamn alien invaders. I want a report on the Dubreck hacker on my desk in thirty."

Halloway seemed to shrink inside his lime green jumpsuit. "Yes, sir."

"When you're done with that you hook up with Silby on the 'links from the Stewart break-in. And when you're done with that, I'll let you know. Scram."

Halloway scrammed, flicking one mortified glance at Eve as he scrambled out and back toward his cube.

"Does the heart good," Feeney said with a sigh, "to peel the skin off a skinny butt in the morning. What's up with you?"

"What was his score on Crusader?"

"Got up to fifty-six mil on Commando level." Feeney sniffed. "Damn near nipped my record and that's been standing for three years, four months, and twenty-two days. Little putz."

She strolled in, sat on the corner of his

desk, and copped a handful of the candied almonds he kept in a bowl. "You hear about Trueheart?"

"No. Been buried." His baggy face creased with concern. "What?"

She told him, leaving out nothing as they both munched on nuts. Feeney dragged a hand through his explosion of ginger hair. "Gonna be tough on him."

"Builds fucking character," she muttered. "He's giving it to me straight, Feeney. Kid would sooner swallow a live rat than lie to me. But it doesn't hold up. I brought Cogburn's data and communication center in. I was hoping you could bump it up to priority. Look, I know you're swamped," she added before he could speak. "But I want all the ammunition I can get for this. And there's something on there. I know there is. This Purity business smells bad."

"Can't give you McNab. Already got him juggling. Halloway," he said and brightened. "I just don't think that boy has enough to do. I'll put him on it. A little overtime should be good for him."

"And help protect your high score."

"Goes without saying." But the humor on

his face faded quickly. "IAB's going to take some hard shoves at that kid."

"I know it. I'm going to see if I can deflect a few of them." She pushed off the desk. "I'm going to go harass Morris. If my hunch holds up, Trueheart's off the sharpest hook."

Chapter 3

When Eve swung back into Homicide to snap up Peabody, several of the detectives in the bullpen sent meaningful looks her way.

"Rat in the hole," Baxter commented as he walked past her, and jerked his head toward her office.

"Thanks." She hooked her thumbs in the front pockets of her trousers and headed into her office.

Lieutenant Don Webster sat in her single spare chair, his polished shoes kicked up on her cluttered desk. He was drinking her coffee.

"Hey, Dallas. Been a little while."

"But somehow never long enough." She knocked his feet off her desk. "Is that my coffee in that mug?"

He took a long sip, let out a happy sigh. "It must be nice, being able to call up the real thing whenever you're in the mood. How is Roarke these days?"

"Is this a social call? Because I don't have time to chat. I'm on duty."

"Not social, but it could be friendly." He moved his shoulders when her expression stayed set and stony. "Or not. Gotta say though, you're looking just swell."

She reached behind her, shut the door. "You'd have gotten the report of the incident occurring yesterday between nineteen hundred and nineteen-thirty involving a uniformed officer assigned to Central who, while off-duty, responded to—"

"Dallas." Webster held up a hand. "I got the report. I know the incident. I know Officer Troy Trueheart—hell of a name, huh—is in Testing at this time. Internal Affairs will interview the subject and investigate the termination after the results of said Testing are evaluated."

"He's twenty-two years old. He's still

green but he's solid. I'm asking you to go easy on him."

Irritation settled over his face. Toughened it. "You think I get up in the morning thinking about how many cops I can destroy that day?"

"I don't know what you or the rest of your pack think about." She started to order coffee for herself, then spun around. "I thought you were coming back. I thought you'd decided to be a cop again."

"I am a goddamn cop."

"After all that dirt came out from inside IAB—"

"That's why I stayed in." He said it quietly, and cut off her tirade. "I thought about it." He pushed a hand through his wavy brown hair. "I thought about it long and hard. I believe in the Bureau, Dallas."

"How? Why?"

"Checks and balances. We need checks and balances. When there's power there's corruption. They go hand-in-hand. A wrong cop's got no right to a badge. But he deserves having another cop see it's taken from him."

"I've got no use for dirty cops." Annoyed with the world in general, she took the coffee mug from him and drank. "Damn it, Webster, you were good on the street."

It gave him a quick zip to hear her say it. To know she meant it. "I'm good in the Bureau. I think I make a difference."

"By hammering at a rookie like Trueheart because he did what he had to do to protect a civilian and himself?"

"You know, the first thing I did when I went back into IAB was move out all the racks, thumbscrews, and other torture devices. I read the report, Dallas. It's clear there was immediate jeopardy. But there are holes, and there are questions. You know it."

"I'm looking into it. Let me clear it up."

"You know. I'd love to do you a favor, just so you'd owe me one. But he has to be interviewed, he has to make a statement. He can have his rep there. He can have you there. Jesus, Dallas, we're not looking to fuck this kid over. But when a uniform terminates using his weapon it has to be reviewed."

"He's clean, Webster. He's goddamn spanking clean."

"Then he's got nothing to worry about. I'll take it personally if that means anything to you."

"I guess it does."

"You tell Roarke you were tagging me for this? Or is he going to get riled up so I have to kick his ass again?"

"Oh, is that what you were doing when you had to be carried out of the room unconscious?"

"I like to remember it that I was just getting my second wind."

Webster rubbed a hand over his jaw. He could still remember what Roarke's fist had felt like plowing into it. Like a well-aimed brick.

"Whatever works for you. And I don't report to Roarke."

"You go on thinking that." He took the coffee back from her, finished it off. "You're so married I see little lovebirds circling over your head."

It mortified, right down to her toes. "Roarke's not the only one who can knock you unconscious."

"I really like the look of you." He grinned when her eyes narrowed. "Just looking," he assured her. "No touching. Learned my lesson there. You can trust me to keep it clean, personally and professionally. That good enough for you?"

"If it wasn't, I wouldn't have called you."

"Check. I'll be in touch." He opened the door, glanced back. He really did like the look of her—lean and tough and sexy. "Thanks for the coffee."

Alone, she shook her head. She could hear the noise level drop into silence from the bullpen as Webster walked through it. He'd chosen a very hard road, she thought. A badge who policed other badges was regarded with suspicion, derision, and fear.

A slippery line to walk. She supposed, all in all, she liked him well enough to hope he kept his balance.

She checked her wrist unit, judged how much longer Trueheart would be in Testing. More than enough time, she thought, for her to browbeat Morris for results on Cogburn.

They were stacked and racked and packed in the morgue. Rarely in eleven years on the job had Eve seen so many corpses in one place at one time.

A trio of the bagged and tagged were laid out on gurneys and shoved against the wall outside of one of the autopsy suites.

Take a number, she thought. Too late to

be protected, but you'll be served eventually.

As Eve strode down the bright white corridor of the dead, Peabody hustled beside her.

"Man, this place is always a little spooky, but this is beyond. You know how you half expect one of these bags to sit up and grab at you?"

"No. Wait out here. If one of them makes a run for it, give me a call."

"I don't think that's particularly funny." And watching the still black bags warily, Peabody took her post at the door.

Inside Morris was busy at work, a laser scalpel midway through the Y cut on one of the six bodies splayed out on tables.

He wore goggles over his pleasant face, a plastic hood over his long, dark braided hair, and a clear protective coat over a natty navy blue suit.

"What's the point in having voice mail if you don't talk to it?" Eve demanded.

"A lot of unexpected company dropped in this morning, due to an airtram collision. Didn't you catch the report? Bodies dropping out of the sky like flying monkeys."

"If they could fly they wouldn't be bagged and tagged. How many?"

"Twelve dead, six injured. Some jerk in an airmini rammed it. Tram pilot managed to hold the controls most of the way down, but people panicked. Add to that the knife fight at a club that took both participants and one bystander, the Jane Doe female found stuffed in a recycler, and your everyday bashings, bludgeonings, and brutalities and we've got ourselves a full house."

"I've got a police termination with some questions. Rookie uniform stuns crazy guy, crazy guy dies. No sign of stunner contact on vic. Stunner confiscated from officer was set on low."

"Then it didn't kill him."

"He's dead as the rest of your guests."

Morris completed his Y cut. "Only way a noncontact zap with a uniform stunner would take out a man, crazy or not, would be if said potential crazy man had a respiratory or neurological condition of such seriousness that the electronic jolt acerbated it and led to termination."

It was exactly what she'd wanted to hear. "If that's the case, it's not actually a termination by maximum force."

"Technically, no. However—"

"Technically will do. Be a pal, Morris, take a look at him. It's Trueheart."

Morris looked up and shoved the goggles up. "The kid with the peach fuzz on his face that looks like a screen ad for toothpaste?"

"That's the one. He's in Testing. IAB's next. And something doesn't hang about the way this went down. He could use a break."

"Let me look him up."

"He's over there. Number four in line." She jerked a thumb.

"Let me pull the report up."

"I can—"

"Let me read it." Morris cut her off with a wave of the hand and moved over to the data center. "Name of crazy dead guy?"

"Cogburn, Louis K."

Morris called up the field report. As he read, he hummed to himself. It was some catchy little tune, vaguely familiar to her. And it started playing around in her head in a way that told her it would be stuck there for hours.

"Illegals dealer," Morris began. "Could've been oversampling, heart or neurological damage possible. Bleeding from ears, nose, broken blood vessels in the eyes. Hmm."

He moved to the table where Louie K. was laid out, skinny and naked. He refit the goggles, lowered his face so close to Louie's it looked as though he was about to kiss the dead.

"Record on," he said and began to dictate preliminary data, visual findings.

"Well, let's open him up, see what we see. You going to hang for this?"

"Yeah, if it's quick."

"One doesn't rush genius, Dallas." He picked up a skull saw, set it to whirl.

Eve often wondered why anyone chose this particular line of work, or how they could be so cheerful when going about it. At least the air in the room was cool, she thought and wandered over to study the offerings of the little fridgie. She settled for a tube of ginger ale before walking back to Morris.

"What do you—"

"Ssh!"

She scowled, but subsided. Morris was usually chatty when he worked. In this case he went about the job in silence, referring to the inside of Cogburn's skull, to the computer imagery on the screen beside the table.

She studied it herself, but saw nothing but shapes and colors.

"You do a medical search on this guy?"

"Yeah. He hasn't been in for any sort of work or check in a couple of years. Nothing popped."

"Oh yeah, something popped. His brain, and no standard stunner did this damage. No tumor that I can see. No clotting. If it was an embolism there should be ... What we've got is severe intercranial pressure. His brain's massively swollen."

"Preexisting?"

"I can't tell, not yet. This is going to take time. Fascinating. Pop's just what this brain did. Like an overinflated balloon. I can tell you that in my opinion this wasn't done by any weapon. It's internal."

"Medical then."

"I'm not going to confirm that. I'm going to run some tests." He shooed her away. "I'll contact you when I have something solid."

"Give me something."

"I can tell you it appears this guy's brain was in serious condition, an ongoing condition prior to any act by your officer last evening. What happened here didn't happen as a result of a stun. It didn't happen if he'd stuck a police issue laser in the guy's ear and blasted away. I can't say if the stun caused some sort of chain reaction that led to early termination. But from the looks of this brain, this guy would've been dead within an hour. I'll let you know when I figure out how and why. Now go and let me work."

Eve bypassed the seal on Cogburn's apartment. The stench, the stale, trapped heat punched like a dirty fist when she opened the door.

"God. That's foul."

"Oh yeah." Peabody turned her head, sucked in what she imagined was her last easy breath, then followed Eve inside.

"Go ahead and open the window while we're in here. It's got to be better than working in a closed box."

"What are we looking for?"

"Morris's prelim is leaning toward preexisting condition. We may find something in here to verify that, to indicate he was self-medicating. The place looks like he was off, sick. That's what struck me from the first. He's a creep, but a tidy, organized creep. Keeps his nest neat ordinarily. But the last several days, he's falling down on the domestic front. Keeping up with his business though. You're sick, you're hot, you're irritable. Neighbor hassles you, you crack. Makes better sense."

"But, well, it doesn't really matter why Cogburn had batting practice on his neighbor."

"It always matters why," Eve answered. "Ralph Wooster's dead, and Cogburn's paid for it. But it matters why."

She opened drawers she'd opened and searched the day before. "Maybe he had a hard-on for Wooster all along. Maybe he wanted to shag Ralph's woman, or owed him money. And now he's feeling like shit and old Ralph's hammering on his door and yelling at him."

She crouched down, shined a penlight deep into the recesses of a cupboard. "Point is, something made him snap, go postal. Could be his brain was frying. Morris said he was a dead man."

"Even so, Trueheart's in Testing." Peabody glanced at her wrist unit. "Or just coming out of it. He'll have to face IAB whether or not Cogburn had a preexisting."

"Yeah, but he'll feel better if it comes out he gave the guy the standard and acceptable stuns, and a preexisting was the root or cause of death. We get him that, he won't get the mandatory thirty-day vacation."

She stayed crouched, frowning into space. "Anyway, I don't like how it feels. Just don't like it."

"What's that song you're humming?"

Eve stopped, cursed herself, straightened. "I don't know. Damn Morris. Let's knock on doors."

It was amazing how many people lost their sense of hearing or their ability to communicate in coherent sentences when a badge was involved.

More than half the doors Eve knocked on remained firmly shut, and whatever sounds emitting from inside were stifled instantly. The doors that opened revealed people no more helpful, with responses that ranged from *I dunno* to *I didn't hear nothing from nobody*.

On the first floor, in apartment 11F, Eve's dwindling patience was rewarded.

The blonde was young and looked half asleep. She wore a tiny pair of white panties and a thin tank. She yawned hugely in Eve's face, then blinked at the badge when it was shoved in front of her.

"My license is paid up. I got six more months till renewal, and I just had my mandatory health check. I got the okay."

"Good to know." As licensed companions went this one was on the young side and still looked fresh. The license was likely in its first year. "I'm not here about that. This concerns what happened on the fourth floor yesterday."

"Oh! Wow! That was sure something. I hid in the closet until the screaming stopped. I was really scared. There was a big fight and people got killed and stuff."

"Did you know either of the men who got killed?"

"Sort of."

"Can we come inside, Miss . . ."

"Oh, oh, I'm Reenie, Reenie Pike—well Pikowski, but I'm changing it to Pike because, you know, it's sexier. I guess so— about coming in. My trainer said how we were supposed to cooperate with the police so we didn't get rousted and stuff."

She was, Eve thought, the Trueheart of the licensed companion crowd. Still shiny and innocent despite her chosen occupation. "That's a good policy, Reenie. Why don't we all have some cooperation. Inside."

"Okay, but the place is kinda messy. I sleep during the day, mostly, especially since it's so hot. Super hasn't fixed the climate control. I don't think that's right."

"Maybe I can talk to him for you," Eve offered as she eased inside the door.

"Really? That would be great. It's hard to bring clients back here because it's too hot for sex and stuff, and I'm only licensed for street work and most street clients don't want to pop for a hotel room and stuff. You know?"

The furniture was spare, the layout identical to Cogburn's. Disorder came from scattered clothes in bright, come-hither colors, in the trio of wigs tossed about like tangled scalps and the army of cosmetic enhancements jumbled on the chest under the window.

The air was hot enough to bake cookies.

"What can you tell me about Louis Cogburn?" Eve began.

"He liked it straight and quick. No fancy stuff."

"That's really interesting, Reenie, but I wasn't really asking about his sexual preferences. But since you mention it, was he a regular client?"

"Sort of." She moved around the room, picking up clothes, tossing them into a closet. "Once every couple weeks since I moved in. He was real polite about it, said how it was nice having an lc right in the building. He said how we could work out a trade, but I told him I'd sooner the money 'cause I'm saving up for on-call status, and I don't do illegals and stuff. Oh." She slapped a hand on her mouth. "I didn't mean to say about him dealing, but I guess it's okay since he's dead."

"And stuff. Yeah, we know about his business. Did he ever fight with any of the other tenants before yesterday?"

"Oh no, nuh-uh. He was real quiet, and like I said, polite and stuff. Kept to himself mostly."

"Did he ever mention Ralph Wooster or Suzanne Cohen to you, any problem or grudge he had regarding them?"

"Nuh-uh. I sort of know Suze. Sort of. I mean to say hello to, and howzit. And just a few days ago we sat out on the stoop and had a brew 'cause it was so hot inside. She's nice. She said how she and Ralph were thinking about getting married and stuff. She works at a 24/7 around the corner and he does the bouncing at a club. I forget which one. Maybe I should go see her in the hospital."

"I bet she'd appreciate that. Did you notice anything different about Mr. Cogburn in the last few days?"

"Sort of. Hey, you want a cold drink? I got some Fizzy Lemon."

"No, that's okay. You go ahead."

"I could use some water," Peabody put in. "If you don't mind."

"Sure, okay. Is it hard being a cop and stuff?"

"It can be." Eve watched Reenie's pert little butt lift as she bent down to find her Fizzy Lemon in the fridgie. "But it shows you . . . all sides of the human condition."

"You see lots as an Ic, too."

"What did you see different about Mr. Cogburn recently?"

"Well . . ." Reenie came back with a glass of water for Peabody, then took a moment to sip delicately at her soft drink. "Take the day Suze and I were on the stoop. Louie K. walked up on his way in. He looked kinda bad, you know all pale and sweaty and tuck-

ered out and stuff. So I said, you know, hot
enough for you? And he gave me this real
nasty look and told me I should keep my
mouth shut if all I could say was something
stupid."

Her unpainted lips moved into a pretty little pout. "Really hurt my feelings, but you
know, Louie K.'s just not mean like that and
he really didn't look good, so I said, aw,
Louie K., you look all worn out. You want
some of my brew? And for a minute, he
looked like he was gonna be nasty again,
and Suze got all stiff. But then he sort of
rubbed at his face and said how he was
sorry he said that, and how the heat was
getting to him and he had this bad headache
and stuff. I said I had some blockers if he
wanted, which, I guess, was stupid, too,
'cause of his business. But he didn't say so
and just said how he'd maybe lay down
awhile and try to sleep off the headache."

She paused a minute as if thinking it
through. "And like that," she concluded.

"Did you see him between that time and
yesterday?"

"Not to see. But I heard him yesterday
morning. I was sleeping, but he woke me up
pounding on the super's door and yelling at

him to fix the climate control. He was cursing up a streak, which wasn't something you heard him do a whole lot, but the super didn't open the door, and Louie K., he went on back up, not out like he did most days."

"He went back up to his apartment after trying the super."

"Yeah, and that's kinda strange 'cause Louie K. was really, you know, like disciplined about work. I don't think he'd gone out for a while, now that you mention it. Anyway I was getting dressed yesterday when I heard all the yelling and the crashing upstairs. I only peeked out for a second, and saw that cute cop come running in. Then I hid in the closet. The cute cop was calling out for somebody to call 911. I guess I should've, but I was awfully scared and stuff."

"You heard the responding officer call for someone to call for police backup?"

Reenie bowed her head. "Yeah. I'm sorry I didn't help, but I thought somebody else would and I was scared. I guess it wouldn't have made a difference anyway because it all got over pretty fast. The cop guy, the cute guy, I think he's a real hero to go up there the way he did when everybody else stayed inside where it was safe. Maybe, if you see him and stuff you could tell him I said so. And I feel bad I didn't help."

"Sure," Eve replied. "I'll let him know."

Rather than write an updated report, Eve opted to go straight to Commander Whitney with an oral. She had to wheedle a five-minute window through the commander's assistant but she was willing to take what she could get for the impact of a face-to-face.

"Thank you for making time, Commander."

"If I could make time, my day would be a lot less harried. Make it fast, Lieutenant."

He continued to read whatever data was on his desk screen. His profile was stony. The bulk of him suited the large and currently cluttered desk as did the weight of his command. Both that bulk and that weight, Eve had reason to know, carried steely muscle.

"Regarding the incident involving Officer Trueheart, sir. I've gathered additional data, which indicates the terminated assailant may have suffered from a preexisting that caused his death. ME Morris is still running tests but has stated that due to this condition the subject would have died within the hour."

"Morris shot me a brief prelim on that. You have loyal associates, Dallas."

"Sir. Trueheart has completed Testing by now. Results should be in by morning. I'd like to postpone any IAB involvement until the investigation into yesterday's incident shows clearly if any such involvement is warranted or necessary."

Whitney turned to her now, his wide, dark face closed. "Lieutenant, do you have any reason to believe that a standard IAB investigation and interview will cast any shadow on the actions taken by this officer?"

"No, Commander."

"Then let it ride. Let it ride," he repeated before she could speak. "Let the boy stand for himself. Let him clear himself. He'll be the better for it. Having you in his corner is one thing. Having you stand in a shield is another entirely."

"I'm not trying to . . ." She trailed off, realizing she was doing just that. "Permission to speak frankly, Commander."

"As long as it's brief."

"I feel some responsibility as I brought Trueheart in from his former detail. A few months ago he was seriously injured on one of my ops. He follows orders to the letter and he has a lot of spine. But his instincts are still developing, and his skin's still thin. I just don't want to see him take any more hits over this than he deserves."

"If he can't stand up to it, better he finds out now. You know that, Dallas."

"If there's a preexisting, mandatory thirty day can be waived. You know that, Commander, as you know the emotional and mental distress even a by-the-book suspension can bring on. He responded to a call for help. He put himself on the line, without hesitation."

"He failed to call for backup."

"Yes, sir, he did. Did you ever fail to call for backup?"

Whitney's eyebrows lifted. "If I did, I deserved to get kicked for it."

"I'll kick him."

"I'll consider the waiver, Lieutenant, once all data and results are in and studied."

"Thank you, sir."

Huddled in his cube, Halloway ran another series of scans on the Cogburn unit. And groused.

Play a little Crusader on your break, and you get all the shit details dumped on you. Who the hell cared about the data stored on the drive of a dead kiddie dealer's unit? What was Feeney going to do? Tattle on the pint-sized clients to their mommies?

Four hours, he thought, and popped a blocker for the vicious headache trumpeting inside his skull. Four frigging hours dicking with useless data on a useless second-rate unit all because bigshot Dallas comes begging to bigshot Feeney.

He sat back, rubbed his blurry eyes.

He couldn't get past the shield on this Purity transmission. Cogburn hadn't generated the message. That much he'd verified. It had come from outside, but so the fuck what?

Absolute Purity. Probably some sort of baby lotion.

His head was killing him. And God, it was hot in here. Damn climate control must've gone out again. Nobody did their jobs anymore. Nobody but him.

He shoved away from the desk, pushed out of his cube, desperate for water, for air.

He elbowed other cops out of his way, earned himself some inventive suggestions on self-gratification.

At the water cooler, he glugged down cup after cup as he tracked the movements of his associates.

Look at them. Like a bunch of ants in a nest. Somebody ought to do the world a favor and squash some ants.

"Hey, Halloway." McNab bounced in fresh from a field assignment. "How's it going? Heard you caught a shit detail."

"Fuck you, asshole."

Temper rolled over McNab's face, but then he noted Halloway's pallor, and the beads of sweat. "You look a little wasted. Maybe you should take a break."

Halloway downed more water. "Somebody's gonna get wasted. Get off my case before I show the rest of these dickweeds what a pansy Feeney's pet really is."

"You got a problem with me?" If so, it was a new one. To that point McNab and Halloway had flowed along smoothly. "We can take it down to the gym and work it out. See who's the pansy of EDD."

Feeney swept in, stopped by the cooler when he felt the hot wall of tension. "McNab, I want that report ten minutes ago. Halloway, you got all this time to stand around the cooler I can find more for you to do. Move it."

"Later," Halloway muttered under his breath, and stalked back to his cube with his head raging.

Chapter 4

With Peabody in tow, Eve stopped by the hospital for a followup interview with Suzanne Cohen. The woman was weepy and despondent, having discovered her affection for Ralph ran considerably deeper now that he was dead.

But she had nothing appreciable to add to the mix. Her version of the incident on the stoop followed Reenie's, as did her basic take on Louie K.

He was quiet, except for his music, and kept mostly to himself.

"Isn't that always the way?" Eve noted. "Every time you've got some guy going on a spree that ends in blood, people say he was quiet and kept to himself. Just once, I'd like to hear how he was a maniac who ate live snakes."

"There was that guy last year who bit off the heads of pigeons before he jumped off the roof of his apartment building."

"Yeah, but he only splattered himself, and we didn't catch that one. No point in trying to cheer me up with pigeon eaters." Despondent herself, Eve pulled out her beeping communicator. "Dallas."

"Thought you'd want an update," Morris began. "I'm still running tests, and results in are largely inconclusive."

"Boy, that sure perks me up."

"Patience, Dallas, patience." His face was glowing the way some people glowed when they claimed to have found Jesus, Eve thought.

"What we've got here is worthy of a write-up in medical journals across the land. This guy's brain is fascinating. Like it was under attack from the inside. But there's no tumor, no mass, no sign of disease as such."

"But there's damage. Brain damage."

"I'll say. Like someone set microscopic

charges inside it. Biff, bam, boom. You know how I likened it to an overinflated balloon?"

"Yeah."

"Picture this balloon, in an enclosed space, in this case, the skull. Balloon swells, bigger, bigger. Space stays the same. It keeps pushing, expanding, but it's got no place to go. Pressure builds, builds, builds. Capillaries burst. Ping, ping, ping. Nose bleeds, ear bleeds until . . . Pop!"

"That's a really pretty image."

"Poor sucker had to be suffering from major headaches. The Mount Vesuvius of headaches. I've sent tissue to the lab for further analysis, and I'm calling in a neurologist."

"Would this damage have caused his sudden violent behavior?"

"I can't tell you that, not conclusively. But the pain may have pushed him over the edge. Pain's nature's warning system. Ouch, something wrong with me. Enough pain though, can drive you crazy. And, an invasive body such as a tumor in the brain can cause aberrant behavior. This brain was, unquestionably, invaded."

"By what?"

"The best I can tell you is it looks like

some sort of neurological virus. Pinning that down isn't going to be quick work."

"Okay, get me what you can when you can." She clicked off. "Looks like it's moving out of the area of police problem and into medical problem. We'll close it up. Subject, suffering from as yet undiagnosed neurological disorder, assaults and kills neighbor, attacks another. Police response results in death of assailant. Trueheart's just got to hold on through the IAB bullshit."

"Are you going to let him know the guy was mostly dead before the stun?"

"Yeah, but he should handle IAB first. Whitney's right. I go standing in front of him, it makes him look weak."

"He's not, you know." Peabody smiled a little. "He's just . . . pure."

"Yeah, well, his purity's a little soiled now, and he'll probably be better off. We'll swing into EDD and see if they've pinned down the other Purity. I want to tie this up and put it away."

In his cube, Halloway raged and he sweated and he worked. He didn't know he was dying, but he knew, he knew *damn well* he was being abused.

He couldn't remember, not exactly, why he had this old and crappy data center on his work counter. But he remembered, oh he remembered, the way Feeney had slapped at him, how Feeney had humiliated him.

And McNab, that asshole, breezing up and sneering. Laughing at him behind his back. Laughing right in his face. Why was he the one who always got the plum assignments? Those plums should go to Colleen Halloway's son, Kevin. And they would if that backstabber McNab didn't kiss Feeney's ass every chance he got.

They were holding him down, holding him back. Both of them, he thought as he swiped his forearm over his sweat-drenched face. Trying to ruin him.

They weren't going to get away with it.

God. God! He wanted to go home, go to bed. He wanted to be alone in his own place, away from this heat, away from this noise, away from the pain.

His vision blurred as he stared down into the guts of the unit Feeney had ordered him to work on.

And he saw McNab's guts spread out and gleaming under his hands.

Take it down to the gym? He let out a little

snort that ended on a sob. Hell with that! Hell with them. He pushed to his feet, closed his hand over his holstered weapon. Drew it.

They'd handle this here and now. Like men.

Eve stepped into the glide. "I don't need you for this, Peabody."

"Sir, I'm your faithful aide. I feel obliged to stay close to your side."

"If you think you're coming up to EDD with me so you can play grab-ass with McNab, you're very much mistaken, faithful aide."

"The thought never crossed my mind."

"Is that so? Why are your pants on fire?"

Peabody grinned. "They're not because I'm not lying. I was thinking of pat-ass, not grab-ass. His is so skinny it's kind of tough to grab a good handful."

She hopped off beside Eve, and since she thought she saw her lieutenant's mouth twitch in what might have been a smile rather than the usual muscle tic during such conversations, she pushed.

"And I can get a firsthand on the status of Cogburn's unit, write that area of the report for you. As your faithful and hardworking aide."

"That's a good bribe, Peabody. You make me proud."

"I've learned from the master."

They finished the hike across the breeze-way that connected EDD, turned toward the detectives' sector. And all hell broke loose.

Shouts, the distinctive hum of a fired weapon, the scramble of feet. Eve's weapon was in her hand, and she was running be-fore she heard the first crash.

A cop rolled out of the doorway as others came rushing down corridors.

"He zapped him! Jesus Christ, he zapped him. Call for medical."

"Who's down? Detective, give me the sit-uation."

"I—God. McNab's down."

Eve grabbed Peabody's arm as her aide started to spring forward. "Hold!" she or-dered as the muscles trembled under her hand. "Officer down, officer down!" she snapped into her communicator. "EDD, De-tectives' level. Give me the goddamn situa-tion."

"I don't know! Halloway, he just walked up to McNab's cube. Zapped him, then everybody's running and Halloway's screaming, firing streams. He's got the captain. I saw him take the captain."

"Keep out!" Eve strode to the door, ordered the cops who poured out of doors and hallways to stay clear. "We've got a potential hostage situation, at least one wounded. I need this area secured. I need a negotiator. Peabody, inform the commander of this situation."

"Yes, sir." Tears gathered in the corners of her eyes. "McNab."

"We're going in. Draw your weapon." She eased closer, lowering her voice for Peabody alone. "If you can't handle this, say so now. You won't help them if you can't maintain."

"I can. I will." Fear had already blown through her, and out again. "We have to get in there."

"Hold fire," Eve called out. "Hold fire."

She went in slow, sweeping first. Cops were scattered, cubes blasted, some of them still smoking. She saw a clutch of them huddled on the floor—McNab's cube—she noted, and felt a gathering of ice in her belly. More were outside of Feeney's office, shouting through the door.

"I'm Lieutenant Dallas!" she had to shout to be heard. "I'm in charge here until Commander Whitney takes over this situation. You men, get away from that door."

"He's got the captain! He's got the captain in there."

"Get the hell away from the door. Now! What's McNab's status?"

She could see him now, lying unconscious, his face white as bone. She said nothing when Peabody dropped down beside him, checked his pulse.

"He's alive." Peabody responded shakily. "Pulse is thready."

"Didn't take a full stun. Detective Gates." A woman with zebra-striped hair stepped forward. "I saw Halloway walk up to the cube. Something off about it, then I saw the weapon. I yelled something. McNab looked around, saw, he shoved off his chair and Halloway's stream took him down. It was bad. It was bad, but I don't think it was a full stun."

"Medical's on the way. I need eyes in Feeney's office. Get me eyes in there. For now, get me to a 'link station so I can talk to him. Peabody, assess how many are wounded and in what condition."

She snagged a 'link, ordered transmission to Feeney's. It beeped, beeped, beeped. And her heart thundered.

"This is Captain Fucking Halloway." Halloway's face, nearly as white as McNab's, filled the screen. The whites of his eyes were cracked with red lines, and a dribble of blood leaked from his nose. "I'm in charge here!"

He screamed it, then stepped back so Eve saw him holding his weapon under Feeney's jaw.

One stream, she thought numb with fear, instant death.

"This is Lieutenant Dallas."

"I know who the hell you are. Grandstander. I outrank you now. What the hell do you want?"

"It's what you want that's at issue, Halloway."

"*Captain* Halloway."

"Captain." Her eyes met Feeney's. A thousand messages passed between them in a split second. "If you'd tell me, sir, what it is you want, what seems to be the problem, we can clear everything up without further violence. You don't want to hurt Captain

Feeney. I won't be able to help you get what you want if you hurt Captain Feeney."

"You need to talk to us, son." Feeney's voice was calm as a lake. "Tell us what the problem is."

"You're the problem, and I'm not your son. So shut up! Shut up!" He jerked Feeney's head back with his weapon, and broke transmission.

Every cell in Eve's body screamed to rush the door. Every instinct, every hour of training, ordered her to hold back.

"Eyes. Get me eyes in there now! I want all available data on Halloway. If he's married, get his wife in here or on a 'link. Get me his mother, his brother, his priest. Whoever he's most likely to listen to. I want all nonessential personnel out of this area. Who in here knows Halloway best?"

Shocked faces, grim faces, angry faces looked back at her. It was Gates who finally spoke. "I guess we all thought we knew him. This doesn't make sense, Lieutenant."

"Talk to him." Eve pointed to the 'link. "Keep it calm and friendly. You ask him what he wants, what we can do for him. Don't criticize him. Don't say anything to set him off. Just keep him talking."

She turned away, moving just out of range and pulled out her communicator. "Commander."

"On my way." His face might have been carved in granite. "Situation?"

She relayed it, fast and brief.

"Negotiator is also on his way. What do you need?"

"Sharpshooters. I'm getting eyes, but at this point I can't ascertain target area. Feeney usually keeps his shades up, but they might be lowered. Rushing the room or shutting it down is too risky. He'd drop Feeney before we could get to him."

"I'm two minutes away. Keep him talking. Find out what he wants."

"Yes, sir." She moved back toward the 'link. Gates tapped manually on the keys of a mini-unit.

He's not listening to me. Incoherent, scattered. No answers. Looks sick.

Eve nodded and took over the 'link. "You okay in there, Captain Halloway? Need anything?"

"I need some respect! I'm not going to be ignored."

"I'm not ignoring you. You have my full attention. I am having a little trouble concentrating. If you could ease back on your weapon a little so we can talk this out."

"So you can bust in here?" His laugh was a squeaky wheeze. "I don't think so."

"No one's coming in there. There's no reason we can't resolve this without more injuries. Feeney, you'll give Halloway your word to remain seated and cooperative, won't you?"

Feeney understood the message. Stay where you are as long as possible. "Sure. I'll sit right here while we work this out."

"It's hot in here. It's too goddamn hot in here." As he spoke, Halloway used his free hand to swipe at the blood that trickled out of his nose.

Seeing it, Eve went cold. "I'll have the climate control adjusted." She gestured off-screen to Gates. "We'll cool it down in there for you. You feeling okay otherwise, Halloway?"

"No! No, I'm not feeling okay. This son of a bitch has me working until my damn eyes bleed. My head." He grabbed a handful of his own hair, yanked viciously. "My head's killing me. I'm sick. He made me sick."

"We can get you a medical. Will you let me send a medical in? You don't look well,

Halloway. Let me get you some medical assistance."

"Just leave me alone." When a tear dripped out of his eye, it was tinged with blood. "Leave me alone. I need to think!"

He broke transmission.

"Status," Whitney snapped from behind her.

"He's sick. He's showing the same symptoms demonstrated by Cogburn. I can't explain it, Commander, but he's dying in there, and he could take Feeney with him. We need to get him out, get him medical assistance."

"Lieutenant. Ah, Commander." Another detective hustled up. "We've got your eyes." He managed a wan smile. "And ears with them."

With Whitney, Eve bent over a monitor. She could see the whole of Feeney's office now—the sun and the privacy shades lowered. There would be no outside visual for the sharpshooters. Feeney was in his desk chair, restraints locking his arms to its arms.

Halloway paced behind him, his young, pleasant face ravaged. His own blood smeared it like war paint. He tore at his hair with one hand, waved the weapon wildly with the other.

"I'm the one who knows what I'm doing around here." He raged, kicking Feeney's chair viciously as he passed. "I'm the one who's in charge. You're old and you're stupid, and I'm sick to death of your orders."

Feeney's response was quiet and measured. "I didn't know you were feeling that way. What can I do to make things right with you?"

"You want to make them right? You want to make them right?" He jammed the weapon under Feeney's chin again and had Eve braced to hurl herself at the office door. "We're going to write us a memo, Ry."

"Okay, okay." She let out a long breath. "Keep him busy."

"Sir. Negotiator's on-scene."

"Bring him up-to-date, Dallas," Whitney ordered. "Then we structure alternatives."

She briefed the negotiator, set him up with a 'link. And turning, saw Roarke striding through the door. "What the hell are you doing here?"

"Media bulletin." He didn't speak of the terror he'd lived with since hearing the report that there had been weapons fired, officers wounded, and a hostage taken at Cop Central. And from his quick scan of the room, he sized up the most vital aspects of the situation.

His wife was unharmed. And Feeney was missing.

"Feeney?"

"The hostage. I don't have time for you."

He laid a hand on her arm before she could walk away. "What can I do to help?"

She didn't waste time asking how he'd gotten into a secured area in the first place. He was a man who went where he wanted to go. Nor did she ask how he expected to help when the sector was loaded with cops whose job it was to deal with a crisis.

Nobody was better at cutting through a crisis.

"McNab was hit."

"Christ." He turned, as she did, and found Peabody, on the floor with the first medical team.

"I don't know his status. I'd feel better if I knew one way or the other."

"Done." There was anger in him now, a kind of frigid fury more deadly than heat. "Lieutenant, if it's money he wants, the department will have unlimited funds at its disposal."

"Appreciated, but it's not money. Go, give Peabody a shoulder. I need to focus on getting Feeney out of there alive. Roarke. Wait." She scooped a hand through her hair. "Find which cube is Halloway's. He's got a data unit in there. Shut it down. Don't touch it, don't get any closer to it than necessary. Just shut it down."

Inside Feeney's office, Halloway screamed into the 'link. Rusty knifes were slicing their way through his brain. He could feel it bleeding. "You want to talk to me? Then turn the temp down in this furnace. You keep trying to fry me out, I drop this useless old E-fart. I'm not talking to you, asshole. Put Dallas back on. Put that goddamn lying bitch back on. You got ten seconds!"

At the signal, she sprang to the 'link. "I'm here Halloway."

"Didn't I order you to turn the heat down in here? Didn't I give you a direct order?"

"Yes, sir. I followed that order."

"Don't you lie to me. You want me to start on his hands." Halloway pressed his weapon down hard on the back of Feeney's hand. "I give it a good strong jolt, he won't be jerking off with this hand anymore."

"I'll have it turned down farther. Halloway, just listen to me. Look at Feeney. He's not sweating. You can do a temp check. The room's down to sixty-five."

"That's bullshit! I'm burning up in here."

"Because you're sick. You've got some kind of virus, like an infection. You've got a bad headache, haven't you, Halloway? And you've got a nosebleed. It's the infection that's making you feel this way, the infection that's hurting you. You need medical. Let us get you some help, and we'll straighten all this out."

"Why don't you come in, bitch?" His mouth twisted. "Come on in and you'll see how fast we straighten this out."

"I can come in. I can bring you some medicine."

"Fuck you."

"I come in, Halloway, and don't deliver. You'd have two hostages. You're in control. You're in charge. You know Feeney's a friend of mine. I wouldn't do anything to jeopardize his welfare. I can bring you in medication for your headache, and whatever else you want."

"Fuck you," he said again, and broke transmission.

"Bartering another hostage isn't the way to deal in this situation." The negotiator shoved himself between Eve and the 'link. "We don't need any sacrificing, we don't need any hotshots."

"Normally I'd agree with you, but the man holding the cards in there isn't going to listen to the usual lines. First, he's a cop and he knows the routine. Second, he's suffering from some sort of neurological disorder that's affecting his behavior, his judgment, his actions."

"I'm in charge of this negotiation."

"This isn't a pissing contest, damn it. I don't want your job. I want to see both of those cops come out of there in one piece. Commander, I'm sorry, I don't have time to explain it all. Halloway's physical and mental conditions are deteriorating. I don't know how much longer he's got before he loses it completely. But when he does, he's going to take Feeney with him."

"Sharpshooters are in position. They can take him out using an on-screen visual."

"One stun and he's dead. That's what happened with Cogburn. Halloway's still a badge, Commander. And what he's done, what he's doing is not within his control. I want the chance to take him alive."

"You go in," the negotiator said, "and three cops die."

"Or live. I can tranq him. He's in serious pain. If the meds are there, he'll want them. Commander, Feeney trained me, he brought me up. I need to go in."

Whitney stared into her eyes. "Talk him into it. Make it fast."

It took her precious moments of bargaining, but she fell into the rhythm of groveling. That, she realized, was what he needed. Not just to be acknowledged as being in charge, but to be shown absolute subservience.

"He could very well fire on you the minute you're in the door." Roarke spoke softly as she waited for the MTs to prepare the medications and pressure syringes.

"He could."

"But you go in without a vest, without a weapon."

"That was the deal. I know what I'm doing."

"You know what you have to do. There's a subtle and dangerous difference. Eve." He laid a hand on her arm. It took everything inside him not to yank her clear of the room. Get her away. "I know what he means to you. Remember what you mean to me."

"I'm not likely to forget it."

"McNab's condition is serious. He took a hard hit at close range. The MTs were guarded, but he came around briefly before they transported him. It's a good sign."

"Okay." She couldn't think about McNab. Couldn't worry about him now.

"Three others were injured before Halloway grabbed Feeney and used him as a shield into the office. I'd like to know, just for curiosity's sake, how one man takes out four other cops without taking a single hit."

"Jesus, Roarke, this is EDD. Half the cops in here are glorified drones or geeks. You're more likely to see them pulling out an e-pad than a weapon."

"Lieutenant." The MT approached with a clear bag of meds. "Set these up like you wanted. Syringe with the red dot on the depressor's the tranq. Takes a man down in under five seconds. Second's the dummy. Nothing but a mild blocker. Pills are standard blockers, except for the one with the little yellow stripe. That's another tranq. You get him to use either of those, he's down pretty fast. Five seconds."

"Okay, got it. Back in a few minutes," she told Roarke.

"See that you are." And because he didn't give a damn at the moment about her much-prized rep, he yanked her against him and kissed her.

"Jeez. Save it, will you?" But it warmed her, steadied her as she walked over to the 'link and put through the next transmission. "I got your meds, sir." She held up the bag. "Pain blockers, oral and bloodstream. The MT informs me that the syringe will clear up the infection, and take care of your headache fairly quickly."

She held her arms up, turned a slow circle. "I'm not carrying. I know you're in control. I just want to give you what you need to resolve this situation to your satisfaction."

"Damn skippy." He swiped at the blood leaking out of his nose again. He was rocking, rocking, back and forth on his heels as if to soothe away the pain. His sandy hair was standing in mad tufts where he'd yanked at it. Sweat and blood had soaked through the top of his cheery green jumpsuit.

"Come on in, Dallas." His mouth moved into a terrible grin as he levered his weapon under Feeney's jaw again. "I'm going to show you just what I need to resolve this situation to my satisfaction. Keep that 'link open."

He paused, hissed out a breath, then rammed the heel of his free hand against his eye. "Keep that visual so I can see you all the way to the door. Anybody tries to pass you a weapon, this old man is over. Keep your hands up, keep them up where I can see them."

He drilled the heel of his hand against his eye again, the other rolling wildly as he tried to focus on the screen. "My head!"

"I've got the medication to help you." Eve spoke calmly, slowly as she walked to Feeney's office door. On either side of it, just out of visual, were two crisis cops in full riot gear armed with lasers. "I need you to release the locks, sir."

"Anybody tries to rush that door, I take him out."

"I'm coming in alone. I'm not armed. I'm not carrying anything but the medication. You're in control here. Everyone knows you're in control."

"About damn *time*!" He released the locks, then shoved Feeney's head back, digging in with the business end of his weapon.

And now, Eve thought, if she was wrong, everybody died. She eased the door open, then lifting her hands high, nudged it the rest of the way with the toe of her boot.

"I'm alone, Captain Halloway," she said, stepped in, shut the door at her back.

She risked one fast glance at Feeney. She read the anger, the frustration on his face. And saw the bruises gathering under his jaw where Halloway had rammed his weapon time after time.

"Put the bag down on the desk." Halloway licked his dry, cracked lips as she obeyed.

"Take a step back, hands behind your head."

"Yes, sir."

"Why are there two syringes?"

"Sir, the MT said that you might require a second dosage for full relief."

"Come around the desk slow."

She could hear him keening under his breath, like an animal beyond pain.

He couldn't be thirty yet, she thought. He couldn't be thirty and a few hours before

Feeney had dressed him down for fighting virtual aliens.

Blood trickled slowly out of his nose. The left sleeve of his jumpsuit was red from wiping at it. She could smell his sweat, his blood, his fury pumping.

"How many times you have to bang this old bastard to make lieutenant?"

"Sir, Captain Feeney and I have not been intimate."

"Lying bitch." He swung out, backhanding her faster, harder than she'd anticipated. Off balance, she fell back into a chair. "How many times?"

"As many as it took. I lost count."

His head bobbed rapidly. "That's the way it works. Somebody's always screwing somebody so they can screw somebody else over."

"Everyone knows you've achieved your rank and position through your own merits."

"You got that. You fucking-A got that." He pawed a blue blocker out of the bag. "How do I know this isn't poison? Here." He shoved it into Feeney's mouth. "Swallow it! Swallow it or I do her." He swung the weapon toward Eve.

They were close, but not close enough for

her to see if the pill had a thin yellow stripe. She waited, counting off the seconds as Feeney swallowed to see if she'd already lost the gamble.

But his eyes stayed clear. "Halloway." As did his voice. "Everybody here wants to resolve this. You need to tell us what you want so that everybody walks out."

"Shut up." He sliced his weapon down Feeney's cheek with casual violence. Then pawed another pill out of the bag, popped it in his mouth, chewed it like candy.

"Maybe those syringes are poison. Get one out, get one out." He chewed a second pill. "We'll have a little test."

"Yes, sir." She pretended to fumble a bit as she reached in the bag. "I'm sorry. I'm a little nervous." She took out the dummy. "Do you want me to administer this, sir, or would you prefer to do it yourself?"

"You go ahead and administer it. No," he said when she started to rise. "Sit right there. Pump it into yourself. You live through that, maybe you live a little longer."

She kept her eyes on his as she turned the syringe toward her arm, settled it, depressed the plunger.

"I followed your orders, sir. I'm sorry

you're in pain. It's difficult to think clearly when in pain. I hope, after this medication alleviates your physical distress, we'll be able to resolve this situation to your satisfaction."

"You want to make captain, you're going to have to start banging me. I'm in charge now. Get up, get up! Give me the damn syringe. These pills are *useless*."

She stepped forward. There was blood in his ears now. She kept her eyes locked on his as she lifted the syringe. "This will work faster."

She set her thumb on the depressor.

"Poison!" He screamed it, jerked away. "Poison! My head's exploding. I'll kill you. Kill all of you."

She heard the rush at the door, pictured the sharpshooters taking aim. He was a cop, was all she could think as she leaped at him, deflecting his weapon an instant before the stream struck her.

She brought the syringe down on his shoulder and pumped the tranq into him.

"Hold your fire! Hold fire!" She shouted it as Halloway ran in circles around the room, screaming as he ripped at his hair. "I disarmed him. He's unarmed."

The door burst open. She leaped between Halloway and the lasers. "I said hold your goddamn fire."

She whirled around. It was taking longer than five seconds. Halloway was throwing himself against the wall. Shrieking, weeping. Then his body danced, as bodies do when a stream takes them down.

Blood fountained from his nose as he pitched forward.

"Get medical in here," Eve ordered as she rushed over to kneel beside Halloway.

She'd seen death too often to mistake it. But still she checked his pulse.

"Damn it. Damn it." She beat a clenched fist against her knee, looked over to meet the knowledge in Feeney's eyes. "We lost him anyway."

Chapter 5

"He really caught you a good one." Eve crouched down to where Feeney sat under the ministrations of a med-tech. She pursed her lips as she examined the long, shallow gash that scored his cheek. "Been a while since you took one in the face, huh?"

"I don't stick my nose in the knothole as often as other people. You and me, we're going to go a round, Dallas. I taught you better than that. Adding a hostage—"

"Do I look like a hostage? I don't recall getting locked to my desk chair with my own restraints lately."

Feeney sighed. "Dumb luck that worked. And dumb luck—"

"Is a nice bonus to solid police work. Somebody told me that once." She smiled at him, laid a hand over his. Under her touch, his hand turned so their fingers linked.

"Don't think I owe you one. Not for dumb luck. And you make sure your man knows that—ah—business about banging and whatnot was just smoke."

"I know he's seething with a black jealousy and planning on whomping on you, but I'll do what I can to calm him down."

He nodded, but his grin faded as he looked away. "Caught us with our pants down, Dallas. Pants down around our goddamn ankles. I never saw it coming."

"You couldn't have. Couldn't have," she repeated quickly before he could speak. "He was sick, Feeney. Some virus, some infection. I don't know what the hell. Morris is working on it. It's the same deal that happened to the guy Trueheart took out. It's in the computer. It's got to be in the computer."

Jesus, he was tired. Sick and tired. All he could do was shake his head. "That's science fiction crap, Dallas. You don't catch anything but eyestrain from a unit."

"You put Halloway on Cogburn's unit. By the end of the day he's exhibiting the same symptoms as Cogburn. Deduction 101, Feeney, science fiction or not. There's something in that thing, and it goes into quarantine until we've got some answers."

"He was a good kid. He screwed off some, but he was a good kid, and a decent cop. I got on his ass this morning, but he needed a boot. Saw him sniping with McNab this afternoon and . . ."

Feeney rubbed his temples. "Oh Christ."

"They're taking care of McNab. He's going to be okay. He's tougher than he looks. He'd have to be, wouldn't he?" She worked up a smile when she said it and ignored the sick dread in her belly.

"Four of my boys hurt, one of them dead. I've got to know why."

"Yeah, we've got to know why."

She glanced back at Halloway's cube, at the old, broken-down data center on his work counter.

Absolute Purity, she thought.

She went back into Feeney's office. Halloway's body was already bagged. The blood that had burst from him was splattered like some mad drawing on the industrial beige wall.

She gestured to the MT who'd fixed her the tranqs. "What do you make of it?"

He looked down, as she did, at the body bag. "Some sort of rupture. Damned if I know. I've never seen anything like it, not without severe head trauma first. You need the ME's take. Maybe a brain tumor, maybe an embolism, massive stroke. Awful damn young. Couldn't hit thirty."

"Twenty-eight." He had a fiancée who was rushing back from a business trip in East Washington. Parents, and a brother, coming in from Baltimore.

And if she knew Feeney, Detective Kevin Halloway would be buried with all the honors due a badge who'd gone down in the line of duty.

Because that's just what had happened, she thought as they carried the bag away. He'd been doing his job, and had died because of it.

She didn't know how, she didn't know why. But a young EDD man had died today, for the job.

"Lieutenant."

She turned toward the door, and Whitney. "Sir."

"I need your report as soon as possible."

"You'll have it."

"What happened here . . ." He stared at the blood on the wall. "You have answers to that?"

"Some. More questions than answers. We need Morris to examine Halloway immediately. I believe he'll find similar neurological damage as he found in Cogburn. There are answers on Cogburn's data unit, but it can't be examined until some reasonable safety measures are devised. I do know Detective Halloway wasn't responsible for what happened here."

"I have to brief Chief Tibble and the mayor before we speak to the media. I'll let you ride on that one, for now," he added. "For the moment, the official word will be that Detective Halloway was suffering from some as yet undetermined illness that caused his aberrant behavior and resulted in his death."

"As far as I know that's exactly the truth."

"I'm not worried about the truth when it comes to the official word. But I want it, the whole of it. This matter is your only priority. Any and all other investigations you have

ongoing are to be passed on. Find the answers."

He started out, then pivoted back. "Detective McNab regained consciousness. He's
moved up from critical to serious."

"Thank you, sir."

When she walked out of EDD, she spotted
Roarke, leaning idly against a wall and
working with his PPC.

Anyone less like a cop, less like a victim,
she'd never seen. As far as the other element that frequented cop shops, he could
still slide in, silkily though, to that dangerous
group.

He looked up, held out a hand for hers.

"You couldn't have done more than you
did."

"No." She knew that, accepted that. "But
he's still dead. I put the murder weapon at
his head. I didn't know it, couldn't be expected to know it, but that's what I did. And
I don't even know what the weapon is."

She rolled her shoulders. "Anyway,
McNab's awake and moved up to serious. I
figure I ought to swing by and take a look at
him before I head home."

"Interview him?"

"I'll give him some stupid flowers first."

Roarke laughed and had nearly lifted her hand to his lips when she jerked it down. Hissed.

"Darling, you really shouldn't be so shy about public displays of affection."

"Public's one thing, cops're another."

"Don't I know it," he murmured and went with her to the garage level.

"I'll ride along with you. One of us should see that Peabody gets a bit of food or has a shoulder."

"I'll leave that end to you." Eve climbed behind the wheel. "You're better at the 'there-theres' than I am."

He touched the ends of her hair. Just needed to touch. "She held up very well."

"Yeah, she hung."

"It isn't easy, when someone you care about gets hurt or is in danger of being hurt."

She slanted him a look. "People want easy, they should hook up with an office drone not a cop."

"Truer words. But actually, I was thinking how difficult it was for you to stand and watch Feeney being threatened with death for nearly an hour."

"He was handling himself. He knows how

to—" It rushed up through her, grabbed her by the throat with spikey claws. "Okay." At the exit of the garage she stopped, dropped her head on the wheel. "Okay. Scared me. Jesus, Jesus. He knew just where to hold the damn weapon. Just the right point. One jerk and Feeney's gone. Gone in a blink and there's nothing you can do."

"I know." Roarke switched to auto, programmed in the address for the hospital, and leaning over rubbed the back of Eve's neck as the vehicle streamed into traffic. "I know, baby."

"He knew it. We looked at each other, and we both knew. It could be over so fast. No time to say anything, do anything. Damn it."

She laid her head on the seatback, closed her eyes. "I wheedled him into taking that unit, bumping it up in line. I know, I know what happened, what could have happened, wasn't my fault. But there it is anyway. He's got a neck like a stupid rooster. It's got bruises on it where Halloway kept jamming the weapon under his stupid droopy jaw. How many times did his life pass in front of his eyes? Never see his wife again, his kids, grandkids."

"You take on the job, you take on the

risks. Someone's always reminding me of that."

She opened her eyes now, looked at him. "Must be tempting to smack her back for being such a tight-ass know-it-all."

"Oh, infinitely." He played his fingers lightly over her cheek. "But someone's always beating me to it."

She smiled now. "I don't get hit in the face every couple weeks anymore, I don't feel right. I'm okay."

"Yes, you are."

She was steady again when she strode into the hospital admission's lobby. Steady enough to snap like a wolf at the dozen reporters already camped out and trying to sniff out a story.

"No comment."

"Your name was brought up as part of the negotiation team that brought about Captain Ryan Feeney's release. Why was Homicide part of this team?"

"No comment."

"A police source has stated that Detective Kevin Halloway fired on several other detectives, took Captain Feeney hostage within the Electronic Detectives Division of Cop

Central and subsequently was killed during the incident."

She shoved her way through the encroaching reporters, and—oops—knocked over a camera. "Perhaps you didn't hear the *no* portion of the phrase 'no comment.' "

"Did you terminate Detective Halloway in your efforts to obtain Captain Feeney's release?"

She turned at that, her eyes flat as a shark's. "Commander Whitney, along with the chief of police and the Mayor of New York will be briefing the media on today's events within the hour. If you want to feed, go chew on that bone. I'm just here to visit a sick friend."

"Why'd he do it?" someone shouted as she bullied her way to the elevators. "What kind of cops do you have working down there?"

"The kind who lay it down to serve and protect, even when it involves vultures like you. Goddamn it," she muttered the minute she was inside the elevator. She punched the wall, causing the elderly woman half-buried in a flower arrangement to try to melt into the corner of the car. "That's going to be tonight's revolving sound bite. I know better, better than to let them get under my skin."

"It would have to be made of reinforced steel not to get pricked now and then, Lieutenant. And as sound bites go, I thought it a strong and pithy one."

"Pithy, my butt. Damn it, I didn't get what floor he's on."

"I did. Twelve. Madam." Roarke smiled winningly at their elevator companion. "Your floor?"

"I can get off anywhere." She noticed the weapon peeking out from under Eve's jacket. "Anywhere at all."

"It's all right." Smooth and handsome in his business suit, he kept his voice light, friendly. "She's the police. That's a beautiful flower arrangement."

"Yes. Well. My granddaughter just had a baby. A boy."

"Congratulations. You'd like Maternity, I imagine. Ah, six." Once he had their destinations, he turned back to her, careful to keep his body blocking Eve's gun. "I hope mother and son are doing well."

"Yes, thank you. It's my first great-grandchild. They've named him Luke Andrew."

She slid her gaze cautiously toward Eve when the elevator doors opened to six. Holding the flowers like a shield, she scurried out.

"What? Do I look like I stomp on old ladies for recreation?"

Roarke angled his head. "Actually—"

"Just keep that silk tongue of yours still."

"That's not what you said last night."

And because he made her laugh, she was able to head down to McNab's room with less weight on her shoulders. It dropped right back on when she stepped in, saw Peabody sitting by the bed, and McNab in it.

He looked too young, lying there with his eyes closed, face white, so white against white sheets. They'd taken his body adornments, she thought. He looked naked, vulnerable, *wrong* without his complement of earrings.

Skinny shoulders, Eve thought with a wave of worry. The guy had skinny shoulders and they didn't belong under some drab hospital gown. He needed something bright, bold, silly over that half-assed body of his.

His hair was loose so that all that sunny

blond looked too shiny, too healthy against the rest of him.

She hated hospitals. They stripped you down to flesh and bone, left you weak and alone in some narrow bed where machines clocked your every breath.

"Can't we get him out of here?" she heard herself say. "Can't we—"

"I'll arrange it," Roarke whispered in her ear.

Of course he would. He'd arrange everything while she stood here, stuck in the damn doorway. Annoyed with herself, Eve stepped inside. "Peabody."

Peabody's head snapped up. Eve could see she'd been crying. Her hand slid across the sheet, covered McNab's.

"He's out. The doctor says he's doing okay. He took a pretty hard hit, but . . . I appreciate you letting me leave the scene to ride with him."

"I heard he'd come out of it."

"Yeah, he . . ." Peabody stopped, took one long breath, and seemed to draw herself in. "He went in and out a few times. He was vague on what happened, but he was coherent. They didn't find any brain damage. It gave his heart a pretty bad punch, and I think they're a little worried because the beat's still irregular. And his, um, his right side's numb yet. They think that's temporary, but right now he can't move his arm or leg on that side."

"Gonna walk funny." The voice was a bit slurry, but brought everyone's attention to McNab's face. His eyes were still closed, but his mouth curved up, just a little, in an attempt to smile that ripped at Eve's belly.

"You in there, McNab?"

"Yeah." He tried to swallow. "Yeah, Lieutenant, all present and accounted for. She-Body?"

"Right here."

"I could use some water or something. A brew'd be nice."

"You get water." She snatched a covered cup, brought the straw to his lips. After two shallow sips, he turned his head away. "I don't smell any flowers. Guy ends up in the hospital, people are supposed to bring him some damn flowers."

"I got a little distracted on my way to the gift shop." Eve moved over to the right side of the bed. "Had to kick a few reporters."

He opened his eyes. They were green, and they were clouded. From drugs or pain she couldn't be sure, but to Eve's mind one was as bad as the other.

"Did you get the captain out? I can't remember—"

"He'll be coming by to see you as soon as he gets out from under the paperwork. He's fine."

"Halloway."

"He didn't make it."

"Jesus. Jesus." McNab closed his eyes again. "What the hell happened?"

"You tell me."

"I . . . I can't get it clear."

"Take it easy for a while, then we'll talk about it."

"You laying off me that fast? I must be in pretty bad shape. Peabody, if I croak, you get my vid collection."

"That's not funny."

"Okay, okay, you can have all the earrings, too. But my cousin Sheila's going to be pretty pissed. Can somebody help me sit up some here?"

"The doctor said you were supposed to rest." But Peabody was already bringing the bed up to a reclined sitting position.

"If I croak—"

"Will you *stop* saying that."

He managed a grin while Peabody scowled with her face close to his. "How about you lay one on me?"

"I'll lay one on you." She muttered it, then pressed her mouth gently to his.

When she glanced over, she noted Eve was staring fixedly at the ceiling. "Sorry," Peabody murmured. "Just indulging the dying guy."

"No problem." She looked around when she heard Roarke come in. He nodded, then walked to the foot of the bed. "There seems to be an inordinate amount of attractive female medical personnel on this level, Ian. But I don't suppose you've noticed."

"Blast didn't screw up my vision."

"That being the case, you may not want to change locations. Summerset, while efficient, isn't quite so pretty."

"Sorry. Huh?"

"The lieutenant thought you'd be happier recovering elsewhere. We've a room for you at home, but it lacks attractive female medical personnel."

"You'd spring me?" The faintest hint of color crept into his cheeks. "To your place?"

"Your doctor wants another look at you

first, but we should be able to transport you in an hour or two. If that suits you."

"I don't know what to say. That's so solid. Lieutenant—"

"Yeah, yeah." Eve shifted her feet. "Let's see how grateful you are once Summerset's poking at you. I've got stuff to do."

"He looked sick," McNab said and stopped Eve before she turned for the door.

"Halloway?"

"Yeah, I was coming in from a field as-signment, and he was by the cooler. He got really pissy. Mean and aggressive. Not like him. He could be a pain time to time. Full of himself, but we got along. We were in the squad together two years."

He closed his eyes again. "Jesus. I don't get it. He came down on me like he wanted to taste some blood. Wasn't just what he said—you ride each other just for kicks half the time. You know how it is."

"Sure." Eve moved back to the bed. "But this wasn't just riding."

"No. It was how he said it, how he looked at me when he did. Got me hot enough to suggest we go down to the gym and pound on each other, but the captain came in and broke it up. He didn't look good. Halloway.

All sweaty and his eyes were blown. Your eyes get fucked sometimes with all the data, but his were bad. I went back to my cube, he went to his. I forgot about it."

"Did you speak with him again? See him speak or have an altercation with anyone else?"

"No. I had to get this report out. And there was a search and scan on a couple 'links I'd been putting off because they promised to bore my brains out. I got some coffee, bullshitted with Gates. Got stuck with a transmission from some woman who thinks her computer's possessed by aliens. We get those all the time. We've got this routine we walk them through to . . . Doesn't matter. I'm just off that call, and I hear somebody yell. Somebody's yelling in EDD half the time, but this was different. This was trouble. I swung around to see what the hell was going on."

He stopped there. Eve could hear the monitor's rapid beeps. His heart rate was up, she thought. Time to back off.

"Okay, we'll get the rest tomorrow."

"No. No, I remember how it went. I saw him coming at me. It didn't click through all the circuits at once. I mean, jeez, why would Halloway be charging at me with his weapon out? Doesn't compute. His face . . . He looked crazy, and he was already sweeping out streams like some combat cop laying down suppressive fire. Somebody screamed. I jumped up . . . started to jump up. I didn't have my weapon on. Hardly any of us wear it when we're working. I think maybe I was going to dive for cover. I think maybe I started to. Then bam—a couple of elephants plowed into my chest, and I was gone. How many of us did he take out?"

"Three others took jolts, and were treated and released on-scene. You got the worst of it."

"Just my luck. Halloway, he was okay before this. We'd rag on each other now and again, but just the way you do. We didn't have bad blood between us. He liked his work, and there's this skirt he was gone enough over that they were going to get married. He bitched about Feeney sometimes. Thought the captain was old-fashioned or something, but everybody bitches about the ranks off and on. It doesn't make sense he'd come at me that way. Something's wrong about this."

"Something's wrong about it," she agreed.

"I need to be in on the investigation."

Yeah, she thought, he did. In his place, she'd have needed it. "There'll be a full briefing tomorrow, nine hundred, my home office. Meanwhile, you'd better get back in shape because I don't have time to carry you around."

"Yes, sir. Thanks."

"We've got to go stock the AutoChef with gruel and other tasty invalid food. See you around."

"The gruel was a nice touch," Roarke told her as they walked down the hall.

"I thought so."

"Put a nice happy glow on his face."

"Lieutenant! Dallas!"

She turned to see Peabody hustling down the hallway, then took a staggering step back when her aide caught her in a fierce embrace. "Thanks. Thank you."

"Oh, jeez." Mortified, Eve lifted a hand, patted Peabody awkwardly on the back. "Okay."

"His heart stopped. During the transpo. They had to zap him. It was only a few seconds, but I thought: What'll I do? What'll I do? He's such an asshole," Peabody said and burst into tears.

"Man. God. Roarke."

"An interesting and flattering lineup," Roarke said to his wife's strangled call for help. "Here now, darling." Gently, he eased Peabody's death grip on Eve and with his arm around her led her into a small waiting area. He sat her down and dabbed at her cheeks with a handkerchief.

Eve shuffled her feet, then sat. Then rubbed a hand over Peabody's thigh. "You're just going to puff up his ego if he finds out you're crying over him. He's already hard to live with."

"I know. Sorry. It was, I guess it was hearing him say how it went down. It's got my brain all scrambled up."

"There's a lot of that going around."

Peabody managed a watery laugh and laid her head on Roarke's shoulder. Such was her state of mind that the physical contact didn't cause her to experience the usual sexual tingle. "You guys are the ult. Seriously. Taking him in for a few days while his system levels out."

"Well." Eve sighed. Friendship, she thought, could be so damn inconvenient. "He's bound to be pretty demanding. I'm sure as hell not going to be his private nurse. You're going to have to come along and take that duty."

Peabody's lips trembled. Her eyes filled again.

"Don't! Don't do that again. That's an order."

"Yes, sir." She let out an enormous sigh. "I'm going to go stick my head under a faucet before I go back in with him. I'll keep him out of your hair, Dallas."

"See that you do."

Eve sat where she was a moment after Peabody walked out. "Don't make any smart comments about me being a soft touch," Eve warned. "Or you'll be glad we happen to be in a medical facility when you regain full consciousness."

"Wouldn't dream of it." Roarke rubbed a hand over hers. "Lieutenant Softie."

She slanted him a look, but got to her feet without resorting to violence. "Let's get the hell out of here."

She let him drive home because she wanted to think. Electronics weren't her strong suit. In fact, she and technology fought an ongoing war, and so far she'd lost most of the battles.

Feeney was captain of EDD because he

was a good cop, and because he not only understood the strange world of electronics, he had a lifelong love affair with it. She could count on McNab, if he was physically up to it. He brought a young, fresh, innovative hand to the field.

And, after today, she could expect the full cooperation of every cop, drone, and droid in EDD.

But she had one more weapon, and it was sitting beside her, making her clunky departmental vehicle purr like a kitten as it darted through the misery of evening traffic.

She might have been Roarke's wife, and the wheel of the deal was his favorite pastime. Okay, second favorite, she corrected with a smirk. But electronics was his well-loved mistress.

"We need to get into Cogburn's unit," she began. "We need to take it apart and put every chip, every circuit, every board under a scope. And we need to do that fast, without whoever's working on it turning into a homicidal maniac. Any ideas?"

"I might have a few. I might take the time and trouble to refine them, if I were officially attached to the investigation. Expert consultant, civilian."

Yeah, she thought. Always a deal to wheel. "I'll consider it, after I hear the ideas."

"I'll discuss the ideas, after you consider it."

She only scowled and tagged Morris on the in-dash 'link.

His preliminary exam on Halloway showed the same massive intercranial pressure. Unexplained.

Early test results on Cogburn's brain tissue indicated some unidentified viral infection.

She frowned as they drove through the gates toward home. "Computers get viruses."

"Not biological viruses," Roarke pointed out. "A sick computer can and does infect other computers, but not its operator."

"This one did." She was dead sure of it. "Subliminal programming geared to mind control? We've dealt with that kind of thing before."

"We have." And he was considering it. He veered away from the house toward the garage to save Summerset the annoyance of remoting it there later. "As I said, I've some ideas."

She got out in what she thought of as his

vehicular toy warehouse. She'd never understand what one man needed with twenty
cars, three jet-bikes, a minicopter, and a
couple of all-terrains. And that didn't count
the ones he had stashed elsewhere.

"I'll run consultant status by the commander. Temporary consultant status."

"I really think I ought to get a badge this
time." He grabbed her hand. "Let's have a
walk."

"A what?"

"A walk," he repeated, drawing her outside. "It's a nice evening, and will likely be
the last we'll have to ourselves for a bit of
time. I've a yen to take the air with you, Lieutenant." He lowered his head, kissed her
lightly. "Or maybe it's just a yen for you."

Chapter 6

She didn't mind walking. Though she preferred pacing for exercising the brain.

And really, this was more meandering, so
that she had to check her stride twice to cut
it back to his pace.

It was funny, she thought, the way he
could throttle back so seamlessly. From action and stress to ease without any visible
effort. It was a skill she'd never mastered.

The air was heavy with heat, thick with it,
so they were strolling through a warm syrup.
But the sharp white light of afternoon had
mellowed toward a gilded evening light that
was so soft, it felt as if it could be stroked.

Even the heat was different here, she thought. Sucking itself into grass and trees and flowers rather than bouncing off pavement and smashing back into your face.

But there was something . . . something just under the surface of Roarke's placid calm. She could sense the honed edge of it, like a knife wrapped in velvet.

"What's going on?"

"Summer doesn't last very long." He steered her down a stone path she wasn't entirely sure she'd seen before. "It's pleasant to enjoy it while it does. Particularly this time of day. The gardens are at their prime."

She supposed they were, though they always looked spectacular. Even in winter, there was something compelling about the shapes, the textures, the tones. But now it was all color, all scent. Dramatic here with tall, spikey things with brilliant and exotic blooms, charming there with tangled rows of simple blossoms. And all lush and somehow perfect, without giving the appearance that any hand had touched it but Mother Nature's.

"Who does all the work out here, anyway?"

"Elves, of course." He laughed and drew

her into an arbored tunnel where hundreds of roses climbed and dripped onto green, shady ground.

"Imported from Ireland?"

"Naturally."

"It's cool in here." She looked up. Little flickers of sun and sky shone through the ceiling of flowers. "Nature's climate control." She sniffed. "Smells like . . ." Well, roses of course, she thought, but it wasn't that simple. "Smells romantic."

She turned, smiled at him. But he wasn't smiling back.

"What?" Instinctively she looked over her shoulder as if expecting some threat. A snake in the garden. "What is it?"

How could he explain what it was to see her standing there in the dappled, rose-drenched shade, looking baffled, a little confused by the beauty? Tall, lean, her disordered hair streaky from the sun. Wearing her weapon the way another woman might a string of good pearls. With careless confidence and pride.

"Eve." Then he shook his head, stepped to her. Resting his forehead on hers, he ran his hands up and down her arms.

And how could he explain what it had

been to stand by and watch her walk un-armed, unprotected into a room to face a madman alone? To know he might have lost her in an instant.

He knew she'd faced death countless times. Had faced it with her. They'd had each other's blood on their hands before.

He'd held her through dreams more violent and vicious than any human soul should have to bear. He'd walked with her through the nightmare of her past.

But this had been different. She'd been shielded only by her own courage and wit. And standing back, having no choice but to stand aside and watch, and wait, having no choice but to accept it was what she'd had to do had driven an unspeakable fear into his heart like a spike.

He knew it was best for both of them if he didn't speak of it.

But she understood. There were pockets and shadows inside him she still didn't fully comprehend. But she'd come to understand love. It was she who lifted her face to his when he would have drawn back. She who lifted her mouth to his.

He wanted to be tender. It seemed right with the romance of roses, in the gratitude that she was here, whole and safe. But the flood of emotion all but drowned him. Swamped by it, he fisted a hand in the back of her shirt as if it were a line tossed into a raging sea. That storm swept through him and into the kiss.

She waited for the heat of it to drop them both, and for his hand to tear her shirt to ribbons.

But his fingers opened, stroked one hard, possessive line down her back before his hands came up to frame her face.

She could see the tempest in his eyes, swarming in the blue of them with a kind of primal violence that made the breath catch in her throat and her pulse pound in response.

"I need you." His fingers dived into her hair, dragging it back from her face, fisting again. "You can't know what kind of need is in me for you. There are times, do you understand me, I don't want it. I don't want this raging inside me. It won't stop."

His mouth crushed down on hers, and she tasted that need, the fierce and focused intensity of it. And the greed, the desperation of it.

She gave herself over to it without hesitation. Because he was wrong, as he was very rarely wrong. She understood the need, and she understood the frustration of knowing it wouldn't be controlled.

The same war waged in her.

He released her weapon harness, dragged it off, tossed it aside. She only wrapped herself more tightly around him, moaned in drugged pleasure when his mouth, his teeth, fixed on the curve of her throat.

Somewhere a bird was singing its heart out, and the scent of roses grew heavy, hypnotizing. Air that had seemed so cool in the green shade went thick, went hot.

He yanked the shirt over her head, and those hands with their long, clever fingers raced over flesh until she all but felt it melt. But when she tugged at his shirt, he shoved her hands away, locked them together at the wrist behind her back.

He needed control, however fleeting, however tenuous.

"I'm taking you." His voice was as thick as the air. "My way."

"I want—"

"You'll get what you want soon enough."

He unfastened the hook of her trousers. "But I'll have what I want first."

And he wanted her naked.

He leaned in, nipped her bottom lip. "Do off the boots."

"Let go of my hands."

He merely slid his down into the opening of her trousers, tightening his grip on her wrists when her body jerked. "The boots."

He laid his lips on hers, slid his hand over her. His tongue slipping in to soothe, his finger slipping in to arouse with a patient seduction opposed to that steely grip on her wrists.

Even as she murmured a protest, her arms went limp. Dazed, she began toeing off her boots, and the movement of her own body shuddered her over peak.

She was hot and wet and trembling.

He wanted to touch, to taste, to explore and exploit every inch of her. Releasing her hands, he moved down her body. And when his mouth clamped over her, she erupted.

Her hands grabbed at his hair as she choked on gasps. But he only gripped her hips and continued to destroy her.

She was his now. In this garden, in this world. She was his.

Her world was spinning, all the color and scent gone mad around her. His mouth was like a fever, burning against her with a torment so exquisite it felt like death.

She could feel the heat rolling through her again, filling her, pumping into her blood and bone until it burst like a nova and left her shattered.

And still he wouldn't stop.

"I can't. I can't."

"I can."

When the next rush buckled her knees, he pulled her down.

This time he dragged her arms over her head and once again locked her wrists together. "Do you remember the first time I had you? I can't, you said, but you did."

"Damn it." Her body bowed up. "I want you inside me."

"I will be." He closed his free hand over her breast. "I can make you come this way now. You're primed for it. Everything in you is ready for me."

His hand was like magic over her skin. Under it her breast felt impossibly full, unbearably sensitive. And her heart beat like a fist.

"It pleasures me to watch it take you over."

He watched now as the helpless pleasure raced over her face, as her breath came faster through her lips. She bowed up again, a trembling arch. Then burst. Then melted.

He shifted away, began to undress.

She lay sprawled, damp, naked, conquered on the soft green grass. She wore only a long chain from which dripped the fat tear of a diamond, and the simple St. Jude's medal. He'd given her those, symbols and shields. That she would wear them, together, moved him unbearably.

Her arms stayed flung over her head as he'd left them. Surrendered, as she surrendered to no one else.

He was rock hard and desperate to mate.

He straddled her, ran his hands over her face, her throat, her breasts. "Eve."

She saw his face so intense, so strongly beautiful in the deep shade. A trio of thin sunbeams shot down through the leaves and flashed light over his hair.

"I want you to take me. Is that what you need to hear? I want to be taken, as long as it's by you."

He drove himself into her. Shoved her

knees back and drove himself deeper. She cried out, the shock of sensation slicing through her as he plunged.

"Harder," she demanded and yanked until his mouth was on hers again. "Harder."

His body quivered, and control snapped like brittle glass. Caught up in his own madness he ravished her mouth, her body. Pounding as he heard her cry out, pounding as he felt her gather again.

"With me." He took her hands, linking fingers now. "Come with me."

He gave himself, as she had given, so they could take each other.

The blood was still roaring in his ears when he managed to roll, drawing her with him so she was cushioned by his body rather than pinned under it.

The storm inside him had burned itself out. His hand was gentle as he stroked over her back.

"Some walk."

He smiled a little. "Yes, well, a bit of fresh air always does a body good."

"Yeah, I'm sure it was the fresh air that did the trick." She snickered. "Now I get why people go to the countryside for a little R and R."

"I'm feeling pretty rested and relaxed at the moment."

She lifted her head now, studied his face. "Yeah?"

He knew what she was asking. Knew she'd understood. "Yeah. I suppose we'd better tidy ourselves up and get inside. They should be bringing McNab along soon, and I've yet to tell Summerset."

"I'll leave that happy little job to you."

"Coward."

"Bet your ass." She rolled off him, then looked around on the grass for her clothes. "Where the hell's my shirt? Did you eat it?"

"Not to my knowledge." He glanced up, pointed. "There, hanging on the roses."

"The many uses of the garden," she commented as she strode over to tug it free. "Visual and olfactory stimulation, sex 'capades and clothes hanger."

He got up laughing, and the rich, easy sound of it told her they were back on steady ground again.

Once they were inside, Eve made a beeline for the stairs and went straight up to her office. She had work, she told herself. It wasn't that she wanted to avoid whatever conversation Roarke was going to have with Summerset.

Or it wasn't just that.

She put in a call to the commander first. The reluctance she'd shown about having Roarke on board as consultant had been smoke. She'd already planned to tag him for it, officially.

But there wasn't any reason to give him a swelled head about it.

"Permission's already been granted," Whitney told her. "Feeney requested that Roarke be asked to consult. I'm told Detective McNab's been released from the hospital and into your care."

"Not my care—so to speak."

"I've already spoken with his parents. You can expect a transmission from them."

"Ah . . ." Her mind began plotting how to pass that along to Summerset as well. "He's young and he's fit. I expect he'll be back on his feet in a day or two. I'll be working primarily out of my home office, Commander. Unless Feeney feels otherwise, I want Cogburn's unit transferred here."

"That's your call. We have a meeting tomorrow with Chief Tibble, Mayor Peachtree, and Chang, the media liaison. Fourteen hundred, in The Tower. Your presence is required."

"Yes, sir."

"Get me some answers, Lieutenant."

When he broke transmission, she sat down at her desk. She might not have the answers yet, but she could line up all the questions.

She made notes, checked prior notes. Shuffled them together and made fresh ones.

Cogburn, Louis K.—playground illegals. Possible to trace purchase of data unit? Search data entries to determine how often he used it—per week, hours per day.

Sudden violence displayed in primitive, physical bludgeoning. No prior VT indicated through witness statements.

Physical symptoms evident several days before incident, as indicated through witness statements.

ME reports intercranial pressure, abnormal and massive swelling, damaged tissues. Terminal. Physical symptoms: headache, bleeding from nose and ears, sweating.

Halloway, Detective Kevin. EDD detective assigned to search and scan Cogburn unit.

Check how many hours logged on subject unit.

Sudden violence displayed in deployment of police issue. Targets most specifically McNab and Feeney. Associate and direct superior.

Methods of violence suited to personality types? Consult Mira for profile verification.

No prior VT reported.

ME reports same results on prelim as Cogburn. Symptoms displayed match.

Death ensued without outside trauma or force.

Murder weapon=data unit.

It was murder, she thought. Technology was the instrument. But what was the motive?

"Dallas?"

"Huh?" She looked up, scooped her hair back, and stared blankly at Feeney until her mind cleared. "I figured you'd be at home by now."

"Rode over from the hospital with the boy."

His face had a few new sags, Eve noticed, and he looked exhausted. "Go home, Feeney. Give yourself a break."

"You're one to talk." He gestured toward

her notes. "Just wanted to see McNab settled. It was a good thing you did, having him come here. He seems pretty chipper." He dropped into a chair. "Shit, Dallas. Shit. He's half-paralyzed."

"That's temporary. You know it can happen if you take a hit wrong."

"Yeah, yeah. Take it wrong enough, it's permanent. He's twenty-fucking-six years old. You know that?"

It curdled in her belly. "No. I guess I didn't."

"His parents are in Scotland. Spend most summers there. They were set to head back, but he talked them out of it. I think part of him's afraid to have them see him like this. Part of him's afraid he's not going to come all the way back."

"We let him think like that—*we* think like that—we're not helping him."

"I know it. I keep seeing Halloway, the way he looked when he went down." He let out a deep breath. "I had to talk to his family, too. Didn't know what the hell to say to them. And the goddamn reporters, and my squad—my kids."

"Feeney. You've been through a bad one. It's different than when it happens in the field. You should talk to the department shrink." She winced at the look he shot her. "I know how that sounds coming from me, too. But, damn it, you were a hostage, you had a weapon jammed at your throat by one of your own men. You watched him die. If that hasn't screwed with your head, what would? So you should talk to the shrink or . . . Mira. If it were me, I'd go to Mira. She'd keep it off the record if you asked her."

"I don't want to open my head or spill my guts." His voice went tight, wrapped with bands of insult and temper. "I need to work."

"Okay." Recognizing the signs as she'd seen them often enough in her own mirror, she backed off. "We're going to have plenty. I'd as soon work from here for the time being, if it's okay with you. But the first order of business is to rig some sort of shield or filter on that unit. Nobody touches it until we have it shielded."

"From what? How are we supposed to design the right shield when we don't know what it's supposed to block?"

"That's a problem. I expect you and the expert consultant, civilian, you've already requested will figure out something."

He nearly smiled. "Thought that might

burn you a little. But you know damn well he's the best."

"Then put him to work, and get me a shield." She got to her feet. It felt awkward, but it also felt right to cross over to his chair, crouch down until their eyes were level.

"Go home, Feeney. Have a beer, be with your wife. She's a cop's wife, but she's not going to feel easy till she sees you. And you're not going to feel steady until you see her. I need you on this. I need you steady."

There was a lot more said between them that didn't take words. "Kids today," he said at length, "think they know every damn thing."

His hand closed over hers, squeezed once. Then he got up, walked out. Went home.

She sat where he'd sat for a moment, laid her hands where his had laid. Then she got up, walked to her desk. Went back to work.

She brought up Cogburn's data, then Halloway's personal file. She was halfway through a search for any connections when her 'link beeped.

"Dallas."

"Got one you're going to want to see." Baxter's face filled most of the screen, but she could see the movements, hear the sounds of a crime scene behind him.

"I'm on a priority, Baxter. I can't take another case. Handle it."

"You're going to want this. Vic's a fifty-three-year-old male. First glance it looks like somebody got in, attacked him. But you look closer, he did all the damage in here himself. Including slitting his own throat."

"I don't have time for—"

"A lot of premortem bleeding. Ears and nose. And take a look at this."

He turned. She caught glimpses of a spacious room, thoroughly trashed. Then the desk unit that lay screen-up on the floor.

ABSOLUTE PURITY ACHIEVED

"Don't let anyone touch that unit. I'm on my way."

She was halfway out the door when she swore, strode back to the desk to hunt up a memo.

"Listen," she spoke into it as she crossed into Roarke's office. "I got tagged. Related death. I'll be back . . . when I get back. Sorry."

She tossed the memo on his console, then bolted.

Chadwick Fitzhugh had lived, and lived well, in a two-level condominium on the Upper East Side. His profession was, primarily, being the solitary male of the fourth-generation Fitzhughs, which meant he socialized smoothly, looked snappy in a dinner suit, played a mean game of polo, and could, if pressed, discuss stock options.

The family business was money, in all its many forms. And the Fitzhughs had plenty of it.

His hobbies were travel, fashion, gambling, and seducing young boys.

Baxter filled her in on the basic data while Eve studied the bloody mess that was now Chadwick Fitzhugh.

"Name popped on the data search. Known pedophile. Trolled the clubs, surfed the chat rooms," Baxter stated.

"He liked them between fourteen and sixteen. Pattern was to buy them alcohol, Zoner, whatever worked, lure them up here, with the promise of more. Then he'd pull out the toys. Into bondage. He'd do them, whether they were willing or not. Looks like he took vids if his homemade stash is any indication. Then he'd give them some cash, pat them on the head, and tell them if they squawked about it, they'd be in more trouble than he would."

Baxter looked down at the body. "Mostly they believed him."

"If we know this, have record of this, at least one of the kids squawked."

"Yeah, he got reported four times over the last two years." Baxter pulled out a pack of gum from the pocket of his on-duty suit, offered it. "In New York anyway," he continued while he and Eve chewed spearmint contemplatively. "Got charged. Family money and lots of high-dollar lawyers stepped in and made it all go away. Nothing stuck to this creep. World's a better place without him."

Eve grunted and fitting on microgoggles, examined the throat wound. It gaped like a wide, screaming mouth. "No visible hesitation marks."

"When you gotta go, you gotta go."

With a sealed finger, she turned Fitzhugh's head. His ear canal was thick with blood. "Surfed the chat rooms?"

"I got the statement here in the file from

one of the complaints. That's how he roped this one kid anyway. Looked for young boys going through a sexual identity crisis, or those just playing around. Got a playpen upstairs. Room's done in black leather. You got your cuffs, your whips, your ball gags, butt plugs, and various mechanical devices. First-class vid setup."

He tucked his notebook away. "How it looked was he had some kid in here who went bonkers on him. Place is pretty smashed up, and he's got quite the potpourri of illegals around here. But security discs don't show anyone coming in here or going out for the last three days. Not even the dead guy."

"Who called it in?"

"Sister. Lives down on St. Thomas. Guess you've been to the islands plenty now," he added. "Blue water, white sand, mostly naked women. Wouldn't mind trading this heat for some of that."

He gave a wistful sigh, then crouched down beside Eve, careful to keep his cuffs out of the blood. "So anyway, bro here was supposed to fly down today. Big family party or some shit. Doesn't show, she gets worried, gives him a call. He answered—

screaming at her, cursing, nose bleeding like a tap. She figured he was hurt, being attacked, and called it in."

"I'm going to need to talk to her, get a formal statement." With her hands braced on her thighs, Eve looked over at Baxter. "I have to take this one away from you."

"Yeah." He huffed out a breath, pushed to his feet. "Figured. Everybody knows what went down in EDD today." He looked around, frowned at the computer screen. "What the hell's going on?"

"I'm putting together a team to find out." She straightened. "You want in on that?"

He looked back at her. "I want in."

"Then you're in. I need copies of the security discs, Fitzhugh's file, sister's name and location. We talk to neighbors, family, known associates. See if we can determine when Fitzhugh got . . . infected." She scratched her head. "We need to review his personal vid collection."

"Oh yeah, that's my idea of a good time. Watching some creep pork little boys."

"Maybe one of those little boys has been playing with computer programs. This unit needs to be transported to my home office."

"We working this out of your digs?" He brightened immediately. "Solid."

"Nobody messes with it. No search, no scan. It gets shut down and stays shut down until I say otherwise. Same goes for any of the data centers in this place." She looked around. "We're going through this place top to bottom. See if he put anything on hard copy. He gets bagged, sent to Morris, with a red flag."

"Got it. Hey, where's your shadow?"

"My shadow?"

"The inestimable Peabody. She's looking pretty good these days."

"A knothole in an oak tree looks good to you, Baxter."

"Only after a very long, very hard day. How come you didn't bring her in on this?"

"She's in, she's just . . . She's with McNab."

His humor faded. "How's he doing?"

"He's okay. Awake, coherent, good attitude. He's . . ." She shoved her hands in her pockets. "He's having a little trouble with his right side."

"What do you mean, trouble?" But he knew. Every cop knew. "Ah, shit, Dallas.

Goddamn it. Temporary, right? It's just temporary."

"Yeah, they're saying that."

They stood for a moment, in silence. "Let's get to work here," she ordered.

Chapter 7

She found Roarke in his office when she got home. Since it was there, she picked up the coffee at his elbow and drank it straight down like water.

"Dead pedophile. Slit his own throat. Went nuts first, broke up his own fancy apartment. Morris is going to find severe intercranial pressure. The Purity message was on his machine."

"Just the one unit?"

"I don't know yet. I'm having all of them sent here. I've got to find out how those units were compromised. How that causes a human brain to essentially blow up."

"You don't say you have to find out why."

"Purity," she said and sat. "Clean out the dirt and make absolute purity. The world would be better off without them," she said aloud, thinking of Baxter's comment.

"A vigilante group with superior tech knowledge." He nodded. "Halloway was simply a casualty of war. Both of your victims preyed on children."

"Yeah, they were scum, of a particularly disgusting sort."

"But they're your scum now."

"You got it. I'm going to need to go through the known victims of my victims. Kids who might have strong tech skills. More likely, family members who do. Could be we'll find somebody who had a kid messed with by both Cogburn and Fitzhugh."

"Chadwick Fitzhugh?" Roarke picked up his coffee mug, scowled into it, then strode to the AutoChef. "Slimy puddle of piss."

"Hey, just because I drank your coffee, that's no reason for calling me names."

"Fitzhugh. Bloody smug bastard, buggering young boys. Someone ought to've taken a knife to his throat long before this."

"I take it you knew him."

"Well enough to find him revolting in every possible way."

There was a different tone, a different look then when Baxter had described Fitzhugh. A far more dangerous one in that icy control, that musical lilt.

"His family's old money," Roarke continued. "Very uppercrust and pedigreed. Too fine to do business with the likes of me. Though they have done," he added as he turned back. His face was cold now. Warrior cold. "Until this sneaking badger's favored form of entertainment got out and about. Then it was me who wouldn't do business with them. Even a Dublin alley rat's got to have standards."

"Not doing business with him is one thing. And three cheers for you there. Killing him's another."

"Cut his own throat, didn't he?" He took a swig of coffee. "More fitting to my mind if he'd cut off his own balls first. But life isn't always willing to be poetical."

She went cold now, too. As cold as the ice that settled in the pit of her stomach. "No one has the right to stand in judgment, to pull on an executioner's hood without due process."

"There are times, Lieutenant, I'm not so fond of that line of the law as you are. In fact, have the coffee. I think I'll have a drink to toast buggering Fitzhugh's demise."

She rose when he went to a cabinet, opened it, and perused wine bottles in the rack. "If that's your stand, you can't help me on this."

"That's my stand." He selected a good cabernet. An exceptionally good one. "But it doesn't mean I can't and won't help you. Don't ask me to be sorry he's dead, and I won't ask you to be glad of it."

They'd been on opposite sides before, she thought. But this was opposite sides on very, very shaky ground. "Whatever he did, whatever he was, someone murdered him. It's no different from lynching a man or standing him against the wall and blasting him to pieces. The law determines guilt and punishment."

"We're not going to march in file on this one, Eve. And consider this: With all those fine words you've just spoken, aren't you standing there right now, judging me?"

"I don't know." But her belly was beginning to churn. "But I do know I don't want to get this messed up with a personal thing between us."

"We can agree on that." He spoke briskly, as if they were debating differing views on what color to paint the parlor. "I'll do whatever I can to help you find who or what is doing this. Let that be enough."

Watching him drink, she worried it wouldn't be enough. "Do you think murdering him was right?"

"I think it's right he's dead. Is that enough differentiation for you, Lieutenant?"

She didn't know, and felt the ground tremble under her feet. "I've got to put reports together for the morning briefing."

So, he thought, they'd leave it there. For now. "You might call Peabody up to help you. She could use a distraction."

"How's McNab?"

"Settled in. A bit sulky as Summerset put him on light food rather than the steak dinner of his dreams. His attitude's cheerful, but straining around the edges. There's no feeling yet."

"It can take up to twenty-four hours. Usually it's back within one to three, but it . . . Hell."

"We'll look into specialists if need be.

There's a clinic in Switzerland that's had great success in this area."

She nodded. Here, she thought, was a man who believed murder was, given the right circumstances, a viable option. Or, at least, the result of it something worthy of a personal toast. And he could, would, take the time, use his own money without hesitation, to help a friend.

"I'll see if Peabody wants to put some hours in."

It was closing in on two A.M. when she sent Peabody off to bed, and thought about heading toward her own. The door between her office and Roarke's was closed now. And the light over it indicated he was still in there.

Working, she thought. Very likely carving away at business he'd had scheduled for the next day. So he could clear his time for her.

She paced back and forth in front of the door. She wished she could tap someone else. Wished she had another source with half his skill and half his resources she could call on so that they could avoid picking their way over this boggy ground of opposing beliefs.

Picking their way hell. Neither of them had the patience to walk daintily. Some things were bound to get crushed underfoot.

She couldn't afford to worry about it.

She rapped briskly, pushed open the door. "Sorry, just letting you know I'm turning in. Briefing's at nine."

"Mmm-hmm." He continued to study the data on his monitor. "Counteroffer, four point six million, USD. Firm. Terms, ten percent escrowed on verbal agreement, forty on signing, remainder at settlement. Acceptance by . . ." He glanced at his wrist unit. ". . . noon tomorrow, Eastern, or negotiations are ended. Transmit."

He swiveled away, smiled at her. "I'll be along shortly."

"What are you buying?"

"Oh, just a little villa in Tuscany with a rather nice vineyard that's been mismanaged."

"Sounds like a lot of dough for a little villa and a mismanaged vineyard."

"Don't worry, darling. We can still afford those new curtains for the kitchen."

"You know, I don't have to pretend an interest in the stuff you do if you're going to crack wise when I do."

His smile only widened. "You're absolutely right. How rude of me. Would you like to see the cost projections for the rehab? Then there's the vintner's report and the financials from the—"

"Bite me."

"Can I take a raincheck on that? I'd really like to finish this up. If things go well, I think we might be able to squeeze out the coin for a new parlor sofa as well."

"I'm going to bed before I spring a rib laughing at all your funny jokes. Nine, ace. Sharp."

She swung away, then cursed viciously as her desk 'link beeped. "What now?"

She stormed across the room, snarled into the 'link. "Dallas. What?"

"Always such a pleasure to see your cheerful face, Dallas." Nadine Furst, on-air reporter for Channel 75 fluttered her lashes.

"No comment, Nadine. No fucking comment. Go away."

"Hold it, hold it! Don't cut me off. First, just let me say my feelings are crushed that you didn't notice I wasn't around for the excitement today. I just got back in town twenty minutes ago."

"And you called me at two in the morning

to let me know you're home safe and sound?"

"Second," Nadine said coolly. "When going through my mail, messages, deliveries that accumulated during my absence, I came across this." She held up a disc. "The contents are very, very hot, and, I think, of professional interest to you."

"Somebody sends you a sex vid, call Vice."

"It's from a group calling themselves The Purity Seekers."

"Don't use your computer," Eve snapped. "Shut it down now. Don't touch it. Don't run that disc again. I'm on my way."

"Listen—"

But she broke transmission and raced for the door.

"I'll drive." Roarke ran down the steps beside her. "Don't argue. I might be able to find something on her machine or on the disc."

"I wasn't going to argue. I was going to tell you to pick one of your faster toys."

They made it to Nadine's apartment in under eight minutes. "Give the disc to Roarke," Eve demanded the instant Nadine opened the door. "I'm taking you to the nearest health center."

"Just a minute, just a damn minute." She shoved at Eve when Eve grabbed her arm. "The disc isn't infected. They made that clear. Stop dragging me! They want media exposure. They want the public to know their purpose."

Eve pulled back, shut down the image of seeing a friend die screaming. "They want you to air the disc?"

"It's text only. They want me to report. That's what I do." Nadine huffed out a breath, rubbed her arm where Eve's fingers had dug in. "I guess I should appreciate you worrying about my health, but this is going to bruise."

"You'll live." And that was the point. "I need the disc."

Nadine arched one of her perfectly shaped eyebrows. Her attractive, foxy face was every bit as determined as Eve's. She was shorter than Eve, curvy, and no doubt softer. But when it came to a story she could do plenty of ass-kicking herself.

"You're not getting it."

"This is a homicide investigation."

"And it's a story. Freedom of the press,

Dallas, you might have heard of it. The disc was mailed to me."

"I'll get a warrant to confiscate, and to dump your pretty ass in a cage if you withhold evidence and obstruct justice."

Nadine had to rise onto her toes to compensate for the difference in height, but she managed to push her face into Eve's.

"I'm not obstructing anything and you know it. I didn't have to contact you. I could have gone straight to air with this, so just shut down your thrusters, sister."

"Ladies. Ladies." Taking the risk all men fear, Roarke stepped between two snarling women. "Let's just take a deep breath. You both have valid points. It might settle things a bit if we took a look at the disc."

"There's no guarantee it's not infected. I can take it into quarantine."

"You know that's bull." Nadine shook back her streaky blonde mane of hair. "They've got no beef with me. They want what I can give them. Exposure to the public. If you'd read the text, you'll see exactly what I mean. Dallas, they've just gotten started."

"All right, let's take a look. And if we all start bleeding from the ears, hey, the joke's on us."

Nadine led the way through the living area into a large office space done in classy pastels and clean lines. She plopped down at a desk. "Run disc."

"I told you to shut the unit down."

"Just read the damn screen."

Dear Ms. Furst,

We are The Purity Seekers, and are contacting you due to our belief of your respect for the public welfare. We want to assure you that we admire your dedication to your work, and wish you no harm. This disc is clean. You have our word that no harm will come to you through us.

We seek only the purity of justice. A justice that is not, cannot always be served through the confines of law that too often is forced to ignore the victim and serve the criminal. Our police force, our courts, even our government often find their hands tied by the slippery rope of tangled laws designed to protect those who prey on the innocent.

We were formed, and are sworn to serve the innocent.

Some will find our means distressing. Some will find them frightening. No war can, or should be fought without distress or fear.

But most will find our means just and our ends a victory for all who have been lost in a system that no longer serves the common good.

By the time this message reaches you, the first execution will have taken place. Louis K. Cogburn was a blight on society, a man who corrupted and addicted our children. He hunted them on the playgrounds and the schoolyards and the parks of our city, luring those young and innocent bodies and minds with illegals.

He has been charged, he has been tried, he has been sentenced.

He has been executed.

Absolute Purity in the matter of Louis K. Cogburn has been achieved.

He was infected through a technology we have designed and developed. As his soul was blighted, so did we blight his brain, until death.

There is no danger to you, to the innocent, to the public from this infection. We are not terrorists, but guardians who have vowed to serve our neighbors, whatever the cost.

Others have been tried, convicted, and sentenced. We will not stop seeking those who profit by and pleasure themselves on the grief and harm of others until Absolute Purity has been achieved in New York.

We ask you to inform the public of our message, of our goals, and to assure them that we work to protect and preserve the victim who the law cannot serve.

We hope to consider you our media liaison in this matter.

—The Purity Seekers.

"That's tidy, isn't it?" Eve commented. "Real tidy. They don't bother to mention Ralph Wooster, who got his brains bashed in, or Suzanne Cohen, who was beaten unconscious. No talk about a dead cop or one who may be paralyzed. Just how pure and true their goals are to serve the public. What are you going to do?"

"My job," Nadine told her.

"You're going to air this garbage."

"Yes, I'm going to air it. It's news, and it's my job to report the news."

"Nice bump to your ratings."

"I'm going to let that pass," Nadine said after a moment. "Because you've got a dead cop, and another—one I consider a friend— who's hurt. And I'm letting it pass because, yeah, this is going to be a nice bump to the ratings. You're here right now, reading this before I go on the air because I respect you, because you're someone else I consider a friend, and because I happen to believe justice doesn't have shortcuts. If you don't respect me and my purpose, then I've made a mistake."

Eve turned away, kicked a small sofa with enough force to make Nadine wince. "You're the only reporter I've been able to stand, on a professional level, for more than ten minutes."

"Oh my. I'm so very touched."

"Friendship's a separate issue. Let's just stick with the program for now. You're good at your job, and you play it straight."

"Thank you. And right back at you."

"That doesn't mean I'm going to do a happy dance knowing you're going to be broadcasting this crap. Guardians, my ass. You can't put a damn halo on murder."

"Good one. Can I quote you?"

Fury leaped into Eve's eyes. "This is off the record."

"This is all off the record," Nadine agreed calmly. "But you're going to want to go on the record very fast. I need a one-on-one with you, interviews with Whitney, with Tibble, with Feeney, McNab. I need to talk to Halloway's people. Family, friends, associates. I need a statement from the mayor."

"Would you like me to tie a bow around all that for you, Nadine?"

Nadine fisted her hands on her hips. "This is my area, and I know how to play it. If you want this story balanced, if you hope to spin it your way, I need airtime with all the key players."

"Eve." Roarke laid a hand on Eve's rigid shoulder. "She's right. She couldn't be more right. The majority of viewers will be fascinated by this group. They'll look at Cogburn and Fitzhugh—"

"Who's Fitzhugh?" Nadine demanded. "Are you talking about Chadwick Fitzhugh? Is he dead?"

"Shut up," Eve snapped. "Let me think."

"Let me finish," Roarke corrected. "They'll look at the people this group has executed and think: Well, it's no more than they deserved. They were parasites preying on our children."

"Like you," she said before she could stop herself.

Face expressionless, he inclined his head. "If you're hoping yet I'll work my way around to indignation over the death of a swine like Fitzhugh, you're doomed to disappointment. The difference is I saw what happened to a young cop today. What happened to Ian, what might have happened to Feeney. To you. That changes the complexion of this pompous, egocentric, and self-serving statement. But some who hear it will consider this purity group heroes."

"Heroism isn't achieved by remote control," Eve snapped.

"If you keep spouting sound bites like that off the record," Nadine said, "I'm going to break down and cry."

"Then show them up for cowards," Roarke told her. "Let the public see the grief Halloway's family is feeling because their son was an innocent victim. A cop who died in the line of duty because of something this group started. You let them see McNab, young, eager, wounded. You need to use the media as thoroughly, as skillfully as they will."

"I need to find them, I need to stop them,

not play Who's Spinning the Media Wheel now."

"Lieutenant." Roarke squeezed her shoulder. "You need to do both."

"I need that disc."

Nadine ejected it, held it out. "This is the original. I've already made a copy for myself." She smiled as Eve snatched it out of her hand. "It's going to be such fun working with you."

"I don't give you anything on record until I've cleared this with Whitney."

"Go ahead, give him a call. I'd say we could all use some coffee."

"I'll give you a hand with that." Roarke strolled out of the room with her.

Eve took a moment to calm down. She hated knowing Nadine was right. She would have to fight part of this battle on the airwaves.

She used Nadine's 'link to wake up her commander.

"She's been in there a long time." Nadine poured a second cup of coffee.

"You wouldn't break the story at this time of morning." Because Nadine was puffing on one of her herbals, Roarke indulged himself with a cigarette. He preferred real tobacco.

"You'll wait until six to maximize the viewing audience and ratings, catch your competitors unprepared, and thoroughly screw up their first-of-the-day broadcasts."

"You're good at this."

"I've some experience with manipulation."

"I'm giving her ten more minutes, then I have to call into the station, block the time, do the prep, call in an electronic's expert. I don't suppose you'd—"

"I think not. That would be skirting right over the line Eve's already drawn in her mind over this. But I can recommend a couple of names if you don't have anyone particular in mind."

"I was thinking Mya Dubber."

"She's excellent. A solid handle on electronics and a pleasant way of communicating technical jargon in simple terms."

"She works for you, doesn't she?"

"In a freelance capacity, yes."

Unable to sit any longer, Nadine stood up to pace. "She's cutting me close on this. I've got research to do, copy to write, interviews to set up. This story's going to blow everything else off the air. Who's next? That'll be one of the questions. And they'll keep tuning in until there's an answer."

"And my cop will work herself into the ground to try to beat that answer, so there is no next."

"That's why you have to respect her. And that's why she always makes a damn good story. Are you two butting heads over this one?"

He blew out a lazy stream of smoke. "Not heads so much as philosophies. It's more difficult for her to accept mine than it is for me to accept hers. We'll work through it."

"I appreciate you backing me up on this."

"I didn't do it for you," he stated calmly. "I did it for her."

"I know. I appreciate it anyway." Nadine spun around as she heard Eve come in. "Well?"

"You'll get your one-on-ones with me and Whitney asap. The mayor will draft a statement that may be read by the deputy mayor. That's not decided yet. He or she will do some questions, pending approval. We're not going to contact Halloway's family at this hour and add to their distress. If, in the morning, they're willing to speak with you, we'll arrange it. The same goes for Feeney. He had a rough one today," she said before Nadine could speak. "I'm not waking him up for this. You can interview McNab at our place, pending medical clearance. I'll let you know as soon as I can. Chief Tibble will also draft a statement, and consider an interview after he's reviewed all the data. Take it, Nadine, because that's the best you're going to get."

"Have some coffee. I need to make a call and change into wardrobe. We'll do the one-on-ones with you and Whitney in studio. One hour."

She got through it, towing the departmental line throughout the interview. If Nadine wasn't thrilled with the content of the interview, she knew it wasn't the words that would make the segment. It was Lieutenant Eve Dallas herself, looking pale and exhausted and absolutely steady.

To Eve's surprise, Mayor Steven Peachtree arrived just as she was going off-camera. At forty-three, he projected both a youthful and steady image. He was dignified and handsome in a conservative gray suit with a broadcast-ready blue shirt and a tie, perfectly knotted, in tones of both gray and blue.

He came in looking alert and grim with a

small entourage of smartly dressed aides
he ignored the way you ignore your own
shadow.

"Commander." He nodded to Whitney,
and was close enough now that Eve noted
the faint smudges of lost sleep under his
eyes. "I felt this needed to be addressed
personally, and swiftly. I'm told you've also
been consulting with Chang re official statements."

"That's correct. We need unification on
this. A solid line."

"I absolutely agree. The media liaison will
have updated statements for all parties by
eight hundred. Lieutenant."

"Mayor."

"We need swift and decisive action on this
matter. My office is to be kept updated on
every action taken." He glanced toward the
studio. "We're going to keep this goddamn
mess under control. We'll feed Ms. Furst
and the others no more than what we determine is good for public consumption."

"We're not the only ones feeding her," Eve
pointed out.

"I'm aware of that." His voice managed to
be both rich and chilly at the same time.
"Whatever they toss out, we'll spin back. We

can count on Chang for that. You'll work directly with him and Deputy Mayor Franco on media relations."

He glanced at his wrist unit. Frowned. "Keep me informed," he ordered, then strode off to the prep room.

"He's good at this," Whitney told Eve. "He'll come off strong, controlled, and concerned. We're going to need strong image projection to keep this lid from blowing off and spilling the contents all over New York."

"It seems to me the way to keep the lid on is to identify and stop The Purity Seekers."

"That's your priority, Lieutenant. But the job has more than one channel. The memorial service for Detective Halloway is scheduled for tomorrow, ten. Full honors. I want you there."

"Yes, sir. I'll be there."

"Today's meeting has been bumped up to thirteen hundred. Get some sleep," he added before he walked over to take his turn in the studio. "It's going to be a long one."

At home, she fell facedown on the bed for three and a half hours.

The alarm on her wrist unit woke her with its incessant beeping. She crawled out of bed in the dark, stumbled into the shower, and stayed under hot, crisscrossing jets for twenty full minutes.

When she came back in the bedroom, Roarke was just getting up. "Did I wake you? You could catch another half hour."

"I'm fine." He gave her face a critical study, then nodded. "And you look considerably better than you did at four this morning. Why don't you order us up some breakfast while I get a shower?"

"I was just going to grab a bagel at my desk."

"You've changed your mind," he said as he went into the bath. "Because you've remembered that your body needs proper fuel to maintain energy and health and because you'd prefer I not pour a protein shake down your throat as that just starts your day off on the wrong foot. Scrambled eggs would be good, wouldn't they?"

She bared her teeth, but he was already in the shower.

She ate, she told herself, because she was hungry.

And when Roarke buzzed Summerset on the in-house 'link and asked about McNab, she tried to feel optimistic at the information that the patient had spent a restful night.

Just as she struggled against despair when she watched him ride into her office in an electronic wheelchair.

"Hey!" His face was just a little too cheerful. His voice was just a little too bright. "I'm getting me one of these rides when I'm back on my feet. They rule."

"No racing in the corridors."

He grinned at her. "Too late."

"We'll wait for Feeney before I start the briefing," Eve began.

"We caught the morning report on 75, Lieutenant." Peabody's eyes were shadowed, and more than a little desperate when they met Eve's behind McNab's back. "I'd say we got a good start on the briefing."

"I need coffee." She gestured for Roarke to distract McNab, then jerked a thumb toward the kitchen. "You've got to hold up better than this," she told Peabody the minute they were out of earshot. "He's not stupid."

"I know. I'm okay. It's just, when I see him in that chair, I get a little shaky. There's no change. They said he should start to feel a tingling, like you do when your foot's asleep and starts to wake up. That would signal the nerves are coming back. But he's not, they're not."

"Recovery time varies. I've taken a full body blast and had no appreciable numbness within minutes. And I've had a glancing stream hit my arm and put it down for hours."

"He's scared. He's pretending he's not, but he's really scared."

"If he can pretend he's not, so can you. And if you want to do something about the people who put him in that chair—temporarily—then you need to pull it in and focus."

"I know." Peabody drew a deep breath, straightened her shoulders. "I can handle it."

"Good, then get started by handling the coffee."

She walked back out, stopped cold when she saw Feeney in her office doorway. His face was a picture of misery, sorrow, and fury as he stared at the back of McNab's chair.

Eve started to make a sound, anything that would snap him back, but before she could, he hit some internal switch. His face cleared.

"What's all this?" He came in scowling at McNab. "This looks like malingering to me. Trust you to manage to get a toy out of it all."

"Iced, huh?"

"First time you run over my foot, I'm flattening you. Baxter's on his way in. Got coffee?"

"Yeah." Eve nodded. "We got coffee."

By nine-thirty, she'd given the team the basic details. By nine forty-five she'd filled in the gaps, and by ten she'd added a basic theory.

"At least one of the key people in this group has been personally affected by a crime, most likely a crime against a child. Most probably more than one of them. You need like minds to get something like this off the ground. They have superior and as yet unknown electronic abilities, and must have some sort of medical consultant. It's also likely they have contact of some sort with the police or with the judicial system. Or both.

"They're organized, they're articulate, and they're media savvy."

"When you've got a group like this," Baxter said, "you've got those like minds. But you almost always have one or more who's in it for the thrill, the blood, or because they're just seriously wacko."

"Agreed. You can start a search for serious wackos who fit another of the group's profile. They will contact Nadine again," she continued. "They want public attention, and approval."

"They're going to get it." Feeney slurped at his coffee. "This is just the sort of thing that gets people riled up, arguing in the streets, making up T-shirts, taking sides."

"We can't stop the media train, so we do our best to steer it onto our tracks. Nadine wants to interview both you and McNab. You can blow," she said before Feeney could do just that. "But you won't be saying anything I didn't already say or think. The point is, the department believes this will be helpful."

"You think I'm giving this airtime?" Feeney slammed his cup down. "You think I'm going to go on-screen and yammer about what happened yesterday, talk about that boy?"

"What you'll say will help people understand what happened with Halloway." Roarke spoke quietly. "It will make them see him as he was—a good cop who was doing his job. Who was killed in the line of duty by a group of people who want to be perceived as guardians of justice. You'd make them see him as a person."

"I'd like to talk about it." McNab was strapped into the chair. It was something he couldn't ignore no matter how hard he tried. He wasn't just sitting, but secured in. So he wouldn't slump down like a ragdoll, tumble out like a baby.

It burned in his belly along with the fear that he would be strapped in a chair the rest of his life. "If people listen they'd understand he wasn't the one who put me down. It was whoever infected that unit he was working on. Halloway didn't put me in here, and he doesn't deserve anyone thinking he did. So I'd like to do the interview. I'd like to say what I have to say."

"If that's what you want." Feeney picked up his coffee again, drank it to wash away the fist-sized lump in his throat. "Then that's what we'll do."

"The department's issued statements. You'll both need to read them." Eve walked to her desk, gave herself time to settle. "They won't preclude or censor anything you feel you want to say, but they'd like you to get in the bullet points, and some of the language. It's important NYPSD show unity in this regard. Nadine can do the interviews here."

She turned back. "Now maybe we can get down to the business of cop work. We need to determine the nature of the virus in the units, and that can't be done until we have some sort of shield against that virus."

"I've done a bit of work on that," Roarke told her. "And taken the liberty of calling in a technical adviser." He turned to the 'link. "Summerset, send him up."

"You should've cleared this with me," Eve began.

"You need specific skills for this. Feeney and McNab need more than me. And I need more than an assistant. I've someone who's been doing some very innovative work with my R and D departments, and I don't think you'll find anything to worry about regarding his loyalty or his clearance."

Eve looked at the doorway. And her jaw dropped. "Well, for Christ's sake, Roarke, I can't use a kid for this."

Chapter 8

"Genius has no age."

So said Jamie Lingstrom as he strutted into her office on a pair of dilapidated air-boots.

He wore his sandy hair short and spiked on top with a longer hank in the front that flopped over his forehead. The only piercing—apparently—was to accommodate the tiny silver hoop at the tail of his left eyebrow. His face had done some fining down since the last time she'd seen him, and right now his mouth was twisted into a smirk.

He'd always been cocky.

His grandfather had been a cop, who'd

gone down while unofficially investigating a cult. The cult had killed Jamie's sister and had come uncomfortably close to sacrificing Eve.

He'd sprouted up at least two inches. When did kids stop growing? she wondered. He was sixteen—no, likely seventeen by now. And he should have been doing whatever teenagers did rather than standing in her office with that cocky expression.

"Why aren't you in school?"

"I do the home thing mostly, on work program. You get to do hands-on-the-job crap as long as it's with a business that contracts through the school and shit."

Eve turned to Roarke. "One of yours."

"Actually, I have several companies that contract with the education program. The youth of today, after all, is the hope of tomorrow."

"So." Jamie scanned the room then dipped his thumbs into the front pockets of baggy jeans with holes at both knees. "When do we get started?"

"You." Eve jabbed a finger at Roarke. "There." Pointing at his office, she strode in ahead of him, slammed the door smartly.

"What the hell do you think you're doing?"

"Bringing in an expert assistant."

"He's a kid."

"He's a brilliant kid. You do recall how he managed to bypass the security here with a homemade jammer?"

"So he got lucky."

"Luck had nothing to do with it." That particular homemade had been refined, adjusted, expanded. "He has more than a knowledge of electronics—though he has that in spades, I can promise you. He has a feel, an instinct that's very rare."

"I'd like to keep his brain inside his head, at least until he turns twenty-one."

"I've no intention of allowing him to do anything that puts him in physical jeopardy."

"Neither of us intended that last fall, either, but he came damn close. And he's, well, he's like Feeney's family."

"Exactly. It'll give Feeney a lift to work with him. The fact is, Eve, we need someone like him. Someone with an open mind and a quick brain. He won't automatically think a thing can't be done because it's not been done before." Roarke spread his hands. "He'll see possibilities. He wants to be a cop," he added before Eve could speak.

"Yeah, I remember, but—"

"Is determined to be, unless I can bribe him into one of my R and D divisions permanently with great gobs of money." His lips twitched. "Which I'll certainly attempt. At the moment, he plans to ditch any thought of college and leap straight into the Academy when he hits eighteen next year."

"So what. You're hoping to use this assignment to turn him off that idea, into college so you can scoop his genius brain up for your own uses?"

He smiled slowly, and with great charm. "That's a lovely thought. But actually, I thought this would be a valuable experience for him. And we need him. I'm not blowing smoke when I say that. What you need electronically is going to take considerable work and research and experimentation, all of which you required in a compressed time frame. Correct?"

"Yeah, but—"

"Look. I'm your expert consultant for a rather pathetic monetary wage, and under that agreement I have the option of selecting a technical assistant. He's mine."

She blew out a breath, paced to the window. Paced back. "Not just yours. It makes him mine, too. I don't know how to deal with a teenaged type person."

"Ah, well, I'd say you'd deal with him as you deal with everyone else. You order him around, and if he argues or doesn't jump quickly enough you freeze his blood with one of those vicious looks you're so good at and verbally abuse him. It always works so well for you."

"You think so?"

"There, see." He cupped her chin. "There it is now. I can actually feel my blood running cold."

"You can keep him, but he's on probation. And you've waived your pathetic monetary wage."

"Have I?" He frowned. "I can't seem to recall doing so."

"And his fee comes out of your pocket."

He'd already intended to pay Jamie, but knew how to play the game. "That's exceedingly unfair. I'm going to talk to my departmental representative about this high-handed treatment."

"You don't have a departmental rep." She walked back to the door. "You got me."

"To both my joy and sorrow," he replied

behind her back as she strode into her office.

Jamie was crouched between Feeney and McNab, showing off some handheld device. "It'll read every system on the market and some that aren't on it yet," he was saying. "Then it clones . . ."

His head came up, and then his body. The handheld was jammed into his back pocket. "So, hey. We got a deal or what?"

Roarke merely crossed to him, held out a hand.

Shoulders slumping, Jamie pulled the jammer out of his pocket. "I only borrowed one so I could see about fine-tuning a couple of functions."

"Don't hose me, Jamie. And if you continue to borrow equipment, you'll be losing your work program privileges very quickly." The jammer disappeared into one of Roarke's pockets.

"It was my prototype."

And the royalties from it, Roarke mused, would make the boy a very rich young man. But he said nothing, merely lifted an eyebrow and waited for Jamie to squirm.

"Okay, okay. Don't fry your circuits." Sulking, he looked at Roarke, looked at Eve. He was never quite sure which of them was in charge.

Either way, he knew both of them could stomp him flat before he saw them lift a foot.

It'd been easy with his parents before the divorce. His father had been in charge. After, especially after Alice died, Jamie himself had mostly been in charge.

But around here, you just never knew.

"What's the word?" he demanded.

"You're attached as Roarke's tech in a probationary capacity," Eve told him. "You step out of line, over the line, try wiggling under the line, I squash you like a bug. Now, do you see everyone in this room?"

"Yeah, nothing wrong with the orbs. So?"

"They're all the boss of you. Which means, anyone here gives you an order, including telling you to stand on your head and whistle through your teeth, you do it. Clear? Next," she continued before he had time to complain, "all data, all info, all conversations, all actions or proposed actions done or discussed pertaining to this assignment are confidential. You speak of this to no one, including your best pal, your mother, any girl you're hoping to see naked, or your pet poodle."

"I don't blab off," he said with some heat. "I know how it works. And I don't have any lame poodle. Plus, I've seen naked girls." He grinned now. "Including you."

"Careful, lad," Roarke said quietly. "Step carefully."

"You've got a smart mouth. I remember that about you." Deliberately Eve walked a circle around him. "I like a smart mouth, under certain circumstances. So instead of yanking your ears over your head and tying them in a knot, I'm going to overlook that comment. Once. Baxter, take this drone into the work area. Show him the basic setup. If he touches anything, break his fingers."

"You got it. Let's go, kid." When they reached the doorway, Baxter leaned down. "How'd you see her naked?"

"He's going to be trouble," Eve muttered.

"He'll be worth it." Roarke slid a hand over the jammer in his pocket. "Believe me."

"He's a good kid, Dallas." Feeney pushed to his feet. "Smart, and as steady as you get at that age. We'll keep him in line."

"I'm counting on it. I'm dumping him on you e-guys. Nadine and her camera are due in about twenty. She's never late. You both

good to do the one-on-ones downstairs
somewhere?"

"Works for me." McNab glanced toward
Feeney. "I want to get that over, and get on
the job."

"She doesn't come up here," Eve cau-
tioned. "She doesn't go near the kid. Any
progress, any at all, tag me. I've got a meet
downtown at thirteen hundred. I'll be working out of here until then."

"Let's get started." Feeney laid a hand on
McNab's uninjured shoulder. "We'll show
the boy what real EDD men can do."

"Flick Baxter back this way. I need to get
him set up somewhere."

"I'll take care of that. You'll want him on
this level," Roarke assumed.

"Fine. And whatever that is in your pocket,
Ace, keep it there."

He shot her such a hot, suggestive grin
that Peabody was forced to swallow.

"Get the salacious images out of your
head, Peabody," Eve ordered. "We've got
work."

She started Peabody on probability
scans. When you were dealing with brass
and bureaucrats the more data, the more
paper, the better.

Eve began a hunt for known child abusers who'd wiggled through the system and out again.

How did so many of them skate over the law? she wondered.

She backtracked, looking for any connection between one or more of her possibles and each other, between one or more and either Cogburn or Fitzhugh.

Birds of a feather, she mused. Some of them had to have sullied the same nest at one point. It was irritating to have to go by case numbers rather than names, but a great number of the files were sealed. Minor victims often had seals slapped onto their files.

Using numbers, incident reports, descriptions, she whittled it down to a short list, ran probabilities.

Since her short list was over twenty-five possibles, she worked on secondary connections.

Twelve of the minor victims had shared the same child services rep.

CLARISSA   PRICE,   BORN   5-16-2021, QUEENS, NEW YORK. ID NUMBER 8876-LHM-22. MOTHER MURIEL PRICE, FATHER UN-

KNOWN. MARITAL STATUS, SINGLE. EMPLOY-
MENT, CHILD SERVICES, MANHATTAN DIVISION.
EMPLOYED SINCE 2-1-43. CURRENTLY B
LEVEL.

   EDUCATION: MASTER'S DEGREES, SOCIOL-
OGY, PSYCHOLOGY EARNED FROM NYU.

   NO CRIMINAL RECORD.

"Visual," she ordered and studied the image of Clarissa Price. An attractive mixed-race female, with a competent, straight-ahead look about her. Not many in Child Services lasted as long without the job adding lines and layers. But Clarissa's skin was smooth. Her reddish brown hair was curly and worn neatly pulled back at the nape.

Eve called up the home and work addresses, copied and saved the data. Then went hunting again.

This time she found a cop.

Detective Sergeant Thomas Dwier had arrested Cogburn four years earlier on possession with intent. But he'd rushed it, scooping Cogburn up without ascertaining if he'd been carrying. The arrest hadn't stuck.

He'd had better luck with an illegals dealer who supplied the uptown teenage crowd.

But by the time the case had wound itself through the system, it had been pleaded down to possession and the dealer had ended up paying a fine, and walking.

He'd bumped into Fitzhugh as well, taking on a complaint of abduction and rape that had been tossed by the P.A.

Eighteen months before Dwier had worked on a team running a sting on a child pornographer. The woman had run a licensed day care center. The case had gone all the way to trial, resulting in acquittal.

Mary Ellen George, Eve thought, who according to the files, just happened to be a known associate of Chadwick Fitzhugh.

"Saddle up, Peabody." Eve stuck data discs in her bag. "We're going to make a couple of stops before The Tower meeting."

"Mary Ellen George. That was some trial." In the passenger seat, Peabody studied the data Eve had accumulated. "Did you buy that act of hers?"

"What act?"

"That shattered, innocent, schoolmarm act." Peabody glanced over, squinted. "Didn't you catch any of the trial on-screen?"

"I don't watch that crap."

"Well, you must've seen the blips in media reports, read the commentaries and stuff."

"I make it a point to avoid media reports, commentaries, editorials, and so on."

"But, sir, you've got to watch the news on-screen, or read it."

"Why?"

"Well . . . to keep abreast of current events."

"Why?"

"Because, because." Flustered, Peabody pushed back her uniform cap to scratch her head. "Because we live in the world."

"Yes, we do. There doesn't seem to be a thing we can do about it. Now, tell me how watching news blips and the On Trial channel is going to make me a better person."

"Just informed," Peabody answered.

"Seems to me it's only news for a few minutes. Then its old and they have to blast up something else that's news. Vicious cycle if you ask me. I don't get caught up in it because, by definition events that are current today are no longer current tomorrow. And before you know it, it's tomorrow anyway. So you've just wasted all that time getting riled up about something that's past its time when you wake up the next day."

"My head hurts. I know there's a major flaw in everything you just said, but it made my head hurt so I can't think of it."

"Don't worry about it. We'll check out George later. First we take a shot at Clarissa Price."

Parking near the Manhattan Division of Child Services was a joke. The two-level slots the city had put in along the street were jammed with vehicles that looked as if they hadn't dared move out in the last five years. Eve saw at least three with pancake tires and another with a windshield so covered with dust and grime it would've taken a pickax to clear it.

She double-parked, flipped up her ON DUTY sign. And wondered idly just how far traffic would back up before she came out again.

The building was a squat twelve-story box of block construction that surely hadn't seen its proper share of city maintenance dollars since it had been tossed up after the Urban Wars.

The lobby, such as it was, was small and crowded and boasted an ancient manual directory.

"Sixth floor." She walked right by the beleaguered lobby receptionist and onto an elevator. So much, Eve mused, for building security.

And as she'd had personal experience with Child Services, she knew that the kids who'd been sucked into the system could be just as dangerous as the adults who put them there.

She stepped out on six and saw someone had tried to add an illusion of cheer in this area. There was a section under a window with child-sized seating in primary colors and an offering of plastic toys. Across from it were two vid-game units currently under attack by a pair of bored, surly teenagers in rebel black.

She saw one of them gaze up and make her for a cop before his eyes traveled over Peabody's uniform and dismissed them both.

She walked up to him, waited for his lazy glance to meet hers again. Then she leaned over. "Take the knife out of your boot, real slow, and give it to me and I won't run you in for carrying a concealed."

Since it was concealed, and very well in his opinion, he only sneered. "Fuck off."

Eve's hand slapped on the hilt under his

pant's leg seconds before his. "You want trouble with me, I'll oblige. Otherwise, I'll just take this and let you spend your mandatory hour bullshitting your social worker."

She yanked the knife out of his boot, slid it into her own. "Nice blade. Decent balance."

"Cost me seventy-five."

"You got hosed, pal. It's not that good."

She turned her back on him and walked to the young, cheery-faced receptionist. They were always young and cheery-faced because they rarely lasted a year before running away with their idealism shattered behind them.

"I need to see Clarissa Price." Eve laid her badge on the counter.

"Miss Price is in a family session. She should be finished in ten minutes."

"We'll wait." Eve walked back and deliberately dropped into the seat beside Knife Boy.

It took him twenty seconds of pretending indifference to break. "How'd you spot the sticker?"

"That'd be telling."

"Come on."

She'd already spotted the bruises on his

wrists—fresh—and when he shifted saw the old burn marks on his shoulder, only partially hidden by his tough-guy muscle shirt.

That was one thing her father hadn't done to her, she thought. No burns, no scars. Wouldn't want to diminish the value of the merchandise.

"When you made me you moved your right leg back, rotated your ankle to check if the blade was under and secure. You get busted for carrying, they toss you in Juvie. Ever been inside?" The way he shrugged told her he hadn't. Yet. "I have. Whatever deal you've got it's better than being inside. Couple of years, they'll shove you out of the system, and your life's your own. You go inside at this stage, they'll keep tabs on you till you're twenty-one."

Since that was as close to advice or a lecture as she intended to give, she pushed up again and went out to hunt up a vending machine.

By the time she got bad coffee, the receptionist told her Miss Price had five minutes free before her next session.

It was a small office, but again the attempt had been made to brighten it. Art, obviously created by children, was framed to cover two of the walls. Files were neatly stacked on the desk and sat beside a little vase of fresh daisies. Behind them Clarissa looked as neat and competent as her ID photo.

"I'm sorry you had to wait," she began. "I'm afraid Lauren didn't get your name."

"Dallas, Lieutenant Dallas."

"We haven't met on the job?"

"No, I'm Homicide."

"Homicide. I see. What's this about? One of my kids?"

"No, not directly. You worked with some minors who had associations with a playground dealer, Louis K. Cogburn, and an alleged pedophile, Chadwick Fitzhugh."

"I worked with minors who were exploited by those individuals."

"A couple of your case files also intersected with other known or alleged child predators. But at the moment, we're interested in Cogburn, in Fitzhugh."

"Who are dead," Clarissa said flatly. "I heard the report on 75 this morning. Some para-organization is claiming responsibility."

"Terrorist organization," Eve corrected. "Who is also responsible for the death of an unrelated civilian and a police officer. You watch much screen? Sorry." Eve let her lips curve. "Just a personal debate between my aide and myself on the merits of media reports and keeping up with current events."

"I have 75 on most mornings and usually tune in at least briefly in the evenings." She smiled back. "Whose side am I on?"

"Hers." Eve jerked her head toward Peabody. "In any case, I'm primary investigator on these matters and I'm pursuing the possibility of connections between members of the group known as The Purity Seekers and minors who may have been exploited by Cogburn and/or Fitzhugh, as well as other child predators this group may have targeted. As the names of those minors are sealed and many of those who've reached majority have requested they remain sealed, I need your help."

"I can't break confidence with those kids and their families, Lieutenant, to help you in an investigation." She lifted pretty, ringless hands. "There's a reason for those seals. These children have been damaged, and while you have your job, I also have mine. Mine is to protect those children, and to do everything in my power to help them heal."

"Seals can be broken, Miss Price. It'll take

me time, but I can get an order to open the files for this investigation."

"I understand that." Clarissa lifted both hands again. "And when you have that authorization, I'll help you in any way the law allows. But I work with these victims every day, and it's difficult enough to gain the trust of kids who've already been hurt by an adult, to gain the trust of their families, even to find family members who give a damn. I can't help you until I'm ordered to."

"Did you ever have personal contact with Cogburn or Fitzhugh?"

"Professional contact. I gave statements to the P.A. on both men. That is, on the psychological damage done to the minors in my case file who'd had dealings with them. I never spoke with either of them, and I won't pretend to be sorry they're no longer around to hunt more children."

"Mary Ellen George."

Clarissa's face closed up. "She was acquitted."

"Should she have been?"

"A jury of her peers thought so."

"Have you had personal contact with her?"

"Yes. I had occasion to visit and examine

the conditions of her day care facility, and I
cooperated and worked with the police who
ultimately arrested her. She was very con-
vincing. Very . . . motherly."

"But she didn't convince you."

"This job requires a certain instinct, just as
yours does. I knew what she was." A cold
disgust, bordering on rage, hardened Price's
features. "You win battles and you lose
them. Losing's hard, but if you don't move
on to the next in this field, you'll burn out.
And I have to move on to the next now. I
have another session, and I'm already late."

"I appreciate the time." Eve stepped to the
door. "I will get that authorization, Miss
Price."

"When you do, I'm at your disposal."

Outside, Eve ignored the knotted traffic
fighting its way around her vehicle. She
didn't bother to respond to the horns, the
curses, the variety of obscene gestures. She
just climbed in.

"She's by the book," Peabody began as
Eve shoved into traffic. "But she'll be helpful
once you get authorization."

"She's holding more than sealeds under
her hands. She knew who I was and pretended not to."

"How do you know she knew who you were?"

"She watches 75 routinely. You watch 75 routinely, you're going to see me. You sure as hell saw me this morning—during the report she admitted watching—when I did the one-on-one. She played it a little too cautious not mentioning that."

Eve swung west, barely missed nipping the bumper of a Rapid Cab. "Clarissa Price goes to the top of the short list."

Chapter 9

Jamie was working hard to act cool. Everything he wanted in his life had fallen so unexpectedly into his lap he was terrified he'd do something to blow it away again. As far as Jamie was concerned electronics made the world go around. There was only one thing he wanted more than to work with them. That was to work with them as a cop.

Thanks to Roarke, he was getting that chance. Sort of. And on a homicide investigation that was baffling the premium ult cop.

It didn't get better.

Well, it would've been better if he'd had a

badge and rank. But tech assist to the expert consultant was an airboot in the door.

He was going to make it count.

He dug on working with Feeney, that was for sure. Uncle Feen was the total e-cop, with all kinds of stories about shit that went on before there *was* an EDD.

And McNab was totally iced. He talked a lot of trash, but he knew his 'tronics. Jamie thought he was pure hero stuff now that he'd been wounded in the line. Here he was half-frozen and pushing on with the job.

That's what cops did.

That's what Dallas did. Nothing stopped her. No matter what, she stood up. Like she had for his grandfather, and for Alice.

It still hurt, thinking about his sister. He knew his mother was never going to get over it, not all the way over it. Maybe you weren't supposed to.

Sometimes when he looked back to everything that had happened last fall, it was like a dream. Especially the end of it. All the smoke and the fire in that horrible room where that bastard Alban had taken Dallas after he'd drugged her.

Smoke and fire and blood, and the bitch Selina lying dead on the floor. Roarke and

Alban fighting like wild dogs, and Dallas
yelling at him to get the knife, get the knife
to cut her loose from where Alban had
strapped her naked to some kind of altar.

He'd cut the bonds, but he'd felt cold. Cold
all over in spite of the smoke. And naked,
still groggy from the drugs, Dallas had
leaped right off the slab onto Alban's back.

Dreamy, it was all so weird and dreamy.
He'd seen Roarke's fist fly up, knock Alban
unconscious. He'd heard the sirens coming,
he'd heard Roarke and Dallas talking—not
words, just sounds. The fire crackling, the
smoke stinging.

And the knife in his hand.

She'd shouted when she'd seen what he
was going to do. But it was too late. She
couldn't have stopped him. He couldn't have
stopped himself.

The bastard who had killed his family was
dead, and his blood hot on Jamie's hands.

He couldn't remember actually doing it.
Not the moment, not the instant when he'd
plunged the blade into Alban's heart. It was
like some time blip, and he couldn't remember.

But it had happened. It hadn't been a
dream. And Dallas had told Feeney and

Peabody and the other cops who burst in that Alban had been killed during the struggle. She'd grabbed the ritual knife from him, put her own prints on the handle, and lied.

Because she'd stood for him, too.

"Jamie. Stay focused."

He blinked, blushed, and hunched his shoulders at Roarke's brisk order. "Yeah, sure. Right."

He was working on a virus simulation, his third since they'd started.

"These sims aren't going to generate hard data without results of a diagnostic on one of the infected units."

"So you've said, in a variety of ways, six or eight times already."

Jamie swiveled away from his workstation. Behind him Roarke worked on filter construction. He was doing most of the programming manually, with fast flicks and taps of his fingers. In Jamie's estimation, any e-man worth his chips had to be able to do manual as well as voice and should know when one method suited the job better than the other.

Roarke was the ultra mag e-man.

"It'd take me five minutes, tops, to run a diagnostic," Jamie continued.

"No."

"Give me ten and I can locate and isolate the virus."

"No."

"Without an identification on—"

He broke off when Roarke held up a hand and shut his mouth.

He finished the sim, input the resulting data, then started the next program. He let it run on auto as he got up to dig out a tube of Pepsi from the full-sized cooler.

"I'll have one of those," Roarke said without looking around.

Jamie pulled out a second tube. Across the room Feeney and McNab worked on filter analysis. Jamie had never been in a house that boasted its own fully equipped e-lab.

Then again, he'd never been in any other house like this one. What it didn't have, hadn't been invented.

The floor was a steel gray tile. The walls were a pale green and covered with screens. The light came from sky windows, a half a dozen of them, all tinted to cut the glare and heat that could play havoc with the equipment.

And that equipment was so cutting-edge,

the edge hadn't even been cut yet. There were a full dozen data and communication centers, including one of the RX-5000Ks that he'd seen tested in R and D. It wasn't scheduled for release for three months, maybe six. There were three VR stations, a sim tube, a holo unit, with d and c capabilities, and a global and interstellar search-and-scan navigator he was itching to get his hands on.

He glanced toward his own screen, checked the status of his sim run, then sat beside Roarke. He scanned the codes jammed end to end over the screen, calculated.

"If you filter out the sound, blank all frequencies, you won't get the ID or source."

"You've missed something. Look again." Roarke continued to work while Jamie rearranged the codes in his head.

"Okay, okay, but if you flipped this equation, see? And this command. Then—"

"Wait." Roarke's eyes narrowed as he read his own program, considered the direction of Jamie's suggestions.

The boy was good.

"That's better. Yes, that's better yet." He made the adjustments, and with them in mind began on the next series of commands.

"Roarke."

"There's no point in asking me again. Answer's still no."

"Just listen, okay? You always say a guy should be able to make his pitch."

"Nothing more irritating than having your own words tossed back at you." But he stopped, sat back, and took the tube of Pepsi. "Pitch then."

"Okay. Without a diagnostic, with direct data from one of the infected units, we're blind. You can come up with filters, with shields, but no matter how good they are you can't be a hundred percent that they'll shut out the virus. If it *is* a virus, which we don't know without a diagnostic."

"We'll be a great deal more certain of operator safety once we have shields in place. If it's a subliminal, which is the highest probability, using either visual or audio to infect, I've dealt with something similar before and am constructing a series of shields to filter it out."

"Yeah, but similar isn't a hundred percent. So you're still going to be playing odds."

"Son, playing odds is a kind of religion to me."

Jamie grinned, and because he wasn't being dismissed, dug in. "Okay, odds are good, given the log time Detective Halloway had in when he first showed symptoms— and factoring in how long the other bad guy dudes were on—that it takes a couple hours, maybe more to hit the danger zone. Logically, Halloway had the brain eruption faster because he had all this time on at once. Straight computime instead of on and off, tasking, surfing, whatever. And he was *in* the unit, not just working on it."

"And you think I haven't factored that in?"

"If you have, you know I'm right."

"Probably right. Probably is a lot to risk dying for."

"You'd increase success rate if you used the first of the completed filters before going in." Jamie had to fight the urge to wiggle in his seat because he knew he was making progress. "Kept log time to under ten minutes. Ran a medical on the operator while he's on to catch any neurological changes. You got equipment in here that can be rigged to do that."

And Roarke had been considering doing

just that after he'd gotten the boy, and the cops, out of the way.

But perhaps there was a more straightforward method to it all.

"Do you see where I'm going with this filter here?" he asked Jamie.

"Yeah, I got it."

"Finish it," Roarke ordered, then got up to make his pitch to Feeney.

McNab was all for it. Perhaps, Roarke thought, it was an easier matter for youth to gamble with mortality.

"We can do sims, analyses, probabilities for weeks and not have it wrapped," McNab insisted. "The answers are in the infected units, and the only way to get at them is to get at them."

"We haven't put a full day in yet." Feeney knew he was meant to be the voice of reason, but he was itching to tear into one of the infected units. "The more tests and sims we run, the better our chances."

"I'll have a filter—the best I think we can hope for under these conditions—ready to be interfaced within the hour." Roarke glanced back toward Jamie. "We can run sims with it first, bombard one of the units with viruses and subliminals, and see how it holds up. At that point, I'd say it'll be time for a calculated risk."

Feeney dragged out his bag of candied almonds. "The primary won't go for it."

"The primary," Roarke said, coolly dismissing the love of his life, "isn't an e-man."

"No, she sure as hell isn't. Never could get her to have any respect for technology. We finish the filter, run the sims. If it holds up, we go in."

"I'll operate," McNab said quickly.

"No, you won't."

"Captain—"

"You're already on partial medical. Results'd be skewed." It was bullshit, Feeney thought, but he'd be damned if he put McNab on the hot seat. He wasn't losing two men in two days.

"I should get to do it." Jamie swiveled around. "It was my idea."

Roarke barely spared him a glance. "Since we both have to answer to your mother, I won't even acknowledge that bit of stupidity."

"I don't see why—"

"Have you finished that programming, Jamie?" Roarke asked.

"No, but—"

"Finish it." He turned back to Feeney. "I'd say it's down to you and me."

"Just me. I'm the badge."

"An e-man's an e-man, badge or no. We can argue about that, the fact you've got a badge, the fact it's my equipment we're using here. But why don't we settle the matter like Irishmen?"

Both amusement and challenge lit Feeney's face. "You want to fight, or you want to drink?"

Roarke laughed. "I was thinking of the other manner of settling things. Gambling." Roarke dug a coin out of his pocket. "Heads or tails?" he asked. "You call."

Eve considered Chief Tibble a good cop, for a suit.

He was tough, he was honest, and he had a very strong bullshit sensor. He played the politics of his job better than most, and generally kept the mayor and other city officials off the backs of the rank and file.

But when murder came through an item everyone in the city—every voter in the city—owned, when the media was in high gear and one cop took another hostage in

Central, the politicians were going to get their swings in.

Deputy Mayor Jenna Franco was known to swing hard.

Eve hadn't dealt with her personally before, but she'd seen her around City Hall or on-screen. She had the hard polish of a woman who knew it was essential to look her best while doing the job in an arena where votes were often swayed because a candidate was attractive.

She was a small woman who made up for it with snappy-looking three-inch heels. She was a curvy woman who took advantage of what nature or her body sculptor gave her with spiffily tailored suits in bold colors. Today's was power red and matched with a chunky gold necklace and earrings that looked as if they weighed five pounds each.

It made Eve's lobes throb just to look at them.

She looked more like some pampered society matron on her way to a ladies' luncheon than a hard-scrabble politician. And the opponents who'd come to that conclusion had been left in her dust.

That was something Eve could respect.

The fact Peachtree had sent her in his stead said he respected her as well.

With her was Lee Chang, the media liaison. He was short, slim, perfectly groomed in a gray pinstriped suit with his straight black hair slicked back.

He had Asian blood, an Oxford education, and an ability to juggle and spin the facts with expediency until it sounded true.

Eve had never liked him, and the feeling was completely mutual.

"Lieutenant," Tibble began, "we have a problem."

"Yes, sir."

"First, I understand Detective McNab is recuperating from his injuries at your home."

"Yes, sir. We have a medical supervising him—" Though she wasn't sure how she'd explain Summerset if pressed. "We felt he'd be more comfortable in familiar surroundings rather than the hospital."

"And his status this afternoon?"

"There's been no change at this time."

"I see." Tibble remained seated at his desk. "You'll keep this office informed in that area."

"Yes, sir."

"And the status of your investigation."

"I'm pursuing possible connections to the victims that may lead to the identity of members of the group calling themselves The Purity Seekers. Captain Feeney and his e-team are working on devising a shield so that the infected units can be examined and analyzed with reasonable safety. Medical and laboratory tests continue to be run on the victims in an attempt to ascertain the nature and cause of the brain damage that resulted in their deaths."

" 'Reasonable safety.' " Jenna Franco lifted a hand—not like someone asking permission to speak, but as one accustomed to being heard. "What, precisely, does that mean?"

"I'm not an e-man, Ms. Franco. That leg of this investigation is in Captain Feeney's hands. All efforts are concentrated on devising a shield for maximum safety to the operator."

"Lieutenant, we can't have another New York City police officer implode, and potentially kill or injure fellow officers or civilians. I can't go back to the mayor or the media with the term 'reasonable safety.' "

"Ms. Franco, police officers go on shift

every morning with no more than reasonable safety."

"They don't usually fire on their squad room and take their commanding officer hostage."

"No, ma'am, and Detective Halloway's commanding officer is in charge of the team who is working with all possible speed to ensure that doesn't reoccur."

"If I may." Chang's hands remained neatly folded; his face continued to hold a warm and pleasant expression. "It could be said that the police are utilizing all resources in this investigation to identify the source of the alleged electronic infection. The media will, of course, consult electronic experts to help them formulate their questions and to generate discussion and debate on-screen. We will, naturally, do the same."

"And when we discuss and debate on-screen," Eve said tightly, "we give this terrorist group exactly what they want. Attention, screen time. Legitimacy."

"The discussion and debate and questions will take place regardless," Chang told her. "It's essential that we control the tone."

"What's essential is that Purity be stopped."

"That, Lieutenant, we can happily agree is your job, not mine."

"Lieutenant." Whitney didn't raise his voice, but the steel tone of command in it stopped whatever comment Eve was about to make. "The media machine is already rolling. We get on board, or it runs us down."

"Understood, Commander. My team and I will follow the departmental directives for media contact. We'll adhere to the official statement."

"That's not going to be enough," Franco put in. "You're a high-profile cop, Lieutenant, on a high-profile case. The head of EDD and another of your team members were directly involved in the debacle at Central yesterday."

"Deputy Mayor Franco, my lieutenant put her life on the line to defuse that situation."

"Exactly my point, Commander. And due to her key involvement, the public interest in her personal and professional life, we need her on-screen as often as can be managed."

"No."

"Lieutenant."

She forced herself to speak calmly when she turned at Tibble's voice. "No, sir, I will not take my time and energies away from

an investigation to play department mouth-
piece. I will not play a part in giving a group
responsible for the death of a fellow officer
and the possible paralysis of another the attention they seek. I should be out in the field
now, not standing here debating the ramifications of the term 'reasonable safety.' "

"You've used the media when it's suited
you, Lieutenant Dallas."

"Yes, sir. And when I have I've done so
using my own words, not spouting off
scripted pap. And my personal life is just
that, and has nothing to do with this investigation."

"The expert civilian consultant on your
team has a great deal to do with your personal life. Lieutenant," Tibble continued, "I
sympathize with your position, and with your
desire for privacy. But if we don't play this
game well, Purity will not only get their media attention, but will continue to build support. Mr. Chang has the results of polls."

"Polls?" Eve couldn't keep the furious disgust out of her voice. "We took polls?"

"Two of the media services had polls generated before eleven this morning." Chang
took a memo book from his pocket. "The
mayor's office conducted its own, for internal

purposes. When asked if they considered the group known as The Purity Seekers to be a terrorist organization, fifty-eight percent of the respondents said *no*. When asked if they were concerned for their personal safety, forty-three percent responded *yes*. Naturally, we would like to see both those numbers decrease."

"You amaze me," Eve murmured.

"The facts are these," Tibble said. "A strong majority of the public perceive this group exactly as they wish to be perceived. Additional polls show little to no sympathy for Cogburn and Fitzhugh, nor regret for the manner of their deaths. It's neither possible nor politically prudent to attempt to generate sympathy for those individuals. The system is what must be defended."

"And the system must have a face," Chang added. "It must be personalized."

"This is a fine line, Lieutenant," Tibble continued. "If this group is publicly damned with the wrong tone, there could be a panic. Businesses shutting down in fear of using their electronics. Individuals afraid to turn on their data centers. People flooding into health centers and emergency centers because they have a headache or a damn nosebleed."

"We need people and industry to remain calm and secure," Franco put in. "It's essential we show that we're controlling this situation."

"Purity hasn't, thus far, targeted anyone outside a specific profile," Eve began.

"Precisely." Franco nodded. "And that, Lieutenant Dallas, is the key message the mayor, all of us, want to send. The family in the downtown loft has no cause for alarm. The midtown café can continue business as usual. Purity's agenda does not include them."

"So far."

Franco's eyebrows lifted. "Do you have reason to believe otherwise?"

"I have reason to believe vigilantes grow to like their work. That power, unchecked, will corrupt its own agenda. That violence, given impunity and approval, breeds more."

"This is good," Chang said, pulling out his notebook again. "With adjustments—"

"Don't mess with me, Chang, or you'll be eating that book."

"Dallas." Whitney got to his feet. "We're all on the same side. Tools and methods may vary, but the end goal is the same for all of us. Forget the polls and the politics for a moment. You know enough about human nature to understand that without a solid spin, people will begin to see this group as heroes. They'll see criminals, predators who slithered through the system's fingers finally meeting justice. Tonight our children are safe because someone took a stand."

"Justice doesn't hide behind anonymity. It doesn't operate without rules of conduct."

"That, in a nutshell, is the point. Press conference at sixteen-thirty, Central's media center. Be there at sixteen hundred to be briefed and prepped."

"Yes, sir."

"We all have our jobs, Lieutenant." Franco reached down, picked up a sleek leather briefcase. "And portions of those jobs are distasteful or annoying. But at the core, it's the safety of this city that concerns all of us."

"Agreed, ma'am. Fortunately my concern isn't contingent on polls or votes."

Franco's lips curved. "I was told you were a hard-ass. Good. So am I. Chief Tibble, Commander Whitney." She gestured to Chang, then strode out on her snazzy shoes.

"Lieutenant." Tibble remained in his position of power at the desk. "You will be required to work with Deputy Mayor Franco on this situation. I expect you to cooperate with her and the mayor's office, and to afford her the respect that office deserves. Is that understood?"

"Yes, sir."

"The potential for crisis here is layered. Public safety, public trust, financial and political ramifications. Those must all be addressed. The damage to city revenue, to individual businesses, to personal incomes could be serious if the tourist trade decreases because people are afraid to come into the city and use a public data center, if employees refuse to come into work, or use their home offices. If parents refuse to send their children to school or utilize their home-school options out of fear the educational units are infected. The media can swing this sort of thing on a dime. And if you believe this is an area beyond your concern, I'd suggest you ask your husband's opinion."

"My husband's opinion doesn't affect how I carry out my duty, Chief Tibble, nor does it affect the thrust of my investigations."

"Any married individual on or off planet

knows that statement is bullshit, Lieutenant. At this point, you don't have the luxury of ignoring the politics or the media. Welcome to my world." He sat back studying her carefully blank face. "Sometimes, Dallas, you make me tired."

That cracked the mask enough to have her blink at him, once. Slowly. "I apologize, sir."

"No, you don't." He waved a hand at her, then rubbed it over his face. "Now, give me the details of your investigation you didn't want to divulge in front of Franco and Chang."

She started to fill him in. He interrupted once. "A social worker and a cop? How many other ways do you intend to complicate my life?"

"I've yet to speak with Detective Dwier, sir, and have no direct evidence linking him to the organization. But, as I suspect civilian parents of abused minors may also be involved, I'd say the complication level will rise fairly high."

"It'll leak. One of your interviews will go to the media. We'll need damage control."

"Chief Tibble—" When her communicator beeped, she had just enough control of her own to realize she'd just been saved by the bell. "With your permission, sir?"

"Answer it."

"Dallas."

"Dispatch, Dallas, Lieutenant Eve, possible priority homicide, 5151 Riverside Drive. Victim identified as Mary Ellen George. See uniformed officer on-scene."

"Acknowledged." Her face was blank again when she looked back at Tibble. "Things just got more complicated, or more simple, depending on your point of view."

He sighed. "Go."

Tibble pushed to his feet as she strode out. "Fifty that she uses this to ditch the press conference."

"I look like a sucker?" Whitney shook his head. "I'll see she's there. One way or another."

Chapter 10

It had been a long time since Roarke had worked a con as basic as the coin toss. Still all it took was quick fingers and a bit of misdirection.

That boyhood skill had come back to him, smoothly, when Feeney had called heads.

A snatch, a light rub of the thumb over the engraving of the coin to determine which end you needed up, and tails slapped onto the back of his hand.

It was all done fast, and if he did say so himself, very well indeed. Feeney might have been annoyed and suspicious at the results, but a deal was a deal.

Even when the game was fixed.

"We could give it another pass or two," Feeney said when they all stood in the temporary lab with Roarke holding the filter disc. "Could be we'd—"

"Don't be such a mother," Roarke said mildly.

"My life won't be worth piss something happens to you on my watch."

"Well now, cheer up. Had the toss gone the other way, I could say just the same. She'd have my bones for breakfast."

"About that toss . . ." Feeney hadn't seen anything hinky about it, but you could never be sure with Roarke. "I say we do it again, but let Baxter here do the flip."

"I could take that to mean you're calling me a cheat—though you examined the coin yourself, made the choice of heads without prompting. But, seeing as we've a long and friendly history between us, I'll just take it as concern. The deed's done, Feeney, and no Irishman welshes on a bet."

"Don't put me in the middle of this." Baxter kept his hands safely in his pockets. "Whatever the hell happens, Dallas is going to be pissed. So let's do it before she starts busting our balls."

"We get the diagnostic run, we keep our balls." Jamie was in heaven. Not only were they about to do something beyond chilled, but he was standing around talking the trash with cops. "Infected unit's a snail, and the filter program's complex. It's going to take ninety-three seconds to download the shield," he said to Roarke. "If you start the diagnostic while it's loading, you'd—"

"Jamie, are you under the impression that this is, so to speak, my first day on the job?"

"No, but while the diagnostic's running, you want to upload the results onto—"

"Go away."

"Yeah, but—"

"Jamie, lad." Feeney laid a hand on his shoulder. "We'll be monitoring from outside. You can badger the man from there. Ten minutes," Feeney said to Roarke. "Not a second more."

"I'll be running a time sequence."

"No, ten minutes, not a second more." His jaw went firm as stone. "I want your word on it."

"All right. You have it."

As satisfied as he could get, Feeney nodded. "If we see anything worrying in the medical readouts, you'll shut it down."

"If you're thinking I'm willing to have my brains come spilling out my ears, let me reassure you." Then he flashed a grin. "But if such a thing should happen, I'll have the satisfaction of knowing Eve will be sending the lot of you to hell right behind me."

"She'll go easy on me." McNab worked up a smile. "I'm handicapped."

"Don't count on it. Now if you'd all get out, we could get this done before we're all old and gray."

"You'll wait until I give you the go-ahead. I want a check of your medicals first." Feeney stopped at the door, glanced back. "*Slainte.*"

"You can say that again, over a couple of Guinness in just a bit."

When they'd gone out, Roarke engaged the door locks. He didn't want his associates to panic and burst in on him again. Alone, he unbuttoned his shirt, then attached the sensors that would monitor him.

Lost your mind, haven't you? he thought. *Not just working for cops, which is bad enough, but risking your bloody brains for them.*

Life was a damn strange business.

He wouldn't lose his brains, or his life, like a lab rat, if it came to that.

He sat, faced Cogburn's machine, and felt under the work counter, let his fingers play lightly over the weapon he'd secured there.

He'd chosen the nine-millimeter Beretta semiautomatic from his collection. It had been his first gun, acquired at the age of nineteen from the man who'd been pointing it at his head. A banned weapon, of course, even then. But smugglers weren't so picky about such things.

It seemed to him, should things go wrong, a properly ironic cycle if he ended it all by doing himself with the very weapon that had started his collection, and had helped him on the road to riches.

He didn't anticipate anything going wrong. They'd taken all possible precautions, and those who had taken them were some of the best e-men—and boy—available. But there was always a chance, however slim.

If push came to shove, he would decide his own fate.

Then he took his hand away from the cold steel, and put it out of his mind.

"Going to run a check on your vital signs." Roarke glanced up at the wall screen, nodded at Feeney. "Fine. Cut the audio in there when you're done. I don't want all of you nattering at me when I'm working."

He slid his hand into his pocket, rubbed a small gray button between his fingers for luck. For love. It had fallen off the jacket of the very unflattering suit Eve had worn the first time he'd seen her.

"You're good to go," Feeney told him.

"Booting up then. Start the clock."

Mary Ellen George had, thanks to the royalties on the book she'd written on her arrest, trial, and acquittal, and the speaking fees she commanded, lived a very comfortable life in her West Side apartment.

She'd died there, as well, but it hadn't been comfortable.

Unlike Cogburn and Fitzhugh, the signs of her illness weren't violent nor were they destructive. It was apparent she'd taken herself off to bed, dosed herself with over-the-counter medication for several days—then with strong, street versions—during which time she had blocked her 'link calls and had refused to answer her door.

She'd taken a laptop unit into bed with her,

essentially destroying herself, Eve thought, as she tried to heal.

One of her last acts had been to place a hysterical transmission to a former lover, begging him for help, weeping about the screaming in her head.

Her last act had been to fashion her silk sheets into a noose and hang herself.

She wore only a white nightgown, obscenely soiled. Her hair was matted, her nails bitten down below the quick. There were tissues and washcloths, stained with blood, littering the bedside table.

Trying to stop the nosebleeds, Eve concluded, and picked up a medication bottle with sealed fingers. Trying to treat a brain on the point of exploding with ten-dollar blockers.

The laptop was still on the bed, its stark message filling the screen.

ABSOLUTE PURITY ACHIEVED

"Get this screen on record, Peabody. Victim: George, Mary Ellen, female, Caucasian, age forty-two. Body discovered in victim's apartment at fourteen hundred hours, sixteen minutes by building manager, Officer

Debrah Banker and Hippel, Jay, who placed the nine-eleven."

"Record of scene and body complete, Lieutenant."

"Okay, Peabody, let's get her down."

It was an ugly job. Neither of then spoke as they wrestled with the makeshift noose, as they shouldered the deadweight and lowered it to the bed.

"Visual evidence of blood in victim's ears, in nasal passages. Indication of blood vessel eruption in the eyes. No head or facial trauma evident. There are no visible wounds other than the bruising around the neck, which is consistent with strangulation by hanging."

She opened her field kit, took out a gauge. "Time of death established at fourteen-ten."

Eve reached over, shut down the laptop. "Bag this, log it and have it transported to my home office."

Then she stepped back and took a long, careful look at the bedroom. "She didn't exhibit the same level of violence as the other vics. You can see she'd been spending most of her time in here, popping blockers and tranqs, trying to sleep off the pain. She got a little messy, a little careless with housekeeping and appearance, but she didn't run around breaking furniture."

"People handle pain differently," Peabody said as she bagged the laptop. "Like you. You pretend it's not there. Like it's a personal insult and you're going to ignore it so it'll go away. Me, I go straight for the holistic stuff. Early childhood training. But if that doesn't work, it's better living through chemistry. And guys, like my brothers and my dad, they whine. A guy gets sick he reverts to babyhood. Which includes temper tantrums."

"That's interesting, Peabody."

"Well, you know. Testosterone."

"Yeah, I know. In these cases, the two males—three counting Halloway—tried to beat the pain and anyone who got in the way. And the female tried to suppress it with traditional methods. Everybody failed, everybody died. And here's what else everyone did. Burrowed."

"Burrowed, sir?"

"Holed up. Climbed into their nest, or the closest thing to it. Cogburn was locked in his apartment. Maybe if his neighbor hadn't come along, hammering at the door, shouting, cursing at him, he'd have stayed there until he died, or until he killed himself."

She studied the messy, makeshift noose. "Terminate and end the pain. I bet it's programmed into the virus. Fitzhugh, holed up, self-terminated. Halloway, the only one who wasn't a target, the only one who was exposed outside of his own home, burrowed into Feeney's office. If we hadn't kept him busy, I think he'd have offed Feeney, then turned the stream on himself."

"Cogburn and Halloway." Peabody nodded, following the dots. "They were the only two who had contact with anyone during the last stages of the infection. If they hadn't . . ."

"Would they have just opted out, like Mary Ellen George? Shuts herself in, blocks her incomings, ignores anyone who comes to the door. Terminates."

"Wounded animal instinct? The burrowing," Peabody asked.

"Human nature. It's logical. And it makes sense for Purity. They don't want to take out the innocent, just the ones they've judged guilty. They're looking for minimum negative fallout. They want public support for their cause. Even with the incidental casualties, they're starting to get it."

"They won't keep it. No, Dallas, they won't. I'm not going to believe most people really want something like this." She gestured toward the body.

"We had legal executions for what, over two hundred years in the grand old U.S. of A.," Eve reminded her. "Illegal ones have been going on since Cain bashed Abel. Under the polish, Peabody, we're still a primitive species. A violent one."

She thought of Roarke. And sighed. "Turn her over to the ME. Open the scene to the sweepers. I'll be talking to Hippel."

She turned on her own recorder as she walked into the small, cheerful office space off the living area. Officer Baker stood on post while a young black male with a muscular build sat with his head down and his hands dangling between his knees.

Eve wagged a thumb at the doorway, and Baker stepped out.

"Mr. Hippel?"

He lifted his head. His skin was a rich chocolate just now faintly tinged with the green of nausea.

"I've never seen . . . I've never . . . It's the first . . ."

"Do you want some water, Mr. Hippel?"

"No, I . . . The officer got me a glass. My insides are too shaky to drink."

"I need to ask you some questions. I'm Lieutenant Dallas."

"Yeah. I saw you on-screen doing that deal with Nadine Furst." He tried to get his lips to curve up, but they just trembled. "She's hot. I always try to catch her segments."

"She'll be thrilled to hear that." Eve sat down on a small, tufted chair. "Ms. George contacted you."

"Yeah. I hadn't heard from her in a couple weeks. We broke things off. Mutual," he said quickly. "We didn't fight or anything. Just time to move on, that's all. Okay, maybe she was a little steamed. Maybe I wanted to move on more than she did, but we didn't fight. Okay, maybe we had an argument."

He choked on his own guilt, spit out information while Eve sat in silence and let him run through it. "Maybe we yelled at each other some. Jesus, Jesus, she didn't do that because I dumped her, did she?"

"When did the dumping take place, Jay?"

"Maybe two weeks ago. It'd been coming on. I mean, hey, she's a fine-looking, sexy lady and all. Plenty of coin, too. But I'm twenty-four, and she's not. Guy needs a piece or two his own age once in a while, right? Only natural. And Mary Ellen, she was getting a little territorial. Crimping my style, got me?"

"Yeah. The last time you saw her, did you notice anything different about her?"

"Different? No. Same old Mary Ellen."

"She didn't complain of headaches or discomfort."

"She was feeling fine. We went out to a club, had some laughs, got ourselves a privacy room and banged. Came back out for a couple drinks, and she sees me scoping out some skirts and gets steamed. So we had a kind of argument and broke it off."

"And today, when she contacted you?"

"She looked bad. Man. Nose was bleeding, her eyes are all red. She's crying and yelling. I didn't know what the hell."

"What did she say to you?"

"Said I had to help her. 'Somebody's got to help me.' Said she couldn't stand it anymore. 'They're screaming in my head' is what she said. I tried to calm her down, but

I don't even think she heard me. I thought she said: 'They're killing me.' But she was crying so hard, I'm not sure. I thought some-body must be hurting her, all that blood on her face. So I called emergency and got my ass over here. I work just around the corner at the Riverside Café. How I met her. I got here right before the cop, and I'm trying to get them to let me go up. Then the cop came, and we went up, came inside. There she was."

He lowered his head again, this time all the way down between his knees.

When she finished at the scene, she swung by the morgue. Morris already had Mary El-len George's brain removed.

Even for a seasoned homicide cop, the sight of that pulpy mass of gray matter on a sterile scale was a little off-putting.

"Definitely expanded her mind," Morris said. "But it doesn't appear she managed it by reading the great works of literature or exploring other cultures."

"Har-de-har. Tell me you've isolated the cause."

"I can tell you this. Preliminary scan shows a healthy forty-two-year-old female.

Broke her left tibia at one point, healed beautifully. She's had some minor face and body work. Excellent job all around. Have to wait on the tox reports to tell you if she considered her body a temple or believed in chemical enhancements."

"Her body's not a big concern of mine right now. Tell me about her brain."

"Massive swelling that would have resulted in death within hours. Irreversible, in my opinion after the initial spread of infection, which is confirmed on the other brains in question by the neurologist I've brought in. The brain contains no foreign matter, no tumor, no chemical or organic stimulant. The infection, for lack of a better word, remains unidentified."

"You're not making my day here, Morris."

He gave her a little come-ahead with his finger, rinsed his hands, then brought an image onto a monitor. "Here you've got a computerized cross-section of the brain of a normal, healthy fifty-year-old male. Here." He tapped a key. "You've got Cogburn's."

"Christ."

"In a word. You can see the increased mass, the bruising where it was squeezed as the pressure increased. The red areas indicate the infection."

"It spread through, what, more than fifty percent?"

"Fifty-eight. Notice that some of the red is darker than others. Older infection. This would seem to be the area where it began. This leads us to believe it was an initial optical attack, and here . . . audio."

"So, it's caused by something he saw, something he heard."

"He may not have been able to hear or see it—not with ears and eyes. But a bombardment on these two senses into the lobes of the brain that run them."

"Subliminal then."

"Possibly. I can tell you that what we found so far indicates that the infection can and does spread quickly, causing the swelling to increase, sector by sector. Whether it's self-generated or requires further stimuli, we haven't determined. I can tell you that the pain and suffering this process would cause is unspeakable."

"Latest polls say most people don't think that's such a bad thing."

"Most people are, academically at least, barbarians." Morris smiled when she looked at him. "Easy to say 'Off with their heads' when you don't have to stand in the blood and have that head roll between your feet. A little of it splatters on them, they start calling for a cop."

"I don't know, Morris, sometimes it splatters on enough of them, and they get a good taste, they turn into a mob." She dragged out her communicator when it beeped.

"Dallas."

"Lieutenant, you're due at the media center in thirty."

"Commander, I'm at the morgue with the ME, awaiting further tests on Mary Ellen George's brain. I need to finish this consult and update my team. I request that—"

"Denied. In thirty, Dallas. Have your aide transmit your incident report and any additional data to my office ASAP. It will need to be reviewed and disseminated for the media."

When Whitney broke transmission, Morris gave her a little pat on the back. "I know, I know. Sucks sideways."

"They sicced the deputy mayor and Chang on me."

"I wouldn't wonder if Franco and Chang were thinking you'd been sicced on them.

Run along now and go assure the viewing public that the city is safe in your hands."

"If I didn't need you, I'd be tempted to beat you up for that."

She suffered through the preconference briefing, read the newly drafted statements, filed away what she was told could be discussed, what she was told could not. But she bared her teeth when Franco suggested she freshen up before the cameras and try a little lip dye.

"The fact that I have breasts doesn't require me to slap on enhancements."

Franco sighed and waved her hovering aides out of the room. "Lieutenant. I didn't mean that as an insult. We're women, and whatever position of power and authority we hold, we remain women. Some of us are more comfortable with that than others."

"I'm perfectly comfortable being female. I'll do what I'm ordered to do, Deputy Mayor. I don't have to like it. I don't even have to agree with it. I just have to do it. But I sure as hell don't have to doll myself up because you'd prefer a different police image on-screen than what I might present."

"Agreed, agreed, agreed." Franco threw

up her hands. "I apologize for making the insulting suggestion that you might put a little color on your mouth. I don't think of lip dye as a tool of Satan."

"Neither do I. Mostly I just don't like how it looks on me, or the way it tastes."

Franco let out another sigh, sat. "Listen, it's been a rough couple of days for all of us. Likely to get rougher. The mayor wants me to work with you, your boss wants you to work with me. We're stuck here. I don't want to battle with you over every step and detail."

"Then lay off."

"Jesus. Let me say this. You and I are both women with a strong sense of public duty. We're committed to doing our jobs, though we may employ vastly different methods and hold different attitudes. I love New York, Lieutenant. I sincerely love this city, and I'm proud to serve it."

"I don't doubt that, ma'am."

"Jenna. We're working together, call me Jenna. I'll call you Eve."

"No. But you can call me Dallas."

"Ah, and there we have one of our key variations. You hold your line, as a woman, by employing more traditionally male methods. I hold mine with the female. I enjoy exploiting my looks, my femininity for my own uses. It works for me, it's helped me get where I am to present an attractive package over the brains, the ambition, the sweat. Just as your method has worked for you. I distrust women like you. You distrust women like me."

"I distrust politicians in general."

Franco angled her head. "If you're thinking to insult me enough that I'll toss you out of this press conference, let me tell you, in the insult game, cops are amateurs compared to politicians."

She checked her slim, gold wrist unit. "We're due. At least comb your hair."

Keeping her face carefully blank Eve raked her fingers through her hair, twice. "That's it."

Franco paused with her hand on the doorknob, looked Eve up and down. "How in God's name did you manage to snap a man like Roarke?"

Very slowly, Eve got to her feet. "If you're thinking to insult me enough that I plant a fist in your face and get myself removed from this investigation so you can toss the media a more attractive image as primary,

I'll tell you that while it's very tempting, I'm going to see this case through. I'm going to close it. After that, all bets are off."

"Then we understand each other. Whatever our personal feelings, we see this case to closure."

Franco stepped out and was immediately swallowed by her pack of aides.

"Lieutenant! Lieutenant!" Chang trotted after Eve, hustling to catch up with her long, angry strides. "I have your media schedule for tomorrow."

"What the hell are you talking about?"

"Your schedule." He handed her a disc. "You will begin in the seven o'clock hour of Planet with a two-minute interview with K. C. Stewart. This is global and has the highest ratings. At ten, we have arranged for a live feed from your office at Central with the crew from City Beat. Again, this is the highest rated—"

"Chang, do I have to explain to you where this disc is going to end up if you keep talking to me?"

His mouth thinned, then pursed. "This is my job, Lieutenant, and I've worked very hard to arrange for these appearances in order to keep the agendas of the NYPSD and the office of the mayor at the forefront of this media blitz. The latest polls—"

"The latest polls are going to end up in the same place this disc does if you don't get out of my face." Riding on fury, she snapped the disc in half, then whirled around and stormed straight to the commander.

"You either want a cop or a media shill. I won't be both. If, in your opinion, the media perception is more important than my investigation, then respectfully, sir, you're full of shit."

He caught her arm before she could spin away. "One moment, Lieutenant."

"You can write me up, you can bust my rank, but I will not spend the hours I should be in the field doing my job as some talking head on-screen so the mayor's office gets better numbers."

"As long as you're under my command, Lieutenant, you will not tell me what you will or will not do."

Behind her, Chang smirked. Then carefully schooling his face, he held out a copy of the broken disc. "Commander Whitney, as Lieutenant Dallas has damaged her copy, I'll prefer to give you her media schedule for tomorrow."

"What media schedule?"

"We have several important segments booked, including appearances on Planet, City Beat, Del Vincent, and The Evening Report. We're waiting for confirmation on Crime and Punishment and Speak Back."

"You've booked my lieutenant on no less than four media appearances?"

Chang nodded. "We're very pleased with the schedule, but it can be improved. We're arranging a satellite interview from Delta Colony. The ratings are very high there for crime segments."

"Are you aware, Mr. Chang, that Lieutenant Dallas is the primary in charge of a priority homicide investigation?"

"Yes, this is why—"

"Are you also aware that standard procedure requires that your office clear any such demands as this media schedule with my office before confirming the appearances?"

"I believed it was made clear at this afternoon's meeting. The mayor—"

"What was made clear at this morning's meeting was that Lieutenant Dallas would participate in this press conference, and that at my directive she would make herself available for comment to the media. This schedule has not, and will not, be approved by me. I'm not wasting my lieutenant's valuable time on media pandering."

"The mayor's office—"

"Can contact me," Whitney interrupted. "Don't again presume to give one of my cops orders, Chang. You overreach your authority. Now back off. I need to speak to my lieutenant."

"The media conference—"

"I said back off." The flare from Whitney's eyes could have seared through stone. Eve heard Chang scramble back.

"Commander—"

He held up a hand. "You've come perilously close to being written up for insubordination, Lieutenant. I expect better contro from you, and have rarely had the need t remind you of it."

"Yes, sir."

"Moreover, I find myself insulted both a personal and professional level that assumed I had or would approve an asir schedule that pulls you off a priority."

"I apologize, Commander, and can offer the weak excuse that any and all tact with Lee Chang results in my temp insanity."

"Understood." Whitney turned the disc over in his hand. "It surprises me, Dallas, that you didn't shove this down his throat."

"Actually, sir, I had another orifice in mind."

His lips quirked, just slightly. Then he snapped the disc in two, just as she had.

"Thank you, Commander."

"Let's get this damn circus over with, so we can both get back to work."

on
you
ine

only
con-
porary

Chapter 11

She got through it, parroting the departmental chorus. As a result of stifling her own opinion, ignoring her own gut instincts, she stewed in her own simmering juices all the way home.

"Dallas." They were nearly at the gates when Peabody dared to speak. That way, if Eve tossed her bodily out of the car, she wouldn't have far to hike. "Don't take my head off, okay? You did what you had to do."

"What I have to do is investigate the case, and close it."

"Yeah, but sometimes serving the public's

complicated. There are a lot of people who'll sleep easier tonight because they heard their home unit isn't going to fry their brains if they sit down and balance their financials or do some e-mail. If their kid does his school report. That's important."

"I'll tell you what I think." Eve headed toward the gates without dropping speed so that beside her Peabody's heart took a fast spring into her throat. "I think people shouldn't always believe what they hear."

"Sir. I'm not sure I follow you."

"Maybe whoever's manning the switch doesn't like the way Mr. Smith with his pretty wife and charming little girl and small household pet lives his life. Maybe he decides Mr. Smith shouldn't be cruising the porn sites, or stopping off at a strip club after a hard day selling furniture, or occasionally getting zonked on Zoner with his pretty wife. Mr. Smith isn't following all the rules as well as he should be. Time to make an example of Mr. Smith so others like him understand the program."

"But, they're going after known predators. I'm not saying it's right. I'm not saying that, Dallas, because it's not. But it's a really big leap to go from school yard dealers and pe-

dophiles to some guy who tokes some recreational Zoner on Saturday night."

"Is it?" Eve stopped the car at the base of
the front steps. "The law's ignoring Mr.
Smith. It hasn't punished him, just like it
didn't punish the others. Purity punished
them, and a lot of people thought: Hey,
that's not a bad idea. Cops didn't do the job,
so good, somebody else did. Nobody's
thinking, hmm, that Mary Ellen George was
acquitted. Maybe she was innocent."

"She wasn't, so—"

"No, she wasn't, but the next one could
be. The one after that. It's not easy to watch
somebody walk, but it's a hell of a lot easier
than it is to know an innocent didn't. These
people are deciding who's guilty. With what
criteria, what system, what authority? Their
own. They're rolling, Peabody, and public
opinion's rolling with them. Let's see how
happy the public is when it starts coming
into their homes, their lives."

"You really think that'll happen?"

"Damn right it'll happen, unless we stop
them. It'll happen because they're on a mission, and there's nothing more dangerous
than someone on a mission."

She should know, Eve thought as she

slammed out of the car. She'd been on one since she'd picked up a badge.

When she walked in, it was one of the rare times she wasn't annoyed to see Summerset lurking in the foyer.

"Lieutenant, I'd like to have some idea how many of your guests will be staying overnight."

"They're not guests. They're cops and a kid. Head on up, Peabody, I've got something to do here."

"Yes, sir." And assuming that something was to have her usual pissing match with Summerset, Peabody darted up to check on McNab.

"Give me the status on McNab, and give it in English," Eve demanded.

"There's no change."

"That's not enough. Aren't you supposed to be doing something?"

"The nerves and muscles aren't responding to stimuli."

"Maybe we should've left him in the hospital." She paced the foyer. "Maybe we shouldn't have brought him here."

"The simple truth is there would be little more they could do for him there as can be done here during the first twenty-four hours."

"We're past twenty-four," she snapped. "We're over that, and he should have it back." She stopped herself, pulled it back in, and studied Summerset's cadaverous face. "What are his chances? Don't pretty it up. What are his chances of regaining sensation and mobility?"

"They decrease by the hour now. Rapidly."

He watched Eve close her eyes, turn away. But before she did, he saw the raw grief. "Lieutenant. McNab is young and he's fit. Those qualities play strongly in his favor. Being allowed to work at this time helps keep his mind active and off his difficulties. That can't be discounted."

"They'll bounce him on disability, or stick him in a cube doing drone work. He'll never feel like a cop again once that happens. He prances when he walks," she said quietly. "Now he's stuck in that chair. Goddamn it."

"Arrangements have been made with the clinic in Switzerland. I believe Roarke mentioned this." He waited until she turned around, looked at him again. "They'll take him as early as next week. They have an impressive rate of success in regenerating nerves. He must continue his treatments until—"

"What's their rate?"

"Seventy-two percent with injuries similar to McNab's make a full recovery."

"Seventy-two."

"It's not impossible he'll recover naturally. In an hour. A day."

"But his chances of that suck."

"In a word. I am sorry."

"Yeah, so am I." She started up.

"Lieutenant? He's frightened. He's pretending not to be, but he's a very frightened young man."

"They used to put bullets in you," she murmured. "Little steel missiles that ripped through flesh and bone. I wonder, when it comes down to it, if this is any cleaner."

She walked up, and into her office to what appeared to be a recreation break. Her team was spread out, lounging, she thought sourly, while each sucked on the beverage of his choice.

Jamie was feeding Galahad little bits from what seemed to be a sandwich the size of Utah. Perched on the arm of McNab's chair, Peabody filled them in on the details of the media conference.

"Well, this all looks so nice and cozy," she said. "I bet those terrorists are shaking in their boots."

"You gotta rest the brain cells and orbs every few hours," Feeney told her.

She stepped over the feet Roarke had stretched out. He could consider himself lucky, she decided, she didn't give them a good kick. She walked directly to her desk. Sat. "Maybe while you're resting those cells and orbs, someone could take just a moment out of playtime and update me."

"Missed lunch again, didn't you?" Roarke said mildly.

"Yes, I did. It had something to do with the woman who'd hanged herself with her own bedsheets, the pesky little details of serial homicides, an annoying little meeting with city officials—some of whom seem to be more interested in media image than those inconvenient dead people—and the hour or so I was ordered to spend feeding those media hounds."

She bared her teeth in a smile that had Jamie sliding down in his chair. "And how was your day?"

Roarke rose, took half the sandwich Jamie and the cat had yet to devour and set it in front of her. "Eat."

Eve shoved it aside. "Report."

"Now, let's not have any bloodshed." Feeney shook his head. The two of them made him think of a couple of bulls about to ram heads. "We've got some progress for you, which is why we're on break. We built a shield that partially filtered the virus. We think we've nearly isolated the infection on the Cogburn unit. We were able to extrapolate a portion of it. Computer's running an analysis now. Once we've got that, we may be able to simulate the rest of the program without going back into an infected unit."

"How long?"

"I can't give you that. It's a program the likes of which I've never seen. Encoded, failsafed. We're working with the bits and pieces we got out before the sucker self-terminated."

"You lost the unit?"

"That baby is fried," Jamie put in. "Didn't just blast the program, it killed the whole machine. Toasted it. But we got some good data. We'd have had enough to be sure of a sim if Roarke had had another minute— even forty-five seconds, but—"

He trailed off because Eve was getting to her feet. Really slow. Something in the movement made him think of a snake coiling up right before it lashed out with fangs.

"You operated the Cogburn unit?"

"I did, yes."

"You operated an infected unit, using an experimental filter, one that subsequently failed? And you took this step without direct authorization from the primary."

"Dallas." Feeney rose. It was a testament to his courage under fire that he didn't back off when she murdered him with one vicious glare. "The electronic end of this investigation falls on me. The lab work falls under my hand."

"And your hand falls under mine. I should have been notified of this step. You know that."

"It was my call."

"Was it?" She looked back at Roarke as she spoke. "Get out."

No one mistook she meant for Roarke to leave. The general exodus was more of a scramble. And at the doorway, Feeney batted the flat of his hand at the back of Jamie's head.

"What?" Sulkily, Jamie rubbed the spot. "What?"

"I'll tell you what," Feeney muttered and closed the door at his back.

Eve kept the desk between them. She wasn't entirely sure what she might do without the symbolic barrier holding the line. "You may run half the known universe, but you don't run my investigation, my operations, or my team."

"Nor do I have any desire to, Lieutenant." His voice was just as cold, just as hard as hers.

"What the hell do you think you were doing? Exposing yourself to an unidentified infection so you could prove you've got the biggest dick?"

His eyes flashed hot, then chilled. "You've had a very difficult day, so I'll take that into consideration. The filter needed to be tested, the program isolated and analyzed."

"With sims, with computer runs, with—"

"You're not an e-man," he interrupted. "You may be in charge of the investigation, but what goes on in the lab is beyond your scope."

"Don't you tell me what's beyond my scope."

"I am telling you. I could spend the next hour explaining the technical ins and outs of the thing to you, and you wouldn't understand the half of it. It's not your field, but it's one of mine."

"You're a—"

"Don't you toss that civilian bullshit at me, not over this. You wanted my help, so I'm part of this team."

"I can take you off the team."

"Aye, you could." He nodded, then reached out, fisted a hand in her shirtfront and pulled her across the desk. "But you won't, because the dead mean more to you than even your pride."

"They don't mean more than you."

"Well, damn it." He released her, jammed his hands in his pockets. "That was a low blow."

"You had no right to risk yourself. Not even to tell me. You went around me on this, and that pisses me off. You took a chance with your life that I find unacceptable."

"It was necessary. And it wasn't some blind leap, for Christ's sake. I'm not a fool."

He thought of the weapon he'd secreted just in case. And the small gray button he'd rubbed like a charm before he'd begun the work.

No, he wasn't a fool, but he'd felt a bit like one.

"There were four e-men in that lab who agreed the step had to be taken," he continued. "I was monitored, and the exposure was limited to ten minutes."

"The filter blew."

"It did, yes. Blew to hell in just over eight minutes. Jamie has some ideas on that I think are sound."

"How long were you exposed without a shield?"

"Under four minutes. A bit closer to three, actually. No ill effects," he added. "But for a little nagging headache."

He grinned when he said it, and she wanted to strangle him. "That's not funny."

"Maybe not. Sorry. My medicals are clear, and we have a partial picture of the infection. It required a human operator, Eve, one who knows his way inside a computer, and who knows the tricks and blocks a good programmer employs. If I hadn't done it, Feeney would have."

"Is that supposed to make me feel better?

Why didn't he?" she demanded. "He wouldn't have just passed this to you."

"We decided it logically. We flipped a coin."

"You—" She broke off, rubbed her hands roughly over her face. "Somebody implied today I chose to act or think like a man. Boy, was she out of orbit on that."

She dropped her hands. "Whether or not the electronics lab is out of my scope, it is under my authority. I expect and insist on being informed and consulted before any step is taken that carries personal risk to any of my team."

"Agreed. You're right," he said after a moment. "You should've been informed. It can be a tricky balancing act. I'm sorry for my part in cutting you out of the loop."

"Accepted. And though I've about hit my quota of apologizing today, I'll add one more for bringing your dick into the argument."

"Accepted."

"I need to ask you a question."

"All right."

Her stomach was knotted, but she would say the words. She would ask the question. "If you think these people are justified in what they're doing, if you think their targets deserve what they get, why would you risk this? Why would you take this chance with your own welfare to help me stop them?"

"For Christ's sake, Eve, you're like a god-damn chessboard. Black and white." Temper was there, bubbling in a way she knew meant it could spurt out any moment.

"I don't think that's an unreasonable question."

"You wouldn't. Why do you think that I think this is justified? I feel no twinge of remorse or pity for someone like Fitzhugh and suddenly I'm the side of terrorists?"

"I didn't mean it exactly like . . . Maybe I did."

"You think I'm capable of finding any justification in what happened to that poor boy, Halloway?"

"No." She felt vaguely ill. "But the others."

"Perhaps I can believe the pure philosophy of it. That evil, real evil, can and should be destroyed by whatever means possible. But I'm not stupid enough, and not quite egocentric enough to believe there can be purity in the spilling of blood. Or that it can be done, in general, without law and courts and humanity."

"In general."

"You would pin that, wouldn't you?" He nearly laughed. "We can't think just the same on this issue."

"I know that. I guess it shouldn't bother me. But it does. Damn it, Roarke, it does."

"So I see. I can't be pure for you, Eve."

"I don't want that. This whole thing has me tangled up. Maybe because I can't feel pity for someone like Fitzhugh or George either. I can't feel it, and at the same time I'm out-raged, I'm insulted that anyone, *anyone* felt they had the right to sit back and push a button that murdered them. Then call them-selves guardians."

"I'm not saying you're wrong. I don't be-lieve you are. But my morals, we'll say, are more flexible than yours. Even so, to make myself clear to you as you seem to need it, I don't subscribe to their means, their methods, or their agenda. If and when you confront evil, you do it face-to-face and hand-to-hand."

As she did, he thought. As he had himself.

"And you don't flog your message to the public like you were selling a new line of bloody sports cars. Eat some of that sand-wich, will you?"

"I guess maybe we're a little closer on this

than I figured." Steadier, she picked it up, took a bite. "God, what's in this?"

"I'm fairly sure it's everything. The boy eats like food's about to be banned and he best gulp it all down while he can."

She took another bite. "It's pretty good. I think there's corned beef in here. And maybe chocolate."

"Wouldn't surprise me in the least. Are we back on track now, you and me?"

"Yeah. Much as we ever are."

"Before we leave this topic, I'll tell you one more reason I did what I did this afternoon."

"Because you like to show off?"

"Naturally, but that isn't what I was going to say. I did it because whatever else I feel or believe or don't, I believe in you. Now, why don't you have some coffee to wash that back, then we'll show you what we've got."

She wasn't an e-man, but she could follow the basics. Even, if she pushed, the slightly more complex. But when she studied the printout of the data Roarke had been able to access from Cogburn's now-toasted unit, she might have been trying to decipher hieroglyphics.

"It's really jazzed," Jamie told her as he monitored the progress of the decoding program he'd devised. "Totally. Whoever built the program is an ultimate. No Chip Jockey could've done it. It's even beyond Commando level."

"While I agree, I doubt very much if this is the work of one programmer. The one thing we are sure of is this took superior programming knowledge as well as medical. Neurological."

"They'd need a team," Feeney agreed. "A first-class lab, equipment, and deep pockets. Isolation chamber."

"How much do you know, at this point, about how it works?"

"Eyes and ears," Jamie said as he swiveled from one unit to another, tapping keys. "Light and sound."

"Light and sound."

"Spectrum and frequency. You go on, pull up a nice game of World Domination to piss a little time away, and what happens is, you're getting bombarded with light and sound, stuff your eyes and ears can't register on a regular level. You know how they've got those whistles for dogs people can't hear?"

"Yeah, I know how it works."

"Okay, well, as far as I can tell, that's the idea with this virus. We haven't clocked onto the spectrum pattern or the frequencies, but we will. The beauty is, the virus runs through the system, but it doesn't make the computer sick, doesn't screw up any of the programs on it, or any the operator might upload after. It all just cruises along, without a hitch."

"And kills the operator," Eve concluded.

"Kills him dead," Jamie agreed. "We're working on how long it takes, but it needs at least an hour, maybe two to transfer the infection into the old gray matter."

"We haven't confirmed that," Feeney reminded him.

"The first shield failed," McNab added. "But it held long enough that we were able to pull out data that'll help us refine the next one."

"How long?" Eve demanded.

"We can put together another experimental in maybe two hours." McNab shrugged his good shoulder. "Longer if we have to wait until we break the code."

"Man, it is dense." Jamie picked up his Pepsi, slurped. "You break through one tier, and there're six more popping out. I'm going to run a short cut on an alternate unit, see if I can sneak through."

"Do that. And, Jamie." Roarke touched a hand to the boy's shoulder. "We'll need you to bunk here until we've cut through all this."

"Frig-o." He rolled his chair to another workstation, and hunkered down.

"Okay, let me give you the status, then we can all go back to work." Eve waited until attention focused on her. "You." She pointed at Jamie. "You're a drone. Be a drone."

He muttered, curled his lip, but turned back to his monitor.

"The ME's findings to date concur with your theory of audio and visual points of attack. He also reports that once the virus begins to spread, it is, most likely, irreversible. The latest victim, Mary Ellen George, was, according to witness reports, asymptomatic as early as eight days ago. After that point, we've found no one who had any contact with her.

"In analyzing the scene, I concluded that the victim, feeling unwell, took herself to bed, attempting to alleviate discomfort with over-the-counter. She blocked her incomings, pulled down the privacy shades and burrowed. She also took her laptop unit into bed with her, thereby certainly speeding the infection along with continued exposure."

"Fitzhugh locked himself in, too," Feeney offered.

"As did Cogburn, until he was incited by his neighbor. In Halloway's case, he was infected on the job but elected to hunker into your office. We'll assume that seeking this sort of shelter or isolation is also symptomatic."

"Programmed in," Roarke said, "to decrease the chances of outside interference or injuries."

"Agreed. Purity doesn't want hysteria or condemnation from the survivors of innocent victims. It seeks out specific targets. It seeks out media attention. It's playing God and politics."

"A very volatile combination."

"Bet your ass," she said to Roarke. "Which forces the NYPSD to play the same combo. The mayor's office and The Tower are spinning their dish to the media. Deputy Mayor Franco is the spearhead."

"A good choice of symbols," Roarke commented. "Attractive, intelligent, strong without being overbearing."

"So you say," Eve sneered.

"Symbolically speaking. By using her as spokesman rather than the mayor, it generates the impression this is not a crisis but a problem. By pushing you forward, it adds the element of competence and doggedness. The city is in good hands, caring hands. Female hands that, traditionally, tend and nurture as well as protect."

"What a load of horseshit."

"You know, it's not." Baxter spoke up. "Pain in the ass for you, Dallas, no question, but it's a good angle. You both look good on-screen. Nice contrast. Like, I dunno, the warrior and the goddess. Then you've got Whitney, Tibble looking all sober and stern, a few comments from the mayor at his dignified best stating his absolute confidence in the NYPSD and the system, and people feel calm and don't riot in the streets and fuck up traffic."

"Maybe you missed your calling, Baxter. You should be in PR."

"And give up this cushy job and the great salary?"

She laughed. "Horseshit or not, that's the current game plan. And unless we get a substantial break soon, I'm going to end up on the morning shows hyping justice like it was the latest entertainment vid. If that happens, I'll make all of you suffer beyond imagining."

She turned for the door. "Peabody, with me."

She waited until they were back in her office. "Don't hover over McNab like that."

"Sir?"

"You hover over him, you're going to make him think you're worried."

"I am worried. The twenty-four—"

"Worry all you want, dump on me if you need to. But don't let him see it. He's starting to fray, and he's trying hard not to show it. You try just as hard not to show it. If you need to vent, go out there on the kitchen terrace. Scream your lungs out."

"Is that what you do?"

"Sometimes. Sometimes I kick inanimate objects. Sometimes I jump Roarke and have jungle sex. The last," she said after a beat, "is not an option for you."

"But I think it would really make me feel better, and be a more productive member of the investigative team."

"Good, humor is good. Get me coffee."

"Yes, sir. Thanks. It's going to be a minute on the coffee. I think I'll try the terrace thing."

Eve sat, began to thread her way through Mary Ellen George's life.

The sealed files remained sealed. She'd gotten her warrant, and Child Services had immediately trumped it with a temporary restraining order. The TRO would hold her off until lawyers fought it out in court.

Days, she thought. Days lost. Unless she took another route.

Before she did, she'd try a more legitimate angle. For the third time that day, she put in a call to Detective Sergeant Thomas Dwier.

This time she tagged him instead of his voice mail.

"Sergeant, Lieutenant Dallas. I've been trying to tag you."

"I'm in court." He had a tough, lived-in face. "We're on a fifteen. What can I do for you, Lieutenant?"

"I'm primary on the Purity homicides. You hear about that?"

"Who hasn't? You tapping me because of that asshole Fitzhugh?"

"I'm digging for what I can find. I'd like to pick your brain over it. You also were part of the team on Mary Ellen George."

"Yeah, thought we had her solid, but she slithered. What's the connection?"

"She's dead."

"So, the wheel goes round and round. Don't know what I can tell you about either one of them that's not in the files."

"Why don't I buy you a beer after court? I'm jammed up, Dwier. I could use some help."

"Sure, what the hell. You know O'Malley's off of Eighth on Twenty-third?"

"I'll find it."

"Should be done here in an hour."

"I'll meet you at O'Malley's." She glanced at the time. "Seventeen hundred."

"Should work. They're calling us back. Later."

She turned from the 'link as Peabody set a mug of coffee on the desk. "Better?"

"Yeah, I guess. Throat's kinda sore. Your fridgie and your AutoChef are both out of Pepsi."

"Jamie must drink it by the truckload. Tell Summerset, then—"

She broke off when a small tornado burst into her office.

Mavis Freestone moved fast. The two-inch platforms on her purple gel-sandals didn't seem to affect speed or balance. She zoomed into Eve's office, a blur of purple, pink, and possibly puce, all mixed together in a microskirt and tit tube that almost covered the essentials. Her hair was in what appeared to be a half-million braids that echoed the color theme.

She spun to the desk, around it—the squishy gel on her feet making little *sproinging* sounds—and caught Eve in a headlock embrace that cut off all oxygen to the brain.

Eve managed to glug, slap on the arms that pressed on her windpipe.

"This is the *best* day! The most totally mag day ever invented. I love you, Dallas."

"Then why are you trying to kill me?"

"Sorry, sorry." But she squeezed again until Eve's ears began to ring. "I've got to talk to you."

"Can't." Freed, Eve coughed, rubbed at her throat. "Even if I were physically able I'm buried here. I'll call you when I surface."

"I have to. It's important. It's like *vital*. Please, please, please." She bounced as she begged, and the virulent mix of colors on the move made Eve dizzy.

"Two minutes. Talk fast."

"It's private. Sorry, Peabody, but . . . please!"

"Peabody, go find Summerset, tell him to hunt up a cargo plane full of Pepsi."

"Close the door, okay. Would you? Thanks." Still bouncing, Mavis linked her hands, held them between her small, barely restrained breasts. Her fingers winked and glowed with rings. On her left arm some sort of coil snaked from wrist to elbow. Eve wondered if the impression of it would be permanently stamped on her throat.

"Make it fast, Mavis." Eve scooped back her hair, gulped down coffee. "I'm really pressed. Weren't you supposed to be somewhere?"

"FreeStar One. Olympus Resort. Did a week gig at the Apollo Casino. It rocked. I just got back this morning."

"Good. Great." Eve shifted her gaze to her screen, began to process the data in her head. "We'll get together when I'm clear. You can tell me all about it."

"I'm knocked up."

"Fine. We'll cover that. We can—" Her brain simply went on hold, as if someone had flicked a switch that shut down all the circuits. When it clicked back, there seemed to be some sort of blip blanking out basic reasoning functions.

"What did you say?"

"I'm knocked up." Mavis let out a snorting laugh, then slapped her hands over her mouth. Her eyes, as purple as her shoes today, danced like a pair of chorus girls.

"You're . . . You . . ." Stunned into stammering, Eve stared at Mavis's bare midriff, at the trio of belly dangles that sparkled from her navel. "You got something growing in there?"

Her hands still over her mouth, Mavis nodded rapidly. "A baby." The laugh spurted through her fingers. "I've got a baby in there. Is that the ult? Is that beyond the beyond? Feel!" She snagged Eve's hand and pressed it to her belly.

"Oh, Jesus. Maybe I shouldn't touch it."

"It's okay, it's all padded and everything. What do you think?"

"I don't know." Cautious, Eve slid her hand away, tucked it behind her back. Logically she knew pregnancy wasn't contagious, but all the same. "What do you think? I mean, are you . . . did you . . . Damn, I'm not processing yet. Was this, like, an accident?"

"No. We did it on purpose." She scooted her tiny butt onto the desk, swung her pretty legs so the gel sandals bumped and squished against the wood. "We've been trying to procreate for a while. Me and Leonardo are really good at the process. We didn't have any luck at first, but you know, try, try again. We tried a lot," she said on another wild giggle.

"Are you sure you're not just drunk?"

"No, totally pregs." She patted her belly. "Embryo's in and cooking."

"Oh, God, don't say embryo." For some reason the word in combination with the squishy sound of the gel made Eve queasy.

"Come on, we all started out as one."

"Maybe. But I don't like to think about it."

"I'm like totally focused on it now. But wait, because I'm getting ahead of myself. Anyhow, when I was at Olympus, I got this feeling maybe I was baking—I was *whooshing* in the mornings and—"

"Okay, skip that part, too." Definitely queasy now, Eve realized, and made a mental note to sterilize the hand that had pressed against Mavis's bare belly.

"Right, so I took a preg test and it was positive. Then, you know, I got worried I'd messed it up because I wanted it so much, so I took three more. Liftoff."

She pushed off the desk, whirled around the room. "Then I went to the clinic up there, just to be more sure. I didn't want to say anything to my honeydew until I was abso-poso. I'm six weeks into the deal."

"Six weeks."

"We'd tapped out pretty regular, so I figured I was just feeling off at first and I was kind of afraid to do the check because you get so bummed when it's a no-go. But when the *whooshing* kept up—oh, sorry. I just *knew* something was up last week. I just went to the clinic here. Just one more check, you know, do an on planet deal. System's go. I went home and I told Leonardo. He cried."

Eve caught herself rubbing a hand over her heart. "In a good way?"

"Oh yeah. He stopped everything and started right away designing—well not *right* away because we had to celebrate by re-enacting the conception program—but afterward he starting designing me preg clothes for when I get fat. I can't *wait*. Can you imagine?"

"No. It's something else that's beyond my scope. You're really happy?"

"Dallas, every morning when I wake up and puke, I'm so happy I could just . . ." She trailed off and burst into tears.

"Oh God. Oh jeez." Eve sprang up, hurried over, then wasn't quite sure what to do. She tried a hug, intending on keeping it light—just in case—but Mavis grabbed on hard.

"This is the best thing that's ever happened to me, in my whole life. I had to tell Leonardo first, then you. Because you're my best friend. We can tell everybody else now. I want to tell *everybody*. But I had to tell you first."

"Okay, so you're crying because you're happy."

"Yeah. It's so iced. I can have mood swings whenever I want and without chemical assistance. No drinking, which sort of blows, but it's not good for little Eve or Roarke."

Eve pulled back so abruptly, Mavis almost doubled over with laughter. "We're not really going to call the baby that. We're just borrowing them for fun until they can tell us what equipment it's got. You get to call those names for when you and Roarke—"

"Shut up. Don't start down that road. I don't want to hurt a pregnant woman."

She only grinned. "We made a baby. Me and Leonardo made a baby. I'm going to be the best mommy, Dallas. I'm going to totally rock."

"Yeah." Eve ran her hand over the thick, colorful braids. "You will."

Chapter 12

Eve was a lot steadier walking into a bar that smelled of cop than she was hugging a pregnant woman.

You knew what to expect at a cop bar— good, greasy food, alcohol without the frills, and people who made you for what you were the minute you walked in the door.

The lights were low. Conversations didn't pause when she stepped inside, but she felt the subtle shifting of bodies. Then the flip back to business as usual when they recognized her as one of their own.

She spotted Dwier at the end of the bar, already half-done with his first glass of beer and the shallow black bowl of pretzels in front of him.

She walked down, slid onto a stool beside him. It was apparent he'd staked a claim on it as every other seat in the joint was occupied.

"Detective Sergeant Dwier." She held out a hand. "Lieutenant Dallas."

"Metcha," he said over his pretzels, then washed them down with a deep sip of beer.

"They spring you early from court?"

"Yeah. Supposed to get to me today. Didn't. Now I gotta give them more time tomorrow. Fricking lawyers."

"What's the case?"

"Assault with deadly and theft."

"Mugging?"

"Yeah. Guy mugs this suit coming out of a late meeting over on Lex. Gets his wrist piece, his wallet, wedding ring, and what all, then bashes him upside the head anyhow 'cause the guy asks him not to take the wedding ring. Got him cold hocking the wrist piece. Mope says, Oh hey, this? I found this on the street. Vic picks his face outta lineup, mope says, Mistaken identity. Got some bleeding heart PD who's trying to push that. Claiming the vic, seeing as he got his brains rattled, can't properly ID. Saying the wrist piece can't be directly tied to the crime as it's a common brand and style."

"How's it shaping up?"

"Shit." He popped more pretzels, chomped down. "Waste of my time and the tax dollar. Mope's got three priors. Figure they'd plead down if the PD wasn't so green and stupid. You drinking?"

"Yeah, I'll have a beer." She signaled the bartender by holding up two fingers. "I appreciate you taking the time here, Dwier."

"Don't mind wasting it over a beer. You read the files. Data's there."

"Sometimes the files miss impressions."

"You want my impression of Fitzhugh and George? They'd have to crawl up to reach scum level. Fitzhugh . . ." Dwier polished off the first beer. "Arrogant bastard. Never even broke a sweat when we hauled him in. Just sat there, smirking, hiding behind his high-dollar lawyers. Smart enough to keep his mouth shut, but you could see it in his eyes. He sat there thinking, You cops can't touch me. Turned out he was right."

"You talked to the vics, to their parents?"

"Yeah." He blew out a breath. "It was

tough. Sex crimes are always dicey, but when it's minors . . . You know how it is?"

"Yeah." She'd been a minor. And when she'd been in that hospital bed, broken, she'd read in the eyes of the cop who'd tried to talk to her what she was reading in Dwier's now. A weary pity.

"Any of the family members strike you as the type to go after Fitzhugh? Anyone talk about seeking revenge outside the law?"

"You blame them?"

"This isn't about my personal feelings or yours, it's about an investigation. Fitzhugh was executed, so was George, so were the others. It's my job to find out who's pulling the switch."

"I wouldn't want your job." He snagged the second beer. "Nobody who worked the Fitzhugh case, or the George, is going to cry any tears over this."

"I'm not asking for tears, I'm asking for information. I'm asking a fellow officer to reach out."

He brooded into the beer, then took the first foamy sip. "I can't say as any of the vics or family members acted in any way you wouldn't expect. Most of these people were shattered. Kids he raped ran the gamut from embarrassed, scared, and guilty. Family that came in, filed the complaint was torn to pieces. Kid was shaking in his socks. But they wanted to do the right thing. They wanted him put away so he couldn't get his hands on the next kid."

"Can you give me a name?"

His gaze shifted to hers. There was no pity in it now. "Names are sealed. You know that."

"Child Services put a TRO on my warrant to open the sealeds. I've got a terrorist organization with technology superior to anything my experts have seen executing at will. There are connections between the victims, and I think one of those connections is their victims."

"I'm not giving you names. And I'll tell you straight, I hope they squash your warrant. I don't want to see those people pulled through this crap again. You've got a job to do, and word is you're good at it. I can't give you more help than I have. I appreciate the beer."

"Okay." She stood up, pulled out credits. "Do you know Clarissa Price at Children's Services?"

"Sure." Dwier reached for more pretzels.

"She repped some of the vics from these cases. If you're thinking of finessing names from her, you're wasting your time. She won't shake."

"Dedicated type?"

"You bet."

"Dedicated enough to go outside the system if she doesn't like how it's working?"

His eyes stayed flat. "If I had to say, I'd say she's by-the-book. Not everybody always likes the way it reads, but it's the book. Until a better one gets written anyway. Let me ask you something."

"Sure."

"Murder cops are different. Anybody on the job knows that. But doesn't it stick in your craw to be working for scum like this?"

"I don't pick the dead I stand for, Dwier. They pick me. Good luck in court tomorrow."

She walked out, then simply sat in her vehicle. There was quite a bit sticking in her craw, she thought. The latest was her instincts telling her that a man who'd been a pretty good cop had crossed a line along the way.

If Dwier wasn't already a member of Purity, he was a prime candidate for application.

• • •

When Eve walked back into the house, Mira was coming down the stairs.

"Eve. I thought I'd miss you."

"Did we have a consult scheduled?"

"No, though I did drop off the profile you'd wanted." Mira stopped at the base of the steps, one pretty hand on the gleaming wood of the banister. Her warm brown hair was a soft wave around a soft, feminine face. Her mouth was a pale creamy rose, her eyes a clear summer blue.

Her suit had a fluid drape and was the color of sunflowers. It was, Eve supposed, stylish in some classic sense, and was matched with Mira's favored pearls.

She looked perfect, essentially female, utterly comforting. And was one of the top criminal profilers in the country as well as the psychiatric specialist attached to the NYPSD.

"Thanks, but you didn't have to go out of your way."

"I was coming by anyway. I wanted to see McNab."

"Oh." Instantly Eve's hands sought her pockets. "Well."

"I wonder if I might speak with you for a

few minutes. There's that lovely garden terrace off the parlor. I'd love to sit outside."

"Ah." Eve's mind strained toward her office, toward her work. "Sure. Fine."

"Would you care for some refreshment,
Doctor?" Summerset lurked at the edge of
the foyer. "Some tea? Perhaps some wine."

"Thank you. I'd love a glass of wine."

Before she could comment, Mira slid an
arm through Eve's and walked toward the
parlor. "I know you have work. I promise not
to keep you long. You've had a difficult day.
The media conference couldn't have been
pleasant for you."

"That's a master understatement." Eve
opened the terrace doors, stepped out.

Like everything of Roarke's, the spot was
beautifully planned and executed.

The terrace itself was constructed of
stones, various shapes, sizes, tones all
smoothed into a fluid curve that blended into
garden paths. There were two glass and
iron tables set among pots where flowers
flooded or dwarf trees speared. Beyond the
curve, gardens exploded with summer.

The evening sun spilled pale gold onto the
stones and through a trellis wild with vines
and vivid blue blossoms.

"Such a charming spot." Mira took a seat at one of the tables. Sighed. "I'm afraid I'd find myself sitting out here every chance I got, daydreaming." She smiled. "Do you ever daydream, Eve?"

"I guess." She sat, wondered if she should read Dwier's file again. "Not so much, really."

"You should. It's good for you. When I was a girl, I used to curl up on the window seat in my father's library. I could dream away an afternoon if left to myself. He's a teacher. Did I ever tell you that? He met my mother when he sliced his hand cutting tomatoes for a sandwich. He's always been a bit clumsy. She was a young resident, doing her ER rotation. And he hit on her."

She laughed a little, lifted her face to the sun. The heat baked through her skin, into her bones. "So odd to think of that. And sweet. They're both semiretired now. They live in Connecticut with their ancient dog Spike and have a little vegetable garden so they can raise tomatoes."

"That's nice." And it was. It was also baffling.

"You're wondering why I'm telling you all this. Thank you, Summerset," she said when he set two glasses of wine and a small tray of canapés on the table. "How lovely."

"Enjoy. Just let me know if I can bring you anything else."

"No particular reason," she said to Eve when Summerset went back in the house. "I suppose the tranquility of this spot made me think of them, appreciate them. Not everyone has such a steady, undemanding childhood."

"I don't have time for a session," Eve began, but Mira covered her hand.

"I wasn't speaking only of you. The children who were damaged by these people will have a great deal to overcome. You understand that."

"And I'd understand killing what hurts you?"

"This is a different matter, and I wondered if you'd been able to separate it. What you did was done in pain and fear and immediacy. To protect yourself, to save yourself. What's being done here is cold, calculating, thorough. It's organized and it's pompous, for lack of a better word. This isn't self-defense. It's arrogance."

The tension in Eve's shoulders eased. "I was beginning to wonder if anyone else saw it. Starting to wonder if I was drawing a hard line on this because if I didn't, it made what happened with me the same."

"You killed to live. This group is living to kill."

"I'd like to see that on a goddamn media release." Eve lifted her glass, drank.

"Whoever formed the group, whoever holds the top position of authority, is intelligent, organized, and persuasive. Others would have to be brought in, recruited for the highly specialized technical positions. They understand the power of the media. They need public support."

"They're beating that drum pretty good."

"Yes, so far. I don't think this infection used to terminate is a coincidence. It's another symbol. Our children have been infected by these monsters. Now we infect them because the law could not, would not. The use of the word *guardian*, another symbol. We'll protect you. You're safe now that we're here."

"How long before they expand their horizons?"

"Unchecked?" Mira picked up a small disc of bread and creamy cheese. "Groups tend to evolve. Successful groups tend to seek out other ways to use their skills and their influence. The child predator today, the acquitted killer tomorrow. The street thief, the chemi-head. If New York is to be pure, these infections must be eliminated."

"I think at least one cop's involved. A social worker. Some of the families the victim's messed with."

Mira nodded as if she'd expected nothing else. "Look for people with connections to your victims who hold high-level skills. Neurology, computer science, physics, sociology, psychiatry. And look for wealth. The research and equipment needed here would require heavy funding. You can expect another death and another statement very soon. They need to keep this story in the forefront. Purity is on a mission, Eve, and it's using our children to drive it."

"They'll have to put a spin on what happened with Halloway—with Feeney and McNab."

"Yes." Mira watched a hummingbird, iridescent as a jewel, dart in for a blossom with a blur of wings. "I'm sure it will be very well-written."

Eve ran her glass in small circles on the tabletop. "Roarke and I have gone around

on this some. We're close to the same line,
I guess, but not quite on the same side of
it."

"I'd say that was a good thing."

Surprised, Eve looked up. "How?"

"You're not the same person, Eve, nor
would either of you want to be. Seeing this
from two sides would, I'd think, help keep
you both honest. And interested."

"Maybe. We pissed each other off."

"Another part of marriage."

"It's a damn big slice of ours." But her
shoulders relaxed a little. "Keep each other
honest," she murmured. "Maybe. So . . . Did
you talk to Feeney?"

"He isn't ready. He's handling himself
well. The work heals him, as it does you."

"What about McNab?"

"I can't tell you specifics about what we
discussed. It's confidential."

"Okay." Eve stared at the tangled vines
and bold blue flowers. "Can you tell me . . .
do you think I should cut him loose from duty
on this? Roarke can get him into this Swiss
clinic, one that specializes in this sort of injury, next week, but in the meantime, maybe
he shouldn't be on the job. Maybe he should
be with his family or something."

"He is with his family. By keeping him on the team, by continuing to value his input, his resources, you're helping him to cope. What you're doing for him right now is help-ing a great deal more than anything I can do. Roarke's made arrangements with the Jonas-Ludworg Clinic? How typical of him."

"It's a good place, right?"

"There is none better."

"Okay." She pressed the heels of her hands to her forehead. "That's good."

"You've had a lousy day, haven't you?"

"Oh, yeah."

"I hope some better news comes along."

"I got some news anyway." She dropped her hands. "Mavis is knocked up."

"Oh my God. Mavis was attacked?"

"No, it was Leonardo."

Mira clutched a hand to her breast. Shock radiated onto her face. "Leonardo? Leo-nardo *beat* Mavis?"

"Beat her? No, he banged her. You know, knocked her up." Confused, Eve shook her head, then began to laugh as the light dawned. "Sperm meets egg," she managed as she had her first genuine laugh of the day. "She's pregnant."

"Pregnant? Mavis is pregnant? Knocked

up. Lord, I'd forgotten that term. This *is* news. Are they pleased?"

"Circling Pluto. He's already designing her fat clothes."

"Oh my. Won't that be a sight to see. When is she due?"

"Due for what? Oh, right. She said she should pop by March. She's writing a song about it. Knocked Up By Love."

"Sounds like another hit. They'll make wonderful and unique parents. How do you feel about it? Aunt Eve?"

There was a jolt, dead center of the belly. "I feel like if anybody calls me that, I'll have to hurt them. Even you."

With a laugh, Mira sat back. "This will all be fascinating to watch. If you speak with Mavis again before I do, be sure to give her my love and congratulations."

"Sure. No problem." Eve snuck another look at her wrist unit.

"And I can see you're anxious to get back to work. Would you mind if I just sat here a while longer, finished my wine?"

"No, go ahead. I've really got to get back to it."

"Good luck." When Eve went in, Mira sipped her wine, looked at the flowers and the bright, bright bird. And daydreamed a little.

Eve stopped by the lab first, then just backed out again. There was some discussion, debate, or argument going on in the sort of tech jargon that invariably gave her a headache.

Deciding they'd let her know something when they had something to let her know, she swung into the room Baxter was using as an office.

"What's the word?"

"I've got many names connected to one or more of the vics that are in the system. Cops, lawyers, Child Services, medicals, the handful of complainants that weren't sealed. Broke that down to names that popped on at least two of the vics and ran those. Just zipped the data to your unit. Our pal Nadine Furst covered the George trial. That putz Chang's down as media liaison."

"I guess that figures." She sat on the edge of his desk. "What's your gut?"

"That if we've got any family members involved, and we do, they're in the sealeds. You're stewing about it; you're carrying wounds over it; you want your privacy."

"Yeah, that's mine, too. And if you're going to talk to anyone about it, about what you're carrying, it's going to be somebody who was there with you. Somebody who knows and stood for you and yours."

"You're looking at Clarissa Price."

"And looking hard. You know anything about DS Dwier, out of the Sixteenth?"

"Nothing I didn't read in his file when he popped. Want me to ask around?"

"Yeah, quietly." She hesitated. "Does it bother you?"

"Looking at another badge?" Baxter puffed out his lean cheeks. "Yeah, some. It's supposed to bother us. Otherwise, we'd all be IAB, wouldn't we?"

"There you go. You can bend the line. You can even move it a little sometimes. But you can't break it. Break it, and you're not us anymore. You're them. Dwier broke it, Baxter. That's my gut."

She pushed off the desk, walked around the room. "You've used Trueheart a few times, right?"

"A couple. Good kid. Fresh as a daisy yet, but eager."

"If I brought him in on this, would you use him?"

"I've got no problem dumping some . . ." He sat back, cleared his throat. "You asking me to train him?"

"No, just . . . okay, yes. Sort of. You're second grade, so you qualify, and he could use somebody to work him, rub some of the dew off him without dulling the shine. Interested?"

"Maybe. I'll take him on this one—contingency. We'll see how we fit."

"Good." She started for the door, then stopped. "Baxter, why'd you transfer in from AntiCrime?"

"Couldn't get close enough to you, honey." He winked suggestively, and when she just stared blandly, shrugged. "Got restless. Wanted Homicide. Never a dull moment."

"You can say that again."

"Never a—"

"You're such a jerk," she replied. And turning ran straight into Roarke.

The man could move like a ghost.

"Sorry to break up this tender moment," he began. "But we've got a second shield ready. We're about to run it with one of the Fitzhugh units."

"Who won the coin toss?"

He smiled. "It was agreed, after some debate, that the initial operator would continue in that function. Do you want to observe from in here, or your office?"

"We'll use mine. It's bigger." She closed a hand over his wrist. "No heroics."

"I'd never qualify for hero status."

"I order a shutdown, you shut down." Her hand slipped down until their fingers linked. "You got that?"

"Loud and clear. You're in charge, Lieutenant."

Eve drank coffee because she wanted something to do with her hands. Feeney sat at her desk, manning a secondary unit they'd brought in as a control. If something went wrong in the lab, he could crash the system remotely.

Jamie hovered over him, so close they looked like one body with two heads.

"Why can't we do the whole thing remote?" Eve asked.

"You lose operator instinct," McNab told her. "You got him right there, at the infected unit. He can make judgment calls in a blink."

"Besides—ow." Jamie rubbed his belly where Feeney's elbow had landed.

"Besides what?" Eve demanded. "Don't pull this e-solidarity crap with me. McNab?"

"Okay, okay, in simple terms we can't be sure the shield will filter out the infection during an interface. It could, probably would, spread from one unit to another. We figure that's how it pumped into the eight units we hauled out of Fitzhugh's place. Infect one, infect all. Efficient, time-saving, and thorough. So if we try a remote, it could leak into the other unit, potentially through the whole system."

"We need more data to confirm," Jamie piped up. "Then we'll create a shield to handle that area. Priority was shielding the operator while he extracts the data. When you're dealing with a remote, and a multi-system network, the units have a language. They, like, talk to each other, right? The infected unit's got a different language, compatible, but different. Like, I dunno, Spanish and Portuguese or something."

"Okay." Eve nodded. "I get that. Keep going."

"Me and McNab, we're working on what you could call a translation deal. Then we can zap it in, run sims. We'll shield the whole system. We figure we'll be able to link to CompuGuard and shield the whole damn city."

"Getting ahead of yourself, Jamie. One thing at a time." Feeney glanced up at the wall screen where they could see Roarke attaching the sensors.

"Gonna run your medicals. You copy?"

"Yes."

"Medicals normal. You're good to go."

"Booting."

Eve never took her attention away from the screen. Roarke had tied his hair back as he often did when he was working. And his shirt was carelessly open. His hands were quick and steady as he slid the disc into its slot.

"Loading the filter. Estimate seventy-two seconds to upload on this unit. Loading Jamie's code breaker. Forty-five. Running diagnostic from point of last attempt. Multi-tasking with search and scan for any pro-grams loaded within the last two weeks."

He was working manually, with those quick and steady hands, relaying his inten-tions in a voice that was brisk and cool, and beautiful.

"Disc and hard copy of data requested, as accessed. Upload complete. We're shielded.

There now, Jamie. Fine job. Data's coming up readable. Here now, what's this? You see the data on monitor, Feeney?"

"Yeah, yeah, wait. Hmmm."

"What?" Eve shook McNab's good shoulder. "What are they talking about?"

"Ssh!" Such was his concentration, he didn't notice her jaw drop at his command as he drove his chair closer to the screen. "That is so total." Forgetting himself, he started to push himself up. And his dead hand slid off the arm of the chair.

For a moment, he simply froze, and Eve's throat filled at the look of shocked panic on his face. Then he adjusted the chair smoothly, bringing it to a different position so he was higher and straighter, with a better view of the monitor.

The room was full of jargon again, rapid questions, comments, observations as foreign to her as Greek.

"Somebody speak in English, damn it."

"It's bloody brilliant. I shouldn't have missed this on the first pass." Roarke reached over to another control, keyed in commands by feel. "Ah, bugger it. She's trying to fail-safe. Not yet, you bitch, I'm not done with you."

"Shield's breaking up," Feeney warned him.

"Shut down," Eve ordered. "Shut it down."

"It's still at ninety percent. Hold your jets there, Lieutenant."

Before she could repeat the order, Feeney interrupted. "He's all right yet, Dallas. Medicals are holding. Son of a bitch's pulse barely shows a blip. He must run on ice. Roarke, go to shell. Try the—"

"I'm in the flaming shell." His voice was a mutter, and Irish now as a shamrock. "And I've already tried that. Clever bastard. Look here, look at this. It's voice printed. Can't override manually. Fuck it, there she goes."

Eve saw his monitor erupt with jags of black and white. He flipped out data discs an instant before a nasty grinding sound came through the speakers, and a small, gray plume of smoke puffed out of the back of the machine.

"Toasted," Jamie said.

Chapter 13

"Unit's a dead loss." Roarke had yet to button his shirt, however he had removed the sensors. "But it gave its life for a good cause."

He turned one of the discs in his hand. "These should be clean—nothing on that program was geared to the external drive. But they should be labeled and set aside for testing after we've managed to extract the entire program. Hard copy will do for now. Jamie, you can start imputting the data in the morning."

"I can start now."

"You'll have some supper, then a two-hour recreation break. If you feel like putting an hour in after that—an hour only—that's fine. In bed, lights out, by midnight. If you don't rest your brain, it won't be of any use to me."

"Man, my mother isn't even that strict."

"I'm not your mother. Feeney—"

"You don't want to tell me when to go to bed, kid. I'm old enough to be *your* mother."

"I was going to ask if you could do with a meal. I imagine we all could."

"Hold it. Just hold it." Frustrated, Eve held up both hands. "Nobody eats anything until I get an explanation. What did you get, and what does it mean? And if I hear one word of computerese, everybody gets rabbit food."

"Talk about strict," Jamie countered.

"Tell me," ordered Eve.

"He got the frequency," McNab told her. "And the spectrum. Another minute, tops, we'd've had the pulse and speed."

"Basically, Lieutenant." Roarke tugged the band out of his hair so it fell like black rain. "With a little more finessing, we've got your virus."

"Did you get the method of infection?" she asked.

"Possibly. There's data to analyze, but from the look I could get on the scroll, I'm putting my money on the simplicity of e-mail."

"They e-mailed it? Fucking e-mail?" Eve had wanted simple, but this . . . this was almost insulting. "You can't infect that way. CompuGuard—"

"Has never seen the likes of this," Roarke interrupted. "My guess would be . . ." He trailed off, gestured. "Go ahead, Jamie, before you erupt."

"Okay, see what it looks like—and I have to figure out how to do it—is they cloaked a doc, micro'ed and stealthed—"

"Do you want to eat radishes and lettuce?" Eve asked mildly.

"Right." He adjusted his brain to lay terms. "So they attached the virus to the e-mail, only it didn't show up as having an attachment, doesn't alert the receiver. Sender can check if it went in just by doing the standard scan on when the mail was read. Had to download fast, really fast, without showing the operator what it was doing. It had to talk to the unit, temporarily at least shut down the prompts and alerts for a download. Then it filed itself, as a document, an invisible document in the main drive program. It wouldn't register on a standard doc search and scan. It doesn't ID. It's just there, like lurking and doing its job. It's way radical."

"Okay, I follow that." Eve looked at Roarke. "If this could be done, how come you didn't know about it?"

"Lieutenant, I am chagrined."

"Me, I'm just starved." Jamie patted his belly. "Got any pepperoni pizza?"

Eve had a couple of slices herself, bided her time through the noisy, confused meal, let her mind drift to the case, away from it, back again.

She wasn't sure when it struck her— maybe when Feeney casually speared some of the pasta off Roarke's plate, or when Jamie dumped another slice of pizza on McNab's as he stretched across the table for another for himself. Maybe it had always been there, and just chose that moment to clarify.

Mira had said it on the terrace. Family.

This was what families did, she realized. This was what she'd never experienced as a child. Noisy, messy dinners with everyone talking over everyone else, which wasn't as annoying as it should've been.

Stupid jokes and casual insults.

She wasn't quite sure what to make of it when it applied to herself, but she could see what it might do to that pattern when something or someone damaged a part of the whole.

It would fall apart. Temporarily for those who were strong enough to glue it all back into pattern or make another. Permanently for those who couldn't. Or wouldn't.

She glanced at McNab. Even here, with all the chatter, there was a smear of worry over it all. If that one part of them stayed broken, the rest would tumble down like tiles. They'd form a new pattern—that was the job—but they'd never forget the way it had been.

She pushed back from the table. "I've got some stuff I need to do."

"The Walking Dead said there was chocolate cake."

"Jamie," Roarke said mildly.

"Sorry," Jamie said reluctantly. "Mister Walking Dead, also known as Summerset, said there was chocolate cake."

"And if you eat it all, I'll kill you in your

sleep. Then you can join The Walking Dead. Roarke, I need to talk to you."

As they started out, she heard Jamie ask: "Think they're gonna go do it?" And heard the quick slap of Feeney's hand on the teen-aged skull.

"Are we going to go do it?" Roarke grabbed her hand.

"Want me to have Feeney knock you, too?"

"I'm a bit quicker than Jamie yet. But I take that to mean we're not going back up-stairs for a fast tumble."

"How many times a day do you think about sex?"

He gave her a considering look. "Would that be actively thinking of it, or just having the concept of it lurking there, like Jamie's invisible document?"

"Never mind. Did you see Mira before?"

"I didn't, no. I was in the lab. Sorry I missed her. Peabody said Mavis stopped by as well, and needed a private word with you. Is she all right?"

"She's knocked . . ." She didn't have time for that little routine again. "She's pregnant."

"What?" He stopped in his tracks.

It was always a treat, a rare one, to see

him stupefied. "Totally pregs, as she puts it. On purpose, too."

"Mavis? Our Mavis?"

"One and the same. She came in jumping and spinning and dancing. I don't know if she should be bouncing around like that now. Seems like you could, I don't know, dislodge the thing in there. She's really hyped."

"Well, this is . . . lovely," he decided. "Is she well?"

"I guess. Looks great anyway. Said she was puking in the mornings, but she liked it. I don't get that."

"No, I can't say I do either. We'll take them out to dinner as soon as we're able. I should check on her performance and recording schedule." He knew every bit as much about the care and feeding of expectant mothers as Eve did. Which was nothing. "I don't suppose she should be overdoing."

"If this afternoon was any gauge, she's got enough energy for both of them, and then some."

When they stepped into her office, she shut the door. The action made him lift a brow. "As you've vetoed sex, I assume you want privacy for a less pleasurable reason."

"They're blocking my warrant, and when you've got two bureaucracies duking it out in court, you can die from natural causes before there's a ruling. I had a brief consult with Mira. I've still got to read her profile, but she gave me the gist in the oral. I got Baxter's take."

"Eve, what is it you want me to do that you'd prefer not wanting me to do?"

"People are dying, right now. They don't know it, but they're infected, and for some it's already too late. It's going to keep spreading. A good cop is dead. Another . . . another who's a friend of mine—and Jesus, I can't believe I'm friends with such an idiot— may not walk again under his own power. Some of the answers to who's doing this are in those sealed files."

"Then we'll break the seal."

She stared at him, then cursing, spun away. "And what makes me any different from them? I'm willing to slide around the law because I think I'm right."

"Because they're killing people."

"I can tell myself that. But it's just a matter of degrees."

"The hell it is. You'll always have a conscience, and you'll always question the right

and wrong of it. Worry it to death, and yourself with it. You know how far to push the
line before it breaks, Eve. You'll never break
it. You can't."

She closed her eyes. "I said something
similar to Baxter. They're using the law to
slow me down. I can't let them."

"It would be best if we used the unregistered."

She nodded. "Let's get it done."

The room was accessible only by voice- and
palmprints. Only three people were cleared
for entry.

There was a single window, wide and un-
covered to the dying evening. But she knew
it was privacy treated to prevent anyone
nervy enough to try a flyby from seeing in.

The room itself was designed almost rigidly. This was work space. Serious space.
There was a wide, U-shaped console in
sleek black that commanded all the research, retrieval, communication, and data
systems. Systems unregistered with Compu-
Guard, and therefore illegal.

The first time she'd seen it, well over a
year before, even she'd recognized the level
of equipment as superior to anything in Cen-

tral. Since then, some units had been up-graded.

She imagined there were some toys in here not yet on the market.

There were comp stations with monitors, a holo unit, a smaller auxiliary station, which now boasted its own miniholo.

Crossing the glassed black tile, she studied the new addition. "Never seen one like this."

"Prototype. I wanted to run some tests on it without documenting them. It seems to be working out nicely."

"It's really small."

"We're working on smaller yet. Palm-sized."

She glanced up. "Get out. Palms with full holofunction?"

"Three years, maybe less, and you'll be slipping one into your pocket just like your 'link." He placed his palm on the console's identi-screen. "Roarke. Open operations."

The console came to life with lights. Eve walked over to join him, laid down her palm. "Dallas."

Identification verified, Darling Eve.

She hissed. "Why do you *do* that? It's em-barrassing."

"Darling Eve, the computer, however brilliant, is an inanimate object and can't em-
barrass anyone. Where would you like to
start?"

"Start with Cogburn. He was their first.
You can pull the data off my unit." She gave
Roarke the case number and the file num-
ber for her notes.

He had them accessed, copied, and displayed in almost less time than it had taken
her to give him the numbers.

"You see his sheet? I've made notations
of the case files that connect him to the
other victims through arresting officers, social workers, legal, medical. Baxter's started
interviews where we have vic ID, but he
hasn't gotten a bump."

"Bump."

"The vibe."

"No bump on the vic," Roarke repeated
with a chuckle. "And you threatened rabbit
food for comp jargon."

"Jeez. Upon interviewing identified victims
related to this matter, Detective Baxter
found no connection to The Purity Seekers,
nor felt any indication of connection from
statements, attitude, or background checks."

"I got it the first time, darling, but it's such

fun to hear you explain it to me in such official tones."

"Moving on," she continued. "The incident
reports list interviews with two additional minors. Records sealed."

"It'll take me a few minutes."

"Yeah. I'll get the coffee."

"Let's have some wine instead," he said
as he began to work on a keyboard. "I'd prefer not to get buzzed on caffeine."

"I need to keep sharp."

"Any sharper, you'd be drawing blood.
Now this is interesting."

"What?"

"There's a secondary block on this file.
That's not usual for a standard seal. Damn
good block, too. Well now." He rolled his
shoulders like a boxer about to enter the
ring.

"When was it put on?" She hurried back
to lean over his shoulder. "Can you tell when
it was put on?"

"No talking." He brushed her back, and
continued to work one-handed. "Yes, indeed, I've seen your work before, haven't I?
You're good, very, very good. But . . ."

"He gets to talk," Eve grumbled and because watching the speed of his fingers fly-

ing over keys made her antsy, she went to get the wine.

"Got him." Roarke sat back a moment, reached out a hand without glancing at her to take the glass of wine. "Wouldn't have been quite that quick if I hadn't already dealt with his work on those two units in the lab."

Now, there's a bump, she thought. "You're sure of that?"

"A good compu-jock has a style. Take my word for it, the block was added by the tech who designed the virus. Or techs. I doubt this was the work of one."

"Organized, thorough, and skilled." Eve nodded. "And careful. Let's see who they wanted to hide."

"Screen Three. Display."

"Devin Dukes," Eve read. "Twelve at the time of the incident." She scanned the data quickly to get to the meat. "Okay, Cogburn sold him some Jazz. Parents—Sylvia and Donald—turned it up, confronted the kid, pressed the right buttons, and got the story. Brought the kid in to make the complaint, and DS Dwier caught the case."

"Might've been wiser to leave the cops out of it."

She looked back, coolly. "Excuse me?"

"Just a thought. Dragging the boy into a cop shop, putting him in the system. Put his back up, wouldn't it?"

"A crime had been committed."

"Absolutely. I just wonder if it might have been simpler and cleaner to stand the kid on his head, so to speak, at home initially rather than having him surrounded by badges and reports."

"We rarely torture minors these days. They break down so easy, it's not much fun."

"Torture has a different definition for a boy of twelve. But . . ." He shrugged his shoulders, elegantly. "That's hardly to our point, is it? It seems a relatively small occurrence to go to such trouble to lock away."

"Cogburn was brought in, ID'd, charged," Eve continued. "But the parents had flushed the evidence. Cogburn maintained that he'd been drinking in a bar at the time the kid stated the buy went down. Bartender backs Cogburn. Probably bullshit. Places like that will back Jack The Ripper if Jack spreads enough grease. Dwier messed this up."

Annoyance edged her voice. "He shouldn't have charged Cogburn so fast. Why didn't he work him first, work the bartender? Hang back, scope out his routine, snatch him up doing another deal? Pop a charge on him like that, he lawyers up, clams up. He knows Dwier's got nothing but the kid's word. And see here, you've got the Child Services report. Clarissa Price. Says the minor was reluctant, defiant, uncooperative. Confrontational with parents. Recommends family counseling and yadda-yadda. Dwier needed to sweat Cogburn because his witness was hostile and worthless."

"Which is something like saying his back was up. Look further," he said before she could snarl at him, "into the CS report. Price states the boy's schoolwork has been in steady decline. His attitude at school, and at home, poor. Brooding in his room, picking fights. And so on. The root of the problem wasn't in buying the Jazz, the root was in the boy, and at home."

"Maybe so, but the result was the parents overreacted, the cop jumps too fast, social worker mouths platitudes, and the system fails the kid."

"Is that how you see it?"

"I see Dwier didn't do his damn job on this one, but I don't know how I see the whole picture." She studied the data, absently twirling a lock of Roarke's hair around her finger. "I know they're seeing the last part. System fails. But you're right, this isn't enough to hide. So there's more. Let's dig into Fitzhugh's sheet."

Roarke found more blocks there as well. But he had the groove now and broke them quickly. "Minor complainants, Jansan, Rudolph . . . ah here we are. Sylvia and Donald Dukes, filing on behalf of their fourteen-year-old son, Devin."

"Yeah, yeah, CS rep, Price, investigating officer DS Dwier. Click, click, click."

"There's a—"

"No talking," she ordered.

"Touché," he retorted, and sat back to watch her work.

"Kid ends up at the health center this time. Sodomized, facial bruising, sprained wrist. Tox report . . . got himself Jazzed again, and chased it with alcohol. Got some body piercing now. Cock and nipple ornaments. Dwier catches it again. But look here, Price tagged him, specifically. Something going on between them."

She pulled out her memo book, began to take notes as she scanned data. "Doctor determines rape—Stanford Quillens. We'll see if he pops up again. But they don't shake Fitzhugh's name out of the kid for twenty-four hours. Doesn't want to talk about it. Why do they think you want to talk about it? Gang up on him at home the next day. Price, Dwier, the parents, rape counselor, who's this? Marianna Wilcox. Should've gotten a male counselor. He doesn't want to spill this to a female. Are they just stupid? Computer, copy text of victim interview to my home unit."

But she read it through from where she stood. It gave her a sour taste in the mouth, a greasy feeling in the gut. So many of the questions were familiar. The same had been asked of her once.

WHO DID THIS TO YOU?
WE WANT TO HELP YOU, BUT YOU NEED TO TELL US WHAT HAPPENED.
YOU'LL FEEL BETTER ONCE YOU GET IT OUT.

"Bullshit, bullshit, you don't feel better. Sometimes you never feel better. Why don't they say it like it is? You've been fucked over, kid, and we're real sorry we have to fuck you over again. Tell us how it was, and don't spare the details, so we can write it all up and make it real all over again."

"Eve."

She shook her head fiercely. "They've got good intentions. Most of them anyway. But they don't *know*."

"This boy isn't like you." He was standing behind her now, laid his hands on her shoulders and began to rub. "He's troubled, and looking for trouble. I know about that. Surely he got more than he deserved in that area, but he isn't like you."

She calmed, leaned back against him. "Not like you either. You were smarter, meaner, and you weren't gay."

"No arguing with that." He kissed the top of her head. "His confusion over his sexuality is likely the cause for most of his behavior and the consequences of it."

"That and his parents. You got Donald here, eight years military service. Marines. Once a marine, always a marine. Mom takes the professional mother route. They put you in private schools, three in five years. Pull you out into home schooling two months before the incident with Fitzhugh. He's got a kid brother here. Three years younger. No problem there, at least that's showing up on personal data. But they yank him into home schooling, too. Taking no chances."

"You did note the father's profession?"

"Yeah, computer scientist. Click, click." She turned away to get her coffee, remembered it was wine. Frowning a little, she settled for it.

"Devin rolls on Fitzhugh, claims he was picked up at a club after he snuck out of the house. Admits he showed fake ID, admits he was a little buzzed, and that Fitzhugh says how he's having a party at his place. He goes with him. Most of that's probably solid, but then it gets smokey. He claims Fitzhugh got him stoned, but the tox level's too low for the way he plays it. He was zonked, didn't know what was going on. Fitzhugh got him into the playroom, got him in restraints. He tried to get away, but Fitzhugh overpowered him, knocked him around, then raped him."

"It wouldn't be the first time. Wolves hunt sheep. It's their nature."

"But it didn't go down like that here. Dwier had to know it didn't go down just like that. Maybe it was rape, kid was a minor so consensual or not, Fitzhugh's a pig. But he didn't knock Devin around. The father did. You look at Fitzhugh's sheet. He never beat on his victims. He didn't use force. He used persuasion, bribery, threats. Trying to make the case with force was one of the reasons they lost him."

"So you read this as Dwier, probably along with the Dukes and Price, tried to build their case out of straw, and the wolf blew it down."

She sat on the console. "Lies, half-truths, and lousy police work. I guess that's straw. I'll tell you how it went down. Kid sneaks out of the house. Probably he's done it dozens of time. They try to cage him in, but he's not having it. He's not his goddamn father. He's not his angel-face baby shithead brother. He heads to a club that caters to same-sex orientation. He's not looking for a girl. Fitzhugh's trolling and smells fresh meat. Buys the kid a drink, maybe offers him some illegals. Come up to my place, there's more where that came from. Kid keeps the nice, steady buzz going, and Fitzhugh does what Fitzhugh does. Buzz is wearing off."

"It's no prettier a picture painted your way."

"No prettier," Eve agreed. "But it's the

right picture. Kid's fourteen. He's angry, he's confused, he's ashamed. He goes home, sneaks back in. But he's busted. He smells of the alcohol and the sex, and the father loses his temper. Grabs him by the wrist, slaps him. Tears, shouts, recriminations. Probably some name-calling the father regretted after. Take him to the health center, order him to say the minor injuries were a result of the sexual assault. He's caused the family enough trouble, damn it, and he's going to do what he's told."

"And in the end," Roarke continued, "it fell apart. Fitzhugh walked, because among other things, the others were too busy protecting their image."

"Yeah, which makes me feel better about going over to their place tomorrow and questioning the family. They won't be the only ones. Let's find the others."

"I've set up the search already, adding in George's file." He smiled at her, moved in, nudging her knees apart so he could fit his body between them. "It'll mark blocked sealeds, and I've input the series of commands to bypass the block, open the seal."

"Busy fingers."

"And they've life in them yet." He slid them

under her shirt. "It'll take a bit of time to finish tasking. Just, I'd say, enough time."

"I'm on duty."

"Me, too." He eased in and found, with his mouth, the spot just under her jawline he liked best. "Why don't you give me an order, Lieutenant?" His fingers skimmed over her breasts, her sides, and around her back to dance along her spine.

The thrill rushed after them. She knew what he was doing—washing away the shadows of the picture they'd just painted. Bringing up the strong, clear colors of their own.

"Cut that out." She angled her head so his lips could trail up. "In a minute."

"That's pushing even my speed and agility, but we'll start with a minute." He caught her earlobe between his teeth. "And see how it goes."

Her brain was starting to fog up, her body starting to rev. "God, you're good at this."

"Is that going into my official file as a . . ." His mouth found hers, sank in. ". . . expert consultant, civilian?"

"I'll keep it in my personal records." Her breath caught. How the hell had he gotten her shirt off so fast? "This is . . . we can't do this on a command console."

"I think we could." He'd already unhooked her trousers. "But it does lack a little something. Hitch on," he said, and gave her hips a boost until her legs were wrapped around his waist.

"Minute's gotta be up," she whispered, but couldn't resist nibbling at his throat.

"Let's see if we can make time stop."

He opened a wall panel. A bed slid out. When he tumbled her to the mattress, she kept her legs and arms hooked around him and used the momentum to roll on top of him.

"It's going to be fast," she warned him.

"I can live with that."

She tore open his shirt, ran her hands in one hard sweep over his chest, then lowered to scrape her teeth over flesh.

The taste of him was already a part of her, lived inside her. Still she always wanted more. And took more, crushing her mouth to his until the heat drenched her.

She could feel it pump from him, from her as mouths and hands turned greedy. It fueled her, pulsing through her system like a slap of adrenaline.

When he flipped her to drag at her trousers, she dragged at his. Her heart hammered under his restless mouth. His muscles tensed under her impatient hands.

They tugged, pulled, yanked and ripped so that she was naked and laughing when she rolled again to straddle him. Laughter became a purr of pleasure as she took him inside her.

She clenched around him and drove him mad with need. Rearing up, he clamped his mouth on her breast, sucking her in until it felt as though he could feed on her heartbeat. The flavor, the heat, the scent of mate. She arched, letting him fill her.

Then began to move.

She drove him back, braced her hands on either side of his head and used her hips to set a furious pace.

The thrill, the dark and dangerous edge of it, sliced through him. Her face was alive, so alive with purpose and pleasure. And she rode him as if their lives depended on it.

The air thickened, his vision dimmed. She was a blur of white and gold.

"You go over." Her voice was raw. "You let go."

His body plunged to hers. He thought it

was like being swallowed alive. He heard her cry out as she dived after him.

He drew her down, drew her in while they drifted back.

"Sex is funny," she murmured.

"I'm still laughing."

She snorted and turned her face into the side of his neck for a moment. "Yeah, that was a really good joke, but I meant sometimes it knocks you flat so you feel like you could sleep for a month. Other times it pumps you up so you feel like you could run a marathon. I wonder why that is?"

"I couldn't say, but I have a feeling this one falls into the latter category."

"Yeah, I'm stoked." She shifted, planted a quick, hard kiss on his mouth. "Thanks."

"Oh, whatever I can do to help."

"Well, you can get your great-looking ass up so I can see the rest of the data." She sucked in a cheerful breath, then rolled away. "I want coffee."

"It's going to be a long night. Why don't we get some of that cake to go with it?"

She grabbed her shirt. "Good thinking."

• • •

Between the sex and caffeine, her energy level stayed high until after three A.M. She had six more names on her list, and had no doubt there were more. The game plan was already formed in her head.

She'd start in the morning with the Dukes.

When she reached for yet another cup of coffee, Roarke simply pushed it out of her reach. "You're cut off, Lieutenant, and going off duty."

"I've got another hour in me."

"You don't, no. You've gone pale, which is a sure sign you've hit the wall. You need some sleep or you won't be sharp tomorrow. You'll have to be if you're going to do what I assume you're going to do and push for interviews with these families. Will you take Peabody?"

He asked more to distract her than a need to know. He shut down the equipment, slid an arm around her waist.

"I've been going back and forth on that. If I take her, I'm putting her in the squeeze. If I don't, she'll be pissed and sulk. She's really annoying when she's sulking."

He had her in the elevator before she realized it. Which proved, she supposed, that she'd lost her edge for the night.

"I guess I'll leave it up to her. Or maybe I'll . . ."

"Decide in the morning," he finished, and steered her off to bed.

Chapter 14

McNab wasn't having much luck shutting down for the night. He felt restless and useless lying in bed. In the dark. More aware of the numb parts of him than the rest. Counting off his own heartbeats. Like they were ticks of a clock, he thought, tick-tocking off the rest of his life as half-there, half-gone.

It was easier during the day when the job kept his mind busy, pushed him to think of something other than himself. And that tick-tock. Until he went to reach for something, or stand up or just scratch his own damn ass.

It flooded back then, boy. Like a goddamn tidal wave.

Tick-tock.

If he closed his eyes he could see it all happening again. The shout, the movement, the blur of Halloway's hand lifting the weapon, drawing a bead. And he could feel it again, that icy hot blast kicking him up and back and down. That one instant, just the one, of feeling nothing.

If he'd moved just a little faster, if he'd jumped the other way. If Halloway hadn't fired so close and so clean.

If, if, if.

He knew what his chances of coming back were now. Down to thirty-percent and falling.

He was fucked, and everyone knew it. They didn't have to say it. He could hear them thinking it.

Especially Peabody.

He could practically hear her thinking it in her sleep.

He turned his head, and could see the outline of her in the dark, in the bed beside him.

He thought of the way she'd chattered

away—about the job, the case, the kid Jamie, about a thousand things to avoid any gaps of silence while she'd helped him get undressed for the night.

Christ, he couldn't even unbutton his own pants.

Note to self, he thought sourly. Zippers, Velcro, and tipcot fasteners only in the future.

He'd deal with it. You ran with the data you got. But he'd be damned if she was going to be stuck with him.

He gripped the bedpost with his good hand, tried to lever himself up.

She stirred, shifted, and her voice came out of the dark, too clear for her to have been sleeping.

"What's the matter?"

"Nothing. Just want to get up. I've got it."

"I'll give you a hand. Lights on, ten percent."

"I said I've got it, Peabody."

But she was already out of bed, coming around to his side. "Bet you gotta pee. You and Jamie must've sucked down a gallon of milk each with that cake. I could've told you—"

"Go back to bed."

"Can't sleep anyway. I keep thinking about the case." Her movements were as brisk and practical as her tone as she scooted him up, lifted, shifted, and maneuvered him into his chair. "You have to figure Dallas and Roarke are working on something or they'd have—"

"Sit down."

"I'm going to get some water."

"Sit down, Peabody."

"Sure, okay." She kept the half-smile on her face as she sat on the side of the bed facing him. Was it too much? she wondered. Not enough? Her muscles were so knotted it felt like a troop of Youth Scouts had been practicing for a merit badge with them.

He looked so tired, she thought. So horribly, horribly frail somehow.

"This isn't going to work. We're not going to work."

"That's a stupid thing to be talking about at three in the morning." She started to get up, but he laid his good hand on her knee.

She was wearing a bright red nightshirt, and her toes were painted the same shade. Her hair was messy, her mouth grim.

And McNab realized Roarke had been right in something he'd said once. He was in love with her. That meant he had to do this right.

"Look what I was going to do was pick a fight, piss you off enough so you'd storm out. Not that hard to do. You get bent pretty easy. We'd break it off and go our separate ways. But that doesn't seem right. Besides, you'd have copped to it anyway. So I'm going to play it straight with you, Peabody."

"It's too late to have this kind of argument. I'm tired."

"You weren't sleeping. Neither was I. Come on, She-Body, hear me out." He saw her eyes start to shine and shut his own. "Don't turn on the tap, okay? This already sucks out loud."

"I know what you're going to say. You're messed up, you're impaired and you want to break things off because you don't want to screw up my life. Blah, blah."

She sniffed, swiped a hand under her nose. "You want me to walk away because you can't, so I can have a full, meaningful life without the burden of being stuck with you. Well, get fucked, McNab, because I'm not walking. And you managed to piss me off just fine by thinking I would."

"That covers part of it." He sighed, kept

his hand on her knee. "You wouldn't walk, Peabody. You're solid, and you wouldn't walk when I'm . . . when I'm like this. You'd stick, and you'd keep sticking even if your feelings changed about everything. You're solid, and that's what a solid does. After a while, neither of us would know, not for sure, if you were with me because you wanted to be or because you felt obligated."

She got a stubborn line between her brows and turned her head so that she stared at the wall instead of those sober, serious green eyes. "I'm not listening to this."

"Yeah, you are." He eased back, gripped the arm of the chair with his good hand. "I don't want a medical, and you don't want to be one. For Christ's sake, I wouldn't be able to take a piss on my own if Roarke and Dallas hadn't given me this fucking chair. She's keeping me on the job, and she doesn't have to. I'm not going to forget that."

"You're just feeling sorry for yourself."

"Fucking A." He nearly smiled. "You try going twenty-five percent dead and see how quick you haul out the violins. I'm pissed and I'm scared, and I don't know what the hell I'm going to do tomorrow. If I've got to live like this, then that's the breaks."

He wasn't going to be a whiner, he reminded himself. He was *not* going to be a
whiner. "But I've got a right to set up the
rules, and I don't want you around."

"You don't know you're going to have to
live like this." She threw up her hands, trying
for exasperated while tears burned the back
of her throat. "If it doesn't come back in a
few days, you'll go to that clinic."

"I'll go. I'll owe Dallas and Roarke big for
that, too, but I'll go. And maybe I'll get
lucky."

"They've got a seventy-percent success
rate."

"They got a thirty-percent fail rate. Don't
talk numbers to an e-man, baby. I've got to
focus on myself for a while. I can't think
about how things may or may not work out
with us."

"So we just box that up so you don't have
to worry about it? Now you're a coward,
too."

"Goddamn it! Goddamn it, can't you get
that I need to do this, for you? Can't you give
me a lousy break here?"

"Guess not." Her chin jutted out. "You already had your lousy break. And I'll tell you,
I don't know how things are going to work

out with us either. Half the time I don't know
what the hell I see in you. You're irritating,
you're sloppy, you're skinny, and you sure
don't match my childhood image of Delia's
dream man. But I'm in it now and I make my
own calls. When I want out, I'll get out. Until
then, you can shut up because I'm going
back to bed."

"Guess Roarke's more the image of Delia's dream man," he grumbled.

"Damn right." She swung her legs back
into bed, punched her pillows. "Smooth,
sexy, gorgeous, rich, and dangerous. None
of which you are now, or were before you
got zapped. None of which you can hope to
be once you're up and dancing again either.
Get your own pitiful self back in bed. I'm not
your nursemaid."

He studied her as she laid back, folded
her arms across her chest and glared at the
ceiling.

And he began to smile. "You're good. I
didn't see that coming. Piss me off, insult
me—the not sexy remark is the one that
stung, by the way—and shove the argument
out of its orbit."

"Kiss my ass."

"It's one of my favorite recreational activities. I don't want to fight with you, She-Body. I just think we could both use a little time, a little space. I care about you, Dee. I really care about you."

It made her eyes sting again. He never called her Dee. She kept her lips pressed tightly together, afraid she might start sobbing. Certain the killing expression she worked onto her face would have made her lieutenant proud, she turned her head.

Then she sat up like a rocket coming off the launching pad, and stared. "You're scratching your arm."

"What?"

Very slowly, trembling only a little, she pointed. He followed the direction and saw he'd been scratching absently at his right arm. "So, it itches. What I'm trying to say . . ."

His body went very still. He'd have sworn his own heart stopped. "It itches," he managed. "It feels like a bunch of needles under the skin. Oh Christ."

"It's waking up." She hurled herself out of bed to kneel beside his chair. "What about your leg? Can you feel anything?"

"Yeah, yeah, I—" The itch grew maddening, and his heart began to hammer. "Help me out, will you? Right along the hip. I can't reach. Ahhhh."

"I have to call Summerset."

"Stop scratching and I'll kill you."

"Can you move your fingers, toes, anything?"

"I don't know." He bore down, tried to ignore the sensation in his biceps, in his thigh that was like being pricked with a thousand hot needles. "I don't think so."

"Do you feel this?" She pressed her thumb against his thigh, and thought she felt a muscle quiver.

"Yeah." He fought back the hot flood of emotion that gushed into his throat. "Why don't you shift that grip a few inches to the left? Distract me before I start screaming from this itching."

"Your dick never went numb."

A tear spilled off her cheek, plopped on his hand. And he knew the sweetest sensation he would ever feel was that warm, wet tear against his awakening hand.

"I love you, Peabody."

She looked up at him, with surprise. "Look, don't get crazy—"

"I love you." He laid his good hand on her cheek. "I figured I'd lost my chance to tell you that. I'm not going to risk missing it again. Don't say anything, okay? Maybe you could just give it a chance to settle in."

She moistened her lips. "I could do that. I need to get Summerset up here. He should . . . do something. Probably." When she straightened, her knees wobbled. And she turned and cracked her shin smartly on the bed. "Shit. Shit. Wow."

She limped to the house 'link while McNab scratched his throbbing arm and grinned after her.

By seven-thirty, Eve was pumping in the caffeine again. Second cup in hand, she headed for the lab for a quick check-in with Roarke before the rest of the team poured into her office.

She was nearly through the door when she heard his voice.

She'd heard that icy tone before—the kind that sliced straight through the belly, spilling out the guts before the victim registered the pain.

Though the victim in this case was a minor, nobody was going to call Child Services.

"Is there something about the rules of this

household and your current position in it
that's eluded you?" Roarke posed the question the way a cat lurks outside a mouse-
hole. With lethal patience and the gleam of
fangs.

"Look, what's the BFD?"

And the kid, Eve thought with a shake of
her head, was responding like the mouse
stupid enough to think it could outwait or
outwit the cat. Foolish, foolish boy, she
mused. You are dead meat already.

"You'll mind your tone when you speak to
me, James. I'll tolerate a certain amount of
idiocy from you due to your age, but I'll tolerate no sass whatsoever. Are we clear on
that particular point?"

"Yeah, okay, but I just don't—"

Eve couldn't see Roarke's face, but she
could clearly envision the look in his eye.
One that had Jamie swallowing back whatever he'd been about to say, and revising it.

"Yes, sir."

"That's good. Saves time and heartache.
Now, I'll explain the big fucking deal to you,
in words that should be easily understood.
Because I gave you a specific order, and
when I give specific orders, they're to be fol-

lowed. And that's the end of it. Any part of that hazy for you?"

"People are supposed to think for themselves."

"That they are. And people who work for me are to do as I tell them. Or they don't work for me any longer. If you're going to sulk over it, take yourself off elsewhere so I don't have to look at you."

"I'm almost eighteen."

Roarke eased a hip onto a work counter. "A man, are you? Then behave as one, and not like a boy who's been caught with his hand in the cookie jar."

"I could've gotten more data."

"You could've crashed that impressive brain of yours. The fact is, Jamie, I've plans for you that don't include going to your memorial."

Jamie's shoulders hunched now, his gaze lowered. He kicked idly at the base of the workstation with the toe of his ancient airboot. "I'd've been careful."

"Careful? Careful isn't trying to sneak into the lab in the middle of the night to boot up an infected computer without anyone at control, without anyone monitoring. What that is, is arrogant and it's stupid. I'll tolerate a bit of arrogance, even admire it. But stupidity's another matter. Beyond all that, you disobeyed an order."

"I wanted to help. I just wanted to help."

"You have been, and you'll continue to help if you give me your word you won't try the same thing again. Look at me. You say you want to be a cop. God knows why as you'll work yourself half to death for piss-poor wages and little to no appreciation from the people you swear to protect and serve. A good cop follows orders. He doesn't always agree with them, doesn't always like them, but he follows them."

"I know." The wind seemed to go out of him, slumping his shoulders again. "I screwed up."

"You did indeed. But not as badly as you might. Your word on it, Jamie." Roarke held out a hand. "As a man."

Jamie looked down at the proffered hand. His shoulders straightened, and he clasped it. "I won't do it again. I promise."

"Then that's the end of it. Go, grab some breakfast. We'll be back at this in a half hour."

Eve eased around the corner, waited until Jamie had dashed out and away.

Roarke was already at a workstation when she walked in. She noted he wasn't doing casework, but transmitting some complicated instructions for his broker. When he was done, she opened her mouth to speak, then closed it again when he immediately started another transmission to his admin.

She reminded herself of all the time he was giving her, the work he was juggling, reshuffling, adjusting so he could carve out the time. It helped keep her from grinding her teeth when he followed up the transmission to his admin with one to FreeStar One.

"If you're going to stand back there shuffling your feet, Lieutenant, you might bring me a cup of coffee. I'm going to need another ten minutes here."

He was doing her a favor, she told herself as she choked back the sass and got the coffee. She listened with half an ear as he pulled in transmissions, answered, transferred, instructed and, as far as she could tell, ruled his empire from the workstation more suited to a drone than a king.

"That thing you were bidding on, the office complex. I guess they caved and took your offer."

"Yes."

"And I wasn't shuffling my feet."

"Mentally you were. I'm going to have to take a meeting this afternoon. Shouldn't tie me up more than ninety minutes."

"Whatever it takes. You've already given the department more than it could expect."

"Pay me," he said, and yanked her down for a kiss.

"You work cheap, Ace."

"That was only a deposit. Have you decided how you're going to handle this morning?"

"Pretty much. Before I brief the team, I wanted to say that was a good technique with the kid before. Slap him down, break him, crush him into dust, then build him back up again."

He sampled the coffee. "Heard that did you?"

"I might've added a couple of creative threats. Something that gives a good visual. But all in all, it was very impressive."

"Little peabrain thinking he'd come in, run an infected, and present us with the data this morning. I nearly planted a boot up his ass."

"How did you know he tried?"

"Because I took the precaution of adding

an extra layer of security to the door and locked down all the units." The faintest smile touched the corners of his mouth. "And I expected him to try it as I would've done at his age."

"I'm surprised he didn't get through."

"I've a bit more skill than a teenage boy, thanks."

"Yeah, yeah, and bigger balls, too. I was thinking of that jammer of his. You took the prototype away from him, but I'd've bet a month of my piss-poor wages he had another."

"You mean this?" Roarke pulled it out of his pocket. "I had Summerset toss his room—discreetly. When it wasn't found there, I assumed—correctly—he had it on him. So I picked his pocket on the way into dinner last night. And slipped him another with a few particular defects."

"Defects?"

"Gives you a quick, rather unpleasant little jolt when you begin the cloning function. That was small of me, I suppose. But he needed to be put in his place."

Amused, she clinked her coffee mug to his. "Yeah, all in all, pretty impressive. You want in on this briefing, or do you need some more time to buy Saturn or Venus?"

"I don't buy planets. They're just not cost effective." He rose.

They walked into Eve's office to see Jamie, Feeney, and Baxter chowing down from a table set up in the middle of the room and loaded with food.

"These eggs"—Baxter swallowed, forked up another bite—"are from chickens. Chickens."

"Cluck-cluck." Eve walked over to snag a piece of bacon.

"You fell into gravy with this guy, Dallas. No offense," Baxter said to Roarke, and shoveled in more eggs.

"None taken." Amused, he nodded toward the meat platter. "Have you tried the ham? It's from pig."

"Oink-oink," Jamie said, cracking himself up.

"If we've finished visiting the farm animals, you've got ten minutes to slurp the rest of this up." Eve polished off the slice of bacon. "And Baxter, if you spread it around Central about me falling into gravy, I'll see to it that you never have another chicken egg as long as you live."

She scowled at her wrist unit. "Why aren't Peabody and McNab in here?" She turned, intending to use the house 'link to roust them. Roarke stopped her with a hand to her shoulder.

"Eve." He said it quietly, nudging her around until she faced the door.

Her throat snapped closed. Her hand went to Feeney's shoulder in turn, squeezed hard. They watched McNab walk slowly into the room.

He used a cane. It looked almost stylish somehow—glossy black, silver-tipped. He was sweating. She could see the beads of effort popping out on his face, even as he grinned from ear to ear.

His steps were unsteady, obviously labored. But he was on his feet. Walking.

Peabody was just behind him, struggling not to cry.

Eve felt Feeney's hand come up, close tight over hers.

"It's about time you got up off that lazy ass of yours." His voice was thick, but Feeney was afraid to lift a cup and drink to clear it. His hand was far from steady. "Team's been carrying you long enough."

"I thought about trying to pull it off for one

more day." McNab was out of breath when he reached the table. Still, he reached out with his right hand, closed his fingers over a slice of bacon, lifted it to his mouth. "But I smelled food."

"You wanted breakfast, you should have come in twenty minutes ago." Eve waited until he looked at her. "Better eat fast," she ordered. "We've got work."

"Yes, sir." He tried to sidestep to a chair, wobbled. Eve caught his elbow, held it until he had his balance again.

"Dallas?"

"Detective."

"I figure this is the only chance I'll ever have at this." He gave her a hard, noisy kiss on the mouth that had Baxter applauding.

Eve choked back a laugh and looked at him coolly. "And you think I won't knock you on your ass for that?"

"Not this time." Exhausted, he dropped into a chair. Caught his breath. "Hey, kid, pass those eggs over here before Baxter licks the damn platter."

After breakfast, after the briefing, Eve dismissed her team but for Peabody.

"He looks good," Eve began. "A little worn out, but good."

"Didn't get any sleep. He was pulling the 'woe is me, you've got to go' routine when—"

"The what?"

"He was feeling low and he'd gotten into his head he wanted me to walk so he wouldn't feel like a burden, or I wouldn't feel like it, whatever. We were arguing, and it started. His arm starting itching, then his legs, and then . . . Sorry, I get messed up when I talk about it."

"Okay, then let's not talk about it. Except to say I'm glad he's—" She broke off, pressed her fingers to her eyes and breathed deep.

"Messes you up, too." Peabody sniffled, dug out her handkerchief. "That's so nice."

"We're all glad he's back. Let's leave it alone for now."

She sighed once, then switched gears. "Data has come into my hands through an alternate source. I'm not going to name this source. I intend to act on this data, which includes names and info in sealeds that I do not, as yet, have authority to open."

Peabody sat quietly. She knew what

Roarke and her lieutenant had been working on now. She didn't know how the hell they'd gotten into sealeds. Probably didn't want to know.

"Yes, sir. It seems to me that acting on this data, which came into your hands by an alternate source, would be correct procedure. To ignore the data during an investigation labeled PRIORITY would be dereliction of duty."

"Want to be my rep if they bust me for this?"

"I figure Roarke can hire us the best going."

"You won't be in the line of fire. You can elect to take another assignment."

"Dallas—"

"Or," Eve continued, "you can accompany me, as my aide. And as my aide, your ass will not go in the sling on this. You're just following orders."

"Respectfully, sir, my ass is with yours. If you expect it any other way, you've got the wrong aide."

"I haven't got the wrong aide. We might catch a little heat for this, Peabody, but I don't think it'll burn very hot or very long. I'll fill you in on the way."

• • •

Donald and Sylvia Dukes lived in a tidy, two-story townhouse. Eve noted frilly curtains at the windows and identical white pots of reg-imented red flowers standing on either side of the front door. Like soldiers, she thought, guarding the fort.

She rang the buzzer, took out her badge.

The woman who answered was small, slim, and as ordered as her flowers. She wore a blue-and-white checked dress and there was a white apron tied at her waist. She wore pale rose lip dye, earrings fash-ioned of three small pearls in a triangle, and spotless white canvas shoes.

Without the apron, she would have looked like a woman about to head out for a day of running errands.

"Mrs. Dukes?"

"Yes. What's wrong? What do you want?" Her cautious gaze darted from Eve's face to the badge and back again. Eve could hear the breathy sound of nerves in her voice.

"Nothing's wrong, ma'am. I'd like to ask you some questions. Is it all right if we come in?"

"I'm in the middle of . . . I'm very busy. This isn't a good time."

"I could make an appointment, at your convenience. But I'm here now, and I'll try not to keep you very long."

"Who is it, Sylvia?" Donald Dukes came to the door. He towered over his wife, an athletically lean man of six feet two inches. His sandy hair was fashioned into a short military cut.

"The police," Sylvia began.

"Lieutenant Dallas, NYPSD, and my aide, Officer Peabody. I have some questions, Mr. Dukes. If I could have a few minutes of your time."

"What's this about?"

He'd already shifted his wife aside, and stood blocking the doorway. It wasn't only flowers guarding the fort now, Eve decided.

"It's regarding the deaths of Chadwick Fitzhugh and Louis K. Cogburn."

"That has nothing to do with us."

"Sir, at one time you filed charges, on behalf of your son Devin, against both of these men."

"My son Devin is dead."

He said it so flatly, so coldly, he might have been speaking of the loss of his favorite tie.

"I'm sorry." Eve heard his wife choke off

a sob behind him. Dukes didn't bat an eyelash. "Mr. Dukes, is this something you want
to discuss in the doorway?"

"This is something I don't want to discuss
at all. Devin's files are sealed, Lieutenant.
How did you get our name?"

"Your names came up during the course
of my investigation." Hard-ass to hard-ass
then, Eve decided, staring at him coldly.
"Files can be sealed, Mr. Dukes, but people
talk."

"Dad?" A boy walked halfway down the
stairs. He was tall like his father, his hair as
rigidly shorn. He wore blue trousers, a blue
shirt, both knife-edge sharp. Like a uniform,
Eve decided.

"Joseph, go back upstairs."

"Is something wrong?"

"This doesn't concern you." Dukes
glanced back briefly. "Go upstairs immediately."

"Yes, sir."

"I won't have you disrupting my home," he
said to Eve.

"Would you prefer taking it down to Central?"

"You have no authority to—"

"Yes, sir. I do. And the fact that you're re-

luctant to answer a few routine questions
leads me toward exercising that authority.
This can be simple or complicated. That's
your choice."

"You have five minutes." He stepped
back. "Sylvia, go upstairs with Joseph."

"I require Mrs. Dukes as well."

Eve could see him struggle with fury. Hot
color burned across his cheekbones, and
his jaw worked. This wasn't a man accustomed to having any order questioned,
much less countermanded.

She could go head-to-head with him, or
she could throttle back. She made an instant
and instinctive decision to change tactics.

"Mr. Dukes, I'm sorry to bring this into
your home, to disturb you and your family. I
have to do my job."

"And your job is to question decent citizens over the death of scum?"

"I'm just a foot soldier, following orders."

She saw immediately it had been the right
button. He nodded and without a word
turned and walked into the living area. Sylvia remained standing, her fists clenched,
her knuckles white as her apron.

"Should I . . . would you like some coffee,
or—"

"They aren't guests, Sylvia." Dukes snapped it out. Eve saw his wife flinch as if from a blow.

"Don't trouble yourself, Mrs. Dukes."

The living area was whistle clean. Flanking a sofa done in a pattern of muted blues were two identical tables. On each was a matching lamp. There were two chairs in the same pattern as the sofa, and the green area rug showed not a speck of dust or lint.

There was a vase holding yellow and white flowers arranged too precisely to be cheerful. It was set exactly in the center of the coffee table.

"I won't ask you to sit."

Dukes stood, clasping his hands behind his back at waist level.

Another soldier, Eve thought, prepared for interrogation.

Chapter 15

"Mr. Dukes, it's my understanding that approximately four years ago, your son had occasion to purchase an illegal substance from Louis K. Cogburn."

"That is correct."

"And on learning of this, you reported same to the police, filing an official complaint at that time."

"That is also correct."

"Subsequently charges in this matter against Cogburn were dropped. Can you tell me why?"

"The prosecutor's office refused to follow through." He stayed at attention. "Cogburn was put back on the street where he could continue to corrupt young minds, young bodies."

"I assume your son gave a full statement of the occurence, and with the illegal substance in evidence traced back to Cogburn, it seems unusual that the prosecutor wouldn't press."

Cogburn's lips thinned. "The illegal substance had been destroyed. I would not have it in my home. It seemed my word, my son's word, was not enough against the word of trash."

"I see. That was difficult for you. Frustrating, I'm sure, for your family."

"It was."

It was interesting, Eve thought, that Dukes wore nearly the same blue uniform as his young son. The creases down the center of his trousers were so sharp they looked capable of cutting flesh.

More interesting were the waves of fury rolling off him. Hot, smothering waves of rage barely held in check.

"To your knowledge did your son continue to have dealings with Cogburn?"

"He did not."

But Eve saw the truth on Sylvia's face.

The kid had gone back for more, Eve thought. And everyone knew it.

"I assume Child Services recommended illegals counseling for Devin."

"They did."

Eve waited a beat. "And did he complete the program?"

"I fail to see what this has to do with your investigation, Lieutenant," he said tightly.

She changed tacts again. "Can you tell me about the events surrounding Devin's experience with Chadwick Fitzhugh?"

"The man sexually molested my minor son." The first crack showed in Dukes's composure. But it wasn't grief Eve saw so much as disgust. "He forced himself on my son and engaged in unnatural acts."

"And this molestation took place in Fitzhugh's home?"

"It did."

"How did Devin come to be in Fitzhugh's home?"

"He was lured."

"Did Devin tell you how he was lured?"

"It doesn't matter how. He was molested. It was duly reported to the police. The man responsible was not punished."

"The charges were dropped? Why?"

"Because the law protected the predator and not the prey. Your time is up."

"How and when did Devin die?"

Ignoring the question, Dukes started out of the living room toward the front door.

"I can get that information through public records."

"My son killed himself." Dukes stood with his hands fisted at his sides. "Eight months ago. He pumped his body full of garbage until he died. The system failed to protect him. It failed to assist me in protecting him."

"You have another son. How far would you go to protect him?"

"Joseph will not be corrupted by the cancer that eats away at our society."

"Cancer's a kind of virus, isn't it? You can kill a virus with a virus. Infect the host until the bad cells are destroyed. You're a computer scientist, Mr. Dukes. You know about viruses."

She saw it then—the acknowledgment, even a kind of pride that leaped onto his face, then off again. "I said your time is up."

"So's yours, Mr. Dukes," Eve said quietly. "You're going to want to start making arrangements for your wife and son for when you go down with the rest of Purity."

"Get out of my house. I intend to call my lawyer."

"Good idea. You're going to need one."

When they were back in the car, Peabody frowned back at the house. "Why did you tip him?"

"If he wasn't smart enough to figure out I'm looking at him, and he is, whoever he's going to report this visit to would be. I was tipping the wife."

"You don't think she's part of it?"

"He never touched her, barely looked at her. She's standing there with tears running down her face and he doesn't so much as acknowledge her presence. No, this is his deal. What did you see in that house, Peabody?"

"Well, he rules."

"More than that. It's a fucking barracks, and he's the commander. She answers the door before nine in the morning, dolled up like a woman in a screen ad for AutoChefs. Kid's about fourteen, but he bolts back upstairs at the snap of Dukes's finger. I bet all the beds were already made and you could bounce a five-credit coin off every one of them."

Considering, she headed downtown. "How's a former marine who demands everything around him be squared away going to handle having a son who's *corrupting* his mind and body with illegals? That was his term, right? Just like *unnatural acts* was his term. A chemi-head, homosexual son. Boy, that had to burn his white-bread, homophobic ass."

"Poor kid."

"Yeah, and now his father can use him as a symbol, as an excuse to kill. There are all kinds of cancers," she mumbled. "Dallas," she said when her dash 'link beeped.

"In your vehicle?" Nadine asked. "You may want to pull over somewhere. You're going to want to hear this."

"I can hear and drive at the same time. I'm talented that way."

"I've got another statement from The Purity Seekers. Going to air in fifteen."

"Delay the broadcast. We need to—"

"I can't hold the story for you, Dallas. I won't. I'm giving you a heads up. I'll also air whatever comment you want to make, whatever statement you or NYPSD wants to issue. But this is on in fifteen."

"Damn it." Frustrated, Eve swung toward

the curb, cutting off a cab before she shot up a curbside parking ramp to the crowded second level. "Let's have it."

" 'Citizens of New York,' " Nadine read in perfect on-air pitch, " 'we wish to assure you of your safety and restate to you our promise to seek justice on your behalf. We are committed to our vow to protect the innocent while meting out the due punishment to the guilty that the shackled hands of the law cannot provide.

" 'We are you: your brothers, your sisters, your parents, your child. We are your family as we are your guardians.

" 'Like you, we are saddened by the tragic death of a New York Police and Security officer who died two days ago. Detective Kevin Halloway's death during the performance of his duty is yet another example of the blight that plagues our city. We hold Louis K. Cogburn directly responsible for this despicable crime. If not for Louis Cogburn's previous actions, which made necessary the punishment he received, Detective Kevin Halloway would be alive today, doing what he was allowed to do—within the limitations of our current laws—to serve this city.

" 'We ask you, the citizens of New York, to join us today in a moment of silence for the memory of Detective Halloway. And we offer his family, his friends, his fellow officers our condolences at this grievous time.

" 'Louis Cogburn has been punished. Justice has been served, and will continue to be served.

" 'We send out this warning to all who seek to harm our brothers, to all who prey on our children and the innocents, that our hand will be swift, it will be sure. You will no longer find sanctuary behind the law.

" 'We stand for purity.

" 'We stand for the people of New York.' "

"Smart," Eve said when Nadine finished.

"Very smart. Make yourself one of the people so it doesn't look too much like Big Brother's watching you. Express regret over the death of a cop and point the finger at someone else. Restate your goals so your message is loud and clear, and leave it ringing in your audience's ears that you stand for the people. It's textbook PR."

"Isn't anyone hearing what I'm hearing?" Eve demanded. " 'Don't any of you worry your poor silly heads over any of this. We'll take care of it. We'll decide who's guilty, who's innocent. Who lives, who dies. And if, gee, somebody gets caught in the crossfire, it's not on us.' "

"No, you're not the only one hearing it." Nadine shook her head. "But a lot of people are going to hear just what they want to hear. That's why this is textbook PR, Dallas. It works."

"I'll be damned if they're going to use one of us as a symbol. You want a comment, Nadine, here it is: Lieutenant Eve Dallas, primary investigator on the Purity homicides, states that EDD Detective Kevin Halloway was killed in the line of duty by a terrorist organization calling themselves The Purity Seekers. This organization is suspected of being responsible for the murders of four civilians and a police officer. Lieutenant Dallas further states that she, the members of her investigative team, and every officer, every resource of the New York Police and Security Department will work to uncover, identify, and arrest all members of this terrorist organization so that they may be tried under the codes of this city and if found guilty, be punished to the full extent of the law."

"Got it, got it. Not bad," Nadine said as

she turned back from her recorder. "How about a one-on-one followup?"

"No. I'm busy, Nadine. And I have to help bury a cop today."

They memorialized Kevin Halloway in a bereavement facility downtown only blocks from Cop Central. It had often occurred to Eve when she'd had to pay her respects to other fallen cops there, that whoever had started the business had figured the location near a major cop shop would be a plus.

For Halloway, they'd opened the entire first floor, and still the place was packed. Cops always managed to find the time to wake another cop.

She spotted Mayor Peachtree, tucked in among his entourage as he shook hands and looked properly grim, sympathetic, or understanding.

Eve didn't have anything against him personally, and he seemed to be doing the job with a minimum of fuss and self-aggrandizement. He might have been sincere.

He seemed sincere—sincerely pissed, she thought—when his sparkling gaze locked with hers through the crowd.

There was command in the single, sharp gesture that summoned her to him.

"Mayor."

"Lieutenant." He kept his voice low. It could have been mistaken for reverent in such a place, but she heard the annoyance beneath it. "Your record is impressive. Your superiors have complete faith in your abilities. But you're not simply a police official in this matter. You're a public figure. Your statement to Furst at 75 was neither vetted nor authorized."

"My statement was responsive and accurate."

"Accuracy." He seemed to draw himself in. "Accuracy isn't the issue. Perception, image, and message are. Lieutenant, we need to be a unit, a team, during this crisis."

He laid a hand on her arm. There was warmth in the gesture, a kind of practiced bonhomie, just as the slight curve of his lips was practiced. "I'm depending on you."

"Yes, sir."

He stepped back, was soon swallowed up by his people, and by others who wanted that brief contact with power and celebrity.

Eve preferred Commander Whitney's quiet presence to Peachtree's shining one.

He'd brought his wife, Eve noted. If there was anything Anna Whitney excelled at it was the public and social areas of being a top cop's wife. She wore black, a simple, understated suit, and ranged beside her husband she held a woman's hand in both of hers.

"Halloway's mother." Feeney stepped up to Eve's side. "I've already spoken to her. She asked specifically to meet you."

"Man."

"I know. I hate these things, too. Attractive redhead other side of the chief? Halloway's girl. Name's Lily Doogan. She's pretty ripped up. There are badges here from every borough. That says something."

"Yeah. It says something."

"They got him in the next room. McNab's in there." Feeney let out a long breath. "Got him into a chair. Can't stand easy for long yet. Roarke's in there with him."

"Roarke's here?"

"Yeah." Grief drenched him. "I couldn't stay in there anymore. Just couldn't do it."

"Being here's enough, Feeney."

"Doesn't feel like it. I'll take you over to his mother."

They made their way through the crowd

of mourners, through the muted hum of conversation. The air was heavy with the scent of flowers, dim with the quiet light the grieving seemed to prefer.

"Lieutenant."

Eve turned at the hand on her arm and looked into Jenna Franco's eyes. She didn't see grief in them, but she saw plenty of annoyance. She didn't mask it as smoothly as Peachtree.

"Deputy Mayor."

"I need to speak with you. Privately."

"I have something to do first. You'll have to wait."

She tugged her arm free, turned her back. It was petty, she knew. But since she had a damn good idea what the private chat was going to entail, she doubted she and Jenna Franco were going to waste much time on the amenities.

Eve braced herself before approaching Colleen Halloway. She would probably be in her forties, maybe fifties, Eve calculated, but looked younger. Grief had given her skin a kind of translucence that added a youthful fragility against the unrelieved black of her mourning.

"Lieutenant."

It was Anna Whitney who spoke first. Eve had often found herself on the commander's wife's wrong side. But at the moment there was none of the usual hint of impatience or irritation on her face.

And to Eve's surprise, Anna took her hand and squeezed it.

"Mrs. Whitney."

"Detective Halloway's mother has been hoping to speak with you." Her voice was low, her back turned slightly so that the words were for Eve alone. "Do you know the one thing more difficult than being married to a cop, Lieutenant?"

"No. I always figured that was the short straw."

The faintest smile ghosted around Anna's mouth. "There's one shorter yet. That's giving birth to one. Be careful with her."

"Yes, ma'am."

"Colleen?" With a natural gentleness Eve admired, Anna draped an arm over the woman's shoulders. "This is Lieutenant Dallas. Lieutenant, Kevin's mother."

"Mrs. Halloway. I'm very sorry for your loss."

"Lieutenant Dallas." Colleen gripped Eve's hand. It was stronger, firmer than Eve had expected. "Thank you so much for coming. I wonder—there's a small privacy room upstairs. I wonder if you could spare a few minutes? I'd like to speak with you."

"All right."

She led Eve out of the dim parlor, up a set of stairs. Cops had spilled out, crowded there as well. But they stepped aside, eyes lowered respectfully as Colleen passed.

"My husband would like to meet you as well. And Lily. But I asked them if I could have this time alone with you. They understood."

She opened a door, walked into a small sitting room. More flowers, soft fabrics just a little overdone in style, just a little too dark in their wine-red tones.

"These places are so horribly depressing, aren't they? I wonder why they don't let in the light." Colleen walked to the window, threw open the heavy drapes, and let in the sun. "I suppose a lot of people find comfort in the shadows.

"Do you?" she asked Eve, then shook her head. "My thoughts are rambling. Please, sit down."

Colleen took a chair, sat with her back very straight. "I've seen you on-screen. You always seem so competent, even when it's coverage of one of those social functions you attend with your husband. He's terribly handsome, isn't he?"

"Yes, ma'am."

"It was kind of him to come as well. To make the time, to speak to me, my husband, Lily. Very kind. Kevin spoke of you occasionally. You never worked with him, though, did you?"

"Not directly, no. But I often depend on EDD in my work. Hall . . . Kevin was a valued member of the department."

"He admired you. I wanted to tell you," she added, smiling a little at the blank look on Eve's face. "He sometimes spoke of you working with Captain Feeney and the other young detective, Ian McNab. He was, I think, a little envious of your relationship with both Ian and the captain."

"Mrs. Halloway—"

"I only tell you that so you might understand why he might have said or done the things he said or did when he was in such terrible trouble."

"Mrs. Halloway, I don't need an explanation. Kevin was ill, very ill, and none of what happened after they infected him was any fault of his."

"It's good to hear you say that. I heard the statements this morning. Both of them. I wasn't sure if yours was just the departmental line, or if you meant it."

"I did mean it. Every word of it."

Colleen nodded. Her lips trembled once, then firmed. "I know what you did to try to save Kevin. I know you risked your own life to do so. And I know," she continued as Eve started to speak, "that you'll say you were doing your job. That's what all of you say. But I want to thank you first as a mother, just as a mother."

Her eyes swam and though she blinked to fight the tears, one spilled out and trailed down her cheek. "And I want to thank you for Kevin. Please . . . let me finish."

Still she had to stop for a moment, clear her throat. "My son was proud to be a police officer. He believed in what that stood for, respected it, and gave his best. They might have taken that from him as well as his life if not for you. If not for you, his captain, his commander, his fellow officers . . . that pride and respect might have been taken from him. Instead . . ."

She reached into a small black purse and took out her son's badge. "Instead, there's honor. I'll never forget it." She leaned forward now, her expression intense. "Stop them. You will stop them."

"Yes, ma'am. I'll stop them."

With a nod, Colleen leaned back again. "I've kept you long enough. I'm sure you have a great deal of work. I think I'd like to sit here in the light, for a little while."

Eve rose and went to the door. Then she turned and said what was on her mind. "Mrs. Halloway? He must have been awfully proud of you, too."

Again those lips curved, just a little. Again a single tear spilled down her cheek.

Eve slipped out and closed the door.

She was nearly to the stairs when Franco swooped up. Chang scurried in her wake like a pet dog. "We'll talk now."

When she headed for the privacy room, Eve caught her arm. "Mrs. Halloway's in there."

The impatience on Franco's face faded. Her one last glance at the door was full of sympathy. Then that faded as well as she strode down the hallway, pushed her way into another room.

It was some sort of office, manned at the moment by a young woman at a gleaming wooden breakfront that had been modeled into a workstation.

"I need this space," Franco snapped. "You'll have to leave."

Eve lifted her brows as the girl scrambled out. Franco was a woman who went where she wanted when she wanted. Eve admired the trait.

When Chang closed the door behind them, Franco launched into the attack. "You were instructed to use the official statement when responding to the media. We can't waste time and resources running along behind you and clearing up the mess."

"Then you'd better try to keep up. I got a heads up minutes before the latest statement from Purity was to be aired. I responded to said statement as I deemed appropriate."

"It's not your place to deem what is an appropriate response to the media." This came from Chang, in clipped tones. "It's my job to tell you what's appropriate in this area."

"The last time I looked I don't answer to

you, and should that day ever come, I'll retire."

"Chief Tibble ordered you to cooperate," he reminded her. "Yet you refuse to accept the bookings that were arranged for maximum spin and effect. And now you issue your own statement without clearance. A statement that speaks not just for you, Lieutenant, but for the department. This is not acceptable."

"If the chief or my commander determines I've done or said the unacceptable, then they can dress me down, Chang. You can't."

She took a step toward him, was darkly pleased to see him take one back. "Don't ever try to tell me how to do my job."

"You've never had any respect for me or my position."

Eve angled her head. "And your point is?"

"We'll see what Chief Tibble has to say about this."

"Run along and tattle, you little weasel. And let the grown-ups finish talking." She turned back to Franco, who'd said nothing during the exchange. "You got something else to say to me?"

"Yes, actually. Why don't you give us a minute here, Chang? We'll discuss the rest of this in my office in . . ." She checked the time. "Thirty minutes."

He went out, giving the door a sulky little slam.

"Do you try to irritate people, Dallas, or is it just an innate skill?"

"I guess it's the second, because it comes real easy. Especially with pissants like Chang."

"If I tell you I agree that Chang is an annoying, selfsatisfied, and boring pissant—a statement I will vehemently deny making if repeated—can we table some of the hostility?"

"Why do you use him then?"

"Because he's good. He's very, very good. If I had to like everyone I worked with or who worked for me, I sure as hell wouldn't be in politics. Now, issue one, your statement this morning. Chang feels, and I agree—as does the mayor—that your use of Detective Halloway's death was ill advised."

"My use? Just one damn minute. *They* used him, shirking responsibility for his death. I responded and stuck the responsibility right back up their ass."

"And I understand the instinct that

prompted you to do so. For God's sake, Dallas, do you think I function without a heartbeat? I don't. And that heart breaks for that woman down the hall. Damn it. She's lost her son. I have a son. He's ten. I can't imagine having to say good-bye to him the way Colleen Halloway is saying good-bye today."

"It seems to me it would be harder if people were allowed to think her son died for nothing."

"Didn't he?" Franco retorted, then shook her head. "Oh, I know how you cops think. On the job. I won't argue with you because I don't understand that either. But the point is that the more often his name is said, the more he's made the story, the harder it is to focus the media and the public on the message we want to send. Whatever you might think," she added as she turned back.

"I know more about this than you and Chang knows more than both of us. The second point is no statement should have been made without clearance."

"You won't box me in that way. I'm no media hound, but if and when I feel using it helps my investigation, I'll use it."

"Yet you toss back the bookings Chang

arranged, programming where we'd have some control."

"I'm not sitting in some studio parroting departmental or mayoral approved responses and statements when my time and energies are required in a priority investigation. The fact is, I'm never doing it."

"Yes, so your commander has made clear."

"Then what's the problem?"

"Had to take a shot." Franco spread her hands. "We could use the airtime. The other matter I have to discuss with you is, potentially, a great deal more serious. It's already come to the mayor's ear that you questioned the Dukes this morning in the course of your investigation. A family who also lost their son recently, and who are protected by sealed files."

"He didn't waste any time. The information on the Dukes came into my hands. The connection to two of the victims, as well as Donald Dukes's profession, led me to believe an informal interview was warranted. Are you going to try to tell me how to do my job now?"

"Oh for Christ's sake." Franco threw up

her hands. "Why do you insist on behaving as if we're on opposite sides."

"It feels that way."

"Do you know what will happen if Donald Dukes goes to the media? If he talks about being harassed in his own home by the primary in this already hot-button situation? Their son was hooked on illegals by Cogburn—"

"There's no evidence to support Cogburn was his first dealer."

"It doesn't *matter* if there's evidence," Franco fired back. "This is what would be said. Cogburn hooked an innocent, vulnerable twelve-year-old boy, from a good, solid, churchgoing family. The police failed to make a case. Later, this boy—now troubled, now recalcitrant due to his addiction, falls into the hands of a pedophile. Chadwick Fitzhugh beats and rapes young Devin, now a tender fourteen. The family is shattered, the boy is traumatized, and *again* the police fail to make a case."

"That's not the way it happened."

"That's the way it'll be presented, reported, discussed should they go public. Truth, pieces of the truth, outright lies, it doesn't matter once it's on the air. A picture will be painted, then you'll walk into it, questioning this damaged, grieving family who tried to do the right thing, who put their faith and their son's welfare into the hands of the system only to be failed in the most horrible way. You attempt to implicate them in a homicide investigation. You accuse them of being members of a group you've publicly called terrorists. And you do this in their home. Don't you see how this will play?"

"I'll tell you how it plays, Franco. Donald Dukes couldn't or wouldn't accept his son's sexual orientation—"

"Oh my God, oh my God." Franco pressed her fingers to her temples, seemed to try to drill them through. "You start saying that child was gay, you'll be in a lawsuit, and so will the department, probably the city before I can push you out of the nearest twenty-story window."

"Not if I push you first. In any case, evidence indicates he was gay, or certainly confused about his own sexuality. He never got the chance to make up his mind. His father is rigid, domineering. The kind of guy who's just not going to be wrong. He destroys evidence that may have helped make the case against Cogburn, but it's the system's fault. He edits and changes the facts in the Fitzhugh matter so the case falls apart, and again, it's the system's fault. Now he's found an outlet for his aggressions and his viewpoint: Purity."

"You have proof of all this?"

"Of some. I'll get the rest."

"Dallas, if I'm having a hard time believing any of this, no one else will believe it. In addition, you're speaking of facts and suppositions that were in a sealed. An official and public reprimand from your commander may not be enough to stop legal action, or the media storm."

"If and when my commander deems it necessary to reprimand me, that's his right and that's my problem. The media storm's yours and Chang's. Dukes can start all the legal actions he wants. They're not going to go anywhere once I put him in a cage. Are we done here?"

"You'd better be very sure of yourself," Franco warned.

"I'm sure of the job, and that's the same thing."

Eve walked out. As she started back downstairs, she heard the clear, strong voice of a tenor singing the opening bars of *Danny Boy*.

Cops were always singing *Danny Boy* at funerals, she thought. She'd never known just why.

"Lieutenant." Roarke met her at the base of the stairs.

"I need some air" was all she said, and strode out the door.

Chapter 16

A double-parked delivery van had tied up traffic for what appeared to be a good six blocks. The resulting noise from blasting horns and hurled obscenities turned the air into one long scream of rage.

A glide-cart operator had overcooked and oversauced his kabobs. The stink of the greasy smoke was amazing.

Eve preferred the noise and stench to the murmurs and flowers inside.

She strode straight through the nauseating odor and dug out credits. "Gimme chocolate," she ordered the operator.

"Got sticks. Many ya want?"

"Six."

"Got yer fruitade, got yer Pepsi, got yer Coke, got yer fizzy water. Whatcha want?"

"Just the chocolate."

She tossed him the money, snagged the skinny sticks out of his hand. She bit fiercely into the first. They were already melting in the vicious fist of the heat.

Roarke bought a large water and grabbed a small mountain of napkins. "Hand one over. You'll be sick if you eat them all."

"I'm already sick." But she proved her depthless love by giving him one. "Peach-tree gives me the thirty-second lecture on teamwork, ending in the warm, *we're both just public servants* arm squeeze. Then Chang and Franco jump on my ass about the statement I gave 75 this morning. Not screened, not approved. Let's not confuse the public with the truth. I'm a cop, not a public relations puppet."

"Which I'm sure you pointed out."

"Yeah." She smiled grimly, ate more chocolate. "There was that. Franco doesn't seem to be an idiot, especially for a politician. But she—and all of them—sure seem to be more interested in perception, in image, in spins than in the investigation."

"They wouldn't understand the investigation the way they would perception, image, and spin."

He drank water to wash down what was laughingly called chocolate by the city vendors, then dampened a napkin to get the smear of it off his fingers.

"And they wouldn't understand you and the fact that you care less about media exposure than you do what shirt you put on in the morning," he added, two-pointing the napkin into a recycler. "Which is not at all."

Eve looked down at her shirt. It was white, she thought. It was clean. What else did you need to worry about?

"We'd all be better off if they did what they did, and left me alone to do what I do. I've got suspects, damn it. Price, Dwier, and now the Dukeses. I crack any one of them, and this breaks open."

She started on the third stick. "Dukes called a lawyer. Jumped right on that. Whining harassment, making lawsuit noises that've put Franco and company into orbit."

"Was that unexpected?"

"No, I expected it. I guess I hoped it would hold line until after the memorial." She glanced back at the bereavement center. A few cops were heading out. Back to duty, she thought. Life didn't always go on, but the job did.

"He's in it, Roarke. Dukes. Slides into the profile like it was a tailor-made suit. You know how you handled Jamie this morning, what I said about knocking him back, grinding him into dust, then building him up again? Dukes wouldn't trouble himself with the last part of that cycle. My impression is he made his kid's life a small, personal hell. I'm going to bring him down, and the rest of them with him."

She looked up, picked out the window of the room where she'd sat with Colleen Halloway. "I'm going to stop them. I need you to get me as much data and background on Donald Dukes as you can—within legal bounds."

"If you want it within legal bounds, why ask me instead of Feeney or McNab?"

"Because I may be ordered to back off the Dukes, and if I am I can't ask them. So I'm asking you in case it plays that way. Seems to me a guy with all your companies would always be on the lookout for a good computer scientist. You'd do a background check, em-

ployment check, and so on before you considered hiring anyone on, right?"

"I certainly would. And I might casually
mention some of that information to my
wife." He stroked a finger down her chin.
"That's very clever, Lieutenant."

"I want him in a box, and to get him there,
I need all the angles. I'm going to have an-
other talk with Clarissa Price this afternoon.
She's not going to be happy to see me.
Then I may bounce on to Dwier."

She looked down at her hand. The remaining stick was now a blob, and a dead
loss. "Well, yuck."

She dumped it in a recycler, cleaned her
fingers with the water and napkins Roarke
provided.

"Hey, lady!" A man stuck his head out of
his car window and shouted at her over the
horns. "Why don't you blast that asshole up
there, give the resta us a fricking break?"

"Your weapon's showing," Roarke told
her, and she hitched the thin black jacket
back over it.

A quick scan and she spotted a couple of
uniforms coming out of the center. "Yo!" She
held up her badge. "Roust that delivery jerk

up there. He doesn't move along in one, slap him a ticket."

"You a fricking cop?" the man shouted.

"No, I just like carrying a fricking badge and a blaster. Lay off the horn." She turned back to Roarke, caught him grinning at her. "What?"

"You've got chocolate on your fricking badge, Lieutenant."

"Damn it." She'd nearly wiped it on her trousers before he snatched it out of her hand, used the last of the napkins. "Lift up your chin," he ordered.

"What? Is it on my face?"

"No." He leaned in—the perfect angle—and kissed her. "I just wanted to do that."

"Smart guy. Give me back my shield."

"It's back in your pocket."

She checked, shook her head. "Go use those fast fingers of yours to get me some data. I'm going to go grab Peabody and head to Child Services."

"I'll just see if McNab's ready to go."

"You brought them in the limo, didn't you?" she asked as they walked back.

"Yes, why?"

"You're spoiling my team." She turned toward the door just as Whitney came out.

"Lieutenant, Roarke. I thought you'd left."

"We were about to, Commander, as soon as I round up my team."

"Leave that to Roarke. Walk back to Central with me."

"Yes, sir. Tell Peabody to meet me at Central," Eve told Roarke. She took a step, stopped. "Tell her to walk," she added. "I don't want you dropping her off in the limo."

"As you like, Lieutenant." Roarke skimmed a finger over the dent in her chin. "I'll see you at home. Jack." He nodded at Whitney, then went inside.

"From the looks at this traffic, he wouldn't get a vehicle near Central for the next thirty minutes."

"He'd find a way," Eve replied, "and it makes a damn spectacle."

"I prefer walking when I can manage it," Whitney said as they started down the sidewalk. "You spent some time speaking with Halloway's mother, alone."

"She's got a lot of spine."

"Yes, she does. I believe you also spoke with the mayor."

"Yes, sir."

"He's understandably concerned about this situation."

"I think it's fair to say we're all understandably concerned about this situation."

"Our concerns may demonstrate themselves differently. You also spoke with Chang and the deputy mayor."

"We had words."

Whitney looked over at her. "You had words with a number of people today."

"Yes, sir. I believe the statement I gave Nadine Furst in response to the release by Purity was appropriate. It was also factual. Detective Halloway and his family deserve more than to have him used as a tool by terrorists to spread their message. The job owes him more than that."

"I'm very aware of what the job owes, Lieutenant." He stopped at the crosswalk with a crowd of other pedestrians waiting for the light. "As it happens, I found nothing inappropriate about your statement, nor does the chief. The mayor's office is less satisfied, but Chang is already working to maximize the effect in our favor. It matters," Whitney said, though she hadn't spoken. Hadn't intended to.

The crowd started the surge seconds before the light changed. Both Eve and Whitney moved through it, picking up the pace to break clear.

"I could waste our time giving you the standard lines about politics, media relations, public relations, image and perception, and the often tricky dynamics between the NYPSD and the mayor's office."

Whitney flipped credits out of his pocket and into a beggar's cup without breaking stride. "But I won't. You're aware of all of this already, just as I'm aware you're not particularly concerned with any of that. I will say it will be helpful and it will be simpler for all involved if you cooperated with Chang as much as possible. When it doesn't impede or interfere with your investigation."

"Yes, sir."

"As to the matter of your interview with Donald and Sylvia Dukes this morning."

"It wasn't an interview, Commander, but a few informal questions in their home, and with their permission."

"You can play the semantics game when it suits you. Whatever term used, the files on Devin Dukes were sealed, and remain so at this time."

"Data isn't always accessed through files, sir."

"Yes, you can play the game. Are you willing to divulge your source?"

"No, sir, nor am I required to under Departmental Code 12, Article—"

"Don't quote departmental codes at me, Dallas." He continued to walk easily, despite the pressing heat. But his tone took on an edge. "If it comes to a civil trial, both you and those codes will be tested."

"It won't. Not only will the issue be moot when I charge Donald Dukes with conspiracy to commit, but he's going to need to pool all his legal resources for his defense."

"He's part of it?"

"He's up to his neck."

"The mother?"

Eve shook her head. "I don't think so. She's too passive. I'm doing a background to try to determine how skilled a programmer Duke might be. Regardless, I believe him to be a key player. He wouldn't settle for less. I could break him in Interview. He's angry and he's arrogant, and he needs to be right. He doesn't like women in authority, either, so that'll push. Likes them in their proper place," she continued, half to herself. "Wife's all shined up like a show dog, wearing an apron. Lip dye and earrings at nine in the morning."

"My wife puts on her makeup before breakfast."

"Weird. But nobody intimidates Mrs. Whitney. Nobody pushes her around." Eve caught herself, winced. "No disrespect intended, Commander."

"None taken."

"I need a few more threads to tie Dukes, then I can bring him in."

"Find the threads, and make them strong ones."

"I think he's maintained a relationship with the social worker and the cop who were on his son's case. And I think they're involved. I tie any one of them, I'll tie them all."

They streamed through another intersection, turned west.

"Make sure of it. A mistake will blow this up in our faces and you'll take the brunt of that. On another matter, it was good to see McNab on his feet."

"Yes, sir, very good."

"He looks a little shaky yet."

"I'm keeping his workload light, and Peabody's . . ." She clammed up, redirected. Must be something about walking outside like a couple of tourists that loosened her tongue, she decided. "Peabody's taking up the slack."

"Do you think I'm unaware of the relationship between the EDD detective and your aide, Lieutenant?"

Eve stared straight ahead. "I don't like to talk about it. It makes me twitchy."

"Excuse me?"

"Literally. I get this tic right under my eye every time . . . Never mind. Both Detective McNab and Officer Peabody fulfill their duties in an exemplary fashion. I plan to submit Peabody's name for consideration for promotion to Detective First Grade."

"How many years does she have in?"

"Almost three, and over a year of that in Homicide. Her work and her record warrant the consideration, sir. If you could find time to look at her files, and my evaluations, and if you agree with my recommendation, she could start preparing for the test."

"I'll let you know. Can you spare McNab for an hour, maybe two, this afternoon?"

"Yes, sir, if necessary."

"Then I'm pulling him. He'll do a one-on-one with Furst, in studio, in response to the statements issued this morning."

"Sir, that doesn't go down easy. Putting him on display after his injuries? On the day of Halloway's memorial?"

"This is what's known as compromise, Lieutenant." His tone remained mild, a dash of ice water on the heat of hers. "Power and authority demand compromise. Do you doubt he can handle it? More, do you doubt he'll stand for Halloway?"

"No, sir, I don't doubt it."

"You don't like him being used as a symbol." Whitney moved to the entrance of Cop Central. "But that's what he is. And, Lieutenant, so are you."

Inside, he looked around the enormous lobby with its many data stations, animated locator maps. At the cops, at the victims, at the guilty.

"And so," he said, "is this. This stands for law and order, and it's on display. It is, very simply, on trial due to the manipulations and maneuvers of a group of terrorists. It's more than closing your case. It's winning the verdict. Find the threads. If you're going to take down the father of a dead teenager, be sure you tie them tight."

• • •

She decided to tie other threads by taking the time to write an official report on her morning activities. But when she walked into her office, Don Webster was at her desk.

"I keep finding IAB in my chair, I'm going to have to have it replaced."

"Close the door, Dallas."

"I've got a report to write, then I have to get out in the field."

He got up, closed the door himself. "We'll make this quick. I have to record this conversation."

"What's this conversation, and why do you have to record it?"

"It's in regards to your access of data contained in sealeds. Take a minute to think," he said before she could speak. "Take a minute to think before the recorder goes on."

"I don't need a minute. Turn it on and get this over with. I have a few pesky murders to solve while you're filing your internals."

"This is SOP. You know it. You had to know this was coming."

"To tell you the truth, I didn't think of it." And she'd kick herself for that later. "Had a few things on my mind today."

"Have a seat."

"I'm not required to sit."

"Okay, fine." He turned on his recorder. "Webster, Lieutenant, Donald, attached Internal Affairs Bureau in interview with Dallas, Lieutenant Eve, Homicide, Cop Central, regarding the matter of Dukes, Donald, Sylvia, and minor son Devin, deceased. Lieutenant Dallas, do you wish to engage your departmental representative, or any outside legal representation for this interview?"

"No."

"Did you, in your official capacity, visit the home of Donald and Sylvia Dukes"—he read off the address—"at approximately nine A.M. this morning?"

"Yes."

"Did you, at that time, question the aforementioned individuals regarding incidents that involved their deceased minor son, Devin Dukes?"

"Yes."

He lifted his eyebrows, but whether it was in annoyance or approval of her monosyllabic answers, she didn't know. Or care.

"Were you aware that the data regarding certain incidents pertaining to the minor on which you questioned the Dukes is in sealed files?"

She didn't bat an eyelash. "I was informed

of this by Mr. Dukes at his residence this morning."

"You were not aware previously that this data was protected by seal?"

"I deduced it was."

"How did you come by that deduction?"

"As I could find no open files with the aforesaid data in my search for information in the course of my investigation."

Webster's gaze stayed level with hers. "How did you obtain information on Devin Dukes?"

"Through an outside source."

"From what source did you obtain this protected information?"

"I'm not required to name a source utilized during an investigation, most specifically a priority investigation. This information is protected under Departmental Code Twelve, Article Eighty-Six B."

The monotone of his voice never changed. "You refuse to name your source?"

"Yes. Doing so would compromise the source and my investigation."

"Lieutenant Dallas, did you employ departmental equipment and/or sources to access sealed records?"

"I did not."

"Did you, Lieutenant Dallas, break the seal to Devin Dukes's files?"

"I did not."

"Did you order any member of the NYPSD to do so?"

"No."

"Did you coerce, bribe, threaten, or order any other individual to break the court's seal on these files?"

"No."

"Will you, should it be deemed necessary, submit to Truth Testing on this matter?"

"I will not voluntarily submit to Testing, but will do so if ordered by my superiors."

"Thank you for your cooperation, Lieutenant. Interview end. Record off. Good."

"Is that it?"

"For now. Can I have a hit of your coffee?"

She merely jerked a thumb at the AutoChef.

He walked over, programmed a cup. "If this goes to court, the truth angle would be smart. Would you pass it?"

"The interview's over, Webster. I've got work."

"Look, I snagged this interview duty because I'm trying to give you a hand. IAB doesn't follow through officially on something like this, it smells like coverup. Neither of us needs that."

Some of the anger she'd held in check during the questioning leaked through. "There's a coverup, Webster, but it has to do with Purity hiding files under official seals, doing the legal tango to keep them sealed as long as possible to try to stall or impair this investigation. I got around them, and they don't like it."

"You sniffing at any cops?" When she said nothing, merely sat and turned toward her computer, he kicked her desk. It was a gesture she understood, and had some respect for. "Is it so hard to believe I'm on your side in this?"

"No. But I don't toss cops to IAB. At least not until I'm sure. If I find any who're part of this, I'll carry them to you on my back. But not until I know, without a shadow, they're dirty."

He sipped coffee. She could literally see him using it to calm himself down, smooth out the edges. "If you've got names, I could look into it unofficially."

She studied his profile. He would, she decided. "I believe you, and I appreciate it. But

I've got some angles to work first. If I hit a wall and think you can help, I'll tag you. Are you done with Trueheart?"

"Yeah, he's cleared for duty. Kid didn't deserve to take this spin through the wringer."

"As long as he came out the other side. I've got work, Webster."

He started for the door. "If there are cops in this, I want them."

"Get in line," she answered, then made her first call.

While she waited for a response, she drafted out her report, referring back to her own record to be sure she didn't leave out even the smallest detail.

She refined it, logged it, and transmitted the appropriate copies. When she got clearance, she contacted Trueheart.

"I need a uniform," she said briskly. "Grunt and drone work. Report to Detective Baxter, my home office."

"Sir, I'm assigned to dispatch duty until further notice."

"This is your further notice. I've cleared it. My home office, Officer, ASAP."

"Yes, sir. Thank you, sir."

"See if you thank me after you put in a few hours with Baxter."

She broke transmission then went out to scoop up Peabody.

"Peabody, you're with me."

"Sir." It was all Peabody said until they were in Eve's vehicle. "I didn't want to mention anything inside the building, just in case. Baxter passed some info to me for you. About Detective Sergeant Dwier."

"What he get?"

"He struck up some conversations at the memorial. Place was full of cops, and some of them were from the One-Six. He worked it around to Dwier, and it turned out one of the guys there is in his squad. Seems that Dwier went through a rough patch a few years back. Divorce. Wife moved to Atlanta with his kid, so he doesn't get to see his boy as much as he'd like. He was pretty flattened by it according to this source. But not long after, he met somebody—met her through the job. He's been seeing her regularly, and the last year or so, it seems to be heating up. She works in Child Services."

"Some days, it falls right in your lap."

It was time to visit Clarissa Price.

She'd barely cleared the garage when she got the call.

Absolute Purity had been achieved.

• • •

The new homicide delayed her so that she arrived at Child Services minutes before the doors shut for the day. She bullied her way past the receptionist and strode straight into Clarissa Price's office.

There was blood on Eve's trousers. It barely showed against the black, but she could still smell it.

"I'm sorry, Lieutenant, I can't make time for you." Neat and pretty, Price sat at her desk. Deliberately, she shielded the data on her screen, glanced at her wrist unit. "I have to finish this report, then I have a late appointment."

"You'll make time."

Price's lips firmed, and she folded her hands. "Lieutenant, you've already broken faith by intruding on the Dukes family this morning, and setting a cycle in motion that will bring more grief, and almost certainly litigation, which may involve this facility and me. The very last thing I'm inclined to do is make time for you, or to tolerate you bursting into my office at the end of a very trying day."

"Breaking faith? Is that what you call it?" Eve planted her palms on the desk, leaned in. "And what do you call what Purity's doing? Keeping the faith? I've just come from another of their executions, Ms. Price. The name Nick Greene ring a bell with you? Maybe you heard about him in the course of one of your trying days. Dealt in illegals, porn vids, sex brokering, party favors that aren't in what you'd call the mainstream. A client wanted it, Nick provided. Some of those clients' taste ran to minors. Most of us wouldn't call Nick Greene a real swell guy, but I can guarantee he had a couple of trying days himself just lately."

"If that's your way of telling me someone else has died, that's no business of this office. And if this person has ever come up in the course of the duties performed by Child Services, until I'm served with the proper papers, I can neither confirm nor deny."

"Sooner or later, I'm going to roll over whoever's blocking the warrants. That's a promise. Here's another name that might ring a bell with you. Hannah Wade. Sixteen-year-old mixed race female. Recurrent runaway. Parents gave up the last time she took a walk. My information is she'd been on the street this time about three months. Did some unlicensed hooking, petty dealing, petty theft. Hannah's been in trouble on and off since she was twelve. But she's not going to cause any trouble now. She's dead."

Eve pulled three fresh still photos out of her evidence bag, tossed them on the desk. "She was a lovely girl, according to her ID photo, according to witnesses who'd seen her. Can't tell by these, can you? Nobody looks lovely after they've been stabbed fifty, sixty times."

Her face sickly white, Price shoved at the photos. "I don't know her. You've got no right—"

"Tough looking at the results, isn't it? Not so fucking pure when you look it in the face. I just waded through her blood. That's tough, too. There's a lot of blood in a teen-aged girl, Clarissa. A lot of blood to splash and splatter while she tries to run away from a guy with a knife whose brain's trying to burst out of his skull. A lot of blood to pour and pool when she falls because she can't get away from him."

"She . . . Greene did this to her?"

"No. Purity did this to her." Eve shoved the photos closer to Price. "Take a good look at what they did to her. Their research obviously didn't clue in that she'd shacked with

Greene the last week or two. It didn't identify
a teenaged runaway who was flopping at his
place. Sleeping in his bed while the infection
started to cook in his brain. Maybe in hers,
too. Autopsy will check for that."

"I don't believe you. I want you to leave."

"Nothing's pure, Price, don't you get it?
Nothing comes in or goes out of the world
without a blemish. No system's foolproof.
Only when this one fails, innocent people
die. She was a child. You were supposed to
protect her. But you can't protect them all.
Nobody can protect them all.

"Was it your idea?" Eve asked. "Or were
you recruited? Who's in charge of Purity?"

"I don't have to talk to you." Price was
white around the lips now, and her voice far
from steady. "I don't want to talk to you."

"Dukes helped create the virus. Who
else? Did Dwier pull you into it, or did you
pull him?"

Price shoved back from her desk, pushed
to her feet. Eve could see her hands were
trembling. "Get out."

"I'm bringing this down, and you'll go under with it. You and Dwier. Who the hell do
you think you are? Standing in judgment,
executing by remote control. Then brushing

off the bystanders' deaths as victims of the blight on society. You're the fucking blight, Clarissa. All of you self-righteous, self-appointed guardians."

Eve snatched up Hannah Wade's death photos. "You killed this child. And you'll pay for it."

"I'm—I'm calling a lawyer." But tears were swimming in her eyes, gathering in the corners, ready to spill. "This is harassment."

"You call this harassment?" There was no humor in Eve's smile. It sliced like a thin-bladed axe. "Don't get me started. You've got twenty-four hours to turn yourself in. You come in, you turn evidence, and I'll push for an on planet rehabilitation facility. I come after you in twenty-four hours and one minute, you go into a concrete cage off planet. You'll never see real daylight again."

Eve looked at the time. "Five-twelve tomorrow. Not a minute more."

Chapter 17

Eve knew she'd shaken Clarissa Price, and shaken her hard. She also knew Price wouldn't be calling any lawyer unless he was Purity approved. But she would call Dwier.

She'd seen the horror on Price's face when Price had looked at the crime scene photos of Hannah Wade. There had been shock and disbelief along with it, but it was the horror that would continue to surface. That would eat at Price until she woke screaming in the night.

To keep herself from doing the same, Eve knew she had to do what came next, take the next steps. Focus on the work. That's what she told herself when she pinned the latest photos to the case board in her office.

She couldn't allow her own horror to surface again, to have it slam into her belly as it had when she'd stepped into Greene's Park Avenue condo. The horror that had taken her back, for an instant, to a small, freezing room in Dallas, where the blood had reeked and the knife, covered with it, was clutched in her hand.

Roarke came in, closed the door. Locked it.

"I need the whole team in here, except for Jamie, to update them on the latest homicides."

"In a minute." He crossed to her, took her shoulders, turned her to face him. Her eyes were shadowed. Some was fatigue, he knew. But most of it was the nightmare.

"I can see it in you." He pressed his lips to her brow. "The pain from it."

"It's not getting in my way."

"No, can't have that, can we? Hold on for a minute, Eve. Just for a minute."

His arms were already around her, and now hers wrapped around him in turn. "It wasn't the same. It wasn't anything like the same. But . . . it shoved me back. It shoved me right back there. I stood there, looking down at her, at him. I was so cold. I've seen that kind of thing before, and he hasn't pushed me back there."

"This was a girl. A young girl."

"Older than I was. Twice as old as I was. She could have been me." She let out a long breath after she said it. "That's what I thought when I stood there. When I stood over her. If I hadn't killed him first. If I hadn't gotten away from him, she could've been me."

Steadier, she turned her head on his shoulder, looked back at the board with clear eyes. "Do you see what they did to her?"

As much as he'd seen, as much as he'd done in his life, the image of Hannah Wade still made his blood run cold.

The girl had been hacked to pieces. The shirt and shorts she'd been wearing were in tatters, and soaked red with her own blood.

"You can," he said quietly. "You see it time and time again, and no matter how often you do, it still matters. That's what makes you."

"I need to do this now." Take the step, she thought. Do the work. "I want Jamie kept busy somewhere. He's not going to see this. I'll take the stills of her down between briefings."

"I'll send him off to the pool or the game room, have Summerset monitor him to make sure he stays well away from here until you're done."

She nodded, stepped back. "One thing. Did I coerce, bribe, or threaten you into opening sealed files?"

"No. You asked, with some reluctance and teeth gnashing."

She nearly managed a smile. "Except for the teeth gnashing, that's how I saw it. If 'requested' had been on the list, I still would've said no in the IAB query. I'd've lied. I don't like knowing that, but I can live with it."

She looked back at Hannah Wade's photo. "Yeah, I can live with it."

When her team was assembled she ran the details for them.

"Nick Greene provided services. His employment is listed as an entertainment consultant. While he did have some straight clientele, the bulk of it ran below the surface. Illegals, vids that push code as they tend to involve minors, authentic violence, and bes-

tiality. He also provided unlicensed companions, either sex, for those looking for a little
more than the law allows or who just like the
thrill of breaking it. He's got a sheet, which
indicates he often auditioned these companions personally.

"He'd been picked up for questioning a total of eight times, but never charged. His
business apparently paid well. His digs were
Park Avenue smooth."

"Is he linked to Price or Dwier?" Baxter
asked.

"I don't find their names on any of the
data. I have no doubt he was known to Child
Services. Of the eight times he was hauled
in for questioning, two involved complaints
involving a minor. One of those complaints
is sealed. And under that seal we'll find one
or more members of Purity."

"Lieutenant." Trueheart raised his hand
like a kid at a school desk. "Isn't it possible
Greene was infected because of what he
was alone, without any other connection to
the group?"

"It's too early for them to target that way.
The first wave involves personal agendas."

"Gotta be," Feeney agreed. "You start up
a group like this, people are risking a hell of

a lot. Most aren't going to do it just on a principle. They need some payback first. Have to have incentive for the rank and file. You'll have some raving fanatics, too. Sociopaths who just like the idea of taking somebody out without getting bloody."

"Disciples," Roarke continued, "eager to follow the path. Frustrated cops, city officials, social workers, and the like who've seen the guilty walk away free once too often. And some, I'd think, who are simply intrigued, intellectually, at the idea of this sort of man-made selection."

"They've got their first wave in place." Eve gestured to the board. "Working quickly. My opinion is they've infected or set to infect their entire first wave by this time. Give their membership bulk gratification, quick and multiple successes, and keep the media hot on the story. Focusing on targets who have, in some way, victimized children is very deliberate. Even cops have a different attitude when the victims are children."

She looked at the board again.

"According to statements from the knock-on-doors, Hannah Wade was first seen in the building ten days ago. It's possible she was there longer as her parents haven't seen or heard from her in three months. They didn't bother filing a police or CS report on her this time. She was a habitual runaway. McNab, you'll review the building's security discs and pin down the exact date she took up residence with Greene."

"On that."

"I want to know how often she came and went, and who else visited Greene in the last two weeks. We have a list of her known associates from her parents. Peabody and I will run those. Baxter, see if any of the cops of record who questioned Greene will reach out. Feeney, Roarke, and the kid will continue to work to extract data from the units we've impounded."

"We're eking it out," Feeney told her. "We should have enough to dupe the virus in another eight, ten man-hours."

"Keep me up on that. The Green/Wade hit follows the basic pattern. Greene was holed up in his place for the last five days. Building has live doormen on eight to midnight, in three shifts. Droid handles the graveyard. None of them saw Greene come or go in that space of time. Statements indicate this was unusual for him. He generally went out most days, and at least five nights out of seven. Third shift man verifies Greene brought a girl matching Wade's description home with him ten days ago, and that she appeared to come and go freely from that time. No one recalls seeing her exit or enter yesterday."

She turned. "Crime scene record, screen one."

The image that popped on was stark and grisly. The white-on-white living area was splashed with blood. Broken glass sparkled in thin rivers of it that had snaked and spurted their way over carpet. Overturned tables, a smashed entertainment screen, lush tropical plants that had provided a con-trast to the white but were now uprooted set the stage for the girl's body.

She had been flung facedown, arms and legs spread. Her hair was long and curly and had once been blonde with sapphire high-lights. Some of that gold and blue still showed through the matted blood.

Eve heard her own voice detailing the scene, saw herself step into view, and crouch by the body.

"You can see the illegals scattered over the rug. What appears to have been a hos-pitality bowl was found, broken, in this living area. Traces of substances identified as Jazz and Erotica were still in the damaged bowl. Switch to bedroom record."

The disc shifted, showed a large, sun-washed room done in blacks and reds. The sheets on the bed were torn off. The desk unit's monitor faced the recorder, and read:

ABSOLUTE PURITY ACHIEVED

"A smaller bowl, undamaged, can be seen here on the dresser. Various illegal sub-stances are still in it, and others are on the floor. It appears Greene continued to use while the symptoms of the infection mani-fested. There were traces of blood on the sheets, probably from a nosebleed, and traces of semen indicating he was capable of masturbating or engaging in sexual rela-tions with Wade prior to death. Autopsy will tell us which. Wade's body showed no evi-dence of recent sexual activity."

"Where the hell is he?" Baxter asked.

"We'll get there. Reconstruct tells me, he probably spent some time closed up in the bedroom, popping illegals, jerking off, while in the last hours, Wade entertained herself in the living area. Ate junk food, got buzzed, watched some screen. Greene wouldn't have been good company, but hanging in a Park Avenue condo with easy access to illegals, plenty of food, lots of alcohol, was a better deal than picking up a few tricks on the street, maybe getting busted. She'd tough it out until he came around."

Trueheart raised his hands again. Baxter simply kicked him lightly, shook his head. "Uh-uh," he whispered. "She's in the zone."

"Eight transmissions came in during the last three days. Neither of them answered. They were all for Greene. She wouldn't be interested in playing his admin. At some point this afternoon, she gets up. Maybe she wants to go out, look for some action. Maybe she goes to the bedroom, but he's locked the door. Asshole. Her clothes are in there. How she's supposed to go out if she can't get her clothes, slick up some? She wants him to open the door, open the goddamn door, but he doesn't. She kicks at it, bruises her toes. Pisses her off. Bumps it a couple times with her left hip, bruises that some, too. Fuck him."

She could see it, almost feel the girl's edgy frustration. All buzzed up and nowhere to go. "She heads into the kitchen, looking

for something sweet. You get a sweet attack
with Jazz. Gets herself some ice cream, and
feeling put out, writes ASSHOLE on the
counter in chocolate sauce.

"She turns around, and there he is. He
looks bad, really bad. His nose is bleeding,
his eyes are red. His breath is horrible, and
the rest of him smells like a sewer. Doesn't
look like he's changed out of his underwear
in days. If he thinks she's going to do him
now, he is so wrong."

She brought the kitchen of the condo back
into her head. White and silver and red from
the blood. "She says something, something
a teenager thinks is clever and cutting. He
hits her, hits a good one across the face.
Knocks her back so she bangs her head on
the AutoChef, drops her bowl of ice cream.
It hurts. She hit her head hard enough to
break the skin, enough to leave some skin
and hair on the door of the AutoChef. It blurs
her vision for a second and scares her. But
not as much as seeing Greene take the
knife, the big silver knife, out of the block.

"He slashes at her. She throws her hands
up, and the knife slices across both her
palms. She tries to run, and the blood from
her hands splatters on the white wall. Then

from her shoulder, probably her shoulder as he swipes at her again. He doesn't hack. No down strokes in that room. Just those long, sweeping slashes. Left to right, right to left.

"She's screaming, begging, crying, trying to run. Get away. But those swipes keep catching her. The back, the buttocks, the shoulders again. Through the dining alcove. He opens her up good there, hits an artery and the blood starts spurting. She's dead then. She doesn't know it. She still thinks she can get away. She makes it to the living area before she goes down on that white rug. Crawls a few inches. Then he starts hacking."

"Jesus," McNab said softly, prayerlike.

"He doesn't know who she is, doesn't care." Eve's face was stone-cold as she stared at the screen. "She's stopped screaming, but his head won't. He throws the goodie bowl, smashes the screen, shoves at tables, stabs the sofa a few times. He has to stop the pain. He goes back in the bedroom, but he can't stand it. He shoves open the terrace doors. He's still got the knife, and he looks like he's been painted red. He screams, and screams. At the air traffic, at the street below, at his neighbor who comes out on her terrace two apartments down. She runs back in, locks herself in, and calls the cops. By then it's all over. Bedroom terrace view," she ordered.

He was lying on his back, and looked like a man who'd been swimming in a river of blood.

He'd plunged the knife into his own heart.

"Got your timing."

Wanting to stay with the action in the lab, McNab set up in a corner. He liked listening to the familiar language of compu-jocks as Feeney and Jamie debated the next level, or when Roarke weighed in with an opinion.

They were close, he knew they were right on the verge of duplicating the virus. Once they had it, they could fight it.

Eve walked over to him. She wasn't sure why she'd come into the lab—the last place she was needed. Unless it was to get away from her own thoughts.

"Here's our girl," he continued, taping the image on-screen. "Coming in with Greene. Doorman had it. She doesn't show before this time and date. Perv rubs her ass as they walk in. He's old enough to be her father."

"She walked in of her own free will." Eve

studied the girl's face. The suggestive smirk, the glittering eyes. Oh yeah, she thought. Figured you knew the score. You didn't know a damn thing.

"Yeah, well, doesn't make him less a perv. She pops in and out. Never see her before noon. When she makes the daylight appearances, she's back before nightfall. Usually has a couple bags with her. High-end stores. He must foot the bill for the shopping. She's thinking she's got a good thing going."

"Hmm. They go out together."

"Yeah." He zipped through the disc. "Jumped up for a night out. Look half-buzzed already, all duded out. Up till the six days prior to implosion, they went out every night. We got three visitors during the time frame, all male."

He keyed in to the view outside Greene's condo. "This first one goes in, stays sixteen minutes. Bet the contents of his briefcase switched during that little social call."

"Time to test the merchandise and count the money," Eve agreed. "Do we know if Illegals was tracking this guy?"

"Don't. Can." Unconsciously, McNab flexed his fingers, working on the tingle that hadn't quite faded. "I got some contacts there. Far as I can tell, the perv skimmed the line, kept legitimate business avenues open, didn't deal too heavy."

"Second visitor?"

"Different deal. Stayed ninety-eight minutes. No bag."

Eve studied the second man entering, exiting. "Sex," she said flatly. "What about the third?"

"Forty-minute stay, carried a disc bag in and out. Likes his sex on vids, I guess."

"I know this guy. I know him. Tripps. Deals bootlegged vids. Has a few runners on the street. Yeah, I know him. I'll tap him if I need to, see if he can draw me a picture. Run the other faces for ID in case we need them."

Eve saw him massaging his right thigh as he set up for the search. "No, not now. Morning's soon enough. Pack it in for the night. Why don't you and Peabody go use the pool or something? Or just get out for a while."

"Yeah? Taking pity on the recovering crip?"

"Grab it while you can, pal. It won't last."

He grinned. "I wouldn't mind a little club action. Some music. Not up to dancing yet.

You know what would really do it? Virtual club scene. If we could use the holoroom."

"If you're going to program in some perverted sexual fantasy, I don't want to hear about it."

"Mum's the word."

She went back to her own office and spent the next hour dissecting Nick Greene's life.

College man, a business major who'd started picking up trouble in his teens. Minor possession fines, criminal trespass, bootlegging vids. Always the entrepreneur, she thought.

It had paid off for a while. Classy Park Avenue digs, closet full of snazzy designer duds.

She frowned as she continued through his financials. He'd garaged two high-end vehicles, and had kept a third, and a watercraft, stored at his weekend place in the Hamptons. He had art and jewelry insured in excess of three million.

"Doesn't add up."

She went to the 'link and beeped Roarke. "I need you to look at something in my office."

He came in, looking mildly irritated. "If you

want the job done, Lieutenant, you have to let me do it."

"I need your expert opinion on something else. Look at these assets, reported income, debits. Give me your take."

She had the numbers on-screen, and paced the office while Roarke studied them.

"Obviously someone didn't report all their income. That's shocking."

"Ditch the sarcasm. How much in excess of this could you make from a mid-level illegals business, running a few unlicensed whores, dealing some porn vids, a little sex brokering?"

"I've decided to be flattered rather than insulted that you assumed I'd know of such matters. Depends, of course, on the overhead. You'd have to buy or cook the illegals before you could sell them, outfit and maintain the prostitutes, generate the vids. Then there's the outlay for bribes, security, employees. If you were good at it, had a steady clientele, you'd pull in two or three million in profit."

"Still doesn't add up. He kept it small, exclusive. You don't get busted as hard or as often if you keep it low profile. So say you add the three million to what he reported last year. That keeps him under five million. You could live real comfortable on that."

"Some could. Are we done now?"

"No. You've got five million to play with. Look at his clothing expenditures last year."

Stifling impatience, Roarke scanned the data she shot on-screen. "So he wasn't a snappy dresser."

"But he was. Closet full of designer labels. Had to have a hundred pairs of shoes. Since I live with someone with the same baffling addiction, I can recognize the pricey stuff. There was an easy million in the closet. Probably more."

"He prefers paying cash then," Roarke said, but he was becoming interested despite himself.

"Okay, subtract a million from the five. He has art and baubles insured for over three."

"One rarely buys all their baubles in a single year."

"Yeah, but there're appraisals for over three-quarters of a million last year. No debit entries. Cash again. Subtract another seventy-five. Vid equipment, insured for one point five mil. Two new cams on the list last year to the tune of half a mil. Two garaged vehicles in the city. Annual for that's what, two, three thousand a month, each. One's a XR-7000Z, new last September. What do they run?"

"Ah . . . two hundred K, if he got it loaded."

"Three-bedroom condo on Park. Annual's about the same as the car, right?"

He was doing the math in his head. "Close enough."

"Then you add a five-bedroom beach house in the Hamptons, the slip fee for his watercraft. What's that?"

"Run him near a million."

"Okay. You add in he goes out dining and debauchering almost nightly. Basic living ex- penses over that. What do you get?"

"Either I'm well off on the estimate of his business profit, or he had another source of income."

"Another source." She hitched a hip onto her desk. "Follow me here. You got an un- derground business that caters to fairly ex- clusive clientele. Some of whom might blush if their little hobby came out in the light. You've got expensive taste, and your busi- ness does pretty good, but hell, you want better. What do you do?"

"Blackmail."

"And we have a winner."

"All right, so he ran a shakedown on the side. A profitable one by all accounts. What does that have to do with the matter at hand?"

"The matter at hand is homicide. It's a Purity hit, and it's connected, but you still run it by the numbers. He might have kept his blackmail data in a safebox. If he did, he'd keep it close to home. Easy access. We can check the banks and depositories. But, maybe he kept them even closer to home. I'm going to go check out his place again."

"Want company?"

"Two could toss it faster than one."

He thought she was wasting her time and his. But he supposed the cop in her needed to snip off any loose ends.

And he'd had no intention of letting her go back alone to a place that had taunted her nightmares.

He waited until she bypassed the police seal, uncoded the locks.

The air still carried death. It was the first thing that struck him when he stepped in beside her. The raw, pitiably human stench of it lingered under the odor of chemicals used by the crime scene team and sweepers.

Red stains, splatters, streams were a virulent horror over the white. Walls, carpet, furniture. He could see where the girl had fallen. Could see where she had crawled. Where she had died.

"Christ, how do you face it? How do you look at this and not break?"

"Because it's there whether you look or not. And if you break, you're done."

He touched her arm. He hadn't realized he'd spoken aloud. "Did you need to see this again? To face this again to prove you could?"

"Maybe. But if that was all, I'd've come on my own. Second bedroom and the office are over there. We went through the place thoroughly on the first sweep. But we weren't looking for a hidey-hole. Now we do."

She put Roarke in the second bedroom and started on the office herself. They'd taken the data and communication center away, had gone over the work area, through the closet where Greene had kept his extra supplies.

She did it all again, point by point. There was a safe. One of the crime scene techs had run his scanner over it, tagged the combination. She'd found nothing unexpected in

it. Some cash, disc documents, a little paperwork.

Not enough cash, she thought now. Not
nearly enough. If three clients had come by
in the last few days—at least two of them
when Greene's symptoms would have been
increasing—where was the payoff?

Would he have sent Wade out with cash
to tuck it into a safebox? She didn't think so.
You might bang a teenager, sell her off to
clients, but you didn't put cash in her hand
and wave bye-bye.

She took two paintings and a sculpture off
the wall, searched behind them for panels.

"Bedroom's clean," Roarke told her.

"He's got another safe. He's got a hole.
This is the logical place. The office is the
logical place."

"Maybe it's too logical. First place you
looked, isn't it?"

She stopped scooting along the base-
board and sat back on her heels. "Okay, if
this was your place, where's your stash?"

"If I liked combining business and pleasure, as it appeared he did, the master bedroom."

"Okay, let's try it."

She led the way, then stood in the door-way with him, scanning the room.

"Money doesn't always buy taste, does it, darling?" He shook his head at the black and red decor. "A bit obvious for a passion den."

He wandered to the closet, opened it. "Well, here at least he showed some level of class. Very nice fabrics."

"Yeah, and he died in his underwear. Just goes to show."

"Just what does the city do with this sort of thing?"

"The clothes? If he doesn't have family, heirs, that kind of thing, they're donated to shelters."

He pressed the button that had the first tier of suits revolving to reveal the second. "The sidewalk sleepers are going to be better dressed this year."

He moved the second tier aside, studied the wall of shoes to his right. Smiled. "Here you have it."

"Have what?"

"Give us a minute," he said, running his fingertips along shelves, under them. "Ah, here we are. Let's see."

He depressed a small lever. The lower third of the shelves swung slowly open. He crouched. "Here's your hidey-hole, Lieutenant. And your second safe."

She was already breathing down his neck. "Can you open it?"

"Would that be a rhetorical question?" he chuckled.

"Just open the damn thing."

He drew the jammer he'd taken from Jamie out of his pocket. "Well, this is why you're the cop and I'm not."

"Because you can pop a safe?"

"No. I could teach you to do it quick enough, even without this handy little toy. Because I thought you were wasting time coming back here tonight."

"You still think I'm wasting time."

"I suppose I do, but you've found your safe." The display on the jammer began to flash, numbers zipping by in a blur. Then a series of them locked on. The safe hummed once, then clicked.

"Abracadabra," Roarke stated, and opened it.

"Now that's more like it." Hunkered down beside him, Eve studied the neat stacks of cash. "This is how he stayed out of a cage so long. No credit, no e-transfers. Cash on the line. And a file box, loaded with discs and vids."

"Best of all." Roarke reached in, took out a PPC. "His personal palm, very likely un-infected and chock-full of interesting data."

"Let's load it up, get it in." She pulled out her memo book.

"What're you doing?"

"Logging the entry. I better not see any of that green stuff or those baubles go into your pockets, Ace."

"Now I'm offended." He straightened, brushed at his shirt. "If I nipped anything, you can bet your ass you wouldn't see me do it."

Chapter 18

Eve started running the discs as soon as she got back into her office. She set the ones labeled FINANCIALS and BOOKKEEPING aside. They could wait.

She passed the PPC onto Roarke to take to the lab for testing. In short order she found herself listening to what had been Greene's daily journal.

He mentioned clients, but always by initials or an obvious nickname. Lardbutt had made his monthly payment. G.G. had begged for another extension. He made entries on shopping, on the club scene, on sexual exploits. They were all recorded in a tone of disdainful humor and derision.

Greene had despised the people he'd served.

So he'd blackmailed them, Eve mused. Squeezing them until he'd eventually become them. Wealthy, bored, and perverted.

Brought home a nice piece of ass today, he noted on the day he'd hooked up with Hannah Wade. *I've been watching her for a few days. She hangs around the clubs, targets her mark, and talks him into getting her in. Straight up to a privacy room most times. When she's done, she cruises the club looking for action. I decided to give her some. I've got clients who'll pay top for a session with this little number. She knows the score. Figure I'll keep her up here a couple weeks, enjoy the fringe benefits, class her up some. Outfit her right, she could pass for about fourteen. H.C.'s been asking for some new young meat. I just brought home the cow.*

"Creep," Eve said aloud, and ran through the week's journal. She hit the next level two days after he'd brought Wade home.

Fucking headache. Fucking headache all day. Zoner barely touches it. Got meetings today. Can't miss. Told G.G. to come up with payment plus penalty by tomorrow or her loving husband's going to get a delivery. Wonder how he'll feel about seeing his wife do the nasty with a St. Bernard?

Assholes. She tries to screw me over, she'll be sorry.

There was more of the same over the next three days. Increasingly angry entries, full of vague threats, complaints, frustration. He talked about the headaches, and for the first time mentioned a nosebleed.

On the day before his death, the disc was full of weeping, of pounding as if he were beating a fist against the wall.

Trying to screw me over. Everybody's trying to screw me over. I'll kill them first. Kill them. Locked her out, locked the little bitch out. She thinks I don't know. Oh God, oh God, oh God, my head. She put something in my head! Can't let her see. Can't let anybody see. Stay inside. Safe inside. I gotta sleep. I gotta sleep. Make it go away! Lock it up. I have to lock everything up tight. She won't get what's mine. Little whore-bitch.

Eve filed the disc, walked into the kitchen for coffee. Then she just pulled open the terrace doors and breathed.

It was easy to see how Greene's infection had progressed. Paranoia, anger, fear. The symptoms had started shortly after he'd installed Wade in the condo, so he'd believed she was responsible for them.

In his sick way, he'd killed her in self-defense.

She got her coffee, went back to her desk to make notes. Then, though her head was buzzing with a combination of caffeine, fatigue, and stress, she started on the videos.

It was clear how Greene bumped his income up several brackets. The videos were not only technically well-done, but showed a strangely creative sense of theater.

If you liked your entertainment raw and perverse.

"Still at it?" Roarke walked in, headed straight into the kitchen without glancing at the screen. "Will you have some wine now?"

"Oh yeah. I could use a drink."

"I've sent the others on their way. You'll have your little nightcap here, Lieutenant, then I'm going to . . ."

He trailed off as he came back with two glasses of wine. What was playing on-screen had even his jaded eyes widening. "What is that? A small bear?"

"No, I think it's a really big dog. A St. Bernard."

He took a sip of wine, walked closer. "I believe you're right. Someone should report this activity to the Animal Rights League or whatever it is. Although . . . hmmm. He certainly seems to be enjoying himself if the size of his . . . Mother of God."

"Gimme that wine." She grabbed it, drank deep. "There's sick and there's sick. This one goes off the scale. I've got no term for it. You recognize the woman romping with Fido?"

"It's a bit hard to tell, under the circumstances."

"Greene lists her as G.G. I ran an image search on her while she was rubbing butter all over herself to help get Fido in the game. Gretta Gowan, wife of Jonah Gowan. That's Professor Jonah Gowan, of NYU. He's head of the Sociology Department. A staunch Conservative Party member and a Methodist deacon. Want to bet Clarissa Price took some of his classes?"

"Never bet against the house," Roarke declared, fascinated despite himself with the on-screen action.

"She recruited him into Purity, or he did her. I'd bet on that one. Anyway, Gretta there is the mother of two and—whoa, that is just nasty! Gretta chairs several committees, including the garden club, which would no doubt frown on her deep affection for canines."

"There's a log entry on the PPC—it's clean by the way—for G.G. Six thousand paid in six days before the murders."

"Fits with his journal. This vid wasn't done at his place," Eve said. "Some of the others I've viewed were. He used the second bedroom. They're tamer than this. Group sex with costumes, bondage, and role-playing. One used a teenaged girl. I ran her image, too. She popped as another runaway. Greene knew how to sniff them out. Copy disc, log to file."

Roarke let out a long breath. "How about we run a nice classic comedy to cleanse the palate?"

"I want to finish this tonight. At least get the IDs."

"For what purpose, Eve?"

"To know for one thing." She filed the disc,

selected another. "And second, to see if I find a link."

"Do you really think terrorists are killing all these people so they can get rid of a black-mailer?"

"No, but I think each one of the victims was carefully selected, and with Greene the blackmail was part of it. Maybe just a bonus, but part of it. Run disc. You don't have to stay for this."

"If you can stomach it, I can."

"Home again," Eve said, recognizing the bedroom in Greene's condo. "My guess is he rigged the cameras before the client came in, ran them by remote until the ses-sion was over. Did the editing, made a copy. Gives that to the client with a demand for payments. Probably lost clients that way, but he kept the income. No overhead at all. Just pure profit. Here we go, curtain up."

A woman stepped in from the adjoining bath. A rather elegant woman in a killer black dress with long, lush waves of icy blonde hair spilling over the shoulders. Her legs were sheathed in black hose, her feet tucked into mile-high heels.

She wore a diamond choker, and her lips were bloody-murder red.

"Looks familiar," Eve began. "Which is she? Client or hooker?"

"Want an image search?"

"Let it run awhile first."

A man stepped in from the outer door. He was stripped to the waist, bulging in tight black leather. His chest gleamed with oil. His hair was slicked back from a striking face sharp of bone. There was a tattoo under his left nipple. When Eve froze and enhanced the image, she saw it was a tiny skull.

He ran a slim riding crop through his fingers.

"Roseanna." He spoke the name, and the woman lifted a hand to the diamond choker at her throat.

"How did you get in?"

"Role-playing," Eve said. "We run a search on both of them." She froze the disc again, blocked faces, started the task.

"Eve?"

"Hmm?"

"Take a good look at her."

"I am. I know that face. Continue disc play."

With a half-smile on his face, Roarke

leaned against the desk. "Take a better look."

Frowning, Eve watched the scene play out. The man ran the riding crop down the woman's center. She shuddered. She turned as if to run. He dragged her back. Long, sloppy kiss. Lots of hands.

Hands.

Eve straightened with a snap. "That's not a woman."

Distracted, Eve watched the bare-chested man yank the dress down to the blonde's waist. Beneath was a black lace waist cincher. Though the breasts that spilled over it were full and lush, Eve had no doubt they were just another part of the costume.

The man dealt a couple of sharp slaps to the buttocks when his partner struggled.

There was moaning now, breathy protests. The dress spilled to the floor.

"Looks pretty good for a guy," Eve observed. The legs were slim, set off with thigh-high black hose, old-fashioned garters. Too much shoulder though, she mused, and the hands were too big. She could see the hint of an Adam's apple beneath the glittering choker.

In her mind she erased the wig, the red

lips, the heavily accented eyes, and tried to see beneath the female artifice. She *knew* that face.

And when it filled the screen, flushed with excitement as the camera zoomed it, she heard the click.

"Oh good God."

"Did you make him? I'm not quite there yet. Give me another minute." But when the bare-chested man pushed his captive down to the knees, exposed himself, Roarke winced. "Never mind, as I'd soon skip this part. It doesn't—ah well."

He blew out a breath as the face filled the screen again, another angle as the eyes, crystal blue, stared up—full of hunger.

"Yes, indeed, I'd as soon skip watching his honor the mayor give leather boy a blow job."

He turned away from the screen, caught Eve's chin in his hand. "That's why you're the cop, all right. You weren't wasting anyone's time. That'll teach me to doubt you."

"I have to watch the rest of it."

"Must you?"

"I take this in tomorrow, I have to know what I'm dealing with. This isn't your average transvestite. This tosses Peachtree right into the middle of a sex scandal, and a major homicide investigation."

"Then I'm getting another drink." He took her glass. "For both of us."

"Smart," she said later. "Greene caters to a small clientele—rich with whacked whims. Out of that exclusive club, he handpicks a smaller group. A handful of people who've used his services, built a certain level of trust in him, who can't afford even a whiff of scandal. The payments are high, but none of them too high for these select few to afford. You got an even dozen paying out an average fee of twenty-five thousand a month, you rake in . . ."

"An extra three million six annually. Nobody's squeezed so hard they'll pop, and you live in luxury."

"And from what I can tell from his records, most he was blackmailing continued as clients."

"The devil you know," Roarke decided. "Are you putting the mayor in Purity?"

"I don't know. But I've sure got enough to ask him about it, don't I?"

"You'll be putting your hand in the fire, Lieutenant."

"Yeah, I got that, too." She pinched the bridge of her nose to relieve the pressure of a building headache. "Has to be on a need-to-know. Media gets a whiff of the scent, it's a disaster. Shit, I voted for the guy."

"He might've gotten more votes yet if he'd campaigned in that little black dress. Very attractive." Roarke only grinned when she stared at him. "I'd say it's time for bed. We're tired."

"You start talking about guys in black dresses looking pretty, you're more than tired, pal."

"I said attractive," he corrected. "And I meant the dress. I wouldn't mind seeing you in one of those corsets, with spiked heels and little garters."

"Yeah." She yawned as they rode to the bedroom. "You hold your breath on that one."

She was in bed in five minutes, asleep in ten.

When the dream started, she didn't know.

A white room, washed with blood. She could see herself walking through it, her boots splashed with red as she stepped in grisly puddles.

Even in sleep she could smell it.

The girl was facedown on white carpet thick with red blood. Her arm was stretched out, fingers spread as if she reached for something.

But nothing was there.

The knife was there.

In the dream she crouched down, picked up the knife by the hilt.

She felt the slick warm wetness that ran from it onto her hand.

When she looked, it wasn't the girl now, but a baby. Hardly more than a baby. Cut to pieces, curled up tight. Her eyes were like a doll's, staring.

She remembered. She remembered. Such a little thing. So much blood for such a little body. And the man who'd done it, the father, mad on Zeus. The baby screaming, screaming, as Eve had charged up the stairs.

Too late. She'd been too late to save the baby. Killed the father, but lost the child.

She hadn't saved them, the baby, the girl. And their blood was on her hands.

The knife gleamed over her fingers.

The room wasn't white any longer. It was small and dirty and cold. So cold. The red washed in from the light through the window. Over her hands. Little hands now on the hilt of a knife.

When he walked in the door, the red light bounced off his face like a shadow of the blood yet to be spilled.

"Eve." Roarke gathered her close, holding tight when she struggled. Her skin was iced. As she wept in her sleep, it tore his heart to pieces. "Eve, wake up. Come back now. Just a dream." He pressed his lips to her brow, her cheeks. "Just a dream."

"Kill the father, save the child."

"Ssh." He ran his hands soothingly over her back, under the old white shirt she favored for sleeping. "I'm here with you. You're safe."

"So much blood."

"God." He sat up with her, held her in his lap and rocked her in the dark.

"I'm all right." She turned her face into his shoulder. Somehow just the scent of him could center her. "Sorry. I'm okay."

"I'm not, so you can hold on to me awhile."

She slid her arms around his waist. "Something about Hannah Wade, the way . . . the way she died. It reminded me of this little girl. Baby really. The little girl whose father ripped her up. I got there too late."

"Yes, I remember. It was just before we met."

"She haunts me. I couldn't save her, couldn't get to her in time. And I think that maybe if you hadn't come into my life right after, that's the one that might've broken me. But she haunts me, Roarke. A little ghost to add to all the others. To add to myself."

"You remember her, Eve." He brushed his lips over her hair. "Perhaps you're the only one who does."

In the morning, she got up early enough to do a hard, sweaty workout, then took a long swim. She beat off the fatigue and the vague, nagging hangover from the nightmare.

And because she knew he'd keep at her until she gave in anyway, she sat down in the sitting area of the bedroom and ate the oatmeal Roarke ordered for her.

But she cast a suspicious eye on the milky liquid in the glass beside her coffee. "What's that?"

"A protein drink."

"I don't need a protein drink. I'm eating the stupid oatmeal, aren't I?"

"You'll have both." He stroked a hand over

Galahad's head, then gave his attention to Eve rather than the morning financials scrolling by on-screen. "They'll offset the candy bar you probably plan to have for lunch. You didn't sleep well."

"I've got a lot on my mind. How come you don't have to have a protein drink?"

He forked up a section of grapefruit. "Can't abide the stuff. And I'm not the one who's going to have to deal with the mayor today."

"Yeah. I have to get started on that."

"I'm sure he'll find it an even more unpleasant way to start his day than you do yours. Drink up, Lieutenant."

She scowled, but drank. She was actually starting to like whatever he dumped in those mixes. "This data doesn't go to the rest of the team yet. I have to report it to Whitney, probably Tibble, and won't that be fun?"

"We should have your virus fully ID'd today. You're closing in."

"I've been thinking about that, too." She looked toward the data center. "I've been making plenty of noise. They'll know I've got some solid leads now. Could they dump that virus in this system here?"

"This system's security is a great deal

more complex than what you'll find on other home systems."

Galahad inched toward the table, the plates. Roarke merely gave him one cool look. The cat shot up a leg and began to wash as if that had been the plan all along.

"And I've taken separate precautions," he continued, "based on the shield we've been working on in the lab. I can't give you a hundred percent guarantee, but unless they upgrade and modify what they've used to date, no. They can't infect this system."

"Let me take it in another direction. If there was an attempt to infect, can you rig some alarm, some detector, whatever, to alert us to it, maybe track the source?"

"You interest me, Lieutenant. I've already started working on that. It can't be done with any real success until we complete the full ID. But your lab rats have been devising some creative options. Jamie's particularly skilled in this area. I swear, if the boy wasn't determined to be you, he'd make his first billion before . . . well, before I made mine."

"If you could track it from this system, would you be able to track it back from one of the infected units?" She saw the look on his face. "Okay, so I'm one step behind the master geek plan. You get me that today, I might just dig up a pair of garters."

"I want the corset, too. And the shoes."

"You get me a source location, you get the shoes."

"I'm really starting to like this job. You have to wear the shoes the whole time we—"

"Let's not push it, pal." She rose. "I'm going to make this call from my office."

She closed her door. Though she wasn't sure of Whitney's schedule, she assumed he was already on the way in from Westchester. She tried his car 'link, and didn't mind admitting to herself that she'd timed it so she didn't have to tag him at home and chance dealing with his wife.

"Whitney."

"Sir. There's been a development in the investigation that requires your attention, and I believe Chief Tibble's."

"What development?"

"I don't believe I can discuss this over 'link, Commander. My judgment puts this at Code Five."

She saw his eyes narrow. Code Five meant complete media block, and all departmental records would be sealed during the investigation.

"Are you at your home office?"

"Yes, sir. I can be at Central in—"

"No. The chief is closer to you than downtown. For that matter, at this point, so am I. I'll contact him. Expect us within thirty minutes."

"Yes, sir."

"Has your team been informed of this development?"

"No, sir. Just the expert consultant who was working with me when this new development surfaced."

"Keep it that way for now. Out."

Even as the screen blanked, there was a quick knock on her door. Nadine burst in.

"Damn it, Nadine, when I close a door it's because I want it closed. I don't have time for the media. Go away."

"Don't be so hasty." She closed the door at her back, then crossing the room at a clip, tossed a disc to Eve. "I went to a lot of trouble to get that to you and I don't want anyone to know you got it from me."

"Why, and what is it?"

"Why, because it could be perceived as taking media/police relations one step too far. I've a strong feeling the bosses at 75 would think so. What it is, is a copy of the home vid 75 bought *after* what I'm told was a rapid and lively negotiation from a tourist. A tourist who was taking a spin on an air-tram when Nick Greene ran out on his balcony. They're going to air at nine, sharp. I wanted to give you a heads up."

"Channel 75 is going to air a guy killing himself?"

"I'm not saying I approve. I'm not saying I disapprove. This hits at nine, it's going to be big. What I will say, for your ears only, is I disapprove of going public with it without informing the police first. The vid doesn't change the outcome, the investigation, but I don't like the way it might stir up more support for Purity. So I'm giving you time to structure a response."

"Have you looked at this?" Eve held up the disc.

"I ran it on my way over. It's grim, it's ugly. And it makes Greene look like a monster. It's going to be easy to look at it and think: Thank God he's dead."

"Give me the name of the tourist."

"I can't do it." She pushed impatiently at

her mane of hair. "Dallas, even if I knew, I couldn't do it. A source is a source."

"Is this your story?"

"No."

"Then he's not your source."

Nadine shook her head. "I'll only go so far over, same as you. If you're thinking this guy was a plant, I don't see how he could've been. But I'll look into it. I will promise if I smell a setup, I'll spill."

Satisfied, Eve nodded. "Tell me one thing. How much they shell out for this?"

"Dallas—"

"Off the record, Nadine. For both of us. I'm just curious."

"One cool mil for twenty seconds of feed."

"I guess he really hit the jackpot. I know you didn't have to do this. I won't forget it."

"So, you owe me one."

"I don't like to owe. Something's going to bust," she said after a moment. "Likely within the next day or two. Don't bother to ask any questions, I won't answer. When it goes down and I'm cleared to talk about it, I'll give you an exclusive."

"Within an hour after it goes down."

"I can't promise that. At the first possible opportunity."

"Good enough. I've got to go. And I was never here."

When the door was closed again, Eve slid in the new disc, ordered a run.

She saw Greene's balcony, saw the door swing open. He came out fast, he came out bloody. The image bobbled as the operator jerked at what he saw through his viewer, and she heard his gasping oath. But he was cool enough to zoom in.

Yes, he looked like a monster, Eve thought. Blood literally dripping from his fingers, his hair. His mouth was wide, his eyes wild and red as a demon's. He hacked at the air with the knife, beat a fist against his own head.

He raced from one end of the terrace to the other, batting at the air as if swatting at insects. Then gripping the knife in both hands, he threw back his head. And plunged it into his own chest.

"Holy shit." Jamie stood in the doorway leading to Roarke's office. His jaw was slack, his gaze riveted to Eve's view screen.

"Goddamn it. End run. That door was closed."

"Sorry. Roarke asked me to . . . I was just getting something for him and wanted to ask you—doesn't matter." He took a steadying breath, scrubbed the back of his hand over his mouth. "That's the guy from yesterday, right? Yesterday's homicide."

"You should be in the lab."

"I'm part of this team." His chin came up. "My grandfather was a cop, and I'm going to be one. I've seen blood before. I killed a man."

"Shut up." She snapped it out, striding over to close the door behind him. "There's an official report, with my name on it, that states Alban was killed during the struggle to disarm and arrest. You want to fuck me over, Jamie, you keep saying you killed a man."

"I wouldn't do anything to mess you up." Something of what he felt for her, the core of love he tried to bury under a blanket of teenaged cool, surfaced on his face. "I'd never do that, Dallas."

Because she saw it, she eased back before it embarrassed them both. "Okay."

"This is between you and me. I know you kept me out of the briefing yesterday, and I can figure why. You didn't think I should see something like that." He nodded toward the screen. "The new guy, Trueheart, he's what? Three years older than me? Maybe four. What's the difference?"

"He's wearing a uniform."

"So will I."

She studied his face. Something in those gray eyes was already half-cop. "Yeah. Yeah, you will. Look, I'm not saying you can't handle yourself. There's a lot of bad shit out there. You see too much of it too soon, it can swallow you up before you get started."

"I've already seen a lot of it."

"There's more that's just as bad. There's more that's worse. You get through the Academy, you put on the uniform. That's soon enough to start dealing with it."

"Okay."

"Now scram. And do me a favor. I've got a meeting, a private meeting in a few minutes. Keep everyone the hell out of here."

"Sure." He grinned and looked terrifyingly young. "Trueheart's got a little thing for you."

"Get out."

As he laughed, she gave him a shove and shut the door in his face. She went back to her desk, copied the disc for her files, then sealed the other for her commander.

She took the rest of the time to update her evidence log, sealed that as well. Then organized her thoughts.

At the knock on her door, she took a deep breath, and rose to open it for the city's two top cops.

Chapter 19

"During the course of investigating the Greene/Wade homicides," Eve began, "I found Greene's financials didn't jibe with his lifestyle. Even assuming a substantial unreported income through his alleged dealings in illegals and sexual services, purchases, and other assets accumulated over the previous year far exceeded any projected monies."

"You assumed he had another source," Whitney put in.

"Yes, sir. During the initial search and sweep of the premises—"

"Lieutenant." Tibble held up a hand to

stop her. "Is there a reason you're taking us down the long road here?"

"I think my findings in this matter are going to require a solid foundation."

"Fine. But there's no need for the formalities. Just lay it out."

"Yes, sir. We found a safe when we did the first pass. There wasn't enough in it as review of the security tapes showed us three probable deals going down in his digs during the last week. He didn't go out himself, so he wouldn't have made any deposits. The guy dealt in cash primarily. No way he's going to hand his take over to a teenager he found in a club and trust her to dump it into his safebox or dummy account. Had to be another cache in his place, just like there had to be another source of income. Given the type of clientele he serviced, blackmail seemed the most logical sideline."

"You felt this assumed sideline connected with Purity?" Tibble asked her.

"It's not enough to connect, to investigate the big picture. Each case has to be handled individually, by the numbers, or you miss details."

Tibble nodded. "Since we're here, I assume you didn't miss the details."

"I returned to Greene's condo, with the civilian consultant. We located the second safe. I logged those contents at that time, and have updated the log as I reviewed those contents. It contained eight hundred and sixty-five thousand in cash, a code for a safebox at the Security National Bank, 88th Street branch, five data discs, and twelve video discs."

She gestured to her desk. "All contents are logged and sealed, as is my record of their confiscation from the safe."

"Since you're being very cautious, Lieutenant, those contents must be hot."

She met Whitney's eyes. "They are. The data discs contain his underground books. He kept good records. They also contain his daily journals. His deterioration from the infection is well documented on them, demonstrating increasing pain, paranoia, anger and confusion."

"And the vids," Tibble said. "Blackmail?"

"Yes, sir. I did ID search and matches on the individuals recorded by Greene. There's little doubt they were unaware they were being recorded during their activities as said activities were extremely graphic in nature. Some of the recordings take place at an as

yet unknown location, others in the spare
bedroom at Greene's condo. On those vids
are a number of very prominent citizens recorded in compromising, illegal, and/or em-
barrassing sexual situations. Among them
are a criminal court judge, the wife of a college professor and vocal Conservative Party
supporter who I believe I can and will connect to Clarissa Price, a well-known media
personality, and the Mayor of New York."

"Oh, Christ." Tibble stared for a full five
seconds, then pressed his fingers to his
temples. "This is a confirmed ID on Peachtree?"

"Yes, sir. I recognized him, but followed
up with an image scan."

"Then it's a fucking mess." He dropped his
hands. "All right, the idiot cheated on his
wife and got recorded."

"Sir. It's a little more . . . involved than
straight adultery."

"Spell it out, Dallas," Whitney said impatiently. "We're grown-ups here."

"He was dressed in women's clothes and
had a sweaty sexual session with another
man, which included a little dominance and
punishment and, um, oral gratification and
consummation."

"It just gets better and better." As if tired, Tibble sat back, rested his head on the cushion of his chair as he studied the ceiling. "Mayor Steven Peachtree is a transvestite who was being blackmailed by a sex and illegals broker who's now dead, and whose death was precipitated by a terrorist organization now responsible for seven murders."

"In a nutshell," Eve agreed.

"The media gets ahold of this . . ." He shook his head, pushed to his feet. He paced to her window. "It's over for him, one way or the other. Even the talented Chang won't be able to spin him out of the toilet. The city's in enough of an uproar without this. We keep it quiet, for now."

"I need to interview him, Chief, as well as the other individuals on vid."

Tibble looked over his shoulder, studied her face. "You believe Peachtree is involved in Purity? The Mayor, setting a terrorist organization loose on his own city? He may have shown extremely poor judgment in a personal matter, but he's not stupid enough to piss in his own pool."

Why not? she thought. You use a sex broker to fulfill your dream-date fantasy, you're stupid enough for anything. "I can't make that determination until after he's interviewed."

"You want to drag him into a major homicide investigation because he wore a goddamn bra."

She felt her patience drying up, hulling out like a grape in the sun. "Sir, I don't care if he dresses up like a shepherdess and seduces his flock on his downtime. Unless doing so puts him into my case. It's my allegation, as primary in this matter, that Purity has people of power, authority, and influence among their members. My request for a warrant to open sealed juvenile files has been blocked, and continues to be blocked beyond all reasonable objections. Warrants to view files at Child Services have also been blocked or denied. These blocks impede the forward course of my investigation."

"You found a way around them with Dukes."

She took a deep breath. "Yes, sir, I did. And I'll continue to find ways around them. Seven people, including a police officer, are dead. I'll continue to find a way until I have the answers and justice is served. The

Mayor of New York is now a suspect in this investigation whether it suits you or not."

"Chief Tibble." Whitney got to his feet, very nearly gave into the urge to step between them like a referee at a boxing match. "Lieutenant Dallas is right."

Tibble swung his searing gaze onto Whitney. "Do you think I don't know she's right? For Christ's sake, Jack, I've carried tin longer than she's been alive. I know she's right. I also know we'll be digging ourselves out of the fallout for months once this hits. Transvestite terrorist. Sweet Jesus, can you imagine what the media will do with it?"

"The media doesn't concern me."

Tibble turned to Eve. "If you want to climb up the ladder, it better. You'd be wearing bars now if you paid more attention to perception and image. You've made choices that have prevented you from being the youngest female captain in the NYPSD."

"Harry."

Tibble waved off Whitney's quiet objection, turned away again. "I'll apologize for that. This has blindsided me. I work with the man. I can't say we're friends, but we're certainly friendly. I know his family. I believed I knew him. I'd like some coffee. Black, no sugar. If you don't mind."

Eve said nothing, didn't trust herself to speak. Instead she walked into the kitchen, programmed the AutoChef while temper warred with training.

They could take their captain's bars and shove them.

She came back in. As Tibble was once again facing the window, she set his coffee on her desk, then handed Whitney a second cup.

"Am I ordered to ignore the evidence that has come into my hands and detour from the investigative route that leads to Mayor Steven Peachtree?"

"I have no doubt, Lieutenant," Tibble said with his back to the room, "that were I to issue that order you would disobey said command or throw your badge in my face. As I believe you're angry enough at the moment to choose the latter, I'll apologize once again.

"I had no right to personalize this, nor to take my frustrations out on you. I will say there are shades of right, Lieutenant Dallas, and the higher you climb, the more shades there are, and the deeper they get."

"I'm aware of the difficulty of the situation, and your position, Chief Tibble."

"But mostly you think it's bullshit." He spread his lips in the grin that had terrified both cop and criminal over the years. He walked over, picked up his coffee, and drank. "And mostly you're right. No, Lieutenant, you are not ordered to ignore the evidence that came into your hands."

Without thinking, he sat behind her desk. "I am asking you to delay that interview until I speak with the mayor. Any portion of the conversation that is salient to your investigation will be relayed to you. It's not just the man, but the office. The office requires some respect and protection. I hope you can trust me to separate man from office and conduct this preliminary questioning personally."

"I believe you're more than capable of handling such questioning, sir. How do you want me to handle the other individuals identified on the videos?"

"Discreetly. I need copies of those vids, your notes, and files."

"I have them available for you."

He took the evidence bag she offered.

"Jack, it looks like we're going to start the day with some porn."

"I ended mine with it," Eve said and made Tibble roar with laughter.

"Job's never dull."

"How much am I cleared to tell my team?"

"Trust is a two-way street. I leave that to you." He rose. "If Peachtree's part of this, we'll take him down. You have my word on it." He held out a hand.

"We'll take them all down, sir. You've got mine on that."

After they'd left, Eve called Peabody into her office.

"Sit down," she ordered, then as Tibble had done, she took the position of command behind her desk. "New data has come to light that may have a direct bearing on this investigation. I'm not free to share all the details of this data with you at this time, but you'll be accompanying me today on what will be a number of sensitive interviews. Until I give you clearance, you're to say nothing of this to other team members."

"You're not bringing the team in?"

"Not at this time. This is Code Five. Any record I order you to make will be sealed."

Peabody choked back the dozen questions leaping to her tongue. "Yes, sir."

"Before we start on this new round of interviews, we'll do a followup with Dukes. He needs a push. And I figure to round off the day with Price and Dwier. Like, I don't know, bookends."

"Is what's between the bookends connected to the whole?"

"It's all connected. I'll fill you in, as much as I'm able, on the way to the Dukes."

"Blackmail," Peabody said at the first stoplight on route. "Greene sure had his fingers in a lot of nasty pies."

"Lucrative pies. Raked in over three million annually with this scam."

"You think Purity infected him because of the blackmail?"

"Yeah, I do. Look at the others. Those were child predators. Greene, he dealt some in the adolescent arena, but the bulk of his clientele and employees were adults."

"You said you thought Purity would start expanding their criteria."

"And they will. Not this soon. There are plenty more in Fitzhugh's ilk to keep them busy. Greene teeters on the line. I think someone, maybe more than one, had personal reasons for wanting Greene dead. Eliminating another scumbag was a factor, but ditching a blackmail payment, and the threat of exposure, makes a real nice bonus. But it was stupid. A mistake. Killing the blackmailer before you destroy the evidence that ties you to him."

"Can you tell me if Dukes was on the blackmail list?"

"No. But he knows how it's done. He knows who's been infected or scheduled for infection. He's part of the foundation, so we shake him. Or his wife. She's a weak point."

"You think she'll roll on him?"

"She might, if she's scared enough. She's not a player, but she knows Dukes—his schedule, his habits. How else could she tailor the household to suit him? And if he thinks we're pushing her, he might get pissed enough to slip up. He's got a hot button."

Eve hunted up a parking spot, then jaywalked diagonally across the street toward the Dukes's residence. The first thing she noticed were the wilted flowers by the door.

"They're gone."

Peabody followed the direction of Eve's

cold stare. "Maybe she forgot to water them."

"No, she wouldn't forget. Probably has a daily duty list. Damn it. Damn it." She rang the buzzer anyway, waited, rang again.

"Curtains are still at the windows." Peabody craned her neck to see inside. "Furniture's still in there."

"They left it. Got out fast. They were probably packed and gone within twenty-four hours of our first visit."

She started working the street, knocking on doors until one opened for her. She offered her badge to a snowy-haired woman in a pink tracksuit.

"Is something wrong? Has there been an accident? My husband—"

"No, ma'am. Nothing's wrong. I'm sorry to alarm you. I'm looking for some of your neighbors. The Dukes. They don't answer their door."

"The Dukes." She patted her hair as if to stir her thoughts. "I'm not sure I . . . oh, of course. Of course. I saw the story on the media report. Oh dear, you're the policewoman they're going to sue."

"I don't believe any legal action has been taken as yet. Do you know where they are?"

"Goodness. I don't really know them. Pretty young woman. I'd see her walking to the market every Monday and Thursday. Nine-thirty. You could set your wrist unit by her. But now that you mention it, I don't know the last time . . . They lost their older son, didn't they? They only moved in two years ago. I never knew a thing about it. They didn't really talk to any of the neighbors. Some people never do. It's a terrible, terrible thing to lose a child."

"Yes, ma'am."

"I'd see him come and go now and then. Didn't look like a very kind sort of man. On Sundays they'd all go out together. Ten o'clock sharp. To church, I imagine from the way they were dressed. Back by twelve-thirty. You never saw the boy playing outside, with other children. I never saw another child go into that house."

She sighed, staring across the street now. "I suppose they kept him close, afraid something would happen to him, too. Hold on, there's Nita coming out. My jogging partner."

She waved wildly at the woman who came out of a building directly across the street. She, too, wore a tracksuit. In powder blue.

"Nita doesn't miss a trick," the other woman said out of the corner of her mouth. "You ask her about them."

"Getting yourself arrested?" Nita said cheerfully when she joined them. "Better lock her up tight, Officer. Sal's a slippery one."

"We'll talk about slippery later," Sal told her. "They're asking about the Dukes. Two doors down from you."

"They went on a trip a couple days ago. Loaded up the car with suitcases. Wife wasn't too happy about it, if you ask me. She'd been crying. That would've been . . . let me think. Wednesday. Wednesday morning, bright and early. I was out front watering my pots when I saw them loading up."

"Did you notice anyone visiting them prior to that?"

"Saw you," Nita said with a grin. "The morning before. Got the commandant pretty stirred up from what I saw on-screen later."

"Nita."

"Oh, stop fussing, Sal. I didn't like the man and I'm not afraid to say so out loud."

She waved a hand and settled herself in as if for a nice, friendly chat. "I had an old cocker spaniel, old Frankie. Died last year.

A few months before I was out walking him like I did every day, twice a day. Stopped in front of the Dukes place for a minute to talk to a neighbor who was out walking, too. And well, old Frankie did his business there on the edge of their property while I wasn't watching."

She sighed, one long expulsion of air. "Old Frankie. Now I'd've cleaned it up. I cleaned up behind that dog for sixteen years. But the commandant comes to the door and gives me what-for, says he's going to report me. Carries on so you'd think he'd never seen a little poop before. Well, I gave him what-for right back. I don't take that kind of thing from anybody."

She huffed out a breath, obviously still outraged. "He slams the door, I pick up the poop, finish walking old Frankie, and go home. Few minutes later, the beat cop's at my door. Young woman, looked mortified, told me Dukes had called in a complaint. Can you imagine that? Since I'd already flushed away the evidence, nothing came of it. The cop just wanted to let me know he was seeing red, said she'd cooled him off, but maybe it would be best all around if I made sure to keep the dog away from his property."

"Is that the only dealing you had with him?"

"Never spoke another word to the man, nor he to me."

"They lost a child," Sal reminded her. "It can sour a person."

"Some are born sour." Nita nodded to the house across the street. "I'd say that man was."

Eve conducted the first three interviews on Greene's list in the privacy of each subject's home or office. In each case there were varying degrees of denial, outrage, embarrassment, and pleading.

And in the case of Judge Vera Archer, a cold acceptance.

"I'd prefer to continue this discussion without the presence of your uniform, Lieutenant Dallas."

"Peabody, wait outside."

Archer folded her hands on her desk. Her chambers was a streamlined, organized space that suited her image. She was a tall, sternly attractive, rail-thin woman of sixty-three, with short, straight dark hair. She had a reputation for delivering swift and thorough decisions that rarely failed to hold up on appeal.

She brooked no theatrics in her courtroom.

Apparently, Eve thought, she enjoyed them in private. On disc she'd worn a pink ballgown, and had performed a rather glamorous striptease—down to g-string and pasties—for two well-muscled men as a prelude to a very athletic ménage à trois.

"I assumed I'd be dealing with this when I heard Nick Greene had been killed. My private life isn't up for discussion. No laws were broken by me, other than those of common sense."

"Yet you paid Nick Greene seventy-five hundred dollars a month."

"I did. It's not illegal to pay such a fee. And if we determine it as blackmail, the crime was his in extorting such a fee. I'm not going to explain the contents of the disc, nor the motivation behind those contents. I'm entitled to my privacy."

"Yes, Your Honor, and you certainly paid enough for it. However, the contents of that disc, and your payments, are now part of a homicide investigation."

Archer's gaze never wavered. "I was better off with him alive. I could afford the money a great deal more than I can afford the publicity from exposure. The embarrassment to my robes, my husband. I made full disclosure of this matter to my husband nearly a year ago. You can verify that if you deem it necessary, but it is, again, a private matter. I will tell you we agreed to continue the payments."

"You're aware of the circumstances of Nick Greene's death?"

"I am."

"While I sympathize with your desire for privacy, Your Honor, that sympathy doesn't extend over my pursuit of the terrorists who are responsible for his death, and the death of six others to date."

"And how will exposing the contents of that disc aid your pursuit? I must have the respect of my courtroom when I'm on the bench. You pursue, you arrest, but then it's up to the courts to complete the cycle of justice. How can I do that if I'm a laughingstock, an embarrassment?"

"I'll do whatever I can to protect your privacy. Tell me how you came to use Nick Greene's services."

Archer rolled her lips inward into a nearly invisible line. "I'd heard about him through an acquaintance. It seemed harmless, and though his services were admittedly border-line, I made use of them. A release valve, you could say, from the pressures of the job. I made use of them once a month for sev-eral months. Then he gave me a copy of the disc, explained the payment schedule and the consequences of nonpayment. All very reasonable and businesslike."

"You must have been very angry."

"I was angry. More, I felt like a fool. A woman who's lived for more than sixty years, sat on a bench for fourteen, shouldn't be so easily duped. I paid, because one al-ways pays for foolishness, and I stopped us-ing his services."

"Were you afraid he would expose you anyway?"

She angled her head in mock surprise. "And cut off a small but steady income? No."

"Did he ever up the payments or threaten to do so?"

"No. In his way, he was a good business-man. If you bleed too fast and hard, you eviscerate."

Archer lifted her hands, the only excess

motion she'd made throughout the interview. "I didn't even resent the payments. They reminded me I was human. Which is why I used his services to begin with. I needed to be reminded I was human. You've done a background on me. Personal, professional?"

"Yes, Your Honor, an initial run."

"I've served the law, and served it well. My record bears that out. I'm not ready to retire." She glanced over at the small viewing screen on her wall. "I saw the broadcast on 75 this morning. It was a vicious, horrible death they chose for him. He was a blackmailer, and he peddled in what could be called sin, certainly exploited people's secret weaknesses. But he didn't deserve to die as he did. Nor did that child."

She looked at Eve again, her gaze direct and level. "You suspect that I may be a part of these vigilantes calling themselves pure? They stand for everything I abhor, Lieutenant. Everything I've dedicated my life to fighting against. They're bullies and cowards playing God. I'm willing to waive legal representation at this time and submit to a Truth Test. My conditions are that this be done privately, by a single authorized and licensed technician, and that when the results clear me of suspicion, they, as well as the disc and any files pertaining to me in this matter, are sealed."

"I'll agree to those conditions and will arrange it. I can ask Dr. Mira to do the Testing personally."

"Dr. Mira is acceptable."

"I believe the results will put an end to your involvement in this matter, Your Honor."

"Thank you."

"Can I ask your advice and opinion on another matter connected to my investigation?"

"Yes."

"I have requested warrants to open sealed files on juvenile victims that directly pertain to this case. Child Services filed a TRO blocking me from these records and from additional records of their agency. The prosecutor's office engaged in the standard legal wrangle over this. The block remains."

"Sealeds, particularly in the case of minors, are sensitive issues."

"So is serial homicide. So is terrorism. So is obstructing a priority investigation. Time is of the essence, yet an essential tool is being held out of my reach. This isn't a matter of opening sealeds to the public, but to an investigator with probable cause. If this matter was before you, how would you rule?"

Archer leaned back. "Is your probable cause solid, Lieutenant—and don't jive with me."

"It's rock solid. The TRO argues that the sealeds must remain to protect the minors and their families from further distress, to ensure their privacy. The P.A. argues that probable cause in a homicide investigation supersedes, and further argues that the contents of the sealeds will be known only to the investigative team."

"If the arguments are as basic as that, you'd have your warrants in my court. Who signed the initial warrants?"

"Judge Matthews?"

"And he's subsequently held the sealeds?"

"No, Your Honor. The arguments are being presented to Judge Lincoln."

"Lincoln. I see. I'll make a few inquiries."

Eve left the courthouse with Peabody beside her and took a moment in the air. "If she's not clean, I've lost all sense of direction."

"Do we keep working down the list?"

"Yeah, we keep working it. Meanwhile, do a run on Judge Lincoln."

"Another judge? Jeez."

"He's not on Greene's. But he's on Archer's. She's good," Eve said as she got into her vehicle. "But she's not that good. I saw something on her face when I told her he was hearing the arguments over the sealeds."

Frowning, she pulled out her beeping pocket 'link. "Dallas."

"O'Malley's," Dwier said briskly. "Twenty minutes. Come alone."

"The Blue Squirrel," Eve returned, wanting home field advantage. "Fifteen."

She broke transmission.

Chapter 20

Eve didn't frequent the Blue Squirrel as often as she once had. It was a joint with no redeeming qualities, including the food and service. During the day, it catered to a handful of surly regulars and the occasional lost soul who was foolish enough to think he might scope out a cheap meal and a little action.

At night it was usually jammed with people who made the action and were tough enough or crazy enough to risk their lives for what passed for alcohol in such places.

The music was loud, the tables small and

rarely clean, and the air generally permeated with bad booze and stale Zoner.

Eve had an odd affection for it, and was pleased to find it hadn't changed since her last visit.

For a time Mavis had been one of the featured performers, whirling in costumes that defied description and screeching out her music to a packed dance floor where people actually seemed to understand it.

Thinking of Mavis, Eve wondered if impending motherhood would tone her down.

Not a chance.

"Grab a table opposite side," Eve ordered Peabody. "Eat if you dare."

"Their soy fries are only half-bad. I'll risk it."

Eve chose a table in the far corner, slid in. And decided Peabody was right. The fries were only half-bad, and deserved another chance.

She keyed in an order on the menu, and decided not to dance any closer to the edge by risking the coffee. She opted for bottled water, which she feared was bottled in one of the seamy back rooms by flat-nosed men with hairy knuckles.

Seeing no sign of Dwier, she pulled out

her communicator and checked in with Feeney. "What's the status?"

"Nearly there." There was a faint sheen of sweat on his brow and his hair was sticking out in tufts. "Two hours, we'll nail it. What're you working on?"

"In a couple of minutes, lunch. Blue Squirrel."

"You walk on the dark side, Dallas."

"Yeah, that's me. Got a meet with Dwier. He should be coming along shortly. I think he wants to deal."

"I'll give him a damn deal." Feeney blew air out his nose. "You wanna tell me what the brass was doing here this morning?"

"Can't. I have to wait for some information. Bugs me, Feeney, but I can't."

"Hooked a big fish, didn't you, kid? No, don't sweat it," he said. "Just remember, some big fish got teeth."

"I'm careful. Dwier just walked in. Later."

She pocketed the communicator, then waited for him to come to the table.

"I said alone. Ditch the uniform or this ends now."

"The uniform needs to eat. You want to walk, it's your choice." She nipped the bottle of water as it popped out of the serving slot.

"Keep away from the coffee," she said conversationally. "If you want to live."

He dropped into the seat across from her. She wasn't surprised when he ordered bottled brew.

"Your girlfriend tell you about our conversation yesterday?"

"You show some respect when you talk about Clarissa. She's a lady. Your type don't recognize a lady."

"My type recognizes wrong cops, conspirators, killers, fanatics." Watching his face, she took a pull of her water. "I don't care how their skin stretches."

"I want you off her back. I'm giving you one warning on it."

She leaned forward. "You threatening me, Dwier? Are you intimating that if I continue to pursue the line of investigation that involves Clarissa Price, you may attempt to cause me physical harm?"

"What, are you wired?"

"No, I'm not wired. I just want to be real clear on the nature of your warning. That way, I won't be kicking your sorry ass across this sticky floor, out the door, and across the street due to a miscommunication."

"You think you're some badass, don't

you? You homicide cops all think you're so fucking important. Elite or some shit. You come out on the street and wade through the garbage awhile, you pick up the pieces of some kid who's been raped and beat up, or drag through the puke of some asshole teenager who's OD'd on Jazz he got from some vulture working the school yards. See how long you're such a badass."

She felt some sympathy, a sliver of it scraping over her for a cop who'd seen more than he could handle. But there was the line again, the line that could only be moved so far before it fell off the edge.

"Is that why you're part of this, Dwier? Just couldn't handle taking all the steps, seeing some of those steps bust out from under you? Is that why you decided to be judge, jury, and executioner?"

Her fries slid out, and she ignored them. His bottle popped seconds later. He snatched it up, twisted the top with the violence of a man who wished it was a human neck.

"I want you off Clarissa's back."

"You're repeating yourself. Tell me something new."

He took two deep swallows from the bottle. "I'm not saying I got anything to tell you. But if I did, I'd need a deal."

"Can't deal without the cards."

"Don't try to hose me." He snorted at her, and she lost even that sliver of sympathy.

He wasn't just a cop who'd broken under the pressure. He was one who'd puffed up on it and filled himself to bursting—like the thin skin of a balloon—bulging with arrogance, with righteousness.

"I'm a badge. I know how this works. If I had anything to say pertaining to the recent homicides, I'd need immunity for Clarissa and myself regarding any possible involvement."

"Immunity." She leaned back, carefully selected a french fry, studied it. "You just want me to wipe your slate? Seven dead, one a cop, and you want a free ride for yourself and your lady? Just how do you expect me to pull that off for you, Dwier?"

"You'll pull it off. You've got weight."

"Let's put it this way." She drenched the fries with salt. They needed help desperately. "Why do you think I'd use the weight you think I have to help you skate on this?"

"You want the bust. I know your type. The bust comes first. Keep your cases-cleared

percentage high. You figure they'll pin another fucking medal on you."

"You don't know me." Her voice was low
and lethal. "You want a picture in your head,
Dwier? How about this one? A sixteen-year-
old girl, cut into ribbons, her blood all over
the walls following the trail where she'd run
trying to get away from a man who was
driven insane by a group of people who decided he should die. Her name was Hannah
Wade. She was a stupid kid with a bad attitude who ended up in the wrong place at
the wrong time. Like Kevin Halloway, a solid
young cop just doing his job. How do the
people pushing your buttons rate that in
their list of percentages. An acceptable
loss?"

"Clarissa's sick over that girl. She's
busted to pieces over it. Didn't sleep a wink
all night."

Eve felt bile rush into her throat, washed
it back with water. "Remorse will weigh in
with the prosecutor. Maybe you were misled. Maybe both of you were misled by the
people in charge of Purity. You were just
looking for a way to protect the kids on your
watch."

"Yeah." He drank, keyed in the menu for

a second bottle. "If that were the case, it would go toward immunity. The fact, if we did know something relevant, we were willing to give it up—voluntarily."

You puke, she thought, her face blank as a wiped slate. "You know I can't guarantee immunity. That decision doesn't come from me. I can only request it."

"You can push it. You know the buttons."

She looked away from him a moment because knowing she'd try for the deal made her sick. The greater good, she told herself. Sometimes justice couldn't sweep clean.

"I'll push for immunity. But you're off the job, and so's she—"

"You can't—"

"Shut up, Dwier. Just shut up, because what I'm going to lay down here is as good as you're ever going to get. And the offer is one-time only. I put my weight for immunity. Make the case for the P.A. that your information, and Price's, was key to my investigation. If it isn't key, Dwier, this conversation is moot. You and Price walk, no cage time. But you put in for retirement, and she resigns from Child Services. It's up to the P.A. and the brass as to whether you keep your benefits. That's out of my hands. But you walk."

She shoved her plate aside. "You refuse this deal and I give you a vow to hunt you, both of you, until I have enough to put you both over. I'll push for multiple charges, first-degree, conspiracy murder. I'll push for the murder of a police officer. I'll push hard and the two of you will spend the rest of your lives behind bars. The last breath you take will be in a cage. I'll make it my personal mission."

His eyes glittered—temper, terror, alcohol. And, Eve thought with a dull amazement, with insult.

"I got sixteen years in. Sixteen years busting my hump."

"And now you've got five minutes to decide." She pushed up from the table. "Be gone or be ready to talk when I get back."

As she strode across the club, Peabody started to rise. Eve simply shook her head and kept going.

She slammed into what the Squirrel called their rest room. Five narrow stalls and two shallow pits for sinks. She ran the water cold, splashed it on her face again and again until the heat of her anger and disgust chilled.

Face dripping, she lifted her head and stared at herself in the black-flecked mirror. Seven people dead, she thought. Seven. And she was about to help two of the ones responsible ride free so she could stop the others.

Is this what it took to speak for Kevin Halloway, for Hannah Wade? Is this what it took?

Shades of right, Tibble had said. And just now she felt smeared by the shadows.

She scrubbed her face dry, then pulled out her communicator.

"Commander. I need a deal for Thomas Dwier and Clarissa Price."

Dwier was still at the table when she returned and starting on his third bottle. She wondered how long ago he'd drowned his conscience.

"Talk," she said.

"I gotta have some assurances."

"I laid it out for you once, I'm not laying it out again. Talk or walk."

"I want you to understand we did what we had to do. You work to get scum off the street and before you write up your fives, they're back out. The system's gone soft. All this shit about civil rights jammed down our throat, lawyers sliding through the grease, you can't do the job,"

"I don't want the lecture, Dwier. I want data. Who's running the show?"

"I'm gonna tell it my way." He swiped the back of his hand over his mouth, hunched in over the table. "Me and Clarissa, we got close. She's dedicated her life to helping kids, only to see half of them, maybe more, get screwed over by the system. We started going out, mostly just to blow off some steam, and we got close. After what happened with the Dukes kid, she was thinking about packing it in. That one almost broke her. She took a couple weeks' leave to decide what she wanted to do. And . . . Don came to see her."

"Don? Would that be Donald Dukes?"

"Yeah. She was in a rough spot. A rough spot. And he told her about this group who was looking for answers, who was working to find a better way. An underground group."

"Purity?"

"The Purity Seekers. He said a lot of people had gotten together, people like him, like her, other concerned citizens. He asked if she'd come to a meeting."

"Where?"

"Church basement. Downtown. Church of The Savior."

"A church basement?" She didn't know why it offended her sensibilities. She wasn't, never had been, religious. But it appalled something deep inside her. "This runs out of a church?"

"That's one of the meeting sites. We move around, churches and schools. She went to the first one with Don, with Dukes. It brought her back up, pulled her out of the depression. It gave her a grip on things again. I went with her the next time. It makes sense," he insisted. "The program makes sense. You want to clean up the city, you gotta take out the trash. Cops and courts are cuffed. Nobody respects the law because the law doesn't work. It doesn't fucking work, and you know it."

She looked at his face, the flush brought out by beer and righteousness. Not always, she thought. It doesn't always work because it's not going to put you in a cage.

"Who runs the meetings?"

"It's a democracy," Dwier told her with

some pride. "We all have a say. Dukes is one of the founders. We've got cops, doctors, judges, scientists, preachers. We've got thinkers."

"Names."

He dipped his head. Rubbed the bottle over his brow. "We go by first names, but I recognized some, ran some others. You have to know who you're in bed with. Look, we had some glitches with the program. Maybe we pushed things too fast. The techs figured they could delete the virus after Absolute Purity was achieved, but there was some snafu. They're working day and night to fix it. We took up a collection for Halloway. We're making a contribution to the Police Officers' Survivors' Fund in his name."

"I'm sure that'll give his family a lot of comfort, Dwier. Give me names."

"You think it's easy to weasel?" He slammed the nearly empty bottle on the table. "You think it's easy to flip on people you've worked with?"

"Was it easier to kill? Easier to throw a few bucks in the hat for a dead cop because there was a snafu? I don't want to hear about your pain, Dwier, or your skewed

sense of loyalty. I want names. It comes
down to you or them. No names, no deal."

"Bitch."

"Yeah. Keep that in mind. Donald Dukes?
His wife?"

"No. He kept her out of it. He doesn't
much like working with women."

"But he recruited Clarissa."

"I figure there was some pressure on him
to pick her up, since they had a history."
Dwier jerked a shoulder. "Matthew Sawyer,
big-shot doctor out of Kennedy Memorial.
Brain guy. Keith Burns, one of those computer geeks. Worked with Dukes on the virus. He was the kid's, Devin's, godfather.
Stanford Quillens, another doctor. Judge
Lincoln, Angie and Ray Anderson—their kid
got raped by Fitzhugh. Angie runs her own
media consultant firm midtown."

He continued to reel off names. Eve recorded them. He ordered another beer. He
wasn't sloppy yet, she noted. Four beers in
less than an hour and he wasn't showing it.
It told her his body was used to the steady
intake.

There were other doctors, other cops, a
city councilwoman, more programmers, two
former social workers, and a minister.

"That's all I got confirmed. Clarissa might have a couple more."

"What about funding?"

"Everybody kicks in what they can, donates time." He sucked on the bottle. "Some of the members got deep pockets, and put their money where their mouth is. We've got powerful support—political support—and we could've expanded on that without the accidents."

"Who's your political support?"

"The mayor. Peachtree, he doesn't come to the meetings. But he sends statements, and contributions. My take is he lined up Sawyer and Lincoln, Dukes, too."

"Are you telling me this organization generated out of the mayor's office?"

"That's how I see it, yeah. Peachtree wants reform, and he can't get it through the polls. He found another way. He's a goddamn hero."

She stored it, clamped down on another wave of disgust. "How do you select the targets?"

"We put the names, the sheets, to the membership. We vote."

"Who else is nominated?"

"Only got one more infected. We decided

to hold off until we worked out the glitches. Dru Geller. Runs private clubs, sells young meat to patrons. Runaways mostly, she scoops them up and pumps them full of Erotica. Her AP's scheduled within ten hours."

"How do you know when it's achieved?"

"That's mostly tech stuff. Not my area. But we can track usage on their infected unit or units. They ran sims so they know how long it takes to finalize."

"When's the next meeting?"

Dwier closed his eyes. "Tonight, eight. The downtown church."

"Where's Dukes?"

He shook his head. "Safe house, Upstate. Albany. I'm supposed to help work out a re-location. He's still working on the program. Him and Burns and the other techs. They'll have it perfected in a few days. They're sure of it. Nobody anticipated that girl being in Greene's place. How the hell can you antic-ipate something like that? But it comes down to it, she wasn't any different than Greene. Got what she deserved, same as him. Just a little whore—"

She bitch-slapped him. Her hand was up and swinging before she realized the fury had taken over, before he could see it in her eyes and evade. The sharp crack of flesh on flesh slashed through the club. A few people turned their heads, then quickly looked away again.

Eve got to her feet. "Stay where you are. Peabody! You're going in. You can tell your story to the P.A. Price is being picked up right now."

"Just a fucking minute."

"Shut up, you pulsating piece of shit. You'll get your immunity. You're going in now, and staying in until the rest of your self-proclaimed heroes are picked up. There's a black-and-white outside, and a representative of the prosecutor's office. Thomas Dwier, you are now in custody. Surrender your shield and your weapon. Now," she said, laying a hand on his arm. "Or I'll take you down the way I want to instead of by the book you've shown such contempt for."

"People know we were right." He laid his weapon on the table, tossed his badge down beside it. "There are four monsters off the streets thanks to us."

She took his weapon, took his badge. Then hauled him to his feet. "There are all kinds of monsters, Dwier. You don't quite qualify. You're just a weasel. And an embarrassment to the job."

When he was secured in the black-and-white, Eve got into her own vehicle. Then just laid her forehead on the wheel.

"You all right, Dallas?"

"No. No, I'm not all right." She yanked Dwier's badge and weapon from her pocket. "Seal these. I don't want my hands on them again. I got him immunity. I got him a ride. Maybe, maybe I pull him in, hammer at him in Interview, I get him to roll without the deal. But I made the deal, because maybe he doesn't roll, and I can't spare the time to find out."

"The prosecutor wouldn't have dealt immunity if he didn't figure it was the way to go."

"When you want the whole pie, sacrificing one little slice is a reasonable trade. That's how the P.A. figured it. That's how Dwier knew he'd figure it. I wish I could. Get me an address on a Dru Geller. She'll be in the system."

She pulled out her communicator to run the next steps with the commander.

• • •

It took an hour to set it up to her satisfaction. Precious time, but she wasn't losing another cop. Not today.

"We can't be sure what kind of shape she's in," Eve reminded the crisis team she'd handpicked. "We will assume she is violent and armed. Three men on the door, three for the windows. We go in fast. We subdue, secure, and transport. The subject cannot be shocked with standard weapons, even on low setting. The probability is high that the infection has spread to the extent that this would result in termination. We use tranqs, and tranqs only."

She gestured to the apartment blueprint on-screen. "You've familiarized yourselves with the setup. We know the subject is in this location. We don't know where she is within its perimeter, but the highest probability is for the main bedroom, here. Communications are to remain open throughout the op. When the subject is secured, she will be transferred, immediately, to the medical techs, accompanied by two team members during transpo to designated health center where a medical team is waiting."

Maybe they'd save her, Eve thought as she approached the door to Dru Geller's apartment. And maybe they wouldn't. If Dwier's information was accurate, she had under eight hours left. Morris had called the infection irreversible after the initial spread.

She was risking six cops, her aide, and herself over a woman who was in all likelihood already dead.

She drew her tranq-shooter, nodded for the crisis team cop to uncode the locks. "Uncoding," she said quietly into her communicator. "Locks disengaged. Wait for my signal."

She eased the door open. She caught a whiff of spoiled food, of stale urine. The lights were off, the sun shields tight at the windows. The room looked and smelled like a cave.

She gestured, pointing Peabody and the second officer left. She went in fast, low, and right. "Living area clear."

She heard it then, a kind of growling. The sound a rabid dog might make when cornered. "Moving to main bedroom. Hold at the windows."

She took flank at the door, nodded again, then kicked it in.

Dru Geller had her back to the wall. She wore nothing but panties. There was blood on her breasts, breasts scored from her own fingernails. Her nose had bled as well, and the red ran down over her snarling lips, stained her teeth, dripped off her chin.

Eve saw it all in the space of a heartbeat and saw the long-bladed scissors in her hand.

The scissor flew, like an arrow from a bow. Eve pivoted, deployed the tranq. It caught Geller in the left breast. "Now! Go! Hit her again," she ordered as Geller lunged forward.

A second tranq hit her midbody, and still she leaped on Eve like a wildcat, all teeth and nails. She saw the red eyes wheeling, felt the blood drip on her face. Geller howled as a third tranq took her in the right shoulder.

She shut off like a light, red eyes rolling back, limbs going limp.

It took seconds, only seconds. There was a flurry of movement as Geller was rolled away, her unconscious body restrained.

"Get her to the MTs, get her transported," Eve ordered. "Move."

"We got an officer down."

"What?" Wiping the blood from her face, Eve gained her feet, spun around.

And saw Peabody lying on the floor, bleeding, the scissors jammed deep into her shoulder.

"No. Goddamn it. No." She was on her knees in one fast move, and without thinking brushing her hand over Peabody's white face.

"Zigged right, should've zagged left," Peabody managed. She turned her head, stared dully at the bright silver scissors. "It's not too bad, is it? Not too bad."

"No, it's nothing. Get me a medical, now. Right now!" Eve stripped off her jacket, prepared to use it to staunch the flow of blood.

"Pull them out, okay? Wouldja?" Peabody groped for Eve's hand. "It's making me pretty sick, having them sticking out of me."

"Better not. MTs coming up right now. They'll fix you up."

"They'd hit an inch over, the riot vest would've deflected them. What're the chances? Really hurts. Jesus, it really hurts. I'm cold. Just shock, right? Right, Dallas? I'm not dying or anything?"

"You're not dying." She snagged the wrinkled bedspread from one of the crisis team. "I don't have time to waste training another aide."

Eve turned her head as an MT rushed in. "Do something," she ordered.

Ignoring her, he ran a scanner over the point of entry, took Peabody's vital signs. "Okay, Officer. What's your name?"

"Peabody. I'm Peabody. Would you get these goddamn scissors out of me?"

"Sure. I'm going to give you a little something first."

"Gimme lots. Dallas is the one who lives for pain."

He smiled at her, set his pressure syringe.

"She's losing blood," Eve snapped. "Are you just going to let her bleed out on the floor?"

"Just keep the pressure on," he said mildly. "Too bad about that jacket. Looks like nice fabric. I'm going to pull out the invasive object. On three, Peabody, okay?"

"One, two, three."

The MT met Eve's eyes, and mouthed: Hold her down.

Eve felt it in her gut, felt the sharp shock of the blades slicing out of Peabody's flesh. Felt it in the quick jerk of her aide's body against her restraining hands.

Blood flowed over her fingers, warm and wet.

Then she was nudged out of the way, while the MT worked on the wound.

Twenty minutes later she was pacing the ER waiting room. She'd nearly decked the doctor who'd ordered her out of the treatment area. Had restrained herself only because she figured the medical had to be conscious to work on Peabody.

McNab burst through the doors in a limping run, with Roarke right behind him.

"Where is she? What are they doing for her? How bad is it?"

"She's in treatment. They're patching her up. It's just like I told you, McNab. She's got a deep puncture in her shoulder, but it missed the major arteries. They don't think there's any muscle damage. They're going to clean it up, give her some blood and fluids, sew her up. Then they'll probably spring her."

She saw him stare down at her hands. She hadn't taken time to wash the blood off. Cursing herself, she shoved them into her pockets.

"Which treatment room?"

"B. Around the corner to the left."

He rushed off, and Eve scrubbed her

hands over her face. "I can't stay in here," she muttered and hurried outside.

"Is it more serious than you told McNab?" Roarke asked her.

"I don't think so. The MT seemed solid. He said it was too serious to treat and release on-scene, but not major. She lost a lot of blood."

She stared down at her hands.

"You lost a bit yourself." He traced his fingers over her jaw where Geller's nails had swiped.

"It's nothing. Goddamn it, it's nothing." She spun away from him, kicked the tire of an ambulance parked in the bay. "I took her in there."

"Is she less a cop than you?"

"That's not the point. That's not the fucking point." She whirled back. "I took her and six other cops in there. I made the call, I set the op. *I* dodged out of the way when Geller threw the scissors at me."

Because her eyes were swimming, her voice beginning to hitch, he took her shoulders. "And Peabody didn't move as quickly. Is that your fault?"

"It's not about fault. It's about reason. I took her in, took all of them in to secure and transport to medical a woman who's probably going to die anyway. I ordered those people to put their lives on the line for her. A woman who sells little girls. Boy, that's irony for you. I've got Peabody's blood on my hands because of a woman who sells children for sex."

She gripped his shirt, fisted her hands. "For what?" she demanded. "What's the damn point?"

"Lieutenant."

She jerked at McNab's voice, turned quickly.

He'd never seen her cry before. Hadn't known she could. "She's awake. You were right, they're going to spring her. They want to keep her about an hour first. She's still a little groggy. She asked if you were around."

"I'll go in and see her."

"Dallas." McNab moved into her path, took her by the arm. "If you ask her what the point is, she'd tell you. You haven't asked me, but I'll tell you anyway. Because when something has to be done, we're the ones who're supposed to do it. I didn't have to be there to know you went through the door first. So you already know what the point is."

"Maybe I needed somebody to remind me."

Roarke watched her walk back inside. "You're a good man, Ian." He laid a hand on McNab's shoulders. "Let's go buy Peabody some flowers."

"I usually just steal them."

"Let's make an exception for this one."

Chapter 21

Whitney took Eve's report orally, in his office. She was in her shirtsleeves, and the shirt carried a small stain of dried blood.

"Has Peabody been released from the health center?"

"They were preparing to sign her out when I left. She'll need to take a couple days' medical leave."

"See that she has what she needs. Dwier and Price are in custody, and will be held incommunicado until the situation is resolved. We have the location in Albany under surveillance. When you've cleaned up here, Donald Dukes will be taken. We agree that he shouldn't be arrested until after your raid on tonight's meeting?"

"Yes, sir. Dwier and Price were just soldiers. Dukes is one of the generals." The commandant, Eve remembered. "It's probable he remains in contact with other key members of the organization. We let him sit until we've broken its back. Sir, as Dwier has further implicated Mayor Peachtree, I request permission for formal questioning."

"The mayor has agreed to temporary house arrest. His incoming and outgoing transmissions are being monitored. Under advice of counsel he's admitted to the sexual . . . transgression, but continues to deny any association with Purity. Politically, he's finished."

"Politically," Eve began.

"Yes. That's not enough. I won't disagree. However, this evening's op takes priority over questioning him. We'll bag most if not all the other members in this sweep, essentially destroying this organization. That's the first order of business."

"When the mayor's office is a front for terrorists, that's an important piece of business, Commander."

"And will it make a difference to closing

this case if you question him now, or wait until tomorrow?"

She wanted to take him now. She wanted to taste him in her throat. "It could if he gives up additional information."

"I can promise you that with his fleet of attorneys, you'll be in for a long, tough haul getting more than his name. You don't have the time to spare today. He's on ice, Dallas. He's done. Be satisfied with that for a few hours longer. I give you my word that as of ten A.M. tomorrow, he belongs to you."

"Yes, sir. Thank you."

"You've done superior work on this despite a number of difficult obstacles." He hesitated, studying her face. "I'd like to speak to something Chief Tibble said this morning. You deserve the bars, Dallas."

"They don't matter."

"Fuck it. This is between you and me, here in this room. You deserve to wear the bars. You've earned them. If it was only a matter of merit, you would wear them. Regrettably it's not only a matter of merit. Your age is a consideration. What are you, Dallas, thirty?"

"Thirty-one, sir."

He let out a half-laugh. "I've got shirts

older than you. I have to hide them from my wife, but I've got them. Still this is a consideration that could be resolved, even used to advantage, in some circumstances."

"Commander Whitney. I'm aware that my personal life is a factor in this matter. That my marriage to Roarke, who is regarded in some quarters, certainly some within the department, with suspicion—unless he's being useful—is and will be more a detriment to my moving up in rank than the mayor using an illegal sex broker and doing the mambo in women's clothes would be to his future political standing. Chief Tibble was correct. It was my choice."

"I hope you're equally aware that your marriage isn't regarded as a detriment in this office."

"I am."

"Nor, for that matter, by the chief. If it were up to me, you'd have your bars."

"It used to matter to me. It doesn't seem so important anymore. I'd never be able to play the game with the same passion I can put into the job."

"You'll find out differently." His chair creaked when he leaned back. "It's a few years down the road yet, as things stand.

But you will find out differently. Go home, clean up. Gear up. Then go take these bastards down."

Eve decided to follow orders exactly. The minute she got home she headed for the shower. She only wished she could wash away frustration and anger as easily as blood and sweat.

Bracing her hands on the tiles, she lowered her head so the jets of water could beat down over her, drumming out the little aches.

She didn't think. For twenty minutes under the spray she allowed herself to blank. Calmer, she stepped into the drying tube, let the hot air whirl and blow around her. She hitched on a towel, stepped back into the bedroom.

And saw Roarke.

"Sit down, Eve."

Her blood drained. "Peabody."

"No. No, she's doing well. In fact, she's on her way here now. You just need to sit."

"I've got a major op in a few hours. The investigative team deserves to be down on the bust. They need to be briefed."

"It can wait while you take a few more

minutes to settle yourself." He scooped her off her feet.

"Hey! What are you, a damn rabbit. I don't have time for sex."

"If I thought sex was what you needed, we'd be in bed." Instead he dropped her on the couch, sat beside her. "Turn around here. Close your eyes."

"Look, Roarke—oh God." Her eyes fluttered as he dug fingers and thumbs into her shoulders.

"You've knots in here the size of my fist. I could dump a soother into you, but we'll try this instead."

"Yeah? Well, if you don't stop that within fifteen minutes, I'm going to kick your ass."

He bent his head, touched his lips to her knotted shoulder. "I love you, Eve. Every obstinate inch of you."

"I don't feel obstinate. I feel . . ." She felt herself filling up again, doubts and loathing. "I'm not sure of myself. You have to know you're right. Don't you have to know? That asshole Dwier, he knows he's right. Not a doubt in his mind, not a twinge. He's just trying to save his skin, and his woman's."

"A lot of people know they're right, when

what they are is wrong. Having doubts keeps you human."

"Not like this. Not when you start doubting the core. Isn't that how this group pulled people in? The ones who started doubting the core, not trusting it. I traded Dwier for the case today. I gave a wrong cop a walk so I could close it down."

"You had a choice to make."

She reached back, gripped his hand. He'd been one of her choices. The best choice of her life. At least there, she had no doubts. "He said . . . he said they'd taken a collection for Halloway, like a memorial. Like they had a *right*."

Roarke wrapped his arms around her waist, drew her back against him, and let her pour it out. "I'm sitting there, looking at him, listening to his bullshit justifications, the program propaganda, and I remember how Colleen Halloway thanked me. She thanked me and I'm kicking loose one of the people responsible for her son's death."

She pulled up her knees, pressed her face against them. "I'm seeing what happened to Hannah Wade. I see her lying facedown in her own blood. And he says it's too bad about her. Said it was an accident.

But she only got what she deserved because she was just a whore. I want to pound my fists into his flesh for that, beat him senseless for it. But I swing weight with the P.A. to get him immunity so he won't have to pay for it. For any of it. Am I standing for the dead, or am I walking all over them?"

"You know the answer to that." He forced her around. Her cheeks were damp again. "You know the answer in your heart."

"I used to know it in my gut. I used to know it in my *bones*. And I don't know what kind of cop I'm going to make if I don't feel it that way again."

"I don't know this Dwier, but I do know this: He may not live out his life in a cage, but he'll never be free again. I do know you, Eve. Whatever you did, you did for Halloway, for Hannah Wade, and the rest. You bargained your own needs away for theirs."

"I don't know if I did. But I hope to God it was worth it." She used her hands to scrub her cheeks dry. "I'm going to break them tonight. And tomorrow, I'm going to send Peachtree down to hell with them."

She blew out a breath, pushed back her hair. "To do that, I've got to shake this off."

"Would you like some positive news?"

"I could use it."

"We've finished the full ID on the virus. We've duplicated it. Which means we can create a permanent shield against it that allows us full access to the data in the remaining units."

"You can track it back to source?"

"We can. We will. It'll take a bit more time, but we're on our way, well on it, to that point."

"Good. I've got a warrant. One that went through," she added, thinking of Judge Archer. "All Dukes's equipment—whatever's left in his place—is to be confiscated. I need you to dig out transmissions. Somebody gave him the word to run, and where to run to. We're getting Dwier's and Price's, too. Just in case they're holding any names back."

"We'll be busy."

"You and Jamie can put in some time on them tonight while we run the op."

"I recall you saying the investigative team would be in on this bust."

"I can't take the kid on an op." She rose, walked to the closet. "You'd be a lot more valuable to me in the lab. That's not a con, and to prove it, I'm not ordering you to stay."

She grabbed a shirt, turned back. "I'm asking."

"That's tricky of you." He got to his feet. "I'll be your lab rat then, for a bit longer."

"Appreciate it."

"Don't wear those trousers with that shirt. What are you thinking?"

"I'm going to a bust, not a party."

"That's no reason not to look your best. Let's see, what's the well-dressed cop wearing these days to take down a major terrorist organization? You can't go wrong with basic black."

"Is this a joke?" she asked as he selected another shirt.

"Good fashion sense is never a joke." He handed her the shirt, slid a finger down the dent in her chin. "But it's good to see you smile again, Lieutenant. Oh, and wear the black boots, not the brown."

"I don't have any black boots."

He reached in, pulled out a pair of sturdy black leather. "You do now."

Half a block down from the Church of The Savior, Eve sat in the surveillance vehicle and argued with Peabody.

"Look, you're lucky to be here at all. You're on medical leave."

"No, I'm not because I didn't sign off."

"I signed you off."

"I signed me back on."

Eve bared her teeth. "You forgot the 'sir.' "

Peabody's chin jutted. "No, I didn't."

"How about I write you up for insubordination?"

"Go ahead." Peabody folded her arms across her chest. "I can handle it. Just like I can handle this op."

Eve let out a gusty sigh. "Maybe you're right."

Beside her, Feeney shifted his gaze from the monitor toward Eve. And thought: Oh-oh.

"I'm patched up," Peabody claimed, relaxing a little as she saw her opening. "I'm fit for duty. It wasn't that big a deal."

"I guess I'm just overreacting a little." Eve lifted her hands, then pushed to her feet. "You ought to know how you feel, right?"

"Absolutely. Sir," she said.

"Well then." Eve patted Peabody's shoulder lightly. Then squeezed. She watched her aide's color drain, watched her mouth go lax on a shocked and pained *O*. "And how do you feel now?"

"I feel just . . ."

"All patched up?" She watched the sweat pearl on Peabody's brow. "Fit for duty?"

"I'm . . ."

"Sit down. Shut up."

"Yes, sir." At Eve's gentle nudge, Peabody's legs folded. She wasn't sure if she put her head between her knees or Eve did, but either way she was grateful.

"You'll stay in the surveillance vehicle and assist McNab. Any arguments from you, Detective?" she said, looking at McNab.

"No. No, sir, Lieutenant." He patted Peabody on the back. "You okay, honey?"

"No honeys!" Eve pulled at her hair. "There are no honeys on an op, for sweet Christ's sake. Keep it up, just keep it up, and I'm having one of you transferred to Queens."

She turned on her heel, dropped down beside Feeney again. "What's the status?"

"A few early birds going in. Pretty quiet yet." He lowered his voice. "Good job there. She ain't ready to rock yet. Girl's got spine though."

"There'll be other ops," Eve agreed, and

studied the monitor. "There's always another op."

The church was small, an unpretentious building that might have started out white. It was gray now, a soft and dingy gray that boasted a simple black cross. It had no steeple, and only a scattering of windows across the front.

Eve knew what it looked like inside. She'd studied the blueprints and the record Baxter had taken. He'd dressed as a sidewalk sleeper, had stumbled around inside. Though he hadn't been able to get to the basement, he'd gotten a good picture of the main level.

And had copped ten credits from the deacon who'd finally moved him along again.

There were fifty pews, twenty-five to a side. A podium centered at the front. There were two doors off the worship area. Baxter had managed to bungle his way into one, snag a quick record of an office area before the deacon had rushed in to fuss over him.

The equipment in the office was top-of-the-line and several levels over what any little neighborhood church could afford.

There were three outside doors. The front,

the east side, and the rear that led to the basement.

All were covered. When they moved, she thought, they'd surround the building like the rings around Saturn.

"Picking up more chatter now," Feeney told her.

Eve lifted up her earpiece, tuned in.

There was talk about sports. How about those Yankees? Women exchanged recipes and talked child care. Someone mentioned a sale at Barney's.

"Jesus." Feeney shook his head. "Sounds like a damn PTA meeting."

"A what?"

"School deal. Parents, teachers. What kind of terrorists are they?"

"Ordinary people," Eve said. "That's what makes them so dangerous. Most are just regular Joes looking for a way to clean up the streets. I watched this vid with Roarke. This Old West thing. Bad guys kicking ass in this town. Law can't stop them 'cause they kick the law's ass, too. So the people get together, pool some bucks and hire this band of gunslingers—that's a great word, isn't it? Gunslinger."

She savored it for just a moment,

snagged a few of Feeney's candied nuts. "Anyway, they hired these guys to get rid of the other guys. And they do. But then the gunslingers decide, hey, we like it here, so we're going to hang and run things our way. What are you gonna do about that? So the town ends up under their thumb."

"Just trade one gun for another."

"Yeah, plus you lose the bucks, a lot of people who were minding their own get hurt. Ends up this U.S. Marshall type comes in— which should've been done in the first place—and after a lot of shooting, people taking dives off roofs, getting dragged around by horses and shit, he cleans up the place."

"We don't have the horses, but we'll clean up the place tonight."

"Damn right."

They waited. Dull conversation, long silences, quick updates from other units stationed around the perimeter. Cop work, Eve thought, as she sipped black coffee and monitored, was hours of waiting, mountains of paperwork, stretches of unbelievable boredom. And moments, extreme moments where it came down to life and death.

She glanced over at Peabody. Instants, she thought, and inches. And fate.

"They're starting," Feeney said quietly. "Must be all they're expecting tonight. Bastards are starting their death meeting with The Lord's Prayer."

"They're about to have plenty to pray for." Eve got to her feet. "Let's round them up, and take them down."

She ran checks with each unit captain, ordered all positions held while she and Feeney moved in to join Baxter and Trueheart.

Her unit would hit the basement door first.

She gave Baxter's chest a quick poke to make sure he was wearing his riot gear. Grinning, he poked her back. "Damn stuff's heavy, isn't it?"

"Irritates the hell out of me," she admitted. She circled her finger. He turned so she could yank down the concealing flap and reveal the NYPSD emblem on the back of his jacket.

"Meeting's under way," McNab reported through her earpiece. "Judge Lincoln's presiding. They're reading fucking minutes from the last meeting."

"Let's give them a couple minutes," Eve

ordered. "Get more on record. The more we have, the deeper we put them under."

"Lieutenant?" Trueheart whispered, as if already in church. "I want to thank you for allowing me to be a part of this op."

"You're going to suck up," Baxter told him. "You suck up to me now. *I* suck up to Dallas. That's the food chain."

"Opening to new business," McNab reported. "Discussion on Greene termination. Wade termination called unfortunate systemic by-product. Jesus. Single objection from membership."

"Sir?" Peabody's voice came through. "Word just came in. Geller didn't make it."

Eight dead, Eve thought. It ends now. "This meeting's over."

"Locked and loaded," Baxter said.

"All units, go. *Go.*"

She went in the door first, and down a set of old iron stairs. In her mind she pictured other units coming in the front, the side, streaming across the main floor.

Weapon drawn, badge held up, she swung through the doorway into the basement room.

"NYPSD! Nobody moves."

There were some screams, some shouts.

A few people scrambled, either for cover or escape. Secondary units poured in like ants at a picnic. Ants armed with laser rifles and twin-barreled stunners.

"Put your hands up. Hands up," Eve shouted, "or you will be stunned. This building is surrounded. There is no way out. You are under arrest for terrorist acts, for conspiracy to commit murder, for the murder of a police officer, and other charges that will be made known to you."

She moved forward, sweeping faces, movements. Some wept now, and others stood rigid in fury. Still more knelt, hands clasped like martyrs about to be fed to the pagan lions.

"On the floor," she ordered. "On your faces. Hands behind your heads."

She swung hard as she saw Judge Lincoln reach inside his jacket. "Do it," she said softly. "Give me a reason."

His hand dropped. He had a hard face, dark stone with features sharply carved. She had sat in his courtroom, given testimony there. Had trusted him to feed justice.

She took the weapon from under his jacket, patted him down.

"We're the solution," he told her. "We're

courageous enough to act while others sit and wait."

"I bet Hitler said the same thing. On the floor." She pushed him to his knees. "On your face, hands behind you."

She clapped the restraints on him herself. "This is for Colleen Halloway," she said softly in his ear. "She knows more about courage than you ever will. You're a god-damn disgrace."

She got to her feet. "Baxter, read this bunch of heroes their rights."

It was two-thirty when she made it home. But it wasn't fatigue that dogged her now but a weariness so internal it dragged at both body and mind.

She felt none of the rush of victory, the pumping energy from seeing a job through. When she closed the door at her back, she couldn't find it in her to toss an insult at the waiting Summerset.

"Despite the lateness of the hour, am I to expect your houseguests will arrive with their usual desire for refreshments?"

"No. They've got homes of their own, and they're using them."

"You were successful?"

"They scored eight before I stopped them. I guess that would depend on your definition of successful."

"Lieutenant."

Her mind was too shadowed for more than mild irritation. She stopped on the second step, looked back. "What do you want?"

"During the Urban Wars there were a number of civilian-driven organizations. Some risked their own lives to try to protect neighborhoods under siege or to rebuild those that had been decimated. There were many acts of heroism. And there were other groups who were also organized. They sought only to destroy, to punish, to wage other levels of warfare. Some formed their own courts, held trials. Oddly, all of those trials ended with a verdict of guilty, and were swiftly followed by execution.

"Each," he said, "had considerable success with their separate agendas. History is, however, enlightened by one and tainted by the other."

"I'm not looking to make history."

"That's a pity," he said as she continued up the stairs. "Because you've done so tonight."

She went by the lab first, but there was

only Jamie. He was obviously out of work mode and into recreation. There was a graphic of Yankee Stadium on his monitor. He was playing against Baltimore, and the O's were up two runs in the bottom of the sixth.

"Shit, you blind?" He slapped the unit as the ump called a strike on his batter. "That was high and outside, asshole."

"It caught the corner," Eve disagreed. "Nipped the strike zone. Good pitch."

"Like hell." He paused his game, swiveled around. "Wanna take me on? It's better with two reals instead of playing against the comp."

"I'll trounce all over you some other time. Hit the sheets."

"Hey, hey, wait!" He scrambled up. "Aren't you going to tell me how it went down?"

"It went down."

"Well, I *know*. We got the call on it. But no deets. Spill some deets, Dallas."

"Tomorrow. We'll have a full briefing."

"One deet. You give me one, then I got one for you."

"We confiscated discs containing records of every meeting. We've got them sewn up so tight they can't hack their way out of the sack with a broadsword. Give."

"Okay, frig-o. We got some track."

"You found the source?"

"Nothing to it once we cloned. Virus was sent out from the unit confiscated from Dukes's lower level work area. He sent them staggered over a three-day period. He pushed the button on every one of them."

"They brought him in from Albany tonight. He's lawyered up. I'll take him apart tomorrow. Go to bed, kid."

"Got to smash the O's first."

She shrugged. "Whatever." She walked to the door, paused. "Jamie. I was against Roarke bringing you onto the team. I was wrong. You did a stand-up job."

His face brightened like a sun. "Thanks."

She left him to battle the Birds, and went to Roarke's office. He, too, was at his unit, but she doubted he was playing. Whatever his business was, he shut it down when she came in.

"Congratulations, Lieutenant. Where's your team?"

"They were heading to some after-hours place to wind down with a couple of drinks. I passed."

"Then you can have one here with me."
He rose to top off his brandy and pour her
a glass of wine. "We have your source."

"Yeah, Jamie told me. I stopped by the lab
on my way."

"He's still up?"

"Yankees and O's, bottom of the sixth.
He's two down, with two out and a runner
on first."

"Ah, well then." He gave her the wine. "Did
he tell you we also found a number of transmissions? To and from Price and Dwier.
And three, so far, from Mayor Peachtree's
office 'link. The last coming in the afternoon
of your visit to the Dukes house. Text only.
It advises Dukes to take a little holiday with
his family, and gives a suggestion for the
address in Albany. It's carefully worded, but
under the circumstances, damning enough."

"I take Dukes and the mayor tomorrow."
She sat on the arm of a chair, but didn't
drink the wine. "I split up the interviews after
the bust. Gave a push at suspects with various team members and combos. Everybody yelled lawyer, like it was their team
cheer. I broke some pathetic housewife in
under thirty minutes. Spilled her guts while
her lawyer's huffing and puffing about du-

ress. Pleaded her down a couple levels to shut him up, and she rolled over like a puppy."

"You stopped them. You shattered them."

"I took in a judge, two other cops—a retired cop who'd put thirty years in. I took in mothers who were almost as panicked about notifying their child care provider as they were about spending the night in a cage. I took in a boy barely old enough to shave, and a woman who won't see a hundred again. She spit on me." Her voice quavered just a bit on that. "She spit on me when we were putting her in the wagon."

Roarke stroked a hand over her hair, and when she turned her head, cradled her face against his side. "I'm sorry."

"Me, too," she murmured. "I just don't know what I'm sorry about. I've got to go to bed." She eased away, stood. "I'll look over the data you and Jamie extracted in the morning."

"I'll be along when I can. I have a meeting shortly."

"A meeting? It's almost three in the morning."

"It's in Tokyo. We'll do a holoconference."

She nodded, then set the untouched wine

aside. "Were you supposed to be there? In Tokyo?"

"I can be where I want. And I want to be here."

"I've cut into a lot of your time just lately."

He rubbed a thumb over the shadows under her eyes. "You certainly have, and I expect to be properly recompensed." He touched his lips to her forehead. "Now go to bed. I've work here."

"I could come into midtown sometime, and . . . consult."

"I'd like to know what I've done to deserve a threat like that."

It helped to smile. "Or, you know, go shopping with you. Help you pick out a suit or something."

"I felt that chill right down to the bone. Go away, Lieutenant."

"Okay. See you later."

"Mmm." And as his holo unit signaled, he watched her go.

Chapter 22

She woke before dawn, and gauged the time by the quality of the dark. She calculated an hour before daybreak, and thought about trying to zone out again for the best part of that.

She'd slept like a woman in a coma, falling facedown on the bed after stripping down to the skin. She hadn't heard Roarke come to bed. But at least she hadn't dreamed.

She shifted to her side and made out the shape of him. It wasn't often she woke before he did. Because of it she rarely had the opportunity to lay in the dark, in the silence of the house and listen to him sleep.

He slept like a cat, she thought. No, quieter than a cat. The light rumble of snoring she heard was from the other side of the bed where Galahad lay sprawled on his back like roadkill.

It was kind of nice, she decided, with everyone all tucked up safe and warm.

Too nice to waste the best part of the hour she had left for bed sleeping.

She crawled on top of Roarke, found his mouth just where she'd left it. And woke him with heat.

She felt his body throw off sleep. A fingersnap. Brace, assess, relax again.

"Work late?" she asked against his mouth.

"Mmm."

"Sleeping in?"

"Not anymore."

She laughed and scraped her teeth over his jaw. "Just lie back. I'll do the work."

"If you insist."

She was warm and naked and still soft from the night. In the dark before light she moved over him like a dream, all scent and touch and shadow. Her lips and fingers stroked over him, stirring needs that were never quite still.

Her hands cupped his face. Her mouth sank to his.

She sighed into him. He heard something wistful in the sound, and as she lay over him, he traced his hands up and down her back, that long, lean line, as much for comfort as seduction.

His cop, he thought. So troubled. So torn. But here, they were safe and sure. Here, they were right.

He knew, she realized, and turned her face into his throat. He always knew. And the gift of having someone who did, who could, was overwhelming.

"I love you. Roarke. I love you." Her mouth met his again, hotter now, with the first taste of urgency. "I love you. For all the times I forget to say it."

The kiss slid back to sweetness. Her heart beat thick, beat steady against his.

In a long, slow movement, he rolled her to her back. He laid his lips on her collarbone as their legs tangled, as hers parted. He could see her now, the shape of her face, the gleam of her eyes. He slid into her, a satin glide of flesh to flesh. A quick and quiet catch of breath.

Again long, again slow, and deep, with her body rising toward his, with his falling toward hers. She shuddered, and groped for his hands. Their fingers linked; their mouths met.

Overhead, dawn broke.

It was still shy of seven when she studied the data Roarke and Jamie had accessed the night before. She frowned over it, chewed over it. Considered.

"Dukes goes down, all the way down. He has to know it. Essentially, he was the button man. Even without a confession, I'm handing the prosecutor a case he'd have to be a baboon to lose."

"Then why do you look annoyed?"

"I just wonder if this guy knows he was the goat. All along. Whatever, whoever goes down, he takes the heaviest fall. He's the name the media will trumpet, the image of the effigies burned once the crowd turns. If he hadn't figured it out, I might be able to use that to convince him to point the finger at anyone I don't have in the box."

"And they will turn," Roarke agree.

"Yeah they will." She frowned. "Politics," she said softly. "Hell of a game."

She glanced over at Roarke. "I'm going to check out a couple things, then head in to start picking him apart. I want a good chunk of time with him before I pass him to Feeney and move onto Peachtree."

"You're doing Peachtree at Central?"

"His house. His involvement remains Code Five until he's formally charged."

"I want to observe the interviews." He looked over from where he sat on the bed-room sofa, monitoring the stock reports on the mini-unit and the morning media report on the wall screen.

"What's the point?"

"The point is closure. I gave way on the bust last night. I want this."

"What's the matter with you, Ace? You're sprung. Job done, game over. You can spike the ball. You can go back to work and buy . . . Alaska or something."

"I've as much acreage and interest in Alaska as I need for the moment. But if your heart's set on a glacier just send me a memo. You can arrange it, Lieutenant. It's a reasonable enough request."

"For Dukes, yeah, but Peachtree—"

"He's had my support, financially. You're not the only one who's pissed-off by this situation. I want to be there for the end of it."

"Okay. Okay, I'll work it out. But I'm leaving in ten, so you'll have to—"

"Hold on a minute." His gaze narrowed on the wall screen as Nadine Furst came on with a flash bulletin.

"This just in. Forty-three people suspected of being part of the group known as The Purity Seekers were taken into custody last night at the Church of The Savior on Franklin Street. This NYPSD operation was headed by Lieutenant Eve Dallas. Police sources identify some of the suspects arrested as Judge Lincoln, a criminal court judge in this city, Michael and Hester Stanski . . ."

"Where did she get the names!" Eve exploded and barely resisted punching a fist at the screen. "We're not releasing names yet."

"Listen to the rest," Roarke told her. "This can't be it. There's no point in this kind of leak."

"Donald Dukes," Nadine continued, "a former marine sergeant and a computer scientist, was arrested at a private home in Albany and has been taken into custody.

Several charges have been brought against Dukes, including conspiracy to commit murder, in regard to the Purity killings over the past week."

There was a slight pause, then Nadine continued. "But the most disturbing development in the Purity matter is the allegations levied against Mayor Steven Peachtree. Official sources confirm that the Mayor of New York is a prime suspect in the crimes attributed to The Purity Seekers and will be formally questioned this morning. Evidence linking Mayor Peachtree to Purity includes a video of alleged sexual misconduct, which was recovered from the residence of Nick Greene during the investigation of Greene's death. It is suspected that the video was used as part of a blackmail scheme. The mayor could not be reached for comment, nor has his office issued a statement regarding the allegations."

"Son of a bitch." Even as Eve swore, her communicator beeped, as did the bedside 'link, her pocket 'link. She imagined the communication centers in her office, here and at Central, were lit up like Christmas.

"You're in the media storm now, Lieutenant," Roarke told her. "You're going to have to ride it."

Ignoring the 'links, she yanked out her communicator.

"Lieutenant" was all Whitney had to say.

"Yes, sir. I saw it. I don't know where she got it, but I'll find out what I can."

"Fast. Peachtree's lawyers are already out for blood."

"Leak or no leak, Commander, I'm making an arrest today. And it'll stick."

"No media statements," he ordered. "Neither confirm nor deny until I clear it. Take Dukes first, and break him, Dallas. I'll let you know when and where for Peachtree."

"Don't answer the 'links," she told Roarke as she jammed the communicator back in her pocket. "Tell Summerset to screen all transmissions, and to keep Jamie here and under wraps. I don't want him talking to anyone about anything. Not even his mother."

"You think the boy leaked this? Eve—"

"No, he didn't leak it. He's too good a cop already. I know where the leak came from." She snagged a jacket. "This may not be my game, but I know how to play it when I have to. I know how to win it. If you're with me," she added. "You've got five minutes."

• • •

She let him drive and spent the entire time on the 'link, covering the situation with her team, coordinating them and arranging for extra bodies at Central to hold back the media who would certainly be swarming into a pack outside the doors.

Then she tagged Nadine.

"Listen, before you jump on me, I was given that bulletin thirty seconds before air. There wasn't even time to polish the copy. I couldn't have flipped it to you if I'd wanted to."

"Who gave it to you?"

"You're asking me to reveal a source, and you know I won't. But as it happens it was given to me by my producer. I don't know his source. Sources," she amended. "He's never gotten this hot with less than two. All I know is someone high up leaked to him with the stipulation I read the story—he confirmed, and we aired."

"You specifically?"

"That's right."

"Smart," Eve decided.

"Things are popping around here, Dallas. You're going to want to give me a statement ASAP. What evidence do you have linking

Mayor Peachtree to the activities of The Purity Seekers?"

"No comment, Nadine."

"The shit hitting the fan isn't all going to land on Peachtree's face. A lot of it's going to fly into yours." As she spoke, Nadine angled her chair, brought up data manually on her computer screen. "He had a fifty-three percent popularity rating before this. And many of the voters included in that percentage are very vocal, very staunch, and very monied supporters. On the other side's the faction who'll want to lynch him politically, and will use you as the rope."

"No comment. Curious. Which side do you bet on? Supporters or lynching party?"

It was a good angle, she mused, and one it wouldn't hurt her to get a jump on. "He'll resign. No way out of it. Without the dirty details of this sexual misconduct, I can't project. He'll take hits for cheating on his wife, and for any connection with Greene."

"Off the record, Nadine?"

Eve could see Nadine strain against the bonds. "Okay, damn it, off the record."

"If it's a little juicier than cheating? If it involved some sexual kinks?"

"Oh God, you're killing me. If it's good and

juicy, he's probably cooked, at least short term. Convicting him of murder, unless you've got him with fresh blood on his hands, is another matter. Public support will swing both ways, which puts him center ring. People have short memories, and selective ones. They won't necessarily remember if he's guilty or innocent, but they'll remember he did something big. If he doesn't do hard time, if he can slither on the sex, he could run again in a few years. And he'd probably win."

"That's politics," Eve stated. "Later."

"Dallas—"

But Eve cut her off.

"You're pulling on a string, Lieutenant," Roarke said. "I'm beginning to see the shape of the ball it comes from."

"Yeah, let's see how it unravels. Head straight to garage level. Oh, and if you run over any reporters, I give you extra points."

Inside she moved fast. She had Dukes and his team of lawyers in Interview within fifteen minutes. She teamed with Peabody, deliberately choosing to piss Dukes off by having two females go at him.

She turned on the recorder, input the salient data, then sat back. "Let's get started."

"Lieutenant Dallas." The head of the legal team, a broad-shouldered, square-jawed man named Snyder, interrupted. "Mr. Dukes has opted to have all questions and comments directed through and answered by me or one of my associates. As is his right. He prefers not to speak to or be spoken to by you directly."

"No problem. You're going to want to inform your client that with duly executed warrants his data and communication centers were confiscated from his residence in this city, and from the portable registered to him found in the Albany location. Said units were then officially logged. Technicians attached to NYPSD extracted data and transmissions from said units. This data, these transmissions, lock your client in a cage, away from his family, away from his friends, away from whatever has previously passed for his world for the rest of his natural life."

She smiled when she said it, and kept her eyes on Dukes's face. "You can also relate to your client that I'm just as happy about that as I can be. I danced all the way in here this morning. Right, Peabody?"

"You do a mean tango, Lieutenant."

"Your sarcasm is noted on record," Snyder said.

"You betcha."

"If, as you claim, you are in possession of such damning evidence against my client, I fail to see why you're wasting your time in this interview."

"Mostly I wanted to gloat." She grinned. "And, as much as it offends my sensibilities, I'm required to give this asshole—excuse me—your client an opportunity to show remorse, and to cooperate so that such remorse and cooperation may be considered during his sentencing. Have you guys done the math? Eight counts first-degree murder. There's a cop in there, which puts that single count at full life, off planet facility, no possibility of parole."

"Lieutenant." Snyder spread his hands. "You don't have first and you certainly can't hang the cop on my client. The fact is, you don't have any direct evidence linking Donald Dukes to the alleged activities of this supposed organization."

"Either you're as bloody as your client, or he hasn't given you full disclosure. Which do you figure, Peabody?"

"I think we should give Mr. Snyder the

benefit of the doubt. I think Dukes is too puffed up with his own importance to believe he needs to tell his lawyer everything. He likes being in charge too much."

"You think wearing that uniform makes you somebody," Dukes said under his breath.

"Yeah." Peabody edged closer. "It makes me a cop. It makes me somebody who's sworn to protect the public against people like you. It makes me," she said, slapping her palms on the table and pushing her face close to his, "one of the people who walked through the blood you spilled."

"You will not speak directly to my client." Snyder shoved to his feet, and to Eve's delight, Peabody shifted and got up in his face.

"Your client spoke directly to me, on record. He does that, I'm free to respond, on record."

"Now, now, class." Eve clapped her hands once, made a sit-down gesture. "Let's not let our tempers override our manners. If we're going to give Snyder the benefit of the doubt, then we owe it to him, and his associates here, to inform them of the evidence that is now in our hands."

"Maybe we should just toss him to the P.A. Let them sink."

"Peabody, that's very harsh."

"If the two of you think you can run the good cop/bad cop routine on me," Snyder began.

"Wouldn't think of it." Eve grinned fiercely. "And just FYI, I'm the bad cop. I'm always the bad cop."

"Bitch," Dukes muttered.

"See, he knows. To respond to the bitch comment," Eve continued, "let me just say, you ain't seen nothing yet, Don. We ID'd your brainchild. We duped it, and we tracked it back to the source. Your little workshop unit. Your fingerprints, your voice prints, your personal code. You and nobody else. Didn't think we could pull it out, did you?"

Now Eve leaned forward. "I've got a couple of techs at my disposal that make you look like a first-year hacker."

"That's bullshit."

"Infected e-mail transmitted from your unit, by you, to Louis K. Cogburn, eight July 2059, at fourteen hundred hours. Infected e-mail transmitted to Chadwick Fitzhugh, eight July, at twenty-three fourteen."

With her eyes on his, she recited every

transmission she'd committed to memory. She saw the disbelief wash over his face, then the anger flood it.

She wanted the anger.

"We've got you nailed. They knew we'd hang you when we busted this open. You're not a general, Don. You're not even a soldier to the ones running this show. You're the sacrificial lamb."

"You don't know squat. You're nothing but some dried-up female trying to pass for a man."

"Think so? I'll show you my balls, Don, you show me yours."

"I wish to consult with my client," Snyder interrupted. "Privately. I wish to terminate this interview until I've consulted with my client."

"You terminated them, didn't you?" Eve demanded.

"We executed them." Dukes spat it at her, then swiped out an arm, nearly knocking Snyder out of his chair when the lawyer tried to interrupt. "Shut up. Shut the hell up. You're part of the problem. Just like she is. Enough money and you'd defend Satan. You help put garbage back on the street. I don't need you. I don't need anyone."

"Are you dismissing your legal representation at this time, Mr. Dukes?" Eve asked.

"I insist on consulting with—"

"Fuck you." Dukes surged to his feet. His chair shot out, slammed into the wall. "Fuck all of you. We did something great. You think I'm afraid to go to prison for it? I served my country. I served my community."

"How did you serve your community?"

His mouth twisted. "By exterminating cockroaches."

"Mr. Dukes." With admirable calm, Snyder rose. "I'll ask you one more time to afford yourself of your right to remain silent. Lieutenant Dallas will terminate this interview and we'll go to a consult room to discuss—"

"Get the hell out," Dukes ordered without looking at him. "You and your cockroach brothers are fired."

"Let the record show that Snyder and Associates are no longer attorneys of record for Donald Dukes." Snyder picked up his briefcase, signaled to his two associates. "Lieutenant Dallas."

"On the door," she said, and Peabody walked over to open it and let the lawyers out.

"Donald Dukes, did you conspire to murder Louis K. Cogburn?"

His shoulders were back, his head high. And the hate pumped like sweat out of his pores. "You're damn right, I did."

"Did you conspire to murder Chadwick Fitzhugh?"

"I created the virus. Did most of the work myself. She's a beauty. I shot it into him. Into all of them."

"By your conspiracy to cause these deaths, did you in turn cause the death of Detective Kevin Halloway?"

"Yes. What's another dead cop? We took out that bitch George, Greene—along with the whore in training, whatever her name was, and Geller. That cover it?"

"Who gives you your orders?"

"I don't take orders."

"Did you conspire with Mayor Steven Peachtree to murder the individuals named on record?"

"Figure it out."

"I have," she told him. "You're done. I don't need you. Get him out of here, Peabody. Take him down so he can start living the rest of his life in a cage."

He came at her. A silent, panther leap.

Her fist shot out, rammed into his chin. As his head snapped back, she drew her weapon. But Peabody flipped out her stunner and nailed him.

"Damn it." Eve, slapped her hands on her hips when he lay sprawled at her feet. "I wanted to do that."

"So did I, and I beat you. Besides, you got to pop him first. Teamwork."

"Yeah." Eve smiled, but it still didn't reach her eyes. "Nice teamwork, Peabody."

Roarke corroborated the opinion when he met her in her office a few minutes later.

"The two of you played him like a violin. That's superior virtuosity when you figure you'd only met him once before."

"I knew him."

"You did, yes. Knew precisely what would get under his skin and push him to pontificate. Well done, Lieutenant."

"Not yet. It's not done yet." She heard the arguments, the raised voices coming through the bullpen toward her office. "But here comes the next stage. You want to hang in for this?"

"I wouldn't miss it for worlds."

"Of which you own several," she murmured before Chang burst into her office like a tsunami.

"You will issue a statement. I've written it. You'll issue this statement *immediately*, taking full responsibility for passing misinformation to a media representative." He slapped both disc and hard copy down on her desk. His hair was wild; his eyes feral.

"Why would I do that?"

"Because I'm telling you to do it. Because this is the last time you'll undermine my work. The last time you'll make a mockery of what I do."

"What you do is a mockery, Chang."

He took a step toward her. She was fairly certain he envisioned clamping his hands around her throat and squeezing until her eyes popped out. But whether it was the dare in her eyes or Roarke's presence, he resisted.

"You leak a story to the media before its time. You use your influence with an on-air reporter to push forward your own agenda. You create a storm to distract from the fact that you've mishandled your own work. To— to plump and preen yourself before the public while leaving me to clean up the mess behind you. Mayor Peachtree has not been charged. He has not yet been interviewed, yet you've seen to it that he's guilty in the eyes of the public."

"Sure looks that way, doesn't it? One small correction, though. I didn't leak the story."

"You think you can save yourself by lying to me?"

She shifted her body weight, and fascinated, Roarke eased back. He wondered if Chang knew how close he was to annihilation.

"Don't call me a liar, Chang. You of all people."

"Who is it who has a personal relationship with Nadine Furst? Who is it who gives regular favoritism to her and Channel 75, with exclusives and tips?"

"That would be me. And you know why? Because I can trust her to think of more than ratings. That relationship is why whoever leaked this saw that the story went to her. That's your kind of maneuver, Chang."

The hand around the throat image was appealing enough that she used it herself. She caught him one-handed, rapped him back into the wall, and lifted him to his toes. "All this spin, all this storm, all this fallout.

That's going to keep you a very busy boy for a while, isn't it?"

"Get your hands off me. I'll have you arrested for assault."

"Yeah, you can bet a whole squad of cops is going to rush in here to save your oily ass from me. You're going to get a lot of play out of this—fees, bonuses. Add screwing me over to the pie, and it's real tasty. Did you leak the story, Chang?"

He was turning an interesting shade of puce as he batted and shoved at her hand. "Get away, get away!"

"Did you leak the goddamn story?"

"No! This isn't something you leak until you're prepared. Until the spin is in place. You leaked it."

"No, I didn't." She released him so that he dropped to the flats of his feet with two sharp thuds. "Think about that. Now get the hell out of my office."

"I'm filing a complaint." He yanked at his collar. "You'll read the statement or—"

"Bite me," she suggested and shoved him out bodily.

"That was very entertaining," Roarke commented.

"We're not done yet. Act two should be starting any minute."

"Until it does . . ." He smoothed his fingers over the ends of her hair, then slid his hand around the back of her neck. She stiffened, looked so mortally embarrassed that he laughed. "What?"

"I'm on duty here. Just back off. Really." She turned away quickly and moved to the AutoChef. Even as she programmed coffee, she heard the fast, hard click of high heels. "That's my cue."

Franco swept in. She looked every bit as furious as Chang had, if more elegant. "Lieutenant Dallas." She bit down on the words as if she could chew them to bits. She gave Roarke a brisk nod. "I'm sorry, but I need to speak with the lieutenant privately."

"Of course."

"You may want to go give Feeney a hand, Conference Room B," Eve told him. "He's working on some tech stuff you'd be interested in. One level down," Eve added. "Sector Five."

"All right. I'll leave you ladies to your business." With one casual glance at Eve, he slipped out, closed the door.

"You've gone too far this time." Unlike

Chang, Franco kept her voice down, and controlled.

"In what area?"

"Who are you to decide Mayor Peachtree is guilty, to leak information that will ruin his political career, damage his personal life. And all before you've so much as questioned him. You gave him no chance to defend himself."

"Leaking the story screwed him pretty good, didn't it? Coffee?"

"You dare stand there, so arrogant, so goddamn cocky after what you've done?"

"Yeah. Same as you." Eve leaned back on the AutoChef, sipped her coffee. "You leaked the story, Franco."

"Are you mad?"

"No, neither are you. You're a very smart woman. What I can't figure is if you did all this, formed your organization, killed people, ruined a number of lives because you wanted to smear Peachtree or you really believed in what you were doing. I've thought about that a lot this morning, but I'm just not sure. I think it was both."

"If you think you can save yourself by painting me with the same brush you're using to paint the mayor, you're very wrong."

"He didn't make the transmissions."

"What are you talking about?"

"Peachtree didn't make the transmissions from his office to Dukes. You did. You used his office, you used his 'link. The transmission telling Dukes to skip was sent out, from that unit, at sixteen forty-eight. Peachtree left for the day at sixteen forty-two. We have him on security cam. We have him walking out of the building at the time the transmission was generated. Those six minutes make a difference."

Eve gestured with her mug, then took a long sip. "You were still in the office. Dedicated civil servant that you are. His assistant saw you go in a couple minutes after he left. You were the only one who could have contacted Dukes from that unit at that time."

Franco hitched down the jacket of her slate gray suit. "That's nonsense."

"No, that's just niggling details. The kind that usually trip up the bad guy. You probably didn't think we could trace the source, But why chance it? You'd been using the mayor all along, using him as a front. Politics is a weird area for me, but here's how I see it."

Eve walked over, sat on the edge of her

desk. "You want his job. Probably more than that, but Mayor of New York's a good place to start. He's fairly popular. Maybe he'll get another term, and it's a pisser to wait, to play deputy when you can be chief."

"Is that what you think?"

"I think you saw an opportunity to remove an obstacle, even to use that obstacle to further your own ambitions—especially when he makes it easy for you by getting tangled with Nick Greene."

"Mayor Peachtree's sexual leanings should be a private matter."

"Should be. Let's go back awhile before that. You keep up with current events. You keep up with community news, polls, opinions. Kids are being exploited out there— future voters, those kids. Their parents, other parents, other citizens, voters are upset, disillusioned and just plain pissed off. Something should be done, and you're just the gal to do it. A lot of control. A lot of power. You've got a law degree. You know some of that scum is never going to pay. You found a way to make them pay. That's a hell of an accomplishment."

A smile ghosted around Franco's mouth. Her eyes were alive with it—and, Eve noted, with arrogance. "Do you really believe you can make any of this play?"

"I've got Dukes." Eve shrugged a shoulder. "I've got Purity in pieces. You slipping by me isn't so hard to take with more than forty other arrests and a closed case on my record."

"So, this little scenario you're writing here is between us."

"Just you and me. Girl talk. Post-game chatter."

"Then by all means." Franco gestured a go-ahead. "Continue."

"It fell apart on you, Franco, but you still had a button to push. Leak the story. Shove the mayor into the muck. Defend him, but carefully. If he's convicted, you mourn the loss of a man who was corrupted by his own power, his own skewed sense of duty. If he's acquitted, you praise the system for exonerating an innocent man. But either way, you step into his shoes and run the city. Maybe, maybe some of it was about your twisted sense of justice. But under it all, it was just politics."

"You're wrong." Franco wandered over, picked up the second cup of coffee Eve had programmed. "Since it's just the two of us here, since I respect you, I won't say you're wrong about all of it. Purity was a solution. An extermination of a plague. It could be again."

She angled her head. "We could have used someone like you. Pushing to have you as a media symbol wasn't an accident. You have impact, Dallas. With your passion, your skills, your presence, you'd keep the story hot as long as I needed. I think I knew when we met in Tibble's office you'd find a way to break it apart. I had to accept that, deal with that. I always pick my battles."

"Why this one?"

"Every politician needs a platform. This is mine. Dukes wanted to infect you," she added. "But that wasn't the agenda. That wasn't the program. How many innocent children did we save, Dallas?"

"Is that your spin?"

"If I needed one it would be. And it's the truth. Peachtree has good intentions, but he's soft, and he's cautious, politically. And sooner or later he was going to be exposed for his sexuality. Why should I go down with him?"

"So you nominated and pushed on Greene as a twofer. You eliminate another predator, and you see that Peachtree's sexual conduct is exposed, and that he's under suspicion at the same time for multiple murder. It bothered me that no attempt was made to get to the blackmail vids. Didn't make sense, unless you turned it around that the idea was for them to be recovered and used."

"The people on those vids deserve to be exposed. For their weaknesses. For their foolishness, and for their dealings with a man like Greene."

"And you're the judge of all of that, of all of them."

"I am. Or part of a group of people who believe it's time for judgment. You and I, Dallas, we're neither soft nor cautious. We act. We make things happen. I'll be Mayor of New York," she said simply. "And in a few years, governor. From there, East Washington. I will be the third female President of the United States before I'm fifty. I could take you up with me. Wouldn't you like to be New York's top cop, Dallas? Chief of Police Eve Dallas. I can make that happen in five, maybe six years."

"No, thanks. Too much politics for me.

How do you plan to do all this, Franco, from a cage?"

"How are you going to put me in a cage?" she countered. "I've been very careful. As far as that transmission from Peachtree's office, my legal team will get around it. It may have been set and saved for sending. The assistant may have been mistaken about seeing me go into his office at that particular time. It's a very busy place."

"But it wasn't set and saved, and the assistant wasn't mistaken."

"No, but you'll never prove it. Nothing I've said in this room will do you any good. It'll be your word against mine. And at the moment, Dallas, with the very efficient Chang convinced you leaked this story to Furst, with public opinion still deadlocked over Purity, and your part in destroying it, my word's got a lot more juice than yours."

"Maybe. Maybe it does. But your words are going to work just fine." Eve picked up her communicator. "I think that wraps it," she said.

Franco set her cup down with a snap. "You were wired."

"Oh yeah."

"Nothing said here is admissible. You

didn't read me my rights and you entrapped me. Everything I said was said in temper, simply to get back at you for leaking the story."

"Good thinking. We'll see what your lawyers can do with it. Jenna Franco, you're under arrest for conspiracy to murder." As she listed the names, Eve pulled out her restraints. Even as Franco stepped back, the door opened.

The mayor came in first, followed by Whitney and Tibble. "You're a disgrace, Jenna," Peachtree said quietly. "I hope the system you so callously misused gives you full justice."

"I have nothing to say." Franco's face turned to stone as Eve cuffed her. "I want my attorneys. I will not make any statements."

"A little late for that." Eve glanced over as Nadine came to the doorway, her camera behind her. "You get it all?"

"Every word," Nadine assured her. "Live feed. We're through the roof."

"You broadcast . . ." Franco's stony face went sheet white. "You had cameras in here?"

"Just my little spin. Oh, and if you're thinking about getting that tossed, or using it to bite at the NYPSD, I'll remind you that this is my office, and you entered it without invitation. I was under no legal obligation to inform you of security or media presence. Excuse me, gentlemen." Eve maneuvered Franco through the men who crowded into her tiny office. "Peabody."

"Sir." Peabody stepped up from her spot in the hall.

"Read her her rights. Book her."

As Franco was led away, Nadine on her heels shooting questions like laser blasts, Eve could hear Franco's terse and furious: "No comment."

"Lieutenant." Peachtree stepped out. "Well-done. I'd like to thank you for what you did for this department, this city, and for me personally."

"I did my job. If you'd been part of it, I'd've taken you down just as hard."

"Wasn't I?" he said, looking after Franco. "For not seeing what was under my nose?"

"What's under it is usually harder to see than what's in the distance."

"Perhaps." He held out a hand, shook hers. "Chief, Commander. We need to clean this up."

As Tibble passed, he nodded at Eve. "Media conference in one hour. Good work, Lieutenant."

"Thank you, sir."

"You and your team are commended," Whitney told her. "I want your report before the media conference."

"Yes, sir. I'll get right on it."

She'd just sat at her desk when Roarke walked in. "That was quite a show."

"Yeah. Feeding her to the media was just a bonus. I had to put it together pretty fast. Didn't have time to tell you."

"You did," he corrected, "when you looked horrified at the idea of me kissing you in here."

"Yeah, well, the guys in EDD will be snickering over that for days."

"Cameras still on?"

"No."

He leaned down, kissed her, long, slow, and deep.

"There now," he said. "I feel better."

"Enough fooling around, Ace. I've got work. Scram."

"Let me ask you a question first. Do you know you're right?"

She closed her eyes. He always knew.

And when she opened them again, met his, they were clear. "I know I'm right. I feel it in my gut. I feel it in my bones."

"So do I." He walked to the door, glanced back. "Lieutenant?"

"Yeah, what?"

"You're a hell of a cop."

She grinned. "Bet your ass."

She pushed aside her cold coffee, turned to her desk unit. While others played politics, she got back on the job.